LEGEND OF THE FOREST

RAQUEL GABRIELLE

LEGEND OF THE FOREST

RAQUEL GABRIELLE

Dark Storm LLC

Also By Raquel Gabrielle

A Soul Saga Series:

A Hollow Soul

A Soul Forgotten

A Soul Remembered

Standalone:

Legend of the Forest

To childhood and the things that we keep with us as we grow. Always make time for playing, no matter the age. And never let anyone say that you are too old for something.

Prologue
Julie

A circle of rocks flashed in front of her. She stumbled, trying to catch herself on one of the sharp stones. She caught herself before falling. Blood welled up from her palm, the tips of her fingers covered in ink and colored paint. The rustling of her pack bumped against her legs. She pushed some of the rolled up pages back down. Adjusting the strap of the crossbody pack, the weight rested against her hip solidly.

The leaves crunched nearby and a low growl emitted from the bushes.

Her eyes stayed trained on the bush. "Why did I even come here?" Her breath hitched. The hemmed cuff of her baggy brown pants caught on branches and underbrush.

Small sounds fluttered around her. She jumped to the side. A small critter snaked past her, chittering back at her as it climbed up a tree. Her heart pounded hard inside her chest. "What the..." she cut off as she took a deep breath. Holding it in, she tried to calm down.

"Come on, Julie! You can do this," she muttered. "The guards said... stay on the path... we have those... mapped out. We need to explore more," she argued with herself.

Kicking out at the bush, she felt the thistles snag and rip at the fabric, leaving a small tear near the bottom of her pant leg.

Julie walked further into the woods until coming to a clearing. She sat down on a rock, her hands scrambled over the couple of satchels she carried with her. Her hand rushed to the pack on the left, grabbing onto the cloth volume that was hidden inside. The blue azure sky was bright against the greens and browns of the woods. Flipping it open to a blank page; her pen flew across the paper describing what she saw and drawing pictures as she continued to peer around her. A stumpy set of boulders surrounded her, circling around where she sat, hers being the smallest in the group. The stones, though small, reached her waist.

"You want to see more of the woods?" a voice almost like her own whispered over her left shoulder.

Julie whirled to see who said that. No one was there. A black bird cawed in the distance. Her pen blotted the page with ink as a shudder moved through her.

She shook her head and continued to focus on the map she drew.

"I will not go running back scared. I will not," she chanted. She settled in to chart the new area. She hadn't gone too far in, but the trees created a labyrinth. If only she could see a clear view of the sky, then she could get her bearings and go the correct way home.

"Little lamb has lost her way," another rasp, more garbled this time. A bubble of mud popped next to her sturdy black boots. Dirt speckled the leather's sheen.

"Have not," she grumped. She eyed the treetops, hoping the sky would reveal something. Only beams of sunlight glared into her green eyes.

A larger mud bubble floated out of the ground slowly. Julie peered at it cautiously, not knowing if she should run or hide. The dirt exploded and splattered across her front, before she could raise her hand to guard.

She spat on the ground, tasting dirt as she swallowed, trying to rid the taste from her mouth. Snapping the book shut, she placed it back in her satchel. Her tongue moved over her teeth, trying to clear the grime away.

She hissed out in pain and gathered her supplies. Touching the pads of her fingers to her tongue, she noticed blood there. The dirty sludge still caked in her mouth moved and mingled with the blood.

Stop.

She froze mid step, obeying the command. Relaxing her leg, she pushed it down to complete the step. A dull throb began right behind her eye and radiated to the back of her neck. She picked up that same foot and the pressure eased.

"What is happening?" she said in a nervous whisper.

Go to sleep, little lamb, and all will be better when you wake. No more pain, no more fighting, no more struggling to be seen for who you really are.

"I'm so tired." She yawned. Her eyelids slumped down, too heavy to lift back up.

Julie felt something warm wrap around her. It tugged her down, holding her in place as something else came forward to control her.

With force, it pushed her leg down. It rolled her shoulders and stretched her neck to the side; it cracked. With a long slow blink, it made her stand straighter and look around at the deep greens of trees. A half smile pulled at its lips.

"You will be a pleasant and easy enough host for a joy ride. Let's see what kind of disorder we can stir up," she said, but it wasn't her who said it. Something was using her voice and she couldn't stop it.

Her tone going lower than she had ever heard it as the being inside settled with in.

I want to go home. Why didn't I run when I had the chance?

She snarled as she pushed beyond the rock circle and moved away. Fighting every step she made. Her thoughts were chaotic and mingled with this thing that had taken over.

"You happened across my prison, little lamb." It forced her head to look back, her eyes landed on the ring of rocks.

Fear bubbled up, closing off her throat.

"Don't fret, I will be pulled back, but not before I've had my fun."

The thing made her stomp through the underbrush and trudge through the forest, away from the village. Branches and twigs snagged at her limbs and loose clothing, but the pain didn't register.

Shouldn't there be pain? I can see what is happening to me... us... but I don't feel it.

"I will take away your pain. Don't worry, just rest. There is no reason to struggle anymore." It was like it could hear her thoughts. "Human pain is such a trivial thing."

She settled down as if watching a play unfold before her. *Human?* Its phrasing troubled her.

"I will need to be quick and decisive for my plan to work. The spell that holds me is weakening, and is so brittle." It took a deep breath. "Ahhh, they are still here. Let's go see which Old One is still about, shall we?"

Old One's! No. You're just a story. They don't really exist.

Its feet pounded the ground with every step. Birds and animals alike startled from their hiding places and ran away. Sensing the turmoil within. It crashed through the woods, not stopping to talk with her anymore.

Julie nodded off, finding it very hard to stay present when she had no control over things. *I can't give up. No matter how tempting it makes things. Come on Julie.*

A muscular, thin man with golden skin stepped out from behind a tree, blocking the way forward. A bow hung across his chest. He had a green shirt that almost looked to be made up of leaves with brown pants that stretch as he moves. He stepped into the light and hundreds of rainbows glinted off him, blinding them.

It blocked the harsh light with its arm. Crouching down, it grunted in pain. "Must find," it muttered.

"Did Grey tell you to come find me?" he asked.

"Grey said to come find you," it said louder. "The forest... trial..."

"What!?" he said, surprised. "Grey really meant what he sa id..." he said to himself. Clearing his throat, "you have come to take the trial then, human?" he said louder.

Grey? Trial? Was he an Old One too, or one of their descendants? Julie was so frazzled she wished she could scream. Anytime her mouth moved, it was that thing's voice answering, not hers.

She stretched to try to free herself from this thick fog that blanketed her.

"Yes," it said.

"So, you have." He turns down his golden aura. His eyes roved over her, stopping on the splattered bits of mud on her clothes. His top lip raised in disgust. "I'm Haddox."

It stared at him, crouched low, with arms still raised. Leery of what to do or say.

"Well, let's get this over with." Haddox grabbed her elbow and urged her to follow.

No! No! No! I'm not going anywhere, Old One or not. Julie struggled against the thing that held her. She pushed forward with everything she had.

"Sky told us stories about the Old One's. I'm never going home, am I?" Tears raced down her cheeks and her hands shook.

Her body struggled against Haddox's hand and the thing in her mind. Control slipped, "Do not touch me." Ire wrapped around her dull tone.

Haddox dropped her hand quickly. "If you want to go home, then go."

It shook its head slowly.

Julie's mind raced. She had control for a moment, but lost it just as quickly. Moving her body, she kicked, punched, and screamed, but none of that came through to her body. She sat there immobilized. Fear and tears consumed her, she felt so helpless.

A low golden glow emits from Haddox's eyes. "Good." He smiled, big and inviting. "I apologize, this way, please." He motioned with his arm as he walked forward. He kept his eye on her to make sure she still followed.

As they delved further into the thick woods, trees reached out further to the sky. They crossed a stone bridge covered in moss; waters rushed below them. A large stone fortress with multiple levels sat before her. The greens of the forest surrounded it, becoming one. Water cascaded out of the tallest part of the building from further up the mountain that it lay embedded to, it tapered off into the water below. Night was growing closer and lights were lit around the outside, a soft golden glow.

As they came closer, Haddox flexed his muscles as he handled the large ornate stone door. "This is where your first test will be."

Haddox held open the door, stepping aside, waiting for her to enter.

She took a few steps in.

Haddox followed close behind, closing off any escape.

Where am I? What is this strange place? I want to go home!

Julie's thoughts spun in her mind. She struggled against the unforeseen thing holding her body compliant.

Haddox crowded in behind her. His hard chest was warm against her back. He slid around, going further into the barely lit room. A tiny figure emerged from the dark corner of the room with long, brown hair and a simple black dress that hung off her supple form.

"You!" it growled out, clenching its fists tight.

The woman stopped; her bare foot pressed into the soft moss that covered the floor. It looked as it did in the forest. The dark canopy making the light so dull, darkness loomed behind her.

"She says she is the next chosen for the tests," Haddox said.

Its hands shook as they clenched and released over the worn cloth of the bags.

"Has she willingly stepped forward to try the tests?" she asked.

This creature's voice was soothing and musical to Julie's ears. It lulled her, made her feel calm.

Shaking his head. "She has come from the village, said the forest had brought her. Grey sent her to find me. He is still mourning the last one."

Mourning? A shiver ran through her.

She watched as its hand touched something cool and sharp in her bag. Pulling the dagger that had laid hidden in there. Its fingers tightened on the worn leather on the handle, pulling it in front.

They both looked at her as if she were a child.

"Hello, wife!" it barked out.

"Who?" The woman's plump lips puckered in question.

"The barrier is thinning. I will be free soon, and this place will be the first place I run through. Your little game will not help you if you can not finish the tests to strengthen the bond between our kind and them." It brought her wrist forward, pressing the knife into her flesh.

Digging the point into Julie's skin, she watched as a ruby red drop skated down her pale freckled arm.

She struggled against the thing's hold, bending until she broke. Control slipped back to her.

Tears welled up and poured down Julie's face. She took her arm away from the knife, hiding it behind her.

"Help me," Julie whispered out.

Its hand tightened on the knife and pulled it up to Julie's neck, forcing her control back.

"No one here to help you, little lamb," he laughed.

It pulled the knife tightly across Julie's throat, creating a jagged smile. Warm blood flowed out of her, covering her hand. She opened her mouth to talk, but no words followed. The thing leaves her and pain flooded in as she gasped for air. She fell to the ground as her life left her.

"Chaos?" the woman uttered out before all the lights dim and go out.

Haddox backed up. Opening the door, he poked his head out. "The lights went out everywhere."

The woods screamed out as one with the loss of a life, one that barely even had a chance. Animals of all types lend their own voices to the pain. They were restless as they felt the forest shift.

"Another must be chosen," something rough echoed out of the dark woods. "Or the consequences will be dire." A small green butterfly fluttered forward out of the darkness. Trees and leaves quivered around the building. The wind whipped into a frenzy. The butterfly remained unaffected by the howling winds.

"Another!" Haddox called out, his golden hair still shined even in the dark. He crossed his arms over his chest, his muscles twitched. "This will be the second soul from that village. They are not strong enough."

"What did you do!" A tall shadow raced by in a blur around the corner and slipped through, slamming Haddox out of the way. The door was thrown back, banging against the wall; he stopped dead in his tracks as he saw Julie's lifeless body strewn over the floor. "Haddox needs to prepare them better next time." His white eyes are the only thing that doesn't blend into the darkness of the room. "After that first one, I will no longer play these games."

"I did what I was supposed to," grumbled Haddox as he righted himself. A soft glow emits around him, lighting his way. He kneeled next to Julie, picking up her hand and letting it fall to the ground. "You can't blame this on me, Grey!"

"Why? Because you put your all into it?" Grey scoffed. "What? All of five minutes?"

Ignoring him, Haddox takes his time as he looks through the bags that Julie had carried with her. "The village is small. There are few to choose from there. Few even venture past the wall, let alone close enough to it. They will get suspicious if more disappear. Our numbers are not what they used to be. We are not what we used to be!"

"We could always take a guard," Grey said. His Black horns peeked out from the shadows.

"Grey!" Haddox exclaimed.

"Don't pretend that you care," Grey chided. He swiped his tongue over his sharpened teeth, clicking them together. "We haven't played with one of their kind in such a long time."

Haddox glared at Grey as he stood up and faced the woman who was quietly studying Julie. "Ashling, I think what my friend here is trying to say is, what are we looking for?" He smiled.

"A guard will not do. The butterfly will choose," Ashling said. Her dark eyes followed a lone vibrant green butterfly flapping towards Haddox. It dipped and swayed in the night air, floating on the currents. Vines crawled up the walls of the surrounding room around them. The greenery was lush and filled with all colors of greens, browns, and grays.

A low rumble emitted before the ground shook. "The forest calls for someone. It will show you what it needs," Ashling whispered.

"Didn't the forest already choose the last one?" Haddox's face scrunched in confusion. "Grey?"

"What are you talking about?"

"Old One?" Haddox said.

Ashling rose in the air, her long brown hair fanning out around her. The strands of hair rushed out and circled Haddox's throat.

His golden hue that surrounds him flickered as it tightened. More strands follow, wrapping around his body. It pressed in around him.

"Ashling," Grey said.

Her gaze moved to Grey, her hair following as the strands slither over the moss-covered stone.

He stepped out of the shadows into the doorway. He shook his head, holding his tongue. His white eyes stare at Haddox. "Careful, this is her realm. Why do you want answers? Why do you care?" He sneered.

"I don't care for any of them," Haddox spat out.

The tendrils of hair unravel but keep circled around him. "Chaos," Ashling whispered. "Chaos," she repeats.

Haddox stepped away as he stroked his hair, trying to smooth it down. His dull gold glow emitted from his skin once again. "They need us as much as we need them. Stay out of my way, and

I will ensure that I train this next one and make them capable of passing the tests."

"Fine, by all means. Train them how you want." He bowed low to Haddox, the tips of his horns barely slashed over Haddox's shirt. Two of Grey's horns curve up and out from his temple, following the flow of his hair back. They looked slick back, like his black hair. The other two horns were further back and stuck straight up near the middle of his head. A corner of his lip lifted in a snarl. His head came up abruptly. "Don't mess this up. You weren't here yet, but last time we got lucky when Chaos escaped."

Ashling floated forward.

Grey took another step back on the other side of the doorway.

"We need to ensure the Old One's stay in slumber. Life as we know it will be gone if we don't locate another person to take these tests."

Haddox turned his head. Stumbling back, he falls into the archway.

"You perhaps do not remember a time when the Other's ruled, but I do," Grey said. He pressed his finger hard into Haddox's chest, keeping him there so she could not close the door.

The butterfly zipped in between them, fluttering around their heads, getting their attention. A green glow lit behind it, creating a stream for them to follow.

Chapter 1
Mia

Mia's eyelids sprang open. The sky was pitch dark, only the moon shining in through the window lit up the small room. She laid there in the night's silence. Her eyes roamed over the cluttered space.

What woke me?

Raising her head, she heard a rattling noise coming from the window. The wind whistled through the gap between the thin glass pane and the wooden trim. The house groaned out, unhappy with the abuse it received.

She slid from the bed, careful not to step on the many things strewn about on the floor. Her pale blue nightdress caught on twigs sticking out of a basket on her way to the window. She had made it herself from twigs and vines, but it was uneven. Rough around the edges, and being circular, that meant rough around the whole thing. The basket slid closer to the edge of the bench that sat at the foot of her bed. Freezing, she held her position on tiptoes, waiting for it to crash to the floor. Moving carefully, she plucked the cloth from the twigs, scooting it back further on the bench.

She squinted her eyes at the half done project. If she had finished the doll, she might not have had to be so careful. The figure made of twigs lay half done with tufts of hair twisted in between the wooden pieces.

A gust blew hard against the house. A warm but demanding voice whispered through the cracked panes of the window. "Come, child."

Giving a smile, she jumped from her spot, moving away from the bed. Scurrying towards a clear space in front of the window. She braced against the cold glass, putting all her might into pushing the frame up. The window liked to stick, but she had made sure her grunting and the window stayed silent as she whispered out a spell. She didn't need Mother waking up at this time of night.

"Soon," Mia whispered back, letting the salty air whisk her words away from her. She left the window open as she slid to the floor, her hand patting under the bed. It stirred up the dust as she searched the bare wooden floor. Her fingers ran over the smooth cloth as she yanked on the crumpled cloth. Standing up, she had to fight back the sound of a triumphant shout as she bounced from foot to foot.

Dark slacks of soft and well-worn leather ran through her dainty hands. She made quick work of stuffing the bottom of the nightgown into the pants along with muscular legs. Staring outside, she noticed the moon that was almost full dip down closer to the tops of the tall trees. They had a few hours before her mother rose; she liked to be up before the sun. Mia already felt the tension grew between them since her father had gone to sea. The last couple of weeks were not pleasant for either of them.

Tucking a folded note in her pants pocket, she crossed back to the window. Glancing back at the treasures in her room, she saw a plain satchel hanging on the door handle. She shook her head. This time, she would need to forget it. She couldn't risk getting caught again.

Contorting her body out the window, she was as silent as a mouse. She pushed the window down, leaving an inch so she could get back in.

The cool ground made her shiver. She raced across the soft grass, jogging to keep warm.

The wind fluttered around her, pulling and tugging at her clothing. Pushed in the opposite way, she let it guide her to the sandy beaches. Waves tumbled over the sand as she stared out into the inky darkness of the night. The beach curved around the little bay, but if one continued to follow it, they would hit the town. The docks there have lights and lanterns to see by, but this far out near the wall, the darkness surrounded her.

She turned away from her home and followed the beach the other way. Her hand brushed against the rough texture of the wall that surrounded her village. It had been here as long as she had been on this earth. She had only dared to go beyond the wall a handful of times in the past.

The wall didn't look pretty but was needed or so they were told. "Don't worry, Sylvia will show me how to strengthen the barrier tonight." She patted the rough exterior as if it were a living thing. Anything they had built would have been ruined by the elements, let alone the creatures. They needed the spell to strengthen what was there to keep standing.

Taking out the buttery soft wrinkled page, she scanned it.

She had scrawled, "I want to be free," across the page in black blocky lettering. Free of this village. Free of these people. And would have accepted whatever shape it came in as long as it would let her be herself.

She let out a squeal as something from the sea screeched out. Cold white-knuckled fists held tight to the ripped paper. The wind pushed from behind, forcing her into the water. Waves crashed into her legs. A lyrical sound wafted from further out at sea. Humming to the tune, the water tugged and swirled around, ripping the soggy parchment from her hands, taking even that away from her. How could Father leave her here when he knew she was like him? That she craved adventure and sought things that were otherworldly.

A shrill but high-pitched voice carried on the wind, that she could barely hear, "Come to the forest!" it whispered from out in the bay. Clicks and a spray of water burst further out in the depths of the ocean.

She almost wanted to dare the ocean to come up and take her here on the spot. But even as spirited as she was, she wouldn't challenge the water at this time of night. Father spun tales of all sorts of stories about the things that swam beneath the surface.

Her mind was plagued with thoughts of what could be awake right now.

"It couldn't be all bad. Right?"

Sylvia, her mentor, warned that tapping into this inner power would draw the attention of others. When the calls could no longer be ignored, she would struggle against her people and the cage built to keep themselves safe.

This close to the wilderness, her own personal refuge beckoned. The magic tugged at her to join the others. She fought a sliver of herself always as she battled to be normal and stay with all that she had ever known in life. Yet, despite those efforts, she couldn't shake the nagging sense that she had never truly belonged.

"Come play with us," the same lyrical voice carried over the wind. It beckoned her. She edged away, back to the safety of the beach. The cold water rolled over her bare toes as she wiggled them in the sand.

"Halt. Who goes there?" A booming man's voice called out behind. His shape was a dark shadow against the wall.

She immediately dropped to the ground, scrambling up the beach into the overgrown grass.

"I said stop!" His hurried steps raced closer. "Who the hell is out at this time of night and so close to the wall?" he huffed. "I swear if it is Ally's daughter again, creepin' about, I will throw her into the sea and let the gods take her."

Her movements stayed small and sure as she crawled through the long grass behind a post and a washed-up boat.

She tried to make sure only to venture close to the wall in between their rounds, but most of the time she forgot to watch for them when the wilds called.

Her heartbeat thudded in her chest, loud and pounding. His boots hit the packed ground of the trail. There was no other place to hide.

"Come out, Mia, I know you're there."

"Why should I? You're just going to throw me out to the sea."

He grumbled as he made his way around the boat. "You want out of this town so bad? Come, let me help you along."

Keeping low to the ground, she slid up the grassy side, away from the beach, keeping the boat between them.

"Look at this cage that surrounds us. Why do we limit ourselves so?" she questioned for the umpteenth time.

"You mean protect us. The other men warned me about you. How you use your wiles on them. It won't work on me."

"I bet it won't. Don't have the right package for you, do I?" she smirked. Her hand slid into her pocket as she stood up, trying to look defenseless. A silky handkerchief met her cool fingers. She pulled it out with care and gave a big smile.

"Exactly..." He coughed and whispered something under his breath. "Wait, a moment that isn't what I meant. What do you have there?" His heavy stomps squashed the grass between them. Reaching out, his rough hands grabbed her arm firmly.

Up close, she saw his blond hair and beard. His hand squeezed around her arm, making his muscles flex. He was one of the burlier men in the village.

"What do you got there?" He pulled her hand up so he could see what she was holding.

She fell into him, dumping the powder that was wrapped inside.

"So sorry about that. You grabbed me so violently. I must be sleepier than I thought." She rushed to brush any of the dust off her. She blew the remainder off her hands, blowing more on him. Stepping away, she stayed out of the wind.

"I... What..." He glared at her. His eyelids drooped and his hand that held her dropped next to him. His head slowly turned to his hand. "Why?" His eyes widened and his mouth hung open. He crumpled to his knees, his body succumbing to a sudden weakness, as he turned back to Mia with a desperate gaze. His limbs seemed to fold beneath him, leaving him sprawled out on the ground, helpless and bewildered.

She struggled to catch him, lowering him slowly to the ground. He blinked rapidly as he fought the powder. "It's something I have been working on. Almost forgot I kept some for such an occasion." Mia watched his eyes blink rapidly. "Don't worry, you will take a nap for a bit and be back up by first light. Unfortunately for you, though, you won't remember this conversation or much of your night." Giggling, her heart raced with glee at what she was pulling over on him. "Hope you didn't do anything important that you needed to remember."

His fingers scraped through the soft dirt next to him. Mia stood back up and walked away, not worried about the guard any longer.

She made her way to Sylvia's small home. Sylvia's home, like her own, was close to the wall except on the other side of the village. Mia made her way through the town, keeping an eye out to make sure no one spotted her.

Buildings lay dark and silent at this time of night. Hushed whispers and drunken slurs were the only noises she had to worry about.

A loud bang made her heart stop. She slid to the closest house and shrunk down, doing the best to hide herself. A loud meow and hiss echoed from the dark. An orange tabby raced around the corner, taking off down the road.

"Dumb cat, ugh," another woman's voice said. "How could he think I would like such a gaudy piece of jewelry?"

Mia's heart thundered in her ears as she dared a peak at what was happening. She saw another woman that was around Mia's age, standing over the garbage can. She threw something into it.

"He will just have to get me something else. Oh, well." She laughed to herself before turning back to the house to go in.

Mia quickly pulled herself back to avoid being seen. Waiting for the bang of the screen door and the thud of the inner door. She waited a few moments before moving stealthily over to the trash to see what was thrown in. A beaded shell bracelet laid there on top. The turquoise and white beads paired well with the tan and white shells. She scooped it up and pulled it on her wrist. "Well, if she doesn't want it, I like it." People misplaced or threw out things all the time. She couldn't help rooting out treasure in other people's trash.

She made it the rest of the way without incident. Sylvia's house backed up directly to the wall. She couldn't get any closer than she was unless she was on the other side.

Tonight, they would work on something outdoors, so she made her way to the side of the house. A bonfire was already lit and warmed her chilled exterior.

A butterfly was thrashed around by the wind and thrown to the ground in front of Mia.

"You shouldn't be out at night. What kind of creature are you?"

Picking up her foot, she stood poised, ready to strike it with her heel.

"Stop!" Sylvia threw out a slender arm, freezing Mia mid strike as she came out of her house with a bowl. "You mustn't trample on what you don't yet understand. Janani is all around us. She must be respected."

"It's a butterfly. Something isn't right with it. Only moths come out at night."

"Mia, you're not a child anymore. You are a young woman. Even you can understand things are not always what they seem."

"What is it then, if not a butterfly?"

"Something else that watches. The wildness of the Others calls to the wildness in you, doesn't it?" Sylvia coughed out as she passed by, her nails plucked at Mia's damp clothing.

Mia's body relaxed. Changing direction, she stepped away from the butterfly, taking care not to harm it. "What? Or who is Janani?"

"The forest," Sylvia said.

"Do you have more stories of the Others? Or Janani?"

Sylvia laughed as she took the bowl over to the stone table. A purple cloth lays underneath the trinkets and spices strewn about. She could only make out a few things from her training.

"That is your grandmother's expertise. She is the one with the stories. If you know where to look, you will find an abundance of stories."

"I could experience it out there if they would let me." Mia clenched her fists at her side.

"The wall didn't always exist. I remember a time when your grandmother and I were both young. Our town was just getting started then. Before everything changed."

"I can only imagine..." Mia said. Interrupting Sylvia.

Sylvia's darkened gaze roamed over Mia as she stared off at the trees past the wall that they were close to. Her lips twisted up into a smile as she saw Mia yearning for something that this town could not give her.

"Come here, child." Sylvia beckoned to her. "Pick your gift." She pushed the bowl across the table.

She looked down and shuffled through the items. A pinecone sat at the bottom. She pulled it out and let the edges scrape against her fingers. Inhaling, Mia appreciated the scent that came with it. There was a cluster of trees up north towards the entrance to our town.

"How did you get these without the guards harassing you?" Mia wished she were the pinecone, then she could toss herself over the wall. What she had seen from the other side could be dangerous. She hadn't ventured very far. Anxiety had always brought her back to the safety of the village.

"Sometimes you must have friends in high places."

Mia gives a gasp, "Sylvia!"

"They only accept me because I work miracles when their normal medicines don't work and I strengthen the wall to keep them safe. Hush now. That's enough. Let's get to your lesson before we lose the moon."

"Ugh, don't remind me. I have early lessons with my mother, but after that I will get some time with Grandma at the shop to ask her more about the Others."

Sylvia slid the bowl to the side, moving the book in front of them. "You may study the book with me."

Mia fingered the pages of the book, wanting to know more about the craft. She had only begun her training after she last came to get some ointments from Grandmother Sky.

Sylvia slapped her prying hand, smoothing down the pages. "It is considered rude to look at another witch's grimoire. The book, depending on how old it is, can have a mind of its own. Beware, there may be curses set in place for nasty petty thieves."

"But I'm not a thief."

"The book doesn't know that. It only knows you were given this page to gaze upon or the others I have shown you. It knows only because I tell it you may study the book with me. If I were not here, it could act differently."

She would remember that and take care of what her sticky fingers swiped. It hadn't even entered her mind to take anything from Sylvia, but her fingers sometimes did the walking before her mind caught up with what was happening. She never meant ill intent when she took things. Most of the time they were trinkets or baubles, nothing important. Something for her hands to play with when bored.

She bit her lip with worry.

"Come now, let's begin. You can help prepare the spell I will use in the coming night to help strengthen the barrier." She grasped Mia's hand in hers and walked her through the spell and what was needed.

Chapter 2
Mia

"Long ago, when the land was still new, and we first settled here. It was rich with woods and mystery." Sky pounded her wooden cane into the hard floor. Her gnarled hands shook as she spoke. The shawl she had wrapped around her shoulder was colorful. It popped against the dark dress.

"Another Old One's tale," complained a little boy.

Him along with the other children, sat around Grandma Sky. Some other patrons and adults made their way back to the corner of the store, being pulled into another one of her stories.

"That's right Harry, this was before we created the wall that now protects us. We used to play in the woods, but the folk, including children, went missing when the moon was full." Her hands shook as she moved. Her shawl fell from her shoulders.

"Mia, your grandmother is lying. She knows nothing other than this town life like the rest of us. No one has been past the barrier to the woods." The little boy's face scrunched in anger. His fingers plucked at the strands of the rug he sat on.

"Not anyone that has lived to talk about it," Sky grumbled.

Mia straightened up from where she leaned against the front counter. She marched forward; her hands held in tight fists.

"No, she's not!" A tight, dull-red bodice pinched her waist, giving her a figure where there would not be one. Her long skirt of green hues, with hand sewn blue stitching along the bottom, fluttered around her ankles and bare feet.

She tugged at the falling shawl, pulling it back into place. She stood protectively over her grandmother.

Books piled around the circle of kids and adults. Some children huddled behind their parents' legs, while others passionately argued their point. The adults tried to hush and calm the kids, throwing angry eyes at Mia.

This place was the perfect mix of book store meets art and a telling of stories through both.

"Hush Mia, let them speak their minds. It's good for them to tell their side. The power of a voice is nothing to be squandered." She pounded her cane against the wooden floor once again to gain their attention.

This time was usually intended for children, teens, and adults flocked to this place to listen to the stories and history shared by her grandmother. Sky paid great attention to her audience and fed them what they needed. The entire village loved her. Even if her stories strayed on the side of darker times.

"Come here, Harry." Sky motioned the little boy forward.

He climbed to his feet and rushed forward, bouncing on his toes, eager to be moving. "Yes, Sky?" His eyes peered nervously around the circle, unsure if he was being called out for being in trouble or for being good.

Mia stood behind Sky defensively, glaring down at the little brute. His father was not too much older than she was.

Mia bit her tongue, trying not to snap.

You are definitely your father's son. He used to tease me endlessly about being strange.

Harry ducked his head, avoiding Mia's gaze.

"Look at these gnarled hands," Sky soothed the angry rumbles of the crowd.

Harry looked tentatively at Mia before grabbing onto Sky with both of his hands. His little fingers played over her wrinkles, trying to smooth them out. The bones were misshapen, and her hands shook as she tried to straighten the fingers.

Mia gave a small, tight frown as she saw the pain etched into her grandmother's face.

"These hands didn't come with age. I was gifted these hands in the woods beyond our barrier."

People threw worried glances around.

The sun shined brightly into the window of colored glass that sat behind them, making a kaleidoscope of colors reflect on the rug.

"By an Old One?" A little girl peeked out from behind her mother.

"That's right. An Old One caught me. They do not look too fondly on our kind." Sky's lips pressed together in a grim line. "He took advantage of me and the situation. They are powerful and have magics we can only dream of. He was the worst of them and loved to play with his prey."

"What does an Old One look like, Sky?" Harry patted and consoled her.

"The Old Ones are twisted and take on elements of our world. This one was Chaos, and he was a dark, noxious cloud that infected those who breathed him in. Spreading his confusion near and far. He had infected some of their own children, controlling them. He loved to take the thing you loved most and destroy it in front of you."

"What did you love?" Harry asked.

"Was it a prince?" another little girl asked.

"Grandma Sky used to create the most beautiful pieces," Mia answered, raising her head to the stained-glass window behind them. Other forms of her artwork scattered the space, showing animals of great beauty along with the forgotten ones of the woods painted on canvas. "Before they destroyed her hands, Grandma had been very talented."

Sky rubbed her cheek against Mia's arm.

Mia liked this time with her grandma; she felt closer to her when they talked of the forgotten and Old Ones. Her mother was a different story.

"So, they are all bad?" Harry asked.

"Are you all bad?" Sky cocked her head to the side.

He shook his head but stayed quiet.

She wrapped an arm around his shoulders and patted him on the back to go back to where he was sitting. "Did I ever tell you of the time when my son-in-law befriended a water spirit?"

As Sky continued with the story and answering the questions of the children. Mia was pulled away as she caught someone walking through the few stacks of books they had in the shop. The painting of an ethereal woman made of leaves caught her eye. For some reason, it always caught her eye as it hung up near the front of the shop.

"I knew you would be here." A man grabbed her wrist and pulled her to the side in a little nook of books, away from prying eyes.

She pulled away automatically before she saw who it was. The fight left her. Her frown turned into a smile. "Couldn't stay away, could you, John? What would Tina think?" She circled her foot around his leg, running it up his pant, tempting him.

"Probably the same thing Jason would. Or is it Bryan this week?" His lips dipped down to hers as he yanked her closer. His hands bruised her arms, but his excitement was hard against her stomach. Tense with desire, his mouth claimed hers, his kiss passionate and intense.

She hung on to him, kissing him back with force. Her stomach twisted as butterflies fluttered. The thought of being caught thrilled her. She pulled back and gave a soft chortle before stroking the front of his pants. "What does it matter which one I am with this week? You men are all the same. More worried about your own pleasure than mine." Her hand squeezed around him.

He raised her leg higher, spinning around and trapping her against the wall. The shelves hid them. His hand traveled up her skirt, feeling the supple thigh beneath. Her hand pinned to his cock; it jumped in happiness with the rough touch. His fingers brushed against the fabric, toying with her panties underneath. "Mia, you know how much I like it when you make it hurt. Make me hurt for you."

"Only if you do what Bryan can't," she whispered into his ear, biting on the lower part of his lobe.

His lips crashed down on hers. His heat slammed into her, his hand dipping under the band, and teased the curls at her entrance.

Her lips met his fervently, wanting him to make her forget for a little while. Forget this life and village she lived in. And the people who wanted her to act a certain way.

"Mia!" A woman with high cheekbones and a stiff dress slammed the door open, making a loud noise in the small space.

They both froze. They were still hidden. Their breaths were loud in the enclosed space. If she didn't come out, she knew the woman would tear the store apart looking for her.

John slid his hand back out and eased away, dropping her leg. Brushing a teasing kiss, he gave her time to adjust her skirt before moving to the side.

Mia slinked out of the nook into the aisle, avoiding her mother by retreating back to the circle.

All eyes landed on her as she came around the corner of the bookstack. Grandma Sky and children alike, their beady little eyes loud and round in their silence.

Ducking her head, blushing, she rushed to a stack of books, trying to hide behind them and the crowd.

"Don't even try it." Her mother's hard heels hit the wood floor, making a dented scuff. "I will come in there and drag you out if I have to."

"Oooo," the kids all said at once.

"I am busy, Mother," Mia called out. She wrestled with the pile of books beside her.

"Too bad, get over here now," she said with finality. Her nose turned up at the books, her eyes caught on to something outside. She backed up a step and kept herself firmly planted outside the door.

Mia walked back through the bookshelves, meeting John's eyes as she passed the cubby hole. A smile plastered on his face as he mouthed the word, "later."

Mia gave a slight nod and made her way to the door, fluffing out her skirts, knowing the dirt and dust bothered her mother's impeccable eye for detail.

Frowning, her mother's mouth pinched as she noticed Mia's bare feet. "Where are your shoes?"

"At home," Mia whispered.

"Ally, leave the poor girl alone. She was helping me move some items around this morning," Sky echoed in the small area.

"And now she is late for an appointment she knew about weeks ago. She can't go in looking like this. What would they think? They would all but throw her into the woods. She will get into trouble with all her wildness."

Mia's thoughts turn to John and what she wanted to do to him. "Some like that part of me."

Whispering raced across the room.

"Ally, don't frighten the others. We have not practiced that tradition for many decades. They abolished those rules in my time."

"What is she talking about, Sky?" Harry asked.

"We struck a bargain with the Old One's at first. We would send someone to them for our returned safety. That changed after the wall was constructed." Sky's lips pressed into a grim line.

Ally's eyebrows raised. "Maybe so, but that won't keep the creatures at bay, and they will take away naughty women that don't mind their parents." Her eyes pinpointed to Mia, who was standing off to the side.

"I am not a child anymore, Mother," Mia raged. She didn't know why she let her mother get to her. If she would only understand. *Why won't she hear me?*

"If you were not, then you wouldn't need me to remind you of this appointment that we set months ago," she huffed out a breath. "Mia, you need this to find your place."

"I know my place, Mother. You are the only one that is upset with it."

"Upsetting the status quo is not what you want to be known for. You make such pretty things with string you could work in one of the many shops in town." Ally looked down at the blue swirls of string that mark the bottom of her daughter's skirt.

"You make little dolls for all the children. Why can't you work on something like that rather than what is in that mess you call a room?" She shuddered, leaning back against the railing. "I am tired of having this argument with you."

"What does it matter? It's not like I can go anywhere other than here in this village."

"It matters because you have a choice to make. You can not sit on the fence and wait for life to pass you by."

"Not making a choice is a choice," Mia said defiantly.

"Wrong. Not making a choice is for cowards. Or for someone that is an invalid. Are you saying you're not capable of decision making?"

Mia bit her tongue. Fire burned in her chest, and her heart pounded, fighting to pour out of her.

Just because you think I am stuck choosing between two options I don't like; don't think I won't fight to create wiggle room away from them... No, I can't give anything I am planning away. Otherwise, she could destroy everything.

She shakes her head. "I can make decisions. That's not what I'm saying... If you would just listen."

"No one will want you if you continue down this path. You already don't have any friends of your own."

Mia shouldered her way past, leaving the small shop. Slamming the door shut behind her, she cuts off her mother's rant, so others couldn't continue to snoop.

Anger colored her cheeks as she stared. Mia was only a tad taller than her mother, getting her height mostly from Father's side. "Let's go then."

"No, we will make another appointment when you are in more of an agreeable mood. It will be best to put your best foot forward."

She bared her teeth. "You are only putting off the inevitable, Mother. Why else would you have me speaking all these years with someone to help the troubled? You have never had enough to fully commit me."

"I am trying to protect you!" She screeched.

"Protect me from what? You thought Grandma was an outcast, and she found a space for herself." Mia moved past her mother. Her arms and limbs shook. She stomped down the dirt path, feeling better as she connected with the ground and pushed that energy into the soil.

"She is a special case. Another has already spoken for this place, passing her torch to another young man who thrives in the history of this place. Besides, they only come here to be entertained by the strange stories, not that they believe in any of them."

"Good, it should go to someone who will enjoy it as much as she does. She will have plenty of time to teach him. Grandma's path is not mine." Mia danced down the road, needing space away from her mother and the anger that thrived between them. The dirt road was wet in some spots and the mud squished between her toes. A shiver ran up her spine as she giggled with delight.

"What are you doing? Get back over here!"

"I don't want to talk to you about this when you're not willing to hear my side of things. I don't want to deal with this, so I am releasing the anger and problems into the earth and having fun instead."

"You know one day you will have to make tough decisions and you will have to deal with the outcome of those consequences." Ally's eyes traveled the road. The sun was bright and blaring overhead. The weather being most agreeable for this time of year. "We can't have fun whenever we want to."

Mia rolled her eyes at her mother's words. She hoped John would be around later tonight to punish and take out some of this anger on. They would have the most delicious time.

"Rolling your eyes and dancing around the way you do is not becoming of a young lady," Ally said.

Everything inside Mia fought to remain calm. She stopped dancing and let her arms fall by her side.

Ally walked down the packed dirt road as they headed to make a new appointment.

Mia followed sullenly, kicking rocks or twigs to the side as she followed behind.

They stepped out of the side street, where there was a commotion of people in the town square.

Mia slid to a stop, cocking her head to the side. She listened, keeping her eyes trained on the uproar ahead. Men were shouting at one another as they struggled to hold something down. Mia spotted a flash of blue between two of the burly men.

"Come on, men, this is a youngin not even full grown." Another raced around the outer circle, climbing up onto a large cage to open the door up. "The other one took down two brothers in arms. Don't let this one take another."

She watched as the circle of men struggled with something, trying to get it in the cage. The one on top took charge, yelling out orders and demands. He rolled up his long sleeves. His bronzed skin was dark except for the slashes crisscrossed across them. They were in front of a large warehouse type building, one mostly used for storage.

Ally pinched her arm, tugging at the sleeve, pulling her to the side. "I forgot we should go around. It will be quicker passing through here." Pulling away from the crowd, they duck between two houses. Mia's feet slid in the wet grass and mud. Bright flowers populated the ground, keeping it bright in this shadowy walkway. "Mia, Doctor Hink will not be pleased if you track mud into his office!"

A wailing moan uttered from some sort of creature.

Mia's head spun back to the crowd. "Forgot? What was that? What do you know?"

"It's nothing. Now go find a patch of grass to wipe that dirt off. The doctor won't even think to reschedule you if you show up looking a wreck and dirty his rugs." Ally pushed Mia toward the front steps of the house they stood near, blocking the way.

Mia glared at her mother as she twisted around the corner of the house. She wiped most of the dirt away. Holding on to the wooden railing, she took special care to get the rest of the mud between her toes and on the inside of her foot free of the mud.

Angry voices rose from the group, distracting her mother as she made her way down the road.

Mia made no sound as she stood behind her mother. She watched as they hauled the creature away into the main storage shed. That shed was used to store straw or other goods that needed to stay dry during the rainy season.

"Is this all we got from the excursion? They took my sister!" This man was thin and dressed nicely in slacks and a buttoned-up shirt with a nice coat over it. Glasses slid down his nose as he waved a hand at the one in charge. "Those things had their way with her and displayed her body near the wall. All because she wanted to make more maps of the land." A red-faced man bellowed at the two carrying the animal in the large cage. "I want them to pay!"

"Richard, what are you doing here?" The man that had been on top of the cage rushed to him; his next words were low so she could not hear them from this distance. His arms danced as he talked to the angry man. The others dispersed, not wanting to wait around to be yelled at.

"What did they catch? It doesn't look like a sea creature or fish. What happened to Richard's sister?"

"You know, there have been whispers of creatures coming close to the wall again. They are taking extra precautions so that it doesn't escalate. We don't need anything from the woods getting in here and attacking us fine people." Ally sniffed. "It really is horrible what they did to Julie, Richard's sister."

"What kind of animal was this? Maybe they were protecting their young."

"Come now, they are not that bright. They are animals, Mia. They murdered his poor sister for going out there and mapping the land."

"It doesn't sound like you're talking about just animals..."

"Of course it wasn't just animals." Ally stared at Mia, taking a deep breath. "Anything other than us are animals." Ally stood tall and looked down her nose at her.

"And what of the Old One's?"

"Them too." Her eyes turned toward the wall. "Anyway, we have an understanding with them. Or we did... They leave us alone; we leave them alone. We don't enter their domain. You know this."

"Others have gone out there and have come back fine. Hunting parties, guards. In my twenty-one years here in this town, this is the first time I am hearing of someone going missing. Other than second hand stories, where you can't be sure what is truth or tale." Mia threw her arms out.

"No one goes out there alone. Let's not talk of this now," Ally shushes. More and more people walk alongside them as they grow closer to other shops.

"Don't ignore it and sweep it all under the rug. Did that woman show up dead from an animal or something else? What happened to her? I know you make it your business to know what is going on."

"There are only speculations. Maybe if his sister stopped with just mapping our given area and along the coast, she would still be alive. But no, like you, she had to push things. Well, remember that Mia, you could end up dead like her, then where would you be?" Giving a shake of her head, Ally moved down another street, heading to the doctor's place of business.

Mia bit her tongue. What she said didn't matter to her mother.

"Come along," Ally said. Head raised high.

"You won't be able to ignore it forever, Mother."

"Like you want to ignore your choices?"

"I'm not talking about that." Mia ground her teeth. "Either those men went out into the other one's domain and captured that poor creature, or it got in past our impenetrable wall. Which is it?" Tearing her eyes away from the top of the storage building, she continued down the road, following behind.

"If you take from us... No, actually I'm going to do the same as you did and say I don't want to talk about this anymore."

"Come on," Mia complained.

Opening the door to the doctor's office, Ally turned back to her daughter. "Are you willing, then, to talk about your future options?"

"Then you will tell me more?" Mia asked.

Ally stood there, waiting for Mia to decide.

Her lips pressed together. She wanted to stomp through the door and yell at her some more, but she nodded tightly and walked swiftly past her mother.

Chapter 3
Mia

"That was absolutely a waste of time," Mia grumbled to herself. Mother had stayed behind to smooth things over. She stomped her feet as she made her way through the town.

They would have to wait another month before he could fit her in to his schedule. She flipped her hair over her right shoulder; smoothing out the snarls. Dexterous fingers twirled her black hair into a loose braid, keeping it out of her face.

Mia could have gone back to Grandmother's book store and hid out there till it was time to close. She turned away from that direction, wanting instead to go find John. He could help, find some way to destress and forget about her future. Her thoughts were too loud, and she wanted them to be silent, at least for a little while.

She stuffed her hands into her skirts pockets and fiddled with the few trinkets she had picked up that day. A few coins, crumbs of bread, and some white little flowers that she had picked on her way to see Grandma Sky. Taking the one flower out, she picked each of the many little petals off at a time. She strolled through the town in search of John, knowing he would be down by the ships and harbor area. His dad's fish shop was around there and he helped often.

Her thoughts swirled as the sun dipped down in the sky. She made her way down to the wharf. The breeze from the ocean brought salty air she could taste. Raising her chin, she let the wind caress her face.

"Isn't that the bracelet I got you?" John asked.

Mia's eyes traveled over John's strong form. She observed a supple woman snuggled up to his side, clinging onto his arm. Right behind him, there was another man and a girl. He closed the door to the shop they were visiting. He pulled the girl around with him, forming a half circle. With her thoughts taking up her attention, she hadn't noticed them.

A loud gasp. "She stole my bracelet!" The woman that was hanging off John's arm pushed forward and grabbed Mia's arm.

Her eyes widened as she recognized the woman from last night.

John let her go; he eased back against the brick wall of the building behind him. "I thought you said you lost it, Tina." His eyes finally raised to Mia's. He rubbed the front of his forehead, leaning his head back.

Mia turned her head down, hiding a soft sarcastic smile. This was not how she had meant to find him; she grumbled low out of anger and how her luck had been going.

"I thought I had to. But as you can clearly see, she stole it." Tina yanked Mia forward as her other hand reached out to John. "Why would I lie?"

"Because you clearly are." Mia spat out, waiting for her moment to intervene. "You threw it away last night." She wrestled her arm back. "I saw you at the garbage cans."

"You're jealous of what we have, something you could never," Tina huffed.

Mia looked shrewdly at her. "I could have everything you currently have if I really wanted to take it." Her gaze moved to John.

"No, the only way you could ever get jewelry is from the trash, because that's what you are," Tina's friend spoke up. Sashaying her hips as she pointed at her. "It's why you are so unliked by the whole town. We can't trust our items alone with you, let alone our men."

Giving a shake of their heads, both men turned away, talking with one another. Their eyes were downcast, unable to look at any of the women in the group.

Tina dropped John's arm and shuffled forward, hands on her hips. Standing with her friend in front of Mia.

Mia stuffed her hands in her pockets, fiddling with the treasures hidden there. She looked around in search of help if this went south.

"It should have been you that died," Tina said.

Mia froze, cocking her head to the side in confusion. "What do you mean?"

"Instead of Julie, you should have been the one to go out into the forest and get killed. You're always wanting to leave, anyway. What's stopping you?" Tina pushed forward.

Mia backed up a step.

"Tina..." John chided.

"What?" Tina snarled towards John, giving a dirty look.

He raised his hands in front of him and backed away.

Tina plastered a smug smile on her face before she glanced back at Mia. "Don't tell me you're scared?"

Mia couldn't believe how different John was in front of people that were supposedly his friends. It's why they had fun, but that was all it could ever be. Her lips crimped in anger. "I'm not scared. Not all that go outside the wall, perish." Mia burst out.

"How do you know?"

Mia had bitten her lip, not wanting to say any more than she already had.

"Perhaps she heard it from her grandma's stories." John tried to help.

"Is that right?" Tina stepped closer to Mia.

From this close, she saw Tina's eye twitching. "That's right." She gulped. "Not all her stories come with a warning of how not to mess with the Old Ones. Some are of their teachings and what we can learn from them."

"I don't believe her." Tina's friend saddled up next to Mia.

Her eyes scanned the brick wall that was close by.

"Yea, where's your proof? Go out into the forest and bring us back something from there showing us you aren't scared to leave the town." Tina dared.

Mia couldn't tell them she was the proof. She hadn't gathered things from the forest for fear of something being attached to it and coming to attack the town for it back. She wasn't sure what the town would do to her if they knew she had crossed into the forest. Her mother would for sure put her in a cage and throw away the key.

"If you ask me, I don't think she really wants to leave." The friend crossed her arms in front of her chest and stepped into Mia.

She was pushed closer to the wall. "Bree, I think you're right. She wants people to feel sorry for her."

"You're wrong." She did want to leave this place, but how do you leave everything you have ever known? What if she could never see her grandmother or father again?

"Are we?" Tina and Bree said in unison.

"I don't have to explain myself to you. Or anyone else." Mia backed up, coming away from the building.

"You better return what you stole or else." Bree lifted a clenched fist.

"John and Brian will show her what we do to thieves and liars, otherwise." They both snickered.

Mia sucked in a harsh breath. "Fine, take it back." She tore off the bracelet and threw it at Tina.

After throwing the bracelet, she turned to run and could hear them laughing as she raced away. She dashed around the corner; emotion tightened her chest. Fighting the tears that wanted to fall.

Returning to the town square, she slowed to a jog. Stopping at the edge, she noticed the busy crowds. So many people flow around the square. At the center was a statue of the man who had found these lands. Next to it was a grand water fountain. There are many sitting there enjoying a late evening snack. The tavern was the largest building in the square and brought many people in. Since there wasn't much else to do or to go. It was the place to be.

Brushing tears away that had gathered in her eyes but refused to fall. "She is wrong. They are all wrong," Mia muttered defiantly.

Dark clouds moved in with the breeze, the sun sinking behind them, causing the shadows to lengthen. Concealing herself was priority number one, especially with the unshed tears she battled. She had enough of the people from this town, judging her and making it known that she was not a part of them.

As guards passed by the alleyway, she recoiled in fear. The dark shadows swallowed her whole.

"Are we expecting something to attack? Why are we all being asked to do a shift tonight?" She overheard one guard. His voice slurred with drink.

"They want all hands-on deck for the thing we caught. Only a few will be watching the creature, but most of us will be on standby, near or around the wall, just in case."

"In case of what?" He brushed at his tired eyes.

"You heard how big those things can get..." The rest of their words trailed off as they had gone too far.

Mia pulled back her bare feet light on the ground as she made her way back to the building that housed the creature. It was being held furthest from the tavern. The buildings on this side were taller than the smaller shops closer to the bar.

A low mewling sound called out as she neared the shed. She stopped one building over. She walked to the edge, peeking around, getting a good look. There were a set of guards standing at the entrance and others surveying the perimeter.

She walked behind, making her way to the back of the shed. There was less foot traffic in the back, but the guards still patrolled around. She slowed to a lazy walk as she perused the window display of a little shop directly behind the building she needed. The shop contained a variety of clothes and fabrics. Two tall women poured over dresses that they had each tried on. Penny, a friend of Mother's, ran the shop; she loved what she did and could not get enough fashion. She came here wanting to start in a new place and be the talk of the town.

Why anyone would come to this town was beyond Mia. There was nowhere to go other than up and down the coast. Mia thought of going back to the land her grandmother came from. Her father visited there often enough. But the sea didn't call to her as it did to him. Penny liked Mia's sewing ability and what she could design with clothes, but that was as far as it went.

Waiting till the guards moved back to the front, she saw that there were windows that sat high in the shed. Mia looked at the dress shop she stood in front of. This one was right behind and three-storied; she thought it may be close enough that one could jump from the balcony onto the roof of the shed. The sun had vanished and night had moved in. Big dark clouds brought even more coverage; an impending storm blew in from the south.

The air permeated with a sweet smell that came from the flowers. They twisted in a trellis all the way up to the eaves of the roof. The purple flowers hung low on the vine; she tested the wooden trellis to make sure it would hold her weight. Wiggling around it held firm. Her feet were sure on the wood as she climbed. When approaching the third floor, the wooden trellis shook and came apart from the side of the house at the top. She gave a small bark of surprise, trying to lean into the house. She grabbed at the vines, pulling her back in. Barely moving, she reached up, grasping the next rung. She moved slowly and laid flat against the house, trying not to fall.

"Dumb Penny only secured the trellis up to the second floor. No, no, I couldn't think of a reason why it would need to be secured." Grimacing, she grunted the rest of the way, struggling to reach the balcony. Her fingertips brushed against the metal banister as she clutched to it. She breathed a sigh of relief, hauling her body over it, and collapsed on the floor.

She struggled to look through the glass doors, making sure no one was in the room to witness her flailing arms and legs. Her arms shook and sweat poured off her as she took a moment to rest.

"Aro- Aaaaarooooooo- Aaaarorororororo." A keening sound came from the building in front of her.

Something in her felt every one of those painful, lonely cries. It hit a little too close to home because she saw herself in that creature. Mother would also cage her and make her into what she deemed acceptable, regardless of what Mia wanted.

That hurt sound restored her strength to continue. She sat up and eyed the roof of the next building. The entire roof had clay tiles laid, so finding a grip would not be hard. What worried her was this was the landing. The shed's roof was about a floor and a half under the balcony.

She scooched closer to the metal banister, watching the street below, watching the guards and timing them. Mia waited there for a while as she got down their rhythm, timing it perfectly. Her limbs had become cold with the wind that blew through.

She climbed up on the banister, tucking her skirt into the band around her waist. Unsteady legs shook as she readied to jump. Taking a deep inhale, she closed her eyes, centering herself. Calling up strength along with pleading with the elements to help her through this.

Holding onto the roof up above, she stretched out, readying herself. Launching from the railing, she flew across the alleyway. She held her breath as she plummeted to the roof. It came up fast, knocking the wind from her lungs as she landed. Legs dangled off the edge of the roof as she fought to remember how to breathe correctly. A dull throb radiated through her stomach as she kicked her leg up and rolled on to her back. She wheezed in and out, lungs stuttering.

The rough roof was cool against her cheek. Her hands roamed over her side and stomach, lifting the pale shirt she saw red marks. She hoped they wouldn't bruise. She got to her feet and shambled over to the center most window. The others had been closed already for the weather coming in, but one remained open. The clay tiles clicked together, so she had to step carefully and slow. She eased to the side of the window, making sure no one remained on the second floor. She popped her head in the second-floor loft, empty other than some tools and leathers stored there.

"Shut that thing up, Rascal!" A man bellowed at the front of the shed.

Crouching low, she laid on the floor of the loft and rested her ear on the wooden planks.

"I think it fears the storm comin."

Mia scooched to the edge of the loft, a ladder sticking up beside her. She kept low as she listened to the two guards. The dark shadow of one can be seen in between the doorway. The other was already inside, directly below.

"I don't care, we don't need this thing worrying everybody. And don't be fallen asleep like you did last night."

Rascal's rotund form kicked at the hay piled up. It reached the second floor here, but barely. He grumbled, but didn't say anything more. The door slid shut, leaving him alone with the creature.

A loud noise rattled below; the creature growled a warning. Rascal kicked out at the cage, making the beast angry, but quiet for now. Sliding over the second story floor, she watched him.

Mia jumped; her hands brushed some straw off the floor. It fell to the hay bales below.

"Mangy animal. Yous gonna be eaten soon, anyway. Don' know why it matters if it's kept alive." Heavy boots clunk on the wooden floor as another man strolled out from the back.

Her eyes widened as she realized another person was in here with them.

"It's quiet for now," Rascal said.

"Good, it was hard enough gettin' it in here wit' all them people around. We don' need them complainin' bout all the noise."

"Go ahead and git' they only need one of us watching the thing."

The man in question walked with slow, measured steps, his one leg dragging.

He opened and closed the door. Their voices carried up to her, but not clearly. As she laid there, waiting and listening to Rascal settle in. He made quick work of tidying up and then walked the length of the building. There was a room off to the side that he went in and shut the door. Mia counted, making sure he would not come back in.

Rascal's luck was not with him. She wondered if he was on creature duty as a punishment for her sleeping spell from the previous night. They wouldn't be happy the creature got out on his watch.

Moving to the ladder, she made quick work of climbing down to the first floor. Racing over to the cage. The creature in the cage was a brilliant blue with black stripes. There were many hues of blue. They were all deep and vibrant. Most of the blue was dark, especially near the black, and lightened to almost a fluorescent blue.

It cocked its head to the left, watching her as she came closer. Giving a growl, it scooted back in the corner of the cage. A long tongue snuck out as it licked its lips and even up on its nose. Looking back at the door, she paused, making sure the creature would keep quiet before she fiddled with the cage.

Mia hesitated for a moment. How could something so small be dangerous? Maybe if it was a full grown, but this one was still just a baby. Its head came up to her knee. As an adult, its size would be double that. She had pored over every book she could find that was about the outside world. With that, she also had learned these creatures were very territorial, especially over their young. The pack would make its way here in no time.

"I'm going to get you free," Mia whispered. "Don't make any noise." She was more worried about getting caught, more so than anything. She had never done anything like this. So far, she was loving the adrenaline it was pumping through her veins. It gave her a head rush.

Lifting the latch was easy since there was no lock on it. She pulled back on it and opened the cage. The thing sprung at her. She didn't move fast enough as it tackled her to the ground.

Hitting her head on the hard floor, she lifted her arms up in defense. The blue fuzzy fur was soft as she tried to push the thing off her. Sharp teeth sunk into her arm before she could snatch it away. Hissing in and out, she clenched her teeth, trying not to bellow.

"Stop," she hissed. Petting the top of its head, trying to push it to the side.

The thing let go and pounced off her, making a run for it. It dashed around the room, looking for an exit. It crashed into some pails that were in a corner, racing back down the center of the building. Holding up its nose, it sniffed around, searching and curious.

"Hey what's goin' on in there?" Rascal stomped out of the room he was in, the door banging against the wall.

Quickly getting to her feet, she held her arm close to her body. Terrified eyes roamed, tracking it as she ducked back to the ladder. Lifting her arm up, it barely could clutch on to the rung. She would never make it with her arm the way it was. The hay bales stared at her stacked in front of a closed barn window door hatch. Her feet and one good arm scrambled to haul herself up the immense squares of hay to climb to get back to the second-floor loft.

"Mia!" His head whipped back and forth between her and the creature. "What did you do to me yesterday?" His hands clenched into fists. He bolted for her.

"You remember?" She scoffed. She saw her blood was trailing behind her, making it impossible to hide.

"Remember?" he growled and bared his teeth as he advanced on her. "Mia, your name was scratched into the ground where I slept? What did you do?"

Blood dripped down her arm on to the hay. She was out of his reach. She kicked the hay with her bare foot. Hoping to control the blood flow, she attempted to press the arm into her shirt. She scaled the last bale that came even with the second floor, crawling the rest of the way onto the second floor. She stumbled to right herself back up on her feet. Unsure feet danced back and forth across the wooden floors; she was lightheaded.

The creature's pale blue eyes glowed behind Rascal. It hunkered down, hidden in the dark shadows. It eyed Mia, silhouetted against the night sky of the open window.

A cool wind whipped in tufts of hair pulled out of the braid she had made earlier. The creature stopped its scrabbling at the ground and pointed his nose toward the window. A light rain began with fat drops plunking off the clay tiles.

Rascal rushed to the ladder to come up after her. She took off out the window, not wanting to be caught. It was bad enough that he knew it had been her, but he didn't know what had transpired.

Her feet slid on the slippery tiles. The edge of the roof rushed up as her feet slid out over the clearance. She gripped the edge of the beam before the rest of her body went overboard. She hung there for a moment before dropping to the soft mud; it splashed up her ankles. Taking care not to slide, she made her way away from the front of the shed.

Thunder cracked loudly in the sky, covering up the noise from the fall and Rascal's grunting.

She struggled to run, her arm jostling, kept sending sharp pains through it.

The mud squished between her toes as she gripped the earth, forcing herself forward. She heard scrabbling and claws, a soft yip as something hit the ground behind her. She doesn't look back, afraid that they both were on her heels.

Many tensed filled minutes passed, and she was still huffing and puffing as she came to the edge of town. She saw her house in the distance, a medium-sized home with a small cottage set beside it. They lived near the most northeastern part of the wall. Her father enjoyed being the furthest inland that he could. He shipped things from the old country to here, along with catching fish. He desired to position himself as close to the woods as possible, as he rarely saw the inland unless he remained at home.

Racing forward, she set her sights on home and worked to lose anyone behind her.

Chapter 4
Mia

Mia's eyes set upon the small cottage home next to their own. Grandma lived next door so they could keep an eye on her. She raced over the soft wet grass, her heart pounding as she gasped for breath, making her way to the smaller building. The rain was cold and stinging as it battered her.

"Grandma Sky?" Mia called out as she opened the door, the fire already going and warming the small enclosure.

A high-pitched whistle came from the side near a little stove in the homey kitchen. Grandma Sky was there fiddling with two cups and some herbs.

"Come, I was expecting you. Sit at the table and we can have some tea."

Mia looked over her shoulder as she stood there in the door-way, checking to see if the creature had followed her. Rain pelted her back. It made it hard to see more than two feet in front of her. The dark clouds were ominous. Lightning arced high in the sky, lighting up the entire area.

"Arooo - Arrrrrrr - Aroooo," the creature called out from far behind.

The wind howled in answer.

"How did you know I was coming?" She puffed. Walking in water poured off her, creating puddles on the rugs. She slammed the door, shutting out the torrential rain.

"Your mother already was banging around in the kitchen, along with grumbling about you. Could hear her through the wall." Sky brought her cane up and tapped on the wall that was shared. "Things didn't go well?"

Giving a shake of her head, Mia pursed her lips. Old towels were piled by the door in a basket. She took a couple of them to wipe off her feet and dry her damp hair. A large ornate stone cylinder sat in the corner, collecting walking sticks, canes, and umbrellas. Mia struggled to move it a couple of inches from beside the door to in front of it. Blocking the entrance.

There, that should keep anything wanting in, out. "Don't go outside, okay?"

Her arm rubbed against the rough stone, agitating the wound there. She hissed, looking down at the white shirt. It was now completely see through along with a dark red stain on her stomach. She pulled out the long skirt from where she had it stuffed into the band. Dropping it back down to full length. The greens and blues were dark from the mud and rain. The shirt was a bloody mess and would have to be thrown out. No use in saving it. She kept facing the door as she pulled her skirt up, hitching it higher on her stomach to cover the worst of the stain.

The teacups rattled as Sky brought them to the small table in between the kitchen and sitting area. "What happened?"

"It's nothing. How did the rest of story time go?"

Sky gave her a withering stare, her gaze landing on her hurt arm as she held it there, uncovered. "Doesn't look like nothing. Did you get caught taking something that wasn't yours again?"

"Yes, but that isn't what this is about." She motioned to her hurt arm, giving a sheepish look.

"Perhaps caught somewhere you weren't supposed to be?" Sky gave a pointed look.

Mia smiled as she walked over to the warm fire to thaw her icy fingers and dry her clothes. "Hypothetically, that could have happened. Has happened once or twice."

"Were you testing the limits of the wall and guards again?"

"You know the whole point is not to get caught. Telling someone about my adventures could lead to that," Mia threw over her shoulder.

"Well, something caught you." Sky shambled forward the slippers made a soft whispered noise on the rough floor.

Mia waved her hand. "That's beside the point."

Grandma Sky chuckled. "Keep your adventures to yourself, then. I only ask what caused the damage on your arm to better take care of it."

Sky took slow, measured steps over to the sink. She rummaged under it for a moment before bringing out gauze and ointment in a big mason jar. Opening the jar, it stunk up the small enclosure.

"Grandma!" Mia waved a hand in front of her nose, turning her head. "That stuff smells terrible. It's not that bad!"

Sky tsked. "You made your choice, not telling me. Now we know it won't get infected. This stuff can cure a wart on a bullfrog." She knocked her hand against the glass, the rings clinked against it. "To answer your original question, story time went well. I will have a young man helping me soon around the store. So, I won't have work for you to do."

"Mother told me she will probably try to fill my days and nights with things she wants me to do."

Sky crossed behind Mia, landing hard in the wooden chair. "The kids all wanted to know more about the creature I came across and what it was like."

"Did you tell them the name it gave you?"

"Course not. Unlike you, most people don't want to terrify themselves." Sky's gnarled hands struggled with the bandages.

"Most people are boring." Rolling her eyes, Mia crossed to the small sink, running her arm under clean water.

Sky sat the cloth down on the table, scooping out some of the salve to spread over Mia's arm. She spread it over, tugging on the reddened flesh, making sure to get it into the punctured holes.

Gritting her teeth, Mia squeezed the top of her arm, trying to counteract the pain with another that she could focus on.

"What was its name again? I have not heard the story in a long time. Ally refuses to acknowledge that it even happened, let alone listen to the stories you tell."

"Abbadon," Sky said. "A touch of his chaos reached me that day. Your mother worries that it skipped her and will go straight to you. She goes to the extreme when it comes to you. Worrying about you is what she is good at."

"Too good," Mia grumbled.

"You will understand one day." Sky gives a tired sigh, patting Mia's hands.

A numbing sensation seeped into her arm as the ointment began to work. Mia wrapped the bandages slowly around her forearm. Tying it off, she cleaned up the leftover mess. "She needs to worry less."

"If she didn't worry about you, she wouldn't be a very good mother." Sky raised two shaky hands, sipping the cup of tea she had left forgotten on the table.

"If she cared so much, why can't she accept who I am? I am not like the others here." Putting the almost empty jar of salve back, Mia leaned against the sink, looking down at the mess on her clothes.

"It is not her way..."

"Tell me another story of the Old Ones."

"What if I tell you about one of their children instead?"

"They have children?!"

Sky barked out a laugh. Some of her tea sloshed up the sides of the cup, spilling on the warped wood of the table. "Why, of course, they have had children. They are not so different from you and I."

"I guess I felt they were otherworldly, like gods or something. I've never really thought of them like that."

Sky nodded. "Though this descendant had two Old One's for parents."

"How else would that work?"

"A pure blood or direct descendant is made from two Old Ones. But sometimes they would mix with us and create a halfling," Sky explained.

Excitement and eagerness shivered up her spine. Mia hadn't heard a new story in some time, and craved to listen to a new one. "Who was this one born of two Old One's?"

"This one was born of darkness. Everything about him was dark and broody. He dressed in dark colors, surrounding himself in dark shadows. Everything other than his eyes, those were a red, orange color. Even the Old Ones feared him. They say when he came into a room, he sucked all the joy and color out of it and ruined everything he touched."

"If the Old Ones feared him, wouldn't that be good for us?" Mia asked. A shiver ran down her spine as her cold, wet clothes kept her from feeling the warmth of the fire. She didn't know if the tremor came from fear of the unknown or the chill on her skin.

Cocking her head to the side, Sky gave it some thought. "You bring up a good point. Go put on some new clothes and we can talk more about the two horned devil."

Mia nodded. Her chair scraped against the floor as she stood up. Her eyes landed on the almost empty jar. "Do you need me to go to Sylvia's and get more salve soon? How are your other medicines?" Her eyebrows pinched in worry.

"Your mother would be most upset if she knew you had dealings with Sylvia."

"It's not like Sylvia is evil."

"Close enough in your mother's eyes. I had hoped Sylvia would help curb your mother's worries, but I fear it did the opposite." Sky rapped her knuckles on the wood, giving a shake of her head. "Bahh. Yes, I think I will need some things from her soon. I will make you a list."

"Sylvia has taught me many things. Her world is about order and exact measurements. It is fun and interesting, but not something I see myself doing long term. For so much power, it is strict in the regime needed."

Sylvia was great at so many things but she would never go into anything about the creatures that lived in the dark woods or what else may live out there. No, she just focused on talking about the plants, stones and how their spirit could be used.

The thought of what her mother had said to her today put her on edge. Mia felt the constraints of a cage crowd in around her. "This place is strangling me." Her heart beat fast, pounding in her chest. She stifled a cry. Pulling at the collar of her shirt, she loosened it.

"You could have your father's heart and need a sense of adventure on the open seas. When you get back from changing, I can tell you more of the story of the dark one and we can talk more about your future."

"You think I get my adventuring heart from my father?" She had never thought of it that way before. Mia made her way away from the kitchen into the living area. The couch she passed by had old fabric patches filled with threaded designs she had made. Her thoughts turned hopeful, knowing her grandma wanted to see her happy.

"We will think of something. Mia," Sky stopped waiting for Mia to pause, "never stop being you. Your strangeness is unique, and it helps make you strong. Even if others can't accept that."

Mia kept nodding as she moved past the bathroom and bedroom door. There sat a door in the wall. She opened it up carefully, trying to remain as quiet as possible. This door connected their two houses together. Slipping through the door, she shuts the door behind her without a sound. The hallway remained dark as she took cautious steps. The only sound was the creaking of her own footsteps.

She made it to her room, closing herself in. She made quick work of undressing and pulling on a plain shift dress. The dress was a deep blue with stars and a moon embroidered on the bottom near the hem. Though she danced around, her feet did not find the clutter around her room that she was used to. She froze, looking down at the swept floor, searching for feathers and other knickknacks. She muttered to herself and glared at her closed door.

"Mother," she uttered. Heat flushed through her entire body. Letting out a long exhale, she took small steps toward the door.

Her stomach gurgled and cramped. Opening the door, she listened to the house. All was silent. It groaned as it settled in; the wind battering against it. The pitter patter of the rain pounded against the tin roof.

Mia skated past her mother's room on tiptoes, keeping her feet light on the wooden floors. She kept to the side, making sure none of the floorboards creaked.

As she headed to the kitchen, she quickly grabbed some fresh bread she had made earlier. Chomping off a bite, she turned to go back the way she came. She spotted a parchment on the table beside her. Grabbing the paper, she turned to the side and flipped a switch, lighting up the area. Her name sprawled across the top of it in her mother's handwriting. She unfolded the letter to read what she had written to her.

Mia,

I know when you get like this, you either stay over at your grandmother's hut or aren't back till late. I have headed to bed by the time you are reading this and want you to know I do this because I care. If you haven't seen it yet, you will soon. I have cleaned up your room and taken the items you had no care for since they were all over the floor and not put away. This morning was the last straw. I know you snuck out again to go learn from that medicine woman. No daughter of mine is going to be a witch and hated by the entire town. I hear the whispers and what they say about you. You might as well be an Old One if you decide to do that. The doctor we were supposed to see today expressed some in-terest in you if you could tame your wildness a bit. I have allowed him to let his interest grow to give you more time. I persuaded him to give you the time to be wooed by him. That you would come around to his advances in time. It is the only way for you to fit in here. No other will have you. I want you taken care of for fear that we might not always be here when you need us. Do what you must tonight, but come tomorrow, things will change. You will also start work in Penny's shop and will learn from her. The decision is yours, of course, if you want it to be with the doctor. But I am afraid you leave me no choice. You will end up with him, or be locked away for your own good. He will help make you better if I cannot. Please know there are things you don't understand yet, but know I am trying my best to help and keep you safe.

Love,

Your Mother

Mia scrunched up the paper in her fist. She stared at the beige wall. She could not believe what she had read. Thoughts raced through her mind, and her throat tightened with emotion. The urge to scream was so strong she took a huge bite of bread, stuffing her face. The bread tasted like burned ash. As she swallowed the bread, her stomach turned sour at the thought of taking another bite. She then turned the light down low, making it more difficult to read the letter. The letters on the paper blurred together as tears filled her eyes.

"She will never accept me. Never accept anything I try or do. She will force my hand into the pictures she has chosen for me." Tears fell down her cheeks, stifling her cry with her hands over her mouth.

A scratch at the back door caught her attention, stopping her hot tears and sniffles. Everything froze and was quiet for a moment before another scratch. The letter fell from her fingers as she went to the door. Giving the door a curious look, she loosened the tie to move the cloth and look out the window. The darkness made it hard to see what was out there. Cracking it open, icy rain pelted her bare hand. The water was cool against the heat that radiated from her.

A snout pushed hard against the opening. A body wriggled in and slid through before she could close it. Mia jumped back, surprised that the creature from earlier came barreling in, sniffing the ground. Electric blue fur with black stripes streak across the kitchen, heading back to her. Powerful limbs scrambled across the wood as his eyes feast on the hand still holding the bread. Pulling a chair out, she blocked the beast, guarding herself from being attacked.

"You hungry?" she questioned. Wanting to calm the creature long enough to settle down.

Jumping up, its hindquarters remained on the ground; its front paws landed on the chair seat. It used its front two paws to lift itself closer, reaching for the bread that was just out of grasp.

Lifting her hand up, she kept it away. "Food, you want?" She broke off a small piece, placing it right through the back bars of the chair furthest from its teeth. She pulled her hand back through the bars quickly, not wanting to get her fingers bitten off.

With a sniff of the food, a long tongue came out, licked it, and then gobbled it up. Its eyes were dark as it waited there patiently for more.

"Food?" It croaked out when neither one moved for a while.

Dropping the bread all together, Mia's eyes go wide. "Did you just talk?"

"Food!" it said louder, giving a happy howl of excitement as it jumped down, attacking the food that had rolled. The bread disappeared in a matter of minutes. "More?" The creature cocked its head to the side and gave sad eyes.

"Oh, umm. You want more?" Her eyes searched the kitchen. She had not seen any more bread. "Are you a boy or a girl?"

"Boy." He shuffled, coming up behind her.

"Do you have a name?"

"Bloo." He hopped up and down, his nails clicking on the floor.

"Blue, oh, because of your coloring?"

Shaking his head. "Bloooo," he enunciated.

"Bloo?" She shrugged her shoulders, going along with it. Opening a cabinet, she took out some plain cereal and grabbed a handful. She kneeled on the ground, holding her palm out to him. "Can I pet you? Don't eat me, okay?"

"Food?"

"No, I'm not food. But yes, food is here." She placed it on the ground beside her. Bloo's steps were unsure and wary of her movements.

He sniffed the floor around the cereal but did not move closer.

"Why didn't you leave and go back to your family?" Mia asked.

"Abandoned."

"You're all alone?"

"No." Bloo sat down and opened his mouth, showing off his sharp teeth as he yawned.

She grabbed another handful of the cereal and knocked some back into her mouth. She crunched down on the food. "See, it's good." She tossed the rest of what was in her hand on the floor. Her back hit the counter as she slid down to be more on his level.

"You're here. Bloo not alone anymore."

He happily trotted up beside her. She reached out a shaky hand to pet him. His coat was so pretty with the vibrant blue streaks. The black made the blue even more prominent in spots. Scratching his ears, they came to a point. Bloo turned his head as she itched the right spot. Down the middle of its head were two velvety tipped horns, small but pointy. They were rigid beneath the fur.

Once he had eaten all the food, he backed away from her. Pointing his nose up high, he checked out the rest of the room, heading back to the dark hallway. She launched herself at the hallway, blocking off his access.

"No, stay in this room," Mia whispered.

Bloo craned his head to the side, trying to see around her. "Why?"

"Well, because if my mother catches you, she will throw both of us out."

Looking back at the door, it bounced over to it. "Out?"

Glancing at the door, Mia walked over and opened it. "Do you want to go out? To find your home?" He raced back out into the rain, scurrying in the dark, his fur easy to see over the mid length grass.

Stopping, he stuck his head up, looking this way and that. "How?"

"You don't know how to get out of the city?"

A bright light flashed across the sky, but no rumbles followed it.

She chewed on her lip for a moment before her gaze landed on the paper. "Hold on," she called out.

Grabbing the letter, she scanned it one last time before she crumpled it up, letting it fall there on the table. Taking her coat off the hook beside the door, she knew the light dress would not be warm enough in this cool rain.

"I will show you."

She decided against putting boots on and raced into the rain. Bloo bounded off away from her. A light laugh echoed out of her before she could suppress it. Mia raced forward to keep up with his zippy speed. The wind tore at her dark hair; the strands pulled out of the loose braid she had done earlier.

Rising from the hill above, the wall loomed tall and menacing. She had no clue what it had been made with, only that it would stand the test of time along with the magic helping it.

"I hope they have not fixed it since last time." She had not gotten the courage yet to go fully into the woods, but she had ventured onto the other side to ease that building pressure.

Bloo sneezed, shaking his head against the rain.

"Here, here." Mia rushed up to the wall, following it to the closest post. The greenery was already overrunning it and a vine had sprouted up onto the wall. She pressed against it, breaking the foliage as the small part of the wall bent, but not by much. Enough of it to leave a small space at the bottom for something small to push through.

Bloo came over and sniffed the hole, but shook his head at it. "Scared," he uttered.

"I don't blame you; you were in a cage. Here I will go through first and then you can come through." She scooped out some of the dirt, making the hole bigger to get her shoulders through the tight area. The coat sleeves rode up, getting her bandage dirty. Her foot slipped in the mud, she fell and slid away from the wall. The flap of metal snapped shut. Mud coated the back of her coat; she tried to wipe as much of it off as possible.

The rain made the mud so slick. She struggled with the small hill, trying to scale back up it. She gripped her fingers and toes in the mud, glad she didn't bring the boots. That would have made it ten times harder to climb. She trudged back up the small hill and gripped on to the edge, holding it wide open as she could pull on it, the metal not bending as much as she would like. The icy rain mixed with the cold mud on her back made this night unbearable. She longed for the warm fire that grandma Sky was probably already passed out in front of.

Bloo poked his head through the hole, curious. She tried to wait, but the wall wanted to spring back in place. The rough ridge bit into her hands. He took cautious steps, waiting till he was all the way through. The last bit slid through her fingers and snapped close. Her fingers burned as she hissed in pain.

"Follow." Bloo bounded off into the woods, which were a measly few steps away.

Mia hesitated. She had never gone into the deep woods. She always stayed on the trails that were close to the edge of the wall. Only ducking away if a guard patrolled close by.

Taking a step back to the wall, she touched it. It kept her tethered to reality when all she wanted to do was leap into action. Her eyes scanned the greenery. If she stayed here, only heartache and pain would come to her. Her chest squeezed tight at the anguish that clogged her throat. Why couldn't they like her for who she was?

"Please?" Bloo pleaded.

A numb buzzing filled her head as she calmed her torrential thoughts. Everything quieted.

"What could it hurt? It can't be all that bad out here, not compared to what mother has in store for me. It's either this or ship out on a boat back to some land that my grandma escaped from for a reason."

Something out here had called to her; it was time she found out. She would show everyone in town that she wasn't scared and that it wouldn't be a death sentence. Turning back to the woods, she investigated the dark vegetation as the lightning decorated the sky.

"Bloo? Where did you go?" She took a few steps towards the dark branches, trying to spot the little creature.

His light blue fur peeked out of the greenery as he bounded back to her.

"Help, help!" He whined.

Trudging on ahead, her face pinched in worry. "What's wrong? Did you get stuck on something?"

"Friend. Help!" he called out. He circled around her feet, then bounded off to the right, directly into the trees. His fur illuminated the way, making it easier to see him in the dark woods.

"Your friend needs help?" Ducking below a branch, she moved leaves aside, trying to stay with him as he moved more into the dense brush. The rain wasn't as heavy with the thick canopy up above slowing the drops.

She picked up her pace, going at a jog, following him deeper into the thicket. She felt a twang of guilt, but the fresh air and freedom of the night called to her. The strings that had held her back were finally gone as she let herself enjoy.

"I can do this. I will find a way," she said with conviction.

You didn't even pack anything. No food, no shelter, nothing. How far do you think you're going to get?

"I can always come back later when I am done exploring," she argues to herself.

If you don't, get lost.

She grumbled to herself. "Bloo, where did you go?"

"Help me."

She bounded off some rocks and stepped between branches. Glowing flowers lit up a path matching Bloo's steps. He skidded to the left out of sight, giving a growl and yip before a soft thump hit nearby. He whined.

"Bloo, what happened?" Mia rushed forward but stopped before a circle of medium-sized rocks. They came up to her knee, and there at the center was Bloo.

He cried out loudly as his paws tried to pull free of the thick mud and water he had stumbled into.

Reaching out, she caressed the top of the stone. "Circles can be powerful..." A wave crashed over her as her hand connected with the rough rock. The thrill traveled up her arm and down her back, making her feel giddy.

"But are you keeping something in the circle or out?" Mia asked. She slid between the rocks. A wisp of wind blew upward, sending her hair every which way. Pushing through, she took a seat near Bloo, pulling him into her lap and looking over him.

The rain stopped as the clouds cleared. The moon sliced through the leaves. Owls sang out and the forest noises creaked around her. Animals scattered about.

Bloo's face stared up at her as she cradled him in her arms. "You are nice," Bloo said.

She smooshed her face into the top of his head, hugging him close. "You are nice too." She pet him and made sure he was not hurt.

The muddy water underneath crawled up her legs, latching on and taking hold. She sunk further into it before she realized what was happening. Letting Bloo escape her grasp, she made sure he landed on a rock safely away from the sinking mud. Water pooled in the center of the rocks, making the mud less solid. She sunk in faster.

The mud reached up and latched onto her feet so she couldn't kick away. It pulled at her, tugging and dragging into the center of the rocks. Raising her hands, she searched the ground for rope or something to grab onto. If her mother hadn't thrown everything out, she would have brought some of her trinkets with her, then this wouldn't have been a problem.

"Bloo, do you see anything that could help?" she asked, her mind racing at how she could get out of this.

She leaned back, trying to raise her lower half out so she could wiggle free. Instead, the mud has a mind of its own and latched onto her back and arms, sucking her down into its depths. A low rumble shook the earth as something rough wrapped around her legs. She kicked her feet, swishing below her, trying to find purchase on what had her, but they kept sliding and moving away from her.

Whispered voices that were unintelligible and circled around her. Her hair blew around her, getting in her eyes and mouth.

"Chaos," someone hissed. Mud pulled up from the ground in long thin strands as they circled her like snakes. They slithered around her, looking for a weakness.

Raising her hands, she tried to fend them off. Her frozen fingers scrambled for purchase. The vines dodged her feeble attempts, wrapping around her arms, sucking her in. The slime crawled over her body around her arms, lifting the bandages and drilling into the punctured wound left by Bloo.

She yelled out in pain and fought against the thick muddy goop that held her. The mud climbed higher up her chest and neck. Fighting, she strained to free at least one arm.

Bloo barked and growled in the background; she couldn't see him through the stones. A green fleck fluttered in the moonlight's beam. Another night time butterfly? This place was so strange.

As she was being pulled down, everything was covered except her nose and above. Soon she wouldn't be able to breathe. The large yellow green butterfly landed on her forehead. Dust fell around her. Sneezing her head jerked forward, launching the butterfly off her. It caught an airstream gliding around her.

More dust flitted from the butterfly, landing on her and the surrounding ground.

What the hell is this?

"Help," cried Bloo. He was off in the distance.

The dirt below her solidified, stopping her downward descent. The dirt raised up like a cobra ready to strike the butterfly. It took flight, keeping just out of reach but dusting itself with what it was creating with every down thrust of its wings. Launching upward at the butterfly, the snake slowed and froze in midair as the dust hit the wet mud.

The slimy mud snake dried out and became brittle, breaking apart easily. Silence followed the whispers. She kicked her legs and turned up the soil below, emerging from the pit.

Dirt caked under her fingernails as she scrabbled back up. She squirmed and wormed her way between the two rocks, leaving the circle.

Mia glanced back, looking at what could have been her grave. She shuddered to think about what could have happened. Should she go home? Was this going to be the death of her, like the town said it would be? She rested a moment, catching her breath. No, she couldn't think that way. She had to show them.

"Friend?" Bloo yipped at the butterfly, jumping up and trying to catch it.

She laughed as she rolled onto her back, raising her palm, waiting for the butterfly to rest. It was the least she could do after her encounter with whatever that was.

The butterfly landed as its wings slowed their flutter. "I guess you're not so bad," Mia said.

It fluttered once more and raced towards her face, sending dust particles into her eyes. She rubbed as the sting of debris hit them. Wiping them clean, she looked up, eyes streaming. There was a shadow looming over her with four tall horns. She flinched back and crawled away.

Wasn't Grandma Sky going to tell her about a two horned demon? It must be back. Whatever had her in the pit climbed out and was going to take her away.

The butterfly floated away, afraid of her thrashing limbs, and Bloo disappeared into the shrubs nearby. Despite her efforts, she couldn't get up and do the same because her limbs wouldn't cooperate. She kept sliding down in the dirt. She panted, becoming frustrated with how useless her arms were moving.

Her foot came down wrong, and her ankle twisted. Giving out, she fell to the side. Large arms encircled her as her head connected with the ground. Her mind struggled to stay conscious.

"Hush, human. We are not here to harm you." A male voice rumbled softly, piercing her foggy mind. A handsome face came closer to her, one with no horns. He was bright and golden.

So pretty.

"I don't know, Haddox she looks good enough to bite." A man with large horns clicked his teeth together. The shadows near the rocks hid him.

"Back off, Grey. The butterfly and forest have chosen her as our next warrior."

Grey sneered and raised his lip, showing off the glint of sharp teeth as he came out of the shadows.

She wasn't sure what she should do. Her eyes fluttered close, and it took everything in her to raise them back up. "Old Ones?" Mia coughed out before surrendering to unconsciousness.

Chapter 5
Haddox

Haddox looked down at the slight form bundled in his arms. She was so small compared to him, and she was to be their next warrior. Frowning, his eyes scanned their surroundings, searching for threats. They were on the edge of the dark woods. None of their kind traveled this far out anymore. Her village didn't take too kindly to others, especially after they had to take that other woman. The animals had warned them to be on the lookout.

She would have to do, and this time he would make sure she would like and enjoy their kind, so she would help them. She would not throw the game by ending her life, not like the last one.

You started all this.

His thoughts turned dark as he remembered what he had done. What was the forest thinking when choosing their warriors?

He rolled his eyes and stomped over to Grey, who was leaning against the tree.

"Is that?" Grey broke off as Haddox shoved the girl into his arms.

"Here." Haddox shuddered. He cracked his neck to the side. He would have to be close to her all too soon. "Let me check things out to make sure there aren't guards around or anyone missing this one. You get her back to the temple." Part of him hated what he would have to do.

"You said you would watch over her," Grey complained, trying to hand her back.

"And I will. See to her till I get back." This was all Grey's fault, anyway. If it wasn't for him, they wouldn't be in this predicament now. Now he had to play nice with one of their kind and make it believable.

Grey grumbled, holding her body close to his. He waited. "Did she disturb anything?"

Haddox stepped forward, pausing between the stones before entering the circle. He held up a hand, pressing on the barrier to test. "I think we are safe." His hand encountered an unseen obstacle, causing him to take a step back.

Bloo jumped up, snapping at Grey. Growling and barking incessantly, he circled his legs. He leaped up at Grey. "Friend?" Bloo wailed.

Grey bit his teeth at the little mongrel. "Your friend is going to go take some tests. She can't play with you anymore."

"What is one of those doing this far out?" Haddox asked.

"I don't know. This one is young, though. He seems attached to the woman."

Haddox took the bow and arrow he carried from his shoulder and pulled it over his head. Stringing an arrow, he held it at the ready. "You've heard the human tales. They do things for no reason. Maybe they are keeping them as pets now."

"Why is she even out here? Don't they all stay behind the wall?" Grey asked, ignoring Haddox's disdain.

"Why ask me? I don't keep tabs on the humans. I barely want to associate with them," Haddox sniped. "You are the one better at that. With your books."

Baring his teeth. "Don't remind me."

"So ferocious." Haddox rolled his eyes. He stepped lightly around the circle of rocks, testing the barrier. "Poor Grey, a direct descendant with all this power to let a human break you so. What purpose do they serve?"

"Careful there. That kind of thinking lead to the Old One's being locked up as they are," Grey said.

"Don't act like you don't like to play with them..." Haddox gasped as he stepped forward into the circle. A shiver raced across him. Mud and a dark cloud billowed out of the ground, swirling around his feet. The mud sucked at his boots, pulling him under as the ground gave. Falling, he watched as the bow and arrow clattered to the ground beyond his grasp. The mud was up to his chest, making it hard to breathe. The constant golden aura he kept going flickered and dimmed.

"What is it, Haddox?" Grey looked on, worried.

Haddox watched Grey struggle with what to do. His hold on the girl tightened as he walked closer to the circle of stones.

Haddox looked on with disdain. "Worthless!" he scoffed. "What does it look like?"

Why does he not help? Should he not be rushing to my side to help? No, even now he still worries about a human's safety, then his own kind. Haddox couldn't believe his misfortune being paired with Grey.

Haddox's vision blurred; he blinked a few times to clear it. Wiping his eyes with his hands, he glanced down. His boots were on solid ground right at the edge of the circle. He shook his head at the illusion that had felt so real moments ago. Twisting around, he ran worried fingers through his hair. The Bow and arrow still nocked in his left hand. His grip tightened, needing the pain to solidify him in reality.

He was the one to cause illusions he wasn't used to them being so real to him. His lips tightened. Should he ask Grey for help? This was not the first time he had witnessed one of his illusions plaguing him. Grey did all that research day in and day out. Maybe he read something that could help.

"Put friend down," Bloo whined as he backed away from Grey and the stone circle. He rushed to the other side of Grey, circling him. Lunging at him, he nabbed Grey with his sharp teeth, grabbing onto the dark cloak he was wearing. Growling, he hung on by his teeth.

Grey fumbled with the little beast as he held the woman in his arms, careful not to drop her. He spun around, trying to loosen the dragon-like creature, but he did not stop. Bloo's body swayed as his fangs dug in. His feet kicked in the air as he tried to pull Grey's arm away.

Haddox's arm shot out. Grabbing the animal by the back of the scruff, he threw him hard against the ground. Bloo bounced and skittered across the dirt packed ground, rolling to a stop at the base of a tree. He laid there in a heap, whining.

With determination, Haddox moved forward closer to the creature. He pulled back on the string of the bow, drawing the arrow and aiming it dead center at the little furry dragon.

"Haddox!" Grey said in surprise.

Haddox halted abruptly, his gaze fixed on the small lump in front of him. He clenched his hands around the wood and string of the bow. "It attacked you."

"It was protecting her." Grey sidestepped in between Haddox and his prey.

Grey's eyes pierced his. Haddox lowered his bow but kept the arrow knocked in place, holding it by his side. "Fine."

Grey reached for him. Haddox's golden light flickered again.

He shook his head and stepped back, getting as far away as he could. "I said I'm fine keeping your powers to yourself and stop breaking my illusion," Haddox said.

Bloo limped away, staying close to the bushes and partially hiding in the undergrowth.

"You coming, Haddox?" Grey waited to make sure the creature got away before turning back the way they came.

"I'm going to check out the area and cover our tracks so they can't find us. I will be behind you and back before she wakes." Hadn't he already told him that, or was that an illusion? Haddox turned his back to them so they couldn't see the confusion written on his face.

"So, be it."

"Wrong," Bloo wheezed out from behind shrubbery, following his friend and Grey into the dark woods.

Haddox shook his head, knocking the rage and anger that had consumed him away. He had thought his power was growing since he could now do more with it for longer. He had always felt held back or only a part of himself. His human half kept him from achieving his full potential.

"What was that?" He rubbed his fingers against his temple. His eyes focused on the sacred stones that held an Old One. Of course, it had to be the oldest and worst of them. Devouring the distance with his legs, he found himself back at the circle. His hand came up to feel the protective barrier once more. "I need to make sure it's still there, that it was all an illusion."

There was no pressure when he touched his hand to the air between the stones. "What the?" He creeped closer, trying to sense any magic or power in the circle. Walking around the stones, he crouched down in the mud, feeling the rough ridges of the rock. "Where did it go?" Mud snaked up and latched around his hand, pulling him down into the mud face first. It swallowed him down in an instant.

Dirt and gunk covered his mouth. He snapped it close, struggling against what had hooked him. Whispers flooded around him and a dark cloud hovered over his golden light, dimming what he could see.

"I have the knowledge you seek," a gravelly voice taunted.

Haddox froze. He relaxed, cocking his head to the side, waiting to see what this thing wanted. His bow was snaked away from him.

"You are correct that your power is growing and you must use it."

Images flickered through his mind, showing him how the voice wanted him to use that power in the worst way possible.

"All I need is a willing host to help, and I will unlock your potential in ways you have never thought of before. Being the first Old One has its perks. I can help you if you help me."

Haddox knew the stories. Abbadon was the first of their kind to reach this place. He saw the potential and brought more of his kind with him. The temptation was hard to resist, as his lungs longed for fresh, clean air. He kicked out, hitting something hard. Moving his foot slower this time, he found the hard rock and shoved himself up.

"Abbadon," Haddox whispered out as he scrambled his way to the surface. Haddox laid there as images and his mind swirled. The mud receded as the dark cloud enveloped him fully.

"Yes," he hissed.

Chapter 6
Grey

Grey raced forward, the woman in his arms laid limp and cold to the touch. The trees rushed past him; their colors melded together as he sped up. The trees got even larger as they delved deeper into the woods. Buildings intertwined with the trees and bushes, becoming one with each other. There was a balance that most humans had not gravitated towards yet.

He rushed past many others of his kind in various activities. Taking care of their homes and lives as any other person may have. They barely even glanced at him. Whispered voices and hard stares followed him. He couldn't outrun them, let alone his own thoughts.

"It's him... What is he doing out here?"

He ignored them.

Battie, his sister, was who he needed to find. He didn't think she would be in their town center; she much preferred the quiet. Closer to her roots. He couldn't get far enough from his roots. He was glad she didn't suffer as he had.

His eyes danced over a building that was built into a waterfall near the river. The building was perched seamlessly into the landscape, almost as if it was grown from the rock itself. Constant and powerful, the sound of water roared and reverberated through the air. The large building had many levels to it and even climbed up over the waterfall.

In his arms, the woman cried out. He looked down at her, taking her frame in for the first time. He so badly didn't want to be a part of this. She was small compared to him, but most people and others were. A thick layer of dirt covered her long brown coat she wore. The blue dress had some stained spots of reddish brown.

"Grey?" An elderly male who lived on the outskirts stopped him.

"Have you seen Battie?" He slowed to a stop. The creature straggled behind, hardly keeping up. He wheezed in and out as he limped.

"She is at the healing center today. I just came back from there."

He nodded, hiking the woman higher in his arms. Jogging forward, he was caught off guard by two boys playing in a little tree house next to the old man's house.

Terror caught in his throat along with something else he couldn't name. Freezing him in place.

The old man shuffles closer. "Is that the next one?" He brushed her hair aside to get a better glimpse of the woman. "How are you doing, Grey?"

Grey's eyes stared straight ahead at the two boys, his throat constricting tight on his lungs.

"Those are Trey's boys. They are about eight now."

"They look just like him," he wheezed out. Their green wings fluttered as they jumped from branch to branch. Making their way higher up the tree and into the different rooms. That tree had been where Grey would come to teach Trey and Haddox.

"They do. It has not been that long, but the boys seem to do okay, regardless." The man doubled over, coughing.

Grey blinked and remembered the woman in his arms. He hesitated, wanting to set her down to care for the man.

"Nah boy, I'm good. Just clearing the old pipes."

"Boy? I'm older than you."

"Keep tellin' yourself that, but I don't see it. Marnie will be glad to hear that I saw you. We have missed you all this last year."

"I... must... go." Grey set his sights on the path that would take him to the care center.

"Grey, one thing. Because you know she will ask. How are you really doing?"

"I'm alive, ain't I?" He grumbled. "Which is more than I can say for you, old man. Not many more years left in you." He took off without waiting around to hear what was said next. In an attempt to escape that part of his past, he ran as fast as he could. He usually remembered not to come this way, but he had not paid attention as his thoughts had wandered.

"Enough years to still give you a whoopin'," the old man yelled.

He heard surprised laughter and a holler at the two boys in the tree. As he turned with the bend of the path, he disappeared. He slowed his pace to a jog and didn't stop until he reached the healing center, which was right next to where the tests would be given.

"Battie!" Grey yelled out.

"Brother? What happened?" Battie rushed to his side, giving him a once over.

He motioned to the woman in his arms.

Battie motioned him into the closest empty room. Eyes around the center had landed on him. Closing them in the room, she shut out their quiet, whispered questions.

"Wait." Grey hesitated.

The little blue creature hobbled in slowly behind them. He eyed the new woman in a lab coat. Plopping on the ground by the bed, he rested.

Grey laid the woman down on the bed inside the room, making sure not to harm her pet, and turned to his sister. Her black and green hair was up in pigtail buns. The white lab coat didn't hide what she wore beneath. She had on black boots that clomped on the floor as she closed the door and looked leerily at both the animal and the woman.

"You have some unusual friends, brother," Battie said, as she cocked her head.

"Unusual, isn't the half of it." He chortled. "She is the next one that will take the test. The forest chose her."

"Then tell me why, brother, because I feel like this is important. Is she unconscious?"

"She was near Chaos's tomb. Something could have happened to her like the last one..."

"And what are you leaving out?" Battie's hawk-like gaze landed on him.

Walking over to the large clear window, a vine twisted and hung in the corner. His fingers twined with the little greenery. It raised to him but barely. "Can you help her or not?" He grounded out.

"Not," she sang out.

Turning, Grey grabbed her arm. His eyes widened. "Do you want all of them to come back? Do you think she would stay if she had a choice?"

"We would be fine," anger tinged her voice.

Her arm flexed beneath his hand, pulling back. He let her go free. "And what of her?"

"I would go where she went." Battie twirled around the bed and sat down next to the blue fuzzy dragon. "Who is this pretty boy?"

"Bloo," Bloo said, his tail whipping across the floor.

She couldn't really think like that, could she? "Battie," Grey huffed.

"Well, Bloo what happened?"

"Gold boy mean," Bloo whined, curling in to protect his ribs.

If the Old Ones were set free, most of the people in their village would face destruction. Grey wondered what others of their kind thought. Could they put an end to these tests for good?

"Yea, so." Battie gently took Bloo's face in her hands and turned it away. "I'm going to brush my hand against your side and make it all better, okay?"

"Friend?" Bloo questioned.

"Yes, I'm a friend," Battie answered.

"No." Bloo looked at Mia, who laid on the bed, not moving. He butted his nose against Mia's arm. "Friend."

Battie eyed the woman, but nodded her head. "I will look at your friend after we get you feeling better."

"Promise?" He wheezed.

"Promise." She made an elaborate 'x' across her chest.

"Battie, that would mean no more Haddox, no more Trey's children. You can't mean that. The Old Ones would try to eradicate anything that had human DNA." He moved to the woman on the bed, taking the back of his hand to her head. Her temperature plummeted. He helped the woman sit up and maneuvered her arms out of the wet and muddy coat. Grabbing the blanket, he shook it out and laid it over her, trying to do something while his sister took her sweet time.

"What are you spouting about? Of course, I don't mean that," she murmured. Her eyes avoided his as she went still.

The air shimmered with a soft, ethereal glow as her hands brushed the side of Bloo's fur. Light poured out of her hand, it getting brighter as she moved with deliberate, fluid motions. The delicate hue pulsed gently as her very essence poured into the creature.

Grey watched with disbelief; he was in awe of the power that radiated out of her.

Bloo panted and heaved, but as soon as the light winked out, he took deep, settling breaths. He barked joyfully and licked Battie's hand.

"There, there." Her fingers curled into the fur.

"Friend, now," Bloo demanded. He bound away, jumping up on the bed and laid by Mia's feet.

"Yes, I suppose it is time for that." Battie sighed and shook her head and her hands out. "What do we have here, new friend?" She looked over at the woman going through the motions of an assessment.

Grey watched over them, his nose crinkled in thought. "Who did you heal last?"

She waved a hand over her shoulder, ignoring him. "Haddox, friend." She giggled as she lifted the blanket to check on her legs and feet.

"That explains it."

"Explains what?" She threw down the blanket and glared at Grey.

"Why you would say those things?"

"What? My thoughts and ideas?"

"You know, when you heal, you take on some of that person's mindset," Bloo growled. "Or creature's essence. Your voice gets muddled through their thoughts and feelings."

"Not true," she whispered out. Pursing her lips, she rubbed her fingers against her scalp. "No, no, no," she yelled louder and louder with each word. "I.." she sputtered.

"Battie, center yourself."

"Oh, it's that easy!" She groaned out. "Just, just. A minute."

Grey steadied her, grabbing onto her biceps. She hissed in pain; yanking away from him on one side, her hand caressing the black mesh shirt over a hot pink shirt holding her side.

"Share it."

"I can handle it." Battie's piercing blue eyes met his.

A knock rapped on the door before opening a bit. Fiery red hair poked in. "Battie?"

"Not now Leah," Grey burst. His eyes held Battie's. She couldn't keep doing this. He needed her in his life couldn't she understand that. He waited until he heard the soft snick of the door close. "Share the pain." She hesitated. "Now." His fingers dug into her shoulders as he shook her slightly.

Battie placed her hands on his chest. She cocked her head to the side with a wicked glint in her eye. "Careful what you wish for, brother."

A warmth poured into him then turned to a searing pain that dove straight to his ribs. His bones there bent and cracked. He hissed as the pain the person had endured before him became his own to balance. His kind were fast healers; he wouldn't have to deal with it long.

Grey bent at the waist, huddled over her. She danced away, giving a euphoric giggle. "Check the woman, please," he said through clenched teeth.

Battie huffed, stomping over to the bed. She waved her hands over her and then dropped them. "There isn't anything wrong with her."

"What? There must be." He stomped over to her, hovering. "Humans don't just collapse, her temperature plummeted as well."

"It's a cool night, especially with the rain."

The door banged open, Haddox was there in the doorway. "He also frightened the girl into fainting."

"You would." Battie smirked.

"Good, you're back. She is your problem now, remember?" Grey's long legs ate up the distance between them. He waited for Haddox to move from the doorway.

"Battie, will you fetch me when she stirs? I have something to take care of right away."

"Sure, sure."

Grey stared Haddox down, his usual golden eyes dimmed and were a muddy brown.

Haddox stared back, refusing to move. "We all know you care more than you let on. Stay with the girl. I will be back before she wakes." He didn't even wait before turning his back on Grey.

Battie's soft hand pulled his arm back. Grey's clenched fist wanted to beat the smirk off his face.

"There is something wrong with that one."

"Tell me about it. I've been saying that ever since meeting Trey and him."

"Not that." Battie shook her head. "Something more." They both watched him as he walked away with his normal swagger turning back out of the healing center. "What do you think he had to do?" she questioned.

"Probably something with the test and letting those who need to know." He shrugged one side of his shoulder. The fight had gone out of him as he came back into the room. "You can go. I will send someone to fetch him before she wakes." He couldn't tear his eyes from the woman's sleeping form. "Not like she would want to see me, anyway. Too terrifying to look at." He clicked his sharp teeth together.

He fell back into the chair next to the bed, resting while he could. Exhaustion spilled into him as he let the day's excitement wash through him.

Chapter 7
Mia

Her ears perked as she heard whispered voices. Her head ached as she tried to open her eyes. She scrunched them closed tightly. The bright light beaming down on her caused her to shrink and wiggle down in the covers. Yanking them over her head, she turned in bed, away from the voices. If only she could fall back asleep, maybe if she lied here long enough, it would take her back under.

Where the hell was she?

"She's waking up. Make yourself scarce."

"Are you sure, Haddox? You won't mess this up like last time?" another low voice rumbled out.

"Things didn't turn out well when she saw you," Haddox hissed. "Plus, you said you were out of this. Or was that all talk, Grey?"

Haddox, Grey... She had never heard those kinds of names before. What happened? The last she could remember was she was outside the wall in the woods.

Her head pounded in time with their arguing. Without opening her eyes, she covered her ears with her hands, blocking out some of the sound. Her toes stuck out and the cool air hit them. She pulled up her legs, hiding them. She grumbled as she let herself relax into the soft mattress below her. Maybe they didn't mean her harm.

"I know what I said," Grey huffed out.

"The last one didn't like our kind. She failed on purpose. The one before that..." Haddox defended.

Mia held her breath. If she stayed quiet, maybe she could find out more about where she was. Were they talking about Julie or someone else? She froze in fear of what to do. This was much more than one of her grandmother's stories. One wrong move and she could meet an ending she didn't intend. Her mind spiraled with what ifs.

"Did she fail? Or was she pushed to do those things by the Old One?"

"Who knows? Will we ever know what really happened to her or Tre..."

"Do not!" Grey warned.

"I know he was important to you. But he was my brother!" Haddox seethed.

Harsh breaths emanated from his side. She could tell when they talked that one sat close to her and the other was down by her feet. Silence between the two stretched uncomfortably.

"That's fair." The sound of hushed cloth slid against one another as Grey's soft footfalls reverberated further away.

"I will do all that I can to make her succeed in these tests, but to do that, she can't be afraid. Grey, you need to stay away."

Tests? What tests?

"Don't worry, she's all yours."

Mia grunted in discomfort as she pulled some of the blanket away from one eye. She barely opened her eyes in time to see horns and dark clothing disappearing out the doorway, flapping behind someone as they exited.

"Demon?" Mia whispered.

Mia flipped around, not liking the silence at her back. A man stood over her. His hair was honey blond and had a bit of a curl to it. He waited beside her, staring out the open door. He turned to face her and a golden glow emerged around him, highlighting his bronze skin.

"Who are you?" she croaked out. Raising the blanket, she scooted up the bed.

"Here." His boots were caked with dry dirt that flecked off as they thudded on the stone tiles. He moved over to a tall hand carved dresser and grabbed a glass full of clear liquid, bringing it to her.

"Water!"

Her hands shook as she reached out to take the glass. She latched on to it with both hands. Downing the contents, she barely registered the hint of sweetness. Licking her lips, she tried to place the flavor. Her mouth was already watering, wanting another glass.

"That should make you feel better. I am Haddox. We don't get too many of your kind out in our neck of the woods." He smiled.

He sounded like one of the men from her village that was always willing to help. Mother would say he has a great hospitality nature. She stared at him for a minute before remembering that she was outside her village and he was not like any man she had met before. A cold shiver made its way down her spine. They would kill her if she ever got back to town. She couldn't think about what her town or mother would do to her right now; she needed to know what she was doing here.

Staring down at the empty glass, her fingers pressed on it, liking how solid it was under her fingers. "What are you?" she whispered. If he was a descendant of the Old One's, they could be a finicky bunch.

Haddox reached for the glass. "Here I will get you another."

She reluctantly gave it back. The lights overhead beamed down on her, the light intensified.

He crossed the room and whipped up another drink from the cabinet. "Our kind has many names, but I believe your village calls us Old One's."

Her eyes darted around the room in search of safety or a weapon. The room was bare other than the cabinet and dresser drawers and bed. Things looked rustic and made to blend with the surrounding nature.

Haddox raised a placating hand as he walked back to her with the glass in hand. He kept his distance as he reached out, giving her the full glass.

Rubbing her fingers together, she hesitated. Her mouth water's craving the cool liquid.

"You probably have many stories of our kind, but we are not like them. We are the descendants of the Old Ones, but very different from them. They had to be locked away. At least give me a chance. I can show you around here and prove to you our kind is not so bad and how we have changed."

Mia gave a slight nod of her head and reached for the cool glass. She sipped at the sweet drink, slower this time, enjoying the cool sticky feeling on her parched throat. The harsh, bright lights above blurred, shifting into a soft, honeyed glow that seemed to seep into her skin, languid and soothing, like a heavy warmth that numbed her thoughts and body.

Haddox took a seat at the end of the bed, his left leg propped up, bouncing.

She looked down at the blanket pooled in her lap and noticed a plain white dress covering her to about mid-thigh.

"Where are my clothes?" She avoided looking at him.

"You were very dirty and hurt. Battie had to make sure there were no serious injuries and get you cleaned up. She works here in the medical ward."

"Battie?" What a strange name for a girl. This whole place was strange.

"You are probably curious why you are here?" Haddox probed.

"Where is here?" Mia's dark hair spilled over her shoulder. She took another drink, relaxing. Warmth followed the cool liquid, starting a fire in her belly.

"You are in the dark woods."

"Wait. You said you are other…" Her round eyes go wide. "Descendants of the Old Ones?"

"We are. I am." His kind eyes enveloped her as he patted her leg. "If you are up to it. I will take you around and show you our world. Prove to you that you don't need to worry."

Heat arced through her and perspiration beaded up on the back of her neck.

Haddox lowered his head. His blond bangs swooped down, partially covering his eyes. He looked up at her through it. "We need your help."

A pang of sorrow echoed through her. "Help how?" Maybe some of them were being judged for what others had done. She knew what that felt like.

"The Old Ones are cruel and powerful. So powerful we required your help to put them to sleep."

"I've heard the stories."

"They still have them in your village?"

Nodding, the room tilted on its side. She stopped immediately, waiting for the world to right itself.

Haddox scooted further up on the bed. "The Old Ones sleep for now and as long as there is a balance in the world, they stay asleep. If they start to wake, there are tests given to judge the balance of the world. The last two people that attempted the tests could not finish due to unfortunate circumstances."

Tests? Weren't they talking about that before?

Tongue thick in her mouth, she asked. "What kind of unfortunate circumstances?" She tilted the rest of the drink, downing the last of it.

A flurry of people raced past the open door to her room, shouting and giggling. Colorful clothes and streamers twirled around them.

Haddox eyed the crowd, brows turned down in worry. He stood, walked to the door, and stuck his head out, calling to someone in the hallway.

Their hushed voices slurred together, too faint to decipher. An eternity passed as she waited for him.

He returned, a dazzling smile beaming on his face. Offering his hand, he waited.

Smiling back at him, warmth spread to her toes. The blanket was too warm, so she scooted it aside.

"There is a party tonight to celebrate the coming tests and impending victory. Would you like to go check it out?"

"Maybe another night." Reaching out, she held onto his firm hand, using his strength to help her up. His golden hair swayed in the wind, and his dark brown eyes were sweet and kind. Her leg buckled under her.

Haddox was there, holding her to his chest, giving her time.

Her fingers squeezed onto his and her other hand wrapped around his upper bicep caressing the muscles that were well defined there.

"Careful."

"I guess I'm still out of it. Maybe you show me around a little and I get to know you more."

His eyes crinkled in the corners as his lips curled into a slow smile. "If you are sure."

"What will I wear, though? I can't go out in this." Her legs almost gave out, but Haddox's hand held her firm against him.

He twirled her around slowly, golden sparkles rained down around her. "This will do." His eyes travel down and back up again. Appreciating the view.

Looking down at herself once more, a pale blue dress that contrasted with her dark hair and eyes. "I love it." Mia snuggled back against him, leaning into him. He felt nice against her flushed skin.

"I am glad. We have all day; it is still plenty early. Let me show you around." Rubbing Mia's back, he tucked her in under his arm, moving them out into the hallway. "We can worry about getting you ready for the test later."

"When will the test be?" Her stomach turned in worry. Her jumbled thoughts wouldn't cooperate correctly.

"Later tomorrow. Plenty of time to rest and get to know us."

Her hands worried over the light blue cloth. It felt like the cloth of the other plain dress she had been wearing before, but they looked nothing alike.

"Why do I have to do the test?"

"You are so beautiful." His words smoothed over her thoughts. His finger hooked under her chin, turning her face up to his. "Don't you want to help me?"

His lips were inches from hers, the heat of him being close sent a shiver down her spine. If she leaned in, she could press her lips against his. Her mind clouded over. What were they talking about? "Help you," Mia repeated back. The closer she was to him, the more she seemed to lose herself in his presence.

"We can stay in and check out the town on a different day. I wouldn't worry about the tests. Be mindful of your decisions."

She blushed under his piercing gaze. "No, that's okay. I want to see more of this place you call home. Can you tell me more about the tests?" His hand dropped. Pulling back, he continued walking with her.

"Strong choices are a good idea. My brother who got to the third round told me about his first test. I hear they change from person to person, but this will help ease your mind on what is to come."

The hallway buzzed with life as creatures of all sizes moved in a slow, determined procession. Larger beings, hulking and imposing made the ground tremble with each step. Their shapes were varied—some with thick, scaled skin, others cloaked in flowing fur. Amongst them, smaller creatures darted in and out of the gaps between their legs. Most of them had some humanlike qualities, but none of them could easily hide what they were.

She hid in Haddox's side as he guided her out of the building.

"Sorry, I should have warned you. Most descendants are human in appearance, but there are a few of the direct descendants that will be less human looking." He pulled them off to the side of the building into the shade. Flowers tresses laid hung over wooden railings. "Though I don't mind giving you a reason to get closer to me."

Mia chuckled; her eyes took in the greenery that wrapped around buildings. Trees that were as tall as buildings but were married together in a way she had never seen before.

She noticed vines covering the sides of buildings and wrapping around pillars. The pale brown branches and green vines twined around columns that decorate the sides of the path in either direction. Little yellow flowers pop from the green vines, bathing the dark colors in a pop of light.

"We are in the heart of spring. As we continue into summer, you will see more and more flowers sprinkled around these open areas."

"I saw the vines curling inside as well."

"Yes." He gave a wolfish grin. "Many of us here believe in a balance between nature and technology here. We want both to marry together to create a stronger future where both can coexist and make each other stronger."

Chuckling into his arm, she pulled him close, enjoying the tingle that zinged up her arm whenever their skin touched.

His feather light touch pushed into the small of her back, guiding her onto the path. They passed two large stone white doors. "This is where the three tests will occur."

Mia licked her lips and chewed on her bottom lip. The doors were huge. Her head fell back as she saw how tall they were.

"Three?" Her throat closed on her words; she coughed into her hand, pulling away from him. A shiver ran down her back.

Haddox rubbed her back and guided her back into his arms as he leaned back against the pillar. "Yes three. My brother got all the way to the third test before... and the second one ended it before the first test could even start."

"Are the tests hard? No one said anything about dying."

He waved a hand, dismissing the thought. "They are different for each person. Some tests require strength, others need intelligence. It is a tossup. What happens behind the closed doors when the person goes in is between them and that room."

She rubbed her hand over her throat. "And the death part?" She turned into him as her wide eyes met his. "What makes you think I will be successful when two others were not?"

"The forest chose you for a reason." His strong arms wrapped around her, hugging her close.

Mia leaned in against him, her limbs so tired from the previous night.

"She would not steer us wrong."

"She?"

"The forest is woman like, I would say. No one ever really knows when it comes to an elemental spirit."

"What if she chose wrong?" She clutched her hands in worry.

"Can I tell you something?" Haddox faced the sky as he gazed at the top of trees. His thumb brushed over her knuckles.

"What?"

"To be honest, this is the first time I have been through these tests. They are only to be used when there is great tension between our people."

"The Old Ones have been asleep all this time, then?"

"There was one incident a while ago. As it was explained no one questioned if there would be death. We were aware of the outcome if the bonds failed to hold the Old ones in place that there would be countless lives lost."

The leaves rustled as a cool breeze kissed her face. She turned into it, letting the wind blow her hair off her neck. Closing her eyes, she laid her cheek on his chest. Her stomach turned, and the world tipped. She breathed deeply through her nose and breathed out slowly through her pursed lips.

Mia giggled, "I don't know if I can do this," but then she hesitated. The laughter died out.

Haddox drew small circles on her back and swiped her hair to the side. "Do you want to go back?"

His warm embrace filled her with butterfly wings that were fluttering in her stomach. He made her feel good and cherished, made her feel important. Like she was the only one. Rubbing her head against his chest, she shook her head no.

He tucked her in the crook of his arm, reaching away.

Her eyes popped open, curious at what he was doing to disturb their moment. She watched him pluck a dead flower. His fingers twisted at the base of the stem; his hand glowed as he turned the dying flower. The color changed to a grayish hue as it puckered back up and started to open and turn a brilliant white.

Mia's mouth hung open. "What else can you change?"

He smiled and tucked the flower behind her ear.

"As long as you are strong and always choose the strongest choice in your tests, you shouldn't have a problem." His fingers tipped the bottom of her chin up as he leaned down and brought his lips to hers.

She sighed, happy as his warmth mingled with her own, stirring the heat she had already been feeling. A small hiccup erupted out of her mouth, stopping the kiss. "Sorry." She covered her mouth, trying to stifle it. "You aren't like the monsters in our stories."

His eyes turned dark, almost dull, as he pulled away. His boots stomped in the dirt as he crossed into the grass, away from the testing area and path.

Letting out a gasp of surprise. She swiveled around as she tried to keep her legs under her. Her stomach revolted; he had been the only solid thing holding her in place. She wanted to go to him but didn't think she could make it the few steps to him without falling. She could imagine what he already thought of her.

"I didn't mean that you were a monster. There is a power that I sense from you, and you are not like any of the guys in my village. I would know you for what you are, regardless. I mean, you are not..." She throws her hands up, trying to think of a word, "You are different from humans."

"A couple of us have more human strands in our DNA makeup than others. But believe me I am very much other. Want to see?" A wicked glint of his eye watched her from beneath his golden hair as he looked at her from the side.

"Your magic has been so lovely; I would like to see more along with your people and this place, yes." She bounced in place.

"Good, then you can work on making it up to me. Your words wounded me so much." He touched the middle of his chest, giving a pout he looked hurt. "We can spend all day making you forget that my kind are monsters in your stories."

"It is only used as a warning that caution is best when dealing with an unknown."

Haddox reached for her hand, holding her steady. He ran his other hand through the blonde wave of his hair. "Others do not think as you do, darling. They act out of fear and anger at their fear. The forest and others have been attacked because of this, with no warning."

"What if we could change things? Make things better between our people?"

"I would give anything to make that a reality. Let's get past the tests first, though, and show you what your world has been missing with keeping us out."

She suppressed a giggle as she tugged on his hand, his arms there waiting to escort her. They spent much of the day talking and learning from each other. She saw how spread out the houses were from each other. What she saw of the couple of buildings that were separate and grown into the side of the cliff near the waterfall. She could only imagine what the heart of their town looked like.

Chapter 8
Haddox

He was acutely aware of Mia and his surroundings; the sun was starting to dip, and they had spent much of the day walking. He pasted on a smile and ushered her near the hidden grove. "I think you have seen the smaller houses and little groups of buildings on the outskirts. What will really wow you, will be our hidden grove and the city dwelling within."

"A whole city hidden?" Her eyes widened as her head twisted to see where it could be hidden.

"We keep it hidden for good reason, since it is the heart of who we are." He stopped them in front of an archway where vines hang down. The leaves were plentiful and kept what was hidden behind camouflaged. His free hand tapped on the side of his leg as he debated going forward.

Mia rested her head against his arm as they took a pause. She breathed in slowly, sweat beaded off her forehead.

"If you're not up to it tonight, we can always come back another time." Clearing his throat, he let his fingers trickle down the vines, feeling the buzz of the ward standing strong.

Mia puts her hand up next to his, playing with the leaves. "Your city is hidden behind here?" She doubted.

Shaking his head, he laughed through his nose, a half smile plastered on his face. "Something like that. You may not feel it, but there is a barrier there and one that will force you out if you try to go forward."

"I don't think I have the strength to even test it." She settled back in his arms.

Exhaustion flowed through her. Her face and color were pale to earlier. He sighed with relief and walked her slowly down the path. "I have the perfect place for both of us to rest."

Haddox poured more of his magic into the glow that emits from him and warmed his core. He needed her to be strong for the tests. As they returned to the building they had left, he held her close, his body warming hers. He had a room there close to the testing site for cases such as this.

A true illusionist could make her forget about her sickness.

His boot caught on a branch that lay across the path. Stumbling forward, he barely kept them both upright.

Mia laughed as she stumbled into him.

Her soft body melted into his.

She is so thirsty.

Haddox shook his head and righted her before himself. He couldn't screw this up. He needed her to like him. "Sorry about that."

No, you're not. A sharp pain pierced the back of his eye.

You despise her kind and want to see them suffer just as much as I do.

He ran a hand through his soft curls, massaging his head.

"Are you okay?" Mia's soft hands were on his, her fingers long, but her nails were kept short.

He didn't know how she would make it through. They hardly gave them enough time to train, let alone prepare for these tests. "I'm fine," he said in a gruff tone. His thoughts swirled. This voice that was not all together his, urged him on as he tried to stay with Mia.

"Let's go sit and rest for a while. Maybe all this excitement got to both of us today." They make their way back to the care center, the huge stone building carved into the other side of the waterfall.

A pair of young women with iridescent wings giggled as they passed by Haddox and her. Petals of flowers make up their dresses. They screeched and cackled as they looked back and whispered to each other.

Haddox overheard what the girls were saying in their high-pitched voices. "Haddox better not mess this one up. Hopefully she doesn't off herself like the last one. Can they even like us?"

They're right, you know?

He narrowed his eyes and shot a glare their way over Mia's head, giving a hard smile.

Why did they all blame him? He wasn't the reason the other girl hated the Old Ones. It's not like he could have done anything to avoid what happened to her.

"Pay them no mind. They are likely too engrossed in the festivities to even recognize who is in front of them." He bit the inside of his cheek.

Mia's curious eyes looked back at the beautiful young girls, who still shot them glances as they continued down the walkway. Bricked stone gave way to green moss. The sudden transition was jarring beneath her feet. As they entered a vast, opulent room, her eyes widened in wonder. A colossal daisy flower dominated the space, its delicate petals and vibrant center a striking sight.

"A flower?"

The entire floor of the room was blanketed with a lush carpet of green moss, inviting and serene. Haddox kicked the door shut behind her, muffling the distant squeals of laughter and plunging them into a sense of intimate seclusion. A hint of mischief danced in his eyes. "Welcome to my humble abode," he said. His tone was low and teasing. "It's not only a flower, though. Go on, try it." His words were infused with an air of intrigue, beckoning Mia to explore the secrets that lay within the enormous bloom.

He let go of her hand, letting her explore. He walked behind a gold screen wall. Peeking out behind the wall, keeping an eye on her.

Mia stepped onto one of the delicate white petals. The white was soft. Her feet sunk into the plush of the petal. She followed it to the center, anticipating a dusty or pollen-filled interior like a normal flower.

"Is this real?"

His golden eyes concentrated on her as he wove colored threads together to create the perfect illusion for them both.

If you allowed me to take over, I could give you the power you need, so she would never suspect a thing.

Baring his teeth, anger whispered through his veins. No matter what he did, his magic would never be enough, never grow strong enough to be on par with his brethren.

Under his breath, he whispered. "Let me do this my way first. You are only here because I allow it. Lend me a bit of your power to get through this."

I can not lend something without getting something in return.

"Let me guess, there's only one thing you want."

A gruff laughter cackled in his head.

Dark thoughts raced through his mind as he fought to spin the threads into something usable. Mia's eyes were already so heavy it would not take much to bend her mind. He would have to make do with what he had.

"Not a chance." There was no way he would let the creature residing in him take over his body completely. He wasn't weak like a human. He could do the illusions needed to get through these tests and keep her happy and on their side.

Are you sure you can?

Annoyance flared within him, fueling his determination to prove himself to the Old One. What happened on this night would render her helpless with desire towards him. She would crave him with an unrelenting passion, one that would leave her breathless and begging to help him in any way he saw fit.

As Haddox's eyes locked onto Mia, he initiated the intricate dance of magic, his hands weaving a subtle pattern in the air. The room around them began to transform, as vibrant swirls of color erupted into existence, like ethereal brushstrokes on a canvas of reality. The hues deepened, coalescing into a shimmering aura that pulsed with an otherworldly energy. As the magic reached its crescendo, the colors solidified into a tangible form, taking on a life of their own as Haddox imbued it with his will. The air seemed to vibrate with anticipation, as if the very fabric of reality was being reshaped to conform to his vision. With a final whisper of magic, the illusion snapped into focus, assuming a lifelike quality that was almost indistinguishable from reality itself.

The core yellow part of the flower was bright and velvety. She kneeled, dipping her hands into it. It was plush and bounced back against her. Taking her hand back, she flopped into the center, swaying in the middle as it moved with her. It moved up and down with her even after she had stopped moving.

The white flower fell out of her hair and rolled to the side. Reaching for it, she stretched her fingers. It was out of reach. Leaving the standalone flower, she looked over to Haddox, who was walking down the petal. The end of it was coming up behind him. The white petals all pulled up to create a cocoon around them. Tucking them into the dim dome of serenity. He wore a loose shirt showing off a lot of his tanned bronze chest, along with baggy pants made for lounging.

"Did your magic create all this?" she asked in wonder.

"Yes, it can do so much more." Snapping his fingers, little twinkly lights hung midair near the top of the petals that had folded in. He paused before laying down on the soft yellow center. Reaching across her, his body brushed against her sensitive skin. He reached for the flower that had rolled away. Grabbing it, he pointed it at her nose, swiping it over her lips.

Her face flushed, and the heat escalated with each wispy touch.

As he moved the flower down, he followed it, touching his mouth to hers. He leaned against her as he nibbled at her lips.

His body pressed down gently onto hers, feeling her soft body mold to his much. "You crave what I can offer, don't you?" Haddox gave a half smile.

"Yes," she hummed in approval.

He kissed her, claiming her. His tongue delved into her mouth, deepening the kiss and sending shivers of pleasure through her body. She pulled him closer, whimpering into his mouth. The sound sparked something in Haddox, igniting the fierce passion within him. He responded by pressing down on her, his body grinding against hers as he devoured her with kisses. She moaned into his mouth, whimpering for more. Her body bucked against his. A testament to the all-consuming desire that had taken hold of her.

His body pressed against hers, a perfect fit, as he ravaged her mouth. Her hands grew more daring as she reached for him, tugging at his shirt. She looped one of her legs over his hip, pulling him closer, as if trying to merge their bodies into one.

Pressing away from her, he leaned back in the soft center of the flower. "Show me how much I mean to you." The smugness written across his face.

She was so hot and needy. The flower cushion dipped and rolled her. A nervous giggle bubbled up out of her throat as the strong sweet smell of the flower perfumed the area. She rolled in to the side of his body, his arms curled around her settling. Licking her lips, her hands roamed over the front of his pants.

He pushed his hips up to meet her hand. Her fingers snagged on the edge of the band of his pants and pulled them down.

Her eyes widened as she saw his full length. "They don't grow them like that back home," she gasped.

He was already hard and thick. She ran a finger down his length, liking the velvety feel of him. Her tongue tracked where her finger had been.

He moaned with pleasure. Yanking her dark, thick hair into his fist, and held it close to her scalp. With a gentle push, he guided her in the type of rhythm he liked.

"I will show you exactly what you have been missing. Don't worry, my sweet."

Heat flooded through him as he controlled what she did to his body. He brushed his fingers against her cheek as she swirled her tongue on the underside of his cock. A happy thrill rushed through him. She licked and kissed, climbing up his body.

A soft tug at her hair let her know she had crawled as far as she could. He bit his lip as he sat up, molding his lips to hers. His hand massaged the back of her head as he grabbed closer to the base of her skull. He pulled back from the kiss, gazing into her eyes.

"Stay kneeling there. I want to watch as your lips wrap around my cock," he growled, towering over her as he stood.

Grasping the base of his shaft, and with a gentle yet firm motion, he guided it toward her mouth. The tip of his head circled her lips, teasing her with the tip of his soft head.

She couldn't help but dart her tongue out, licking the sensitive skin. Puckering her lips, she waited till he adjusted himself back into place, inserting himself into her hot, wet mouth.

She sank down onto him, her cheeks hollowing as she took him in. He cupped the back of her head, pulling her closer as he whispered urgent demands in her ear. When she coughed, he withdrew momentarily, allowing her to catch her breath before sliding back into the depths of her mouth.

Her hands rose to grasp his thighs, attempting to slow his thrusts as his length proved almost too much for her to handle. But he was relentless, his fingers dancing across her nipple and breast, sending shivers down her spine. As the pleasure built, his thighs began to tremble beneath her touch.

She hummed in pleasure; he could tell her body was warmed up and had ideas of its own. He rushed forward with both hands in her hair, her mouth and tongue fought to swirl around him. Warmth sprayed the back of her throat and left a trail as he slowly pulled out of her. Her tongue swiped up the bottom part of his cock as he let her come up for air.

"If you're a good girl," he rasped out between ragged breaths, "And swallow it all. I will do something just as delicious to you."

Peering down, he watched. Something animalistic in him wanted to break free as she complied with his order. Tears ran down her face, but she was in pure ecstasy.

Swallowing, she opened her mouth to show him what a good girl she was. "Mmm... it's sweet."

"Like candy." He trailed his fingers over her collarbone and breasts. Her nipples pointed through the fabric of the cloth and were easy to pinch and play with. As his hands gently caressed her, Mia let her eyelids drift shut, and a soft, melodious hum escaped her lips. The sweet sound filled the air.

Although he wouldn't make her physically finish what he started, he would accept what she wanted to offer while she was here. He could play with her while they had the time. His power was already peaking, he was getting close to his limit.

"You were so hot as you sucked me down," he said.

Giving a blissful smile, she fell back onto the soft pillow cushion, her hair fanning out from her body.

Settling right beside her, he was hit by her beauty. "Let me give you what you really want." His fingers slid over the dress, barely touching. Brushing them through her hair. Tempting thoughts had spread out before him as her legs fell to each side.

Haddox leaned down to kiss her, letting himself sink into her warm body. He embraced the feeling and let her really see him. Large golden butterfly wings sprouted from his back. Black thick lines colored the inside of the wings that danced and dipped all a crossed it. He shuddered as they flickered. They were like his mother's wings, other than hers were light blue.

"Haddox!" Mia exclaimed as she watched transfixed on the wings forming. Her fingers hovered in the air, wanting to touch. She hesitated, leaving a feather light caress on wings.

A sharp intake of breath speared through him as her fingers touched something that jolted directly south.

"You are... awe-inspiring," she whispered.

You will never be as beautiful as your mother. Or as strong.

"What did you say?" His voice came out strained.

"I said you are beautiful." Her worried gaze met his eyes.

His hands shook as he nodded. Never before had he challenged his magic like this. He wasn't sure of the consequences.

Feeling her against him, he wrapped his arms around her. Pulling the makeshift dress up off her, revealing her slight body to him. His mouth watered as they closed on her pert nipple, letting the dress fall from his fingers.

He bit down, hearing her moan as she rubbed herself against his hardening length.

"Yes," Mia screamed out.

"Wild vixen likes that, don't she?" He flicked his tongue over the hard nipple, changing to the other one. He bit down on it just as hard.

Soft moans poured out of her throat. His cock twitched against her as she softened, her legs cradled his hips.

Her hands roamed up his sides to his back. Her fingers danced against the wings as he sucked on her breast, taking it into his mouth.

"I want you inside me, Haddox. I can't take this heat anymore!" She flung her head back, pushing her breast into his mouth.

His wings spread out massively above them as he flapped them, holding himself over her. Placing a hand over her throat, his hand twitched, wanting to squeeze harder. Her legs came up around his hips, keeping him close. "I tell you what you need, understand?"

"Tell me what I need," she repeated. Her hair twisted beneath her as her body bent to his whim.

"I think you need a good tongue lashing." He licked his way down her flat stomach. Stopping to kiss the sides of her hips, teasing her.

Her legs opened, letting him slide the rest of the way down her body. Her fingers delved into his golden hair, silky against her fingertips. His hair was long enough for her fingers to grip.

His tongue flicked lightly against her sensitive nub. Working his magic, her hands scrunched in his hair, pressing him deeper into her core.

Pulling back up and away, he glared down at her. He widened her legs, forcing her to be even more open than she was. Her hands fell back above her head as she stretched, wriggling before him.

"Listen to me sweetness and I will make sure you get through these trials alive," Haddox said.

Going so slowly, he examined her fully, making her wait for the pleasure only he could give her. His rough hands held her legs the widest they could go. He spread her lips with his fingers, sliding up and down the sides of her. Lowering his mouth to her, his tongue gave short, hard thrusts into her hot, wet channel.

Mia gasped and her back arched up as her legs quaked, struggling to keep up with his fierceness. Stopping, he let her body ease, but as soon as she could catch her breath, he was at her once again, flicking and sucking on her clit. Her head rocked back and forth, her hair spreading out in tangles beneath her as her body tried to keep up with his demands. He stopped, delving deeper as he plunged his tongue into her pussy. Licking and toying with her there. Sliding his hands over her lips, he massaged the wetness around.

Her legs ached to move, his lower arms pressed down on her legs, making her stay. He swiped his tongue up to her clit once more, sucking on it before he thoroughly delved into eating her out, not stopping or taking any more breaks, forcing her body to match his tempo.

Her hands crawled over the bedding, wanting to grab onto something. Her fingertips brushed against the edge of his wings. Making him shudder and rub his face against her wetness. His cock didn't take long before it was standing at attention, ready for her. He felt her shudder, and her moans deepened and increased as her body tried to create hot friction against him.

Haddox's body glided up hers, his mouth closing around her nipple as he sank his teeth in. The sensation sent sparks through her. He lifted one of her legs over his shoulder, opening her up to him, and then slid into her scorching hot depths, her wetness enveloping him like a glove. He drove in all the way to the hilt, filling her completely, before pulling out slowly, almost teasingly.

As he paused at her entrance, he leaned in to soothe the nipple he had bitten, his tongue tracing gentle circles around it before his teeth closed in once more. The sting of pain mingled with pleasure as he thrust back into her with a fierce intensity, their bodies meeting in a rush of heat and desire.

"Yes, Haddox," she moaned.

He slammed into her slowly, keeping an even tempo, pushing in as far as he could go each time. Her head rocked back into the comfy cushion; her breaths were uneven as she gasped. As his cock pushed in and out of her, unrelenting. Grabbing her nipple and pinching it hard in time with his thrusts.

"Yes, what?" He slammed into her.

She tightened around him, clenching down on his cock, wanting and needing more. Her hands came up and gripped his hips as she met his thrust.

"Yes, give me what I need."

"What do you need?" he growled out.

"What you say I do." Her mouth hung open as he slid out of her.

He flipped her onto her stomach, entering her from behind. Deep inside, his cock was tightly enveloped by her hot sheath, the position intensifying the pressure. Her hotness fully slid over his cock he was soaked with how happy he was making her. He pulled her hips up and pushed on her back, forcing her to bend.

"Cross your ankles," he grunted out.

Doing so, he knew she would take more of him as he plunged into her depths. He slid in and out of her building the fire in both of them till they he couldn't take it anymore. She gave a loud, long moan as his hips jackknifed into her one last time and he filled her full.

Resting her head on her arms, a sweet smile fell across her delicious lips. It brought a smile to his face. She closed her eyes and fell into a blissful slumber.

Releasing his hold, he leaned heavily against the wall. He watched as she rolled to her side, snuggling down into the plush bed. His magic, already depleted and used, the dress turned back to what it originally was. Her eyes fluttered as dreams took her over. The sleepiness of the night and the effects of the drinks finally taking their toll on her.

"Sweet dreams, my sweetness," he hissed, showing white teeth in the dim light. "Oh, how easy it would be if I really wanted to." Rubbing his thumb against his bottom lip, he imagined a personal illusion just for him.

Dark thoughts twisted his mind as he shook. Power rose in him, answering the depleted call. Breathing in a deep breath, he smirked. His golden eyes peered down at Mia, pliant and waiting.

Skimming the tips of his fingers from her temple, he brushed them over her tight nipples; they were hard and erect, poking through the cloth. Her mind was sated, but her body was still rearing to go.

Why did you not take her? Take her now.

"She is but a human," he sneered.

He looked on with disgust before getting up and leaving the flower. As he left, the flower rotted and distorted to something darker and more hideous, his magic fully fizzling out. This was not who he thought he would be, but he needed this win.

"Now to go find someone of my kind to actually sate me," he growled, moving his stiff cock in his pants to the side.

Chapter 9
Mia

Waking up in total darkness, she still held a hint of a smile as she thought about what happened between her and Haddox. She could see herself getting addicted to Haddox if he pleased her as much as he did last night. She hadn't been this taken care of for a while now. Most men back in the village did not prioritize the women before they finished themselves. The flower was still closed overhead, and the lights had gone out. She reached out a hand, searching for Haddox, but didn't feel him there. Crawling to the edge of the bed; she heard a giggle and snort followed by hushed voices. Her breath was loud in her ears in the closed off space.

She touched the sides of the petals. A slimy substance coated her fingertips. Bringing her hand back, she sniffed it, trying to determine what was covering the flower. A sickening shiver raced down her spine. The inside was hot; her stomach rolled at the cloying scent. She pushed against the flower until it bent, but the slimy mashed texture coated her hand, pushing through two of the petals. It held tight, but with the goop sliding down, she slipped right through the flower's wall. Her feet slid out from beneath her, falling hard on her butt. The slimy liquid covered her legs as she slid out sticky overall. Looking down, the pale blue dress was gone, and the dirty white plain dress from before covered her. Her head was still woozy but was clearing more than it had been last night. What had been in that drink?

"Haddox?"

Looking back at the flower, it was a bluish green, like the pure white daisy had molded and turned bad. The smell was not pleasant or flowery; she struggled to her feet and scooted away. The closed door hit her back as she met it, the room much smaller than she had remembered it.

"What is going on?" She stared at the horrible scene before her, trying to remember where it all went wrong. "This can't be right."

Hushed voices quieted. Opening the door, she saw Haddox there with some woman. Her slender form was a vision of whimsy and wonder. Mia watched as the woman with vibrant red hair pushed off Haddox's chest, turning. The vibrant locks seemed to glow with an inner light, as if infused with the warm, golden tones of a sunset.

"Go on, get back before it's too late." She called back to him.

Mia's eyes flitted back and forth between Haddox and this woman.

Haddox cleared his throat. "Finally, up, my sweet?" Haddox's eyes landed on hers, but his hand caressed the other woman's lower back as he stepped away. "After all the activity last night, I figured you would sleep in more. You still have a bit of time before the test."

The woman turned back around. "Haddox! You didn't even wait to get her out of her hospital clothes?" She looked Mia up and down.

"What happened to the blue dress?" Mia looked down in confusion, the sticky goop still on her bare legs.

He winked. Strolling up to her, and wrapped his arm around her waist. Shivers ran down her back and something in her stomach settled.

"Let's go get you into some other clothes." He ignored her question.

His hand landed on her ass, making her jump away from his hands. She gave him a peculiar look. "Yes, please," she emphasized. Something felt different, but she didn't know what exactly it was.

"Haddox, you know nothing of clothing, here let me. I will make sure the savior gets where she needs to be." She took two dainty steps before Haddox glared, stopping her in her tracks.

"No Leah, that won't be necessary. I am entrusted to her care." Haddox assured Leah.

"We're all friends here." Leah gave a big smile. "I will ensure she is taken care of. Don't worry, I won't take my eyes off of her."

"Actually, if it's not too much trouble, I would like Leah's help," Mia said. Distance would be good right now. She wasn't sure what to make of Haddox. Last night was amazing, but it wasn't matching up with her perception of him right now.

"Are you sure, my sweetness?" He pulled her close. "Would you like me to get you something to drink?" The back of his fingers caressed her cheek as he gripped her chin, forcing her to look at him.

"No. Nothing to drink." She barely shook her head. She wasn't sure what she had drunk yesterday, but she needed her mind clear before going in to the test. "I need a change of clothes. I would prefer a woman to help me with that part."

"Are you sure?" His hands rested on Mia's upper arms, giving them a little squeeze. He turned her to the side, facing away from Leah. "I wanted to get you ready for the test and go over everything."

Biting her lower lip, she hesitated. "I do want to..."

"Haddox, chill out, ease up on the human, stop being one yourself." She rolled her eyes, shooing his hands away from Mia.

His hands stilled, eyes calculating. "She won't have that much time, but I do have to touch base with Grey. Be back soon." Stepping away, he threw over his shoulder, "I will wait back by the huge white door that we saw last night."

Mia smiled as she remembered last night. "Okay." Glancing down, she noticed the sticky substance still glued to her legs. "Wait, what happened? Why was the flower bed dying in there?"

Leah's slight frame reached Mia's shoulder. Her light fingers grasped hers, towing her away in the opposite direction. Her fingers were tight, like steel on Mia's.

"I will have her back soon," she called back. "What name do you go by, savior?"

"Mia."

They raced across an open entryway that let in the sunbeams of the morning. A few rays caught Leah before she could dash away. A bunch of colored rainbows lit up the square. Mia's hand slipped from hers, coming to a stop as she stared at Leah and the beautiful light display happening.

"Yes come, come. We must get you ready." She grasped her hand once more and tugged her along. "My power here is light, which created the effect of a rainbow."

"Do all of you have powers?" She wanted to reach out and touch the purple flowers that lined the hallway. They flowed over the wall as if it were a living mural.

"Most of us, yes. There are a few humans around, but not many." Leah dashed into a room, this one more girly than the previous one and more cluttered. Clothes laid strewn about, along with trinkets here and there. Kicking them to the side, she stomped through.

Now this was more like it. Mia dodged the clutter with ease as she followed Leah through the room. Her shoulders began to ease as she felt more at home.

Leah's room was normal compared to the flower bed she saw in the last room.

"There isn't much time, but I am guessing Haddox didn't tell you too much about what is going to happen." Leah frowns, going to a basket and picking up swatches of color. She picked each one up and raised it beside Mia's face, shaking her head no.

"Why are you even doing this? Why don't you run back to your village?"

"I was kind of running away from there. I don't really want to go back. Or even if they would accept me back if I did."

Leah's eyebrows knit together in confusion. "But why help us? Why not keep adventuring out there if you want to leave?"

Mia bit her lip.

Leah grabbed a measuring tape and wove it around Mia's waist. She took note of the measurement and moving back to measure another part of her. Motioning with her head, "The washroom is back there. It's a private one, so no worries there."

"I want to know for myself if the stories of the Old Ones are true. I have been constantly judged for being me. What if we are doing the same thing with a story?"

"Hmm," Leah said as she continued to take more measurements and mumbled to herself.

Mia waited till Leah was done measuring before picking her way through the bits and bobbles. Cloth, string, and beads spilled haphazardly across the floor. Paper and sketches tossed and crumbled around a basket, all at various points of being drawn. She reached the washroom, glancing in, hovering at the door. A light beige stone laid at her feet. The room was spacious enough and had a window high up in the wall. She saw and heard trickling water pass over the glass and seep through some of the stone cracks. "I was told the forest picked me."

Mia turned into the washroom and shut Leah out. Enjoying the peace of being alone. Shaking her head, she glanced at her reflection in the mirror. "Why am I helping them?" She took her time washing her hair and her body. Cleaning the sticky mess from her legs. Her hands roamed over her body. She was not sore or aching in the places she thought she would after a night of passion. "Haddox, I wanted to help him." She remembered. Water ran down her body as things started to piece together.

He made everything feel and sound better when he was near. But he wasn't around now. Doubts crept in. She finished up and grabbed one of the fluffy towels that sat on the ledge next to the mirror. Glancing down at the ugly dress, she shuddered, imagining having to put that horrid thing back on. Poking her head out the door, she noticed the room was empty except for Leah, who paced back and forth in front of something she was working on, on a mannequin. Leah's door was shut firmly.

"Are you and Haddox a couple?" Mia blurted out as she opened the door, hugging the towel close.

Leah froze with two color swatches next to her, a yellow and a blue. Turning, she tossed both colors back into the pile. She shook her head as she eyed the mountain of fabrics. Giving a small laugh. "No, he wishes, probably." Her vibrant orange cat-like eyes blinked slowly before going back to the basket and grabbing some ribbon.

"Oh, okay. I saw you two earlier..."

"Embracing when you came out?"

Mia nodded.

"We flirt and toy with one another, but it's nothing serious. We like to have fun." She raced back, holding a dark blue cloth in front of her and something silver trailing behind her.

Mia danced around the items on the floor, making sure not to crush anything. She slinked up beside Leah, watching as her nimble fingers made quick work.

"Here, try this." Leah let the velvet cloth fall from her pinched fingers. "Haddox is more human than most of us here. His father was a human that found his way here and one of the others took him in as a pet."

Mia pulled the gown over her head but stopped when she saw the cloth stitched together. Stepping into the dress, she pulled it up and tugged her dark hair to cascade over one shoulder. "Is that why he looks so normal... not that you aren't beautiful... or normal? It's just..."

"What is normal for one is not for another. Humans are not normal to us here; we celebrate differences in one another. Or at least I do. It's those differences that strengthen us and make us able to go the distance. If we were all the same, we would die out and another species would take our place."

"You remind me of someone."

A smile touched Leah's face as she wrapped the ribbon around Mia's body and did a final touch to the dress. Mia twirled into the fabric as Leah morphed and dragged it where she needed. Creating a cute little dress with shorts-built in. "That is for ease of movement, in case you need it." The silver shone brightly against the dark fabric.

"If you can do this with a mere scrap of cloth, I am afraid of what else you can do," Mia said in wonder.

Leah tilted her head at the dress, frowning. "It's missing something, though." She tapped her pointer finger against her mouth in thought.

Mia twirled, liking the feel of the shorts as the dress came up and spun with her. She walked over to the basket, peeking in to see what else was in there other than ribbons. It was a plain brown basket full of colorful pieces of cloth, buttons, jewels, zippers, and multiple colors of string. She plucked out some string in the color of yellow and white, along with a needle. Sitting back down on the bed, she studies the dark blue front part of the ruffled dress.

Leah's face scrunched up, coming closer and sitting next to her. "What are you doing?"

Threading the needle, Mia started on the first star she will add to the midnight blue skirt. "I'm going to add stars. Plain clothing isn't really my thing. So, when I can, I will sew something into it, creating a picture tapestry in the cloth."

"We have a little time."

"It won't take but a couple of minutes to sew a couple into the fabric. It won't be the best, but will do for now."

Leah looked down at Mia's bare feet and popped back up off the bed. "You will need shoes."

"I'd rather not." She grimaced.

"A human not wearing shoes? Now that sounds strange." Leah stopped before going to a shoe holder that was layered on top of one another, creating a tower.

"I will wear shoes if I must, but if I can get away with it, I'd rather not."

"Do you not like them?" Leah twisted her head back to her in a bird-like posture.

"They are clunky, and it comes between me and the earth. I like to feel the texture of the ground and what I am stepping through. I'm more connected to the world that way." The thread slid through the cloth easily. Starting on the next star, she switched color, this one white instead of the bright yellow. "What can you tell me about these tests? Why do you not interact with our village so we can take down the wall?"

"The last girl didn't last long enough to talk about her test, but the guy before her lasted till the third round. He said they were mainly riddles." Leah's eyes caught on something and swiped it up off the ground. More fabric in a half done state. Tugging at the yarn, she unravels a bit of it and scoots back to the basket and grabs something plopping back down, working on her own thing as Mia worked.

"I know Haddox had a brother that got to the third round, but not of the girl. Where did she come from?"

"That's right, though Grey had a harder time with that death than Haddox did, in my opinion," Leah whispered.

"Who is that? Grey?" Mia interrupted. That was who Haddox had been talking with when she was brought here. She was curious about him.

"Grey, that's weird that you haven't met him. He is the other chosen one who watches over these trials." Her hands fluttered in the air. "No matter, you will meet him later, most likely. He has two sets of horns, very dark, very sinister. Any who, the girl, came from your village. Yours is the closest to here."

"There are other villages? Other than mine?"

A small scuffle at the closed door and then a sharp yip caught Mia's gaze by surprise.

"Bloo?" She raced for the door, fumbling her way to the door.

"Friend!" His small voice hollered through the door.

"What is that?" Leah asked.

Tearing open the door, she let in Bloo; he bounded around the room, coming back to Mia as she shut the door.

"This is Bloo. I kind of helped him escape my village."

Leah raised an eyebrow as Bloo came to sniff her. "It follows you around?"

"I guess so," Mia shrugged, kneeling to Bloo, petting his side. "I've told him to go home at least before coming here."

"Maybe he doesn't know where home is?" Leah questioned.

"Who would know that information?"

"Grey or Battie, they have traveled around the most. They know of all the other villages also?" Leah set the cloth aside and leaned back, her arms catching her weight.

"Right, you were saying there are more than ours?"

"Yes, when your village came to these lands, they had no intention of mixing with our kind, and after what happened, well, let's say we couldn't mend things." Leah frowned.

"What happened?"

"Chaos woke, and he infected someone, and another person got severely hurt. Not before they could help stuff him back into whatever crevice he crawled out of, though."

"Why now? Why is he waking after all this time?"

"Him and others of the old ones are waking. Being divided between us versus humans weakens the spell. They are tired of rest and dream of covering this world in blood once more. They are a bloodthirsty lot and one of the main reasons they had to be put down. We could not conquer them, but could hold them trapped in slumber."

"What if they have changed?" Mia asked, her voice laced with uncertainty.

"Old Ones don't change," Leah replied, her expression grim. "When Chaos last woke, he took over a man and almost destroyed your entire village. A strong, resilient woman was able to fight him. Helping us lay him to rest."

Mia's eyes widened as she stopped petting Bloo. "How did you stop him?" she asked, her voice barely above a whisper.

Leah's gaze turned inward, as if recalling a painful memory. "A powerful spell was used to bind him into the earth surrounded by a circle of rocks."

"I saw such a thing." Mia's voice cracked. She swallowed and tried again. "This circle held great power."

"If it was close to your village." Leah shook her head, stretching as she raised up off the bed. "It's probably the same one."

Mia's hand shook. She clutched Bloo to her side.

He whined in response.

"Don't worry about it. He won't be coming back. He was sealed away by blood; it will take him many lifetimes to get through that alone. He will also have to work his way back from his slumber."

"Who was the woman in the story?" Mia said, rubbing the sewn in star on the nice fabric that feels cool against her skin. She glances at the pattern she had created, a splattering of stars covering the front edge of the dress.

"Sorry, I don't recall." Leah reached down, helping Mia stand up.

"What about the Old One? You said Chaos, but did he go by another name?"

"What does it matter?" Leah waved it away, racing to the door. Poking her head out the doorway, she peered down the hallway before exiting. "Quick, if we don't hurry, Haddox will come get us. We can talk later. I will try to remember the name then."

Bloo raced between Mia's legs and circled Leah as they raced out of this place.

Ringing her sweaty hands, she wiped them on the bottom part of the dress. They hurry back through the twisting hallway and rush across the courtyard, not stopping this time to enjoy the rainbows that splayed out behind Leah as the sun hit her. The white door was larger than she had last remembered. It stood there stark against all the green vines and leaves. The purple flowers that crawled the hallways did not touch this building

Chapter 10
Mia

"Took you long enough," Haddox grunted. With a gentle push, he detached himself from the doors and began to stalk closer, his hips rotating in a smooth, sensual motion. The movement was almost languid, yet it conveyed a sense of coiled energy and anticipation as he prowled nearer, his eyes fixed intently on hers.

"We weren't gone that long. Geez." Leah rolled her eyes as she turned and walked away. "Let me know how everything turns out! I'm going to go have some fun." She called back over her shoulder. Bloo barked and growled at the rainbows she threw out, chasing them as she left. He raced into a bush close by.

Mia waved, her head already spinning with nerves. She spotted a tall, dark shadow that stood behind a pillar. Horns stuck out, giving him away.

Mia eyed the shadow. Was this Grey? Leah said he had horns.

Haddox saddled up next to her, tucking her in under his arm.

Haddox followed Mia's line of sight as she stopped and stared. "That's Grey. He is another that helps see these tests through."

Grey's mouth slashed in a frown; his harsh white eyes had a ring of darkness around them. They traveled to Mia, then Haddox. Her body trembled. He smiled, showing her a toothy grin. His teeth were the stuff of nightmares. With the click of his teeth, he bit at the air between them. Recalling her grandmother's story, Grey could be who the story was about. His eyes weren't red or orange, though.

Mia shuddered, burrowing deeper into Haddox's side.

Haddox chuckled. "Don't worry, he is here to make sure nothing interferes with the trial, then I will make him go away. I will be your guide throughout the entire process."

"Like you could make me do anything," Grey grouched. He stalked forward, clearing the column. His full dark frame intimidated her even in this wide-open walkway. The sharpness of his chin matched his eyes. He opened the massive door; his forearms flexed and showed the muscles hidden on his lanky form. He gave a pointed glare, then turned his head. "Go on."

Haddox pushed Mia forward, his fingers gentle at the small of her back.

She sunk into his side, making sure he was in between them. "You could be nicer."

"I think Haddox is plenty nice for the both of us," Grey rumbled.

Haddox ushered them past Grey, ignoring him. "Once you beat this, we will have a better idea what kind of tests you will be getting. That way, we can plan for the next one accordingly."

He stopped in the doorway, taking her face in his hands. His thumb brushed her cheeks.

She pushed through his hands and hugged him tight. He gave a quick peck on her lips, pouring heated light into her. Her heart fluttered as her stomach dipped. She smiled up at him, feeling the fire quickly begin to stir. Her body flooded with lust as she remembered the night before.

Giving a huff, she turned away from him, walking through the small opening Grey had left her. Grey's dark hand flashed out, catching her wrist gently. His eerie eyes pierced her as she looked frightened, tugging at her wrist. A glimpse of blue fur raced past her, fuzzy and out of focus. Her world tilted as the heat faded and her world became clear.

"Whoa, head rush."

Grey growled. "You can not affect the outcome of the test that way."

"There is nothing wrong with what I did. It only amplifies something that is already there."

"Then there is no reason for it." His cool gaze traveled to Haddox.

Haddox's golden eyes dimmed to a dark, muted color. "Fine, but her loss will not be on my head." Turning from them, he muttered something to himself.

Grey's thumb caressed the underside of Mia's wrists as he held her there while she found her balance.

Mia's heart beat faster, and her breath came out in puffs of air. She looked at the room she already was partially in. The room held a deep, dark jungle. Mia looked around and couldn't see the other walls. *Am I even in a room anymore?*

Her hand dropped as Grey let go and eased the door closed. She guessed he was done with whatever Haddox had done to her. She held her wrist up to the light, scrutinizing it. His touch was gentle even when his tone was harsh.

Every time Haddox wanted something from her, her mind turned to mush around him. She liked the way he made her feel and wanted to explore more with him. Perhaps that was how all Old One's acted. Leah also seemed to enjoy playing with humans. So far, they were different from the stories she had heard about them. She needed this, needed them. She had wanted to be free and have fun for so long.

Hard stone turned under foot pulling her deeper into the room away from the door, away from her escape.

"Who do we have here?" Ghostly whispers surrounded her.

Birds chattered and sang as they flew in between the beams of light that slanted down through the green canopy. Squirrels and other small animals jumped from the tangled branches up above in the trees, racing down to the ground and back up into the foliage.

Mia looked around the vast enclosure, looking for who asked the question.

"Hello? Who's there?" The ground beneath her stopped moving. She backed up a step, wanting to turn back and leave. "What is this place?"

"We are all around, here in my domain." The room changed from a jungle to a warm, inviting cabin in the middle of pine trees. The door was wide open. She saw a fire already lit and there's food and drinks on the table. It looked inviting and reminded her of home. She drifted in and before too long, an old woman shambled through the door behind her. A wind so fierce tried to knock the woman over, but she shut it out with a bang before it could penetrate the warm interior.

As the woman turned from the door, Mia locked eyes with her grandma, Sky. "Grandma?" Her heart sank as she took a cautious step away. Unsure where the exit was since it had been behind her, but now only the wall of the cabin sits there.

"Is that who I am manifesting as?" Sky's arms raised as she looked at the colorful dress that wrapped around her. "Why heavens no, I'm not your grandma. I take the form of who you would be most open to in a time such as this." She stepped around the room lively and bubbly. Her hands are smooth and not gnarled by time or pain. "This is a place you find comfort in?" Disgust encompassed her face as she picked at the scratchy blanket laying over the couch.

It was so strange hearing her grandma's voice come out of something that didn't act like her at all.

"You're not my grandma, so what name can I call you?" Mia stepped to the side, giving her plenty of room to move around the cabin, bringing her closer to the closed door.

"Names! Always wanting to give things names. I forget how your kind likes to operate. Ashling, if you must name me. I am so much more than a name, you know." Her head swiveled back to Mia, pinning her to the spot. Ashling's hands touched her temple, noticing her hair was back in a bun. She unraveled it, letting it loose. Spreading her hands through the thick white hair, she fanned it out around her shoulders.

"Are you my test, Ashling?"

"No, I am the one who partially slumbers, who gives the trial."

"So, it's started then?" Mia asked.

With a nonchalant shrug, Ashling kicked out with one leg, and then the other, her body unfolding into a slow, circular motion as she padded around Mia. Her movements were relaxed and effortless, yet they seemed to convey a sense of quiet power and calculation. "I thought we should talk before it came to that. But if you must hurry your test along, we can get right to it." She snapped her fingers and the cabin all but vanished and two wolves appeared. One was pitch black and dark, showing his teeth and growling. The other was pure white, shaking its head and pawing at the ground like it wanted to run away.

Her stomach swirled as the world turned with the scene. Ashling stood between Mia and the wolves. Mia took a step back. A small circle of green grass surrounded her and Ashling. Right outside the small orb of grass, a snowstorm weathered on. Snow already covered the ground. The wind howled, shoving the snow into drift piles. The cold wind whistled through, but the snow stuck to the protective barrier. Both wolves are waiting in the snow right on the other side of the bubble.

"No, I didn't mean to offend. I was not prepared for what to expect."

"Did the guardians not prepare you?" Her eyes filled with rage as she inspected Mia walking up to her with a weird gait, not a way that a normal person would take.

"Haddox and Grey? I met Grey today before coming in here. Haddox, we spent some time..." Her cheeks blushed under Ashling's watchful gaze. "We didn't talk much about the trials. He said they were different for everyone."

"That's too bad. Perhaps you should ask more questions."

"Is there something you can tell me to help me here?" Mia dug her toes into the warm ground. She stared out at the storm.

"Now is not the time for your questions." Ashling shook her head.

The white wolf hunkered down in the snow, blending with the snowdrifts. Mia quickly lost sight of where he laid down as more snow piled on. The black wolf paced and jumped at the barrier, demanding to be let in.

"What's going to happen?" she whispered. Fear shivered down her back. She hugged her arms around herself, trying to trap her heat close.

"You have to find the right questions and the right people to ask," her voice and body faded from the circle. "Unfortunately for you. That was the wrong question. Now make a choice which wolf will defend you?"

The black one lunged forward as the bubble disappeared, stalking forward. The other hid in the sea of snow that went on forever.

Mia's head whipped back and forth between each animal.

"Decide? How do I make that decision?" Backing away, Mia looked over the snowscape that was barren and plain. There was nothing around, no stick or rocks to defend herself. Her toes chill as the warmth dissipates along with her safety. She was used to not wearing shoes, but snow did not come to their shores. Hardly ever. Her father would talk of it where they had grown up. The temperature almost never dipped that low.

"Decide quickly before it is chosen for you." One last ghostly whisper surrounded her.

The black wolf advanced on her, but she still couldn't see the other one. What if it had run off? "Haddox said to choose strong options and if the black wolf is on my side, then it won't attack me. I choose the black wolf," Mia yelled.

Laughter echoed around the space as the black wolf snapped at her but walked to her side, wrinkling its nose as it licked its lips as the nose rose into the air and sniffed.

"Let us see how your choice does," Ashling whispered eerily.

She stood there waiting, listening. Nothing happened. The wolf looked at her. "What now?"

Ashling didn't answer, no one answered. The wolfs black ears perked up and cocked its head forward as it turned.

"I guess we are on our own, then." Reaching out, Mia took a tentative step forward, wanting to feel the soft fur.

It growled out low before her hand could make contact with the fur. She let her hand fall as she stepped away. Snow had started to pile on the green grass, covering it fully. Her feet going numb. She hopped in place, trying to keep her body warm. She had to get moving. Pine trees out in the distance looked like a viable option to at least keep her out of the wet snow. Trudging past the wolf, she moved in that direction of the trees.

Blue orbs peered out of the white, crystal-like snow in front of Mia. The white wolf sprang up next to her. It had crawled through the snowdrifts, keeping hidden. Dancing away agitated, the fur on the black wolf's spine raised. Growling and licking its lips, showing its pearly white teeth to the enemy.

The black wolf takes off, circling the white one, nipping at its tail and hindquarters, keeping it in line. The dark blur taunted and flashed cruel teeth at the white wolf. Its only mistake was crawling out of its hiding spot.

Pale blue eyes turned cold as the white wolf lashed back at the other, latching on to its throat. It shook as the dark wolf rolled and fought to get free. A loud crunch echoed in the sparse place; the wind died down suddenly. The white wolf crouched over the black still one. Biting down, it finished the kill. All spark of life left the black wolf's eyes.

The blue eyes rise to Mia, staring, judging, deciding. The white wolf was not pure white, as flecks and smears of blood marred its beautiful coat. A snarl rose out of its throat as it stared her down.

Dropping her eyes, she backs away slowly, not staring back. She watched its paws as she backed away. With each step she took, the wolf took a step forward, forgetting about the black wolf that lay dead behind the other wolf.

It launched at her on quick paws. The snow tore up from the ground, brown dirt mixing with the pure snow as the wolf moved. Mia dodged and rolled to the side at the last second. Something hard tugged her head back as a searing pain radiated up her scalp. Gripping her hair, she looked up into the eyes and teeth of the wolf that was chomping at her curls. Its paw came down on her hair, keeping her there.

Scrabbling to yank it away, she struggled not to get any closer. Claws come down on her shoulder, slicing down, easily ripping the fabric and skin beneath.

Screaming out, she flipped onto the wolf's back, wrapping her arms around its humongous neck, barely able to hang on as it bucked to shake her. Her knees gripped the sides, holding close as she herself became feral. Wild with pain, intoxicated with fear, and the want to survive. No, the need to live.

She bit down on the back of its neck, grounding her own flat teeth into its fur. The taste of dirt and hair filled her mouth, along with cold ice that had balled into its fur. Squeezing her arms tight, she held her forearms, locking around its neck. Back claws sliced down her arms that she barely felt. Her numb arms loosened, and she tumbled to the ground. The wolf was too large for her to get a good grip to hang on and the claws were another problem that she couldn't account for.

Mia's arms shook as she tried to raise up. Falling back down into the snow was a comfort to her sore body. The cold barely touched her. What if she rested here for a little while? A dull throb pressed into her stomach. Pulling herself back up, she spotted a thick branch underneath her. She blew at the hair on her face. Calculating what the wolf would do next, her cold fingers wrapped around the thick piece of wood and yanked hard. The wolf pile drive into her side as she pulled the branch free, knocking the wolf to the side. Not stopping to analyze, she jumped on its back, waiting for the next barrel roll. The hard ground did not have enough snow to cushion the blow each time, her own back was littered with scrapes and bruises. She didn't think she could make it past this test, let alone two other ones.

"I'm sorry," Mia whispered out, pouring all her strength into her arms and tightening them. The wolf ducked for one more barrel roll; she pulled the stick across the wolf's airway. Yelling out in pain, she wrapped her legs around its chest and held on, squeezing. She yanked the stick back, crushing its throat. Mia wriggled to keep the wolf in the air and her on her back. She didn't think she could hang on if she took one more crushing blow. She held on, struggling to keep the wolf on its back, its weight too much for her to keep caged. The wolf stumbled and slowed, not able to raise up on its paws.

Lowering onto its belly as it whined and thrashed its head from side to side in one last attempt to release Mia. She pushed down with all her strength, tears rolling down her face as her arms gave out, no longer able to hold on. The wolf puffed in a clean breath of air, laying there tired. Pulling her arms and the branch back to her side, she held onto the stick with one loose hand. Eying the ends to see if there was a point she could use.

"I don't want to fight you." Mia's breath also puffed out; her warm breath could be seen in the cold crisp air.

The wolf gave a heaving snort, struggling out from underneath her. She rolled to the side, letting go of the tufts of fur coiled in her palm.

Holding the stick close to her, blood seeped out of the cuts and slashes crossing down her arms. Noticing the fire burned as the air hit her wounds. Grimacing through the pain, she leaned heavily on the stick and pulled herself up into a crouch. She and the wolf regarded one another with careful eyes. Sizing each other up.

"Interesting," the ghostly voice announced. "Not how I would have dealt with things, but this is your test, not mine. You have survived your first trial." Her booming voice echoed as the wolf disappeared. "There will be a penalty dealt." The image of grandma Sky emerged from the flurries of the snow. A bundle of blue fur hung from her hands by the scruff of its neck.

"Friend," Bloo yipped.

"Bloo? What are you doing here?" Mia asked.

Bloo took a swipe at the hand that held him. Ashling dropped him before he could connect. "The price for cheating..."

"Cheating? I didn't cheat," Mia interrupted.

A cool brow raised. Cocking her head to the side. "Then who?"

Thinking over the events that had happened. "There's no way in this room other than through the door, correct? Wherever that is now."

"Correct." Her eyes shone brighter as her form grew larger.

Bloo growled at Ashling and backed away, wiggling its butt, getting ready to pounce.

"Grey held open the door for me to come in... I thought I had seen something out of the corner of my eye... He must have snuck in then."

"Or Grey let him in, intentionally," Ashling said.

"Bloo, why did you come here?"

"Friend in danger." Bloo stuck his snout in the air and glared at Ashling in the sky.

Ashling crept up to them as her fingers grew longer with her form. Her body morphing and distorting as she towered over Mia and Bloo.

Bloo whined and raced back to Mia, giving a defensive bark. A wind blew in strong, gusts spraying in her face, whipping her hair back.

She couldn't move; she had extinguished all her energy in that fight.

"Bloo didn't interfere with my choice or the fight."

"Because I didn't allow it."

Bloo barked and growled at Ashling, who advanced closer and hovered in the air over them. He yipped and whined, barking as loud as he could, trying to force her back with his little body and big voice.

A large door banged behind her. Rolling to her side, she saw the outline of the door ruining the snowscape façade that was all around them.

Chapter 11
Grey

"What were you thinking?" Grey seethed. His fists curled up as he stared at the shut door that Mia had gone through.

"I was thinking we needed a win!" Haddox grumbled.

Grey heard him shuffle his boots in the dirt pathway. He turned to him, breathing in slow, calming breaths. A speck of gold flared back into Haddox's eyes.

"What is going on with you?" Grey asked.

"Me? What about you? Why are you even here?"

"You know we are both required to be here," Grey said.

Haddox shoved his hands through his blonde hair. Shaking his head, agitated. "After our last talk, I'm surprised you are anywhere near these games. I thought you wanted out."

"I did. I am." Why was he here? Why did he keep getting pulled back in?

Images of golden wings flickered behind Haddox. Some are in the shape of butterfly wings, others are in the shape more like a bird's wings. A soft, golden warm light vibrated around Haddox. He grumbled under his breath.

Stepping forward, Grey reached out to him, pulling his attention back from whatever was distracting him.

"No!" Haddox yelled out, shrinking back away from Grey's reach.

Grey pulled his hand back, not touching him. How could two brothers be so different? Haddox was nothing like Trey. "Your illusions are getting away from you."

"I need to rest," Haddox said.

Grey really looked at him. His eyes were dark, and dull, bruises surrounded them like he had not been sleeping. Haddox slouched against the column of pillars that littered the front of this building.

"I don't need your help or anyone else's."

"I didn't say you did."

"You didn't, did you?" Haddox gave a look of confusion before tipping his head back and closing his eyes.

Mia's form appeared in front of Haddox; she danced and twirled there in the sun. Performing a very seductive dance. A copy of Haddox pulled away from his real body. This one was thicker with muscle and much more than he ever was. His wings were back and the golden glow that surrounded them warmed the already hot day.

Grey watched as Haddox's illusion played out and came into reality. He stepped away, making sure not to break it. Did he do this often? Did he know this was happening? Looking back at Haddox it looked as if he had nodded off.

As he continued to watch, it felt like someone sucker punched him right in the gut as he stared at the illusion of Haddox and Mia embracing the heat of their hands, tugging and petting one another. "Is that what you did to her? Or made her think?" He waved his hand through the illusion, distorting and destroying it.

Haddox's eyes popped open. He stomped forward and shoved Grey back, grabbing his shirt. "I did what was needed."

Grey looked down at him. Rage burned in his gut at the worst possible thoughts of what Haddox was capable of. Was this what would happen if he let someone else take care of things? "Did you do that?" Grey's eyes bore into Haddox, his demeanor rigid and serious. "To her?" He couldn't even say it. He may be a creature of darkness, but that was a different twisted kind that he would never even be tempted towards.

"Do what?"

"You know what?" Grey said through clenched teeth.

"It wasn't real. None of it was real." Haddox unclenched his fists and moved away. The fight in him dying out. "You think you're so much better than everyone else. You are born from the same darkness that we all come from. More so even."

"Does she know that it wasn't real?" He knew who he was. He didn't need Haddox reminding him of where he came from. It didn't mean that he had to feed or give into those to get what he wanted.

Haddox snorted and coughed. "I'm sure you will tell her all about it." He walked away down the hall towards his rooms.

"I'm going to get some rest. I will need it for however you mess things up."

Grey stared at Haddox's slouched back as he walked away. He didn't want to care, but he also didn't want another death on his mind. Trey already plagued his thoughts enough.

Grey's tall form filled the doorway, it wasn't made for someone of his size. He had to stop himself from cracking open the door and stopping the tests from even happening. Several barks and yips disturbed his troubled thoughts. He had looked in the bushes around the area, but as he grew closer to the door, he knew the blue dragon had snuck in there with her.

He had opened the door, hoping to call the animal away without disturbing things, but when he opened the door, his eyes landed on Mia. Her blood was smeared all over her, she was panting and her eyes were wild with fright. His heart stopped as his mind pulled him to another test not long ago where he found a crumpled body at the feet of Haddox, his eyes wild and scared as streams of tears ran down his face.

"Grey!" Ashling yelled out. A tornado gust of wind flew into the doorway, enveloping his tall form, pulling him into her web. He walked calmly into the room as the tornado danced around him, guiding to where she wanted him. "Explain." The wind died down as the wind yanked the door back close, shutting all else out.

"Always good to see you, Ashling," Grey said, tight-lipped.

The wind pulled at his shoulder length black hair, showing the four horns prominently. He stopped in front of Mia and the little creature. She cringed away as he came into full view.

Good, she should fear them. She needed to be far away from this place. Before she ended up like...

The furry blue dragon had his fur standing on end, creating ridges down his back. A low, rumbling growl emanated from his throat. His gaze fixed intently on Grey, but his attention was clearly focused on Ashling, who still hovered above them, her presence commanding his notice.

Grey tucked his dark button-down shirt into his high-waisted pants, causing it to ruffle in the wind.

"He didn't do this either," she panted, hissing as she turned her body so she could look up easier. "He stopped Haddox from doing something to me, said that was cheating." Mia shook her head as she tried to crawl forward, her arms not working properly.

He bit the inside of his cheek. He stepped in between Ashling and Mia, shielding her. No matter how much he wanted to be far from these tests, he couldn't stay away. He was a glutton for punishment. "She is delirious from blood loss and pain. Let me take her to get healed and we can discuss what must be done after."

The wind died down, debris stopped flying around and hitting them. "I thought Haddox was taking this one."

"Do you see him here?" Grey asked.

"Grey," Mia whispered out behind him. But he couldn't possibly have. She was terrified of him.

A tentative hand tugged at the back of his pant leg. He raised an eyebrow, stunned, and shocked as her legs pushed her over the snow filled grass. The cold had turned her lips blue and her body shivered, probably from both it and the pain.

"She needs tending to. Please allow that."

"And what are humans to you? What does it matter?" Ashling cocked her head in the sky, looking down over him. The flurries of the snow slowed, and the wind stopped altogether.

"She matters, you know that. Why else for these tests? You were not like this with Trey's test." He stood in front of Mia, not daring to move out of the way for fear of what Ashling would do. She could be tricky when she was in one of these moods.

"Just checking," she said in a singsong like voice. "Trey was one of us. We knew him, raised him." Ashling disappeared from the sky. "You see," she appeared behind both Mia and Grey, still looking like an elderly woman. "Grey and Haddox are both guardians. They are protectors of the tests and the spelled words that govern our kind."

Bloo turned as the Ashling reappeared and crawled under Mia's outstretched arm. Standing protectively beside her.

Grey turned slowly, making sure to step to the side in case he needed to react.

"What does that mean?" Mia coughed up something dark.

"That means it is their fault if they didn't go over the rules with you," Ashling explained. Her cool eyes sparkled with amusement.

"We are glorified guards for the person taking the tests." He had had enough of this. No one tested him like Ashling did, and she knew it. He walked forward, looking at her decrepit form. "You made sure of that."

"Did I? The previous guardians left their records. You only have to want to find the answer." She looked up at the night sky as if remembering something.

If she only knew. Grey had been through the library many times in search of a way to end these trials, but keep the Old Ones still in slumber. He never knew if Ashling was truly on their side or not. She was an Old One herself. She could be playing both sides.

"Be the guardian you are meant to be," Ashling whispered as she stared at the starry night sky.

"Fine. Did the creature interrupt the test?" he asked. Ashling would not budge on this.

"It was about to..."

"No, Bloo didn't show up until she brought him forward. She showed up after the trial had passed with Bloo in tow," Mia explained. Her fingers gripped onto the blue fur as sweat beaded on her forehead as she struggled to stay semi upright.

Creeping forward, Ashling towered over Mia, bellowing. She kneeled in Mia's line of sight. "Has no one taught you manners?

He was about to crash the test, but I snatched him up, stopping him from doing that. The test remains as it is, but we must administer a consequence."

"I will accept the punishment." Grey's grim face was stoic. She was still stronger than him, even with her stuck in this room.

"No, that's not fair." Mia grabbed onto Ashling's gnarled arm, wanting her attention. "He did nothing."

Ashling's face grew long and morphed, looking nothing like her grandmother's anymore. She stared down at her mouth open wide with lots of needle-like teeth focused on her. "Life is not fair, is it?"

"It's my trial. I will accept the punishment," Mia said.

"The human is unaware of what she is talking about. Let her heal from the trial, as she is already hurt, and I will take the additional damage."

Heaving a sigh, Ashling looked up to the sky as the dark night opened shards of ice and fat flakes of snow. "Bored now." She shrunk down, taking on the body of a child. "Rest." Her arms circled around Mia, helping her lower to the ground as her arms gave out, and she relaxed into Ashling.

Bloo barked but did not attack. "Bloo, help."

Grey kneeled, Bloo came over to him. "Bloo?"

"Yes," he growled. His eyes darted back to Mia, worried.

"You want to help Mia, correct?"

"Yes."

"I need you to not bark right now. We will get her healed, but Ashling requires something first."

"Ass, is mean." Bloo sneezed, plopping his butt down and glaring at Ashling.

Grey smiled at that and hid a chuckle. "That she is."

Mia's eyes were growing tired as her head and neck fell to the side. Not able to hold herself up anymore, she slinks back. Ashling caught and lowered her to the ground.

"There we go much better. Can't have her starting another test before it is time, now, can we?" Ashling said, leaving Mia where she lay and walking closer to Grey, her voice quieting.

Mia struggles to stay awake, barely hearing them over the winds and ice pelting her now frozen form. Her blood slowed and she could barely move.

"Go Bloo, keep her warm while I deal with Ashling." Grey scratched behind the little dragon's ear. He didn't know how Mia had come by one of these, but they could be tricky to work with.

"I am ready," he said. Ashling's height only reached his stomach. She looked so small there next to him.

"You will not be able to sit this one out, Grey. This test requires both guardians. It is why the second one failed as it did."

His teeth clenched, creating a tick along his cheek. "You know, I do not agree with what happened."

"So, you wish for her to follow in your best friends' footsteps?"

He was quiet, not wanting to lie to the Old One, but not willing to explain further. Either way, he would create more problems than help solve.

"Then your punishment is having to be near her. Protect her from your own kind. Those that want the Old One's back will make sure to ruin her at every turn."

He curled his fists as they raise slightly, forgetting who was in front of him for a moment.

"Careful descendent or I will require more than that." She walked up to him and pushed a hand into his chest, her nails biting and sinking in.

He gasped as his hands raised to her small arm, trying to pry her from his chest.

"Ashling," he choked out.

"Careful, dark one. Someone might see you for what you really are." She leaned her head against his chest and shoulder. "I feel it beating there, do you? She is important, cold one. If you do not do this, I left a present to remind you."

"What do you know?" His voice shook with pain. His arm struggled against hers as they dug in deeper.

"I am the epitome of hopes and dreams. Nightmares are only a small caveat of what could be."

"A nightmare you made, Old One!" he yelled out at her. "I will do as you say, but nothing more." He pulled her in, enunciating each syllable. "Nothing more!"

Her hand pulled back out of him, leaving a dark, thick shadow.

Pain sizzled the mark that had been burned, mixing with his blood.

Yanking her hand back, blood covered her wrist and hand. Her tongue grew long and twirled around each of her fingers, licking the blood clean from her hand. Her eyes closed, sighing in relief. "Such delightful flavors you are full of. It has been many moons since I have feasted on anyone of our direct lines."

"There are not many direct descendants left."

"Remember what I said, dark one. Protect her," Ashling cackled as she faded away.

He looked down at Mia's prone form, gathering her body to his. She was limp and had passed out, her skin tinged with blue. She was barely breathing.

"Come, Bloo."

Bloo uncovered Mia's center, growling as he raced around next to Grey, whining. "Friend safe?"

"Yes, she is safe. You can come with and keep an eye on her." Bloo shook his head and perked his ears up, knocking the ice and snow from his fur.

Grey picked her off the ground, holding her close to his body, giving her what little heat he had.

Groaning, Mia turned into Grey's embrace, her cheek resting against his peck. His chest had already healed from Ashling's attack earlier. The shirt, though, was tattered.

"Don't die, okay?" he whispered to Mia's frozen form. Turning to the door, it appeared out of the snow and ice relatively close to them.

Chapter 12
Mia

"No!" Mia yelled. Sitting up in a bed much like the one she had woken up in when first coming here.

A hand touched her shoulder, trying to ease her back.

Mia twisted her neck sharply, seeing a young girl with black, pink, and green hair in space buns on her head. She had metal goggles that were sitting atop her head. Scooting back in the bed, she took a closer look at the woman. She was tall and lanky, Mia had never seen anyone wear clothes like this one did. Her mesh shirt, along with a pink tank top, matched the pink streaks in her hair.

"Hello! Welcome!" She threw her hands up in surprise. "You are safe and back in the medical section. By the way, Haddox took you out of my care way too soon." Her eyes scanned Mia with a harsh glare.

"Where is Grey? What happened to him? Who are you?" This was all too much. As Mia looked around the bland room, her hands pushed her covers off. Both of her hands were wrapped in bandages and she was back in that plain beige dress thing.

"Whoa, hold on there. Grey is fine. I should know he is my brother," she said, her words tumbling out in an excited rush. "Nothing happened to him, at least not more than normal." She chuckled, her eyes sparkling with amusement. "He is around lurking in some dark corner. Don't mind him. He may look scary and sinister, but he isn't like that." She hitched up her leg as she bounced on to the bed.

Staring at this woman, she noticed similar things between them. They were both overly tall. She could have used some of that height herself. They both had similar complexions and a love of dark accents. "You don't have horns."

"I don't?" She cocked her head and shook her hair to the side. "Or can you not see them?" Her hands came up and pressed on the hair that hid a small set of horns. She gave a pointed smile, her teeth as sharp as Grey's.

Mia nodded. She glanced around the room; it was bare like her first room. She needed to stop waking up in this place. "Where's Bloo?"

"The little creature that likes to curl up next to you..." She waited for Mia to nod. "He left not too long ago. I told him I would watch over you and wait till he got back."

Mia fumbled with the blankets, bringing them up and over her shoulders. A chill settled in that she could not shake.

"Right, you asked me my name. My name is Battie. On account I am batty like a fox!" She stood up, threw her hands in the air, and did a little twirl. A crisscross mesh piece of cloth covered each hand past her elbows. One was pink and the other was green, matching the light colors that danced in her dark black hair. "Would you like something to drink?"

Giving a violent shake of her head, she grimaced. "No, not if it's going to make me feel like yesterday."

"What do you mean?" Battie eyed Mia, inspecting her closely.

"I dunno. Like the room was spinning, and I wasn't making the best judgment calls maybe, not to say I didn't want it to happen." Her turbulent mind wandered over what she had done with Haddox and how he had treated her. She had fun, but it felt all unsubstantial and dreamlike now. Her mind spun with confusion as her thoughts turned, trying to make sense of things.

She hissed and grumbled as she stomped around the bed. "Let me get you some water. It won't do anything weird, I promise." Battie walked over to a glass that was waiting on the counter. Bringing it back, she pushed it into Mia's waiting palm.

Mia squinted at the contents. It looked like water, but it did yesterday as well. She raised it to her nose and took a small sniff, not smelling anything off. Bringing the cup to her lips, she tasted a small sip of the water. It was cool and refreshing, not as cloying this time. She scrunched up her face, still not sure if something had been done to it.

"Here." Battie took the glass of water back and downed it in a single gulp, filling it back from the tap as she passed it back to her. "Better?"

Mia nodded and took a small sip, letting it sit on her tongue for a moment before deciding to swallow. It felt nice on her parched throat; she tipped the glass back, taking a bigger gulp than before and downing it greedily.

"Yes much," Mia said. "What was the other drink, the one that was sweet?"

"Who gave that to you?"

Mia bit her lips, afraid to answer the question. What if she said something that she shouldn't and she got in a worse predicament than she already was?

"It's called Nectar of Bliss. It helps you relax and makes you feel warm and good. On a human, it would make you feel really, really good. It has a hint of an aphrodisiac thrown in, but nothing that would make you do something you didn't want to do."

Nodding her head, she averted her gaze. Her fingers fiddled with the glass, twirling it in her hands.

"You let me know if that Haddox comes around bothering you anymore. As your healer, I will not let you out for any reason."

"Oh."

"Oh, what?"

"Healer? What happened to me?" Mia asked.

"After your first trial, you took a pretty bad beating." Battie rubbed at her own arms and shivered as if she could feel the wounds that Mia had taken.

No pain came from her arms. Rubbing at the gauze, she itched to pull the bandages away and see the kind of damage that was done.

"No, dearie." Battie's soft hands came down on hers, settling them. "Leave those be. They have a special healing salve to help with what I could not. Grey left you here in my care, along with the fluff ball of a monster that follows you. Said he had some research to do and I haven't seen him since."

Claws and wolves flit through her mind as she remembered what she had endured. "How am I not in more pain?"

"That is my power. I can heal you and take on some of that pain to make it more bearable."

Mia remembered that there was a penalty that they had discussed without her. She would need to find Grey later and talk with him about that. She wanted to make sure what they agreed to didn't make her pay later down the road.

"Is there something you need?" Battie fiddled with her hands, rubbing them together.

"I was hoping that I could have something done."

"Like what? Maybe I can help." She wiggled her eyebrows up close and personal in Mia's space.

Stretching back and sitting up fully, she reclined against the headboard. "I want to see about getting a haircut."

Battie grabbed a piece of Mia's hair and rubbed it between her fingers in thought. Pulling more of it forward, she inspected the pieces and ends. Years of fiddling with it have frayed and damaged the pieces. "Its beautiful hair, but I can see a cut would be good for it. How short we thinking?"

"I want it gone," Mia said. Haddox had toyed with her hair, running his hands through it.

Battie's mouth hung open, looking at Mia with astonishment. "Why would you do that?"

"It is a hindrance and I need a change. Help me create the person I want to become." She liked having fun specifically with the men back home, but these males were of a different caliber. She needed to show them that she wasn't someone they could push around and have them do what they needed.

Looking down at her own clothes, Battie smiled. "As you can see, I have some expertise in that area. Are we thinking dark and edgy, or more, kill them with jealousy?" Pulling Mia's hair forward, Battie measured it with her fingers on length. "Were you thinking shorter?" She measured with her fingers to Mia's shoulders. "Or all the way off?"

Looking at her arms, she shook her head. "All the way gone." Haddox flashed in her mind again, him over by a mirror crystal clear, then whispered words before a haze came over her. His hand fisted in her hair, controlling. "What did he do to me?" Mia asked.

"What do you mean? Who did what to you? My brother? I'm a healer and can hurry the process for things like scratches and cuts. Grey made sure that you were assigned to me, increasing your chances in this fight. He didn't tell me that there were any other wounds when he brought you."

"No, not Grey." She ran a hand through her hair, stopping to scratch the middle of her head. A feeling as if she were missing something, if only she could reach it. What had Grey been trying to say about him earlier?

"Haddox? He has not been by. Grey didn't mention him at all." Battie shrugged.

She guessed she wasn't as important as Haddox had made her feel the other day. Maybe she was nothing but a means to an end for either of them. Everyone thought they could control her. She hated it when her mother tried to, what made them think she needed controlling. Cutting her hair would make it harder for Haddox, she had to start making better choices.

"Bloo has made it difficult for anyone to stay close to you. He doesn't like very many," Battie said.

Bloo growled in question as he entered the room and raced along the brick stones. He jumped onto the bed.

Battie giggled and booped him on the nose. "Good little one. That's right, rawr back at ya." She curled her fingers at him playfully. Battie pulled on funky goggles that were sitting on top of her head and fixed them over her eyes. They were black with little lime green and pink highlights on the spikes that surround the glasses. "Now let's see." Harnessing the power, she waved her fingers through the air, letting them dance on their own.

Bloo snorted, jumping up on the bed. He circled near Mia's feet before plopping down. Laying his head down on her thigh. Mia petted him as he relaxed against her. His soft fur slipped between her fingers.

"Ahh. Perfect." She pressed her hand forward and then took off the goggles. "Natalia will be here soon to take care of your hair. That way, I can keep you under my wing and make sure you are not getting hurt in the meantime."

Mia's mouth moved to open.

"Yes, yes, you are physically healed, but the healing process takes a toll, and you still need to rest. Don't worry, you will be good enough to party later tonight with your new hair and all. That reminds me, let's get Leah here. She can do pure magic with fabric."

"I met Leah before my tests. She was hanging around Haddox. It is amazing what she can do with clothing."

"That is her one bad quality. She likes to play with him. It's too bad she was one of the better ones here," Battie said.

"Should I get out now while I can? If she is the best, I fear my grandma's stories might be correct." Mia stretched out her legs and uncovered them. Would it even be possible for her to leave?

Battie twisted her head to the side. "Why did you not leave before?"

"Because I didn't want to believe the worst of something I had only heard about in stories. It had been done to me, when they didn't even take the time to understand or know me."

"Really?"

Silence rested around them as Mia gave some real thought to it. "No, or not only that, but living in that village seemed worse than whatever could happen to me out here."

"And now?"

"And now, I don't know."

Battie gazed out the door. "I was like you, wanting adventure and to see what was out there."

"You did?"

She gave a tight-lipped smile. "Traveled around and told stories, something other than healing."

"Why? You are very good at it." Mia lifted her arms, bending them slightly, only feeling a dull ache.

"Healing is a give and take. It robs me of myself and gives me parts of others I come into contact with." She shook her head and blinked away what she was seeing. "I had lost so much of myself last time; I needed to step away and gain what I no longer had. For a long time, it was nice and peaceful, almost. But the... the... Forr..." Battie kept moving her mouth, but no words came out. "Grey actually came and got me when I had given up all hope."

Mia placed a hand on Battie's, comforting her. "You are here now, though."

She came back to herself and smiled. "Yea, I am."

"Grey, where did he go? He doesn't really seem that interested in the trials or me."

"Give him a chance. He went to the library. Most days, he's there conducting more research on the trials. He is interested just distant."

"That's hard to believe," Mia said.

"My brother is stubborn and distant, but he means well."

"Who's ready to party?" Leah interrupted, walking through the door, her red hair bouncing around her face, curled to perfection.

"You know that isn't my scene," Battie stood up from the bed, coming between Mia and her.

Leah crossed her arms. "You need to forget about that. Move on with things. Your brother is even going to be there."

"It's just that simple," Battie said through clenched teeth.

Mia pushed her feet over the edge of the bed and watched them dangle there. "I almost forgot about the party. Battie is having someone come cut my hair. But I would like to go," Mia said. Battie was pretty interesting. There had to be others that weren't that bad as well. She needed to go and meet others. See what this place actually had.

Throwing her arms up, she danced forward, letting her wings flutter, picking her up and carrying her forward. "Finally, someone who likes to have fun." Leah flung her arms around Mia, hugging her. "Let's get you ready to knock some people out. We are going to make you look so good!"

Moving through the throng of people dancing, Mia heard the hard beat come alive as it sung through her, lulling her into letting go of everything.

Mixing with the heat from the surrounding people, the breeze on her neck sent shivers down her back. Her short hair didn't weigh her head down anymore and felt light and freeing. The silkiness of the dress clung to her as she moved. Leah knew what she was doing when it came to an eye stopper, that was for sure. Mia wanted to make a statement tonight, hopefully one that would make Haddox back off. Both him, and Grey would be there tonight, Battie had said. Battie didn't come with, claiming she didn't enjoy going to these things. She would make sure Bloo stayed out of trouble.

Leah showed her where the party was located, but parted ways with her once they were in. She had made a beeline for the bar area and Mia went straight into the mess of people. Lights blinked off and on as they flickered to the beat of the music. She moved with the gyrating group as they moved as one.

Hands and bodies touched hers. Her fingers reached out, touching wings and backs as she learned not all who looked scary were. Not all were humanoid in form. Some had tentacles, others were right out of a horror story. But all seemed to be enjoying themselves.

Fun would be had tonight and she wouldn't think of Haddox or Grey if she could help it.

Chapter 13
Haddox

Haddox spotted Mia with a dancer that was lithe and agile. He spun and leaped across the floor with a fluidity that belied his feline features. His velvet dark fur covered him from head to toe, along with pointed ears. They twitched and swiveled with each beat. His captivating presence twirled her into his arms, drawing her in.

"What did you do to your beautiful hair?" Haddox's disappointed voice carried over the music. He strode forward and yanked Mia close to him, away from another dancer. She should be with him, anyway.

"Hey!" the dancer yelled out, his tail flicked back and forth in time to the tempo of the music.

Haddox gave the would-be lion a look of disdain. He should be so lucky he was allowed to live. The Old Ones had helped the people and creatures of this world move forward. Humans here didn't take kindly to what was done. Called them science experiments.

Give in to my power. And I can make sure she will be yours and pass these tests.

Mia would be his; he had to keep her away from everyone else and make sure she believed only what he wanted her to.

He felt good. Haddox had rested some, gaining his power back as he did so, but this thing - Abbadon didn't let him rest much. Containing him was becoming more cumbersome than he originally thought.

"I hated it! It always got in my way, and with the last challenge, it almost got me killed." Anger bubbled up in her throat, cutting off her words. "You may not care if I live or die, but I do!"

He stepped back, startled at her words; he took in the rest of her outfit. Then rushed her away from the moving mass of dancers, hugging her tight to his chest. His eyes roamed over the people, making sure none looked their way. Just what he needed right now was to be the laughingstock of his kind. He could control one little human. "Of course, I do." He patted her back, frowning over the missing hair.

Pushing him away, she grumbled.

He had a penchant for women with long hair, something that allowed him to exert control and dominance. The thought of grasping those tresses, and using them to manipulate and restrain, was a tantalizing one. As he struggled to placate her and diffuse the tense situation, a surge of rage simmered below the surface, threatening to boil over at any moment.

Grasping at Mia's hand and making their way to a plush couch area, he found Leah sitting there. Leah waved but pouted when he slid in beside her, pulling Mia along. There were many of these couch pod areas all around. Sounds of pleasure emanate from each of them. The crushed red velvet changed colors as the lights strobed back and forth, teasing. The shadows of other bodies, silhouetted against the darkness, appeared to merge with their own, creating an intimate and disorienting sense of proximity.

"I'm bored, Haddox." Leah's eyes scanned the dance floor, already moving on and looking for another partner.

Tugging out of his grip, Mia stopped him from pulling her any closer. "Go back with Leah. I am fine on my own."

Haddox raised his chin and looked off into the distance. "Leah, stay. I think things are going to become a lot more fun for you."

"Bye Haddox." Mia turned.

He reached for her, but she slipped through his fingers into the throng of people. Scanning for her in the crowd, she blended in with the others too well. The lights playing with the shadows and his eyes.

Leah fled out the other side of the circled couch, not waiting for him to come back to her.

Fine, they could leave; he didn't need any of them. He would make Mia pay later for her contempt. A muscle in his cheek twinged, sneering out at the crowd as he plopped down. The crushed velvet cushioning his fall.

Let me give you a taste of what you're missing. Abbadon purred.

He filled Haddox's mind with what he had always wanted. Him wanting to belong, sitting there in his mother's court next to her, along with the other full-blooded Old One descendants. Grey sitting there smiling at him, cheering him on for doing a good job with the trials. Women flocked around him, wanting him to create their dreams with his unlimited power. The power that answered when he called and was able to be pushed when exhausted. Large golden wings shone from his back. And there at the head of everything. His mother flicking a tear from her eye at the sight of his glorious wings. Her own wings were only slightly smaller than his, and a dull bronze where his shone a brilliant gold.

"No," he croaked. His will was at its wit's end.

What is a mere taste worth to you, halfling?

His eyes bounced to the crowd, looking for the missing girls. He had thought all three of them could have fun together, making it easier for him to win over Mia.

What if I said it was my treat?

Sweat dripped down his forehead into his eyes. He wiped it free, his head ached something fierce. The chaos Abbadon harbored stretched out in his mind. Wanting to burst free of Haddox's flesh-covered prison, he watched as his hands shook. Gripping both in a fist, he knocked them against his legs, tapping in time with the beat of the song blaring through the speakers.

"What do you mean your treat?" Haddox said. His voice was swallowed up by the bass and no one paid him any attention.

Exactly what I said, no strings attached. You still get to be my personal prison; you will borrow a bit of my power.

Getting to his feet, he paced the edge of the dance floor, hunting for a flash of one of the girls. Prowling back and forth, the agitation grew as time ticked by. Why was he so bad at this? He had lost both girls, and neither wanted anything to do with him.

It could give you the edge you need to turn things around. Captivate them and show them who you really are.

There he spotted Mia; her short dress being edged up by a pale hand. He watched her as she threw her head back, enjoying the feel of hands on her. The man nuzzled her neck where a black choker sat. The strobe lights made her movements look mechanical. A dark piece of metal flitted between the man's fingers. His eyes followed as the man brought the metal choker to rest around Mia's throat. It was a collar of submission.

How was Mia managing to defy him so brazenly? Did he not warn her about his kind? The thought of being unable to tame a human woman, let alone one of his own, was a humiliating prospect. What would others think if he failed? Leah would be easier, but he needed Mia back under his control for the tests. He couldn't let her get away with defying his every move. He needed to protect what he considered his own, to claim her as his possession.

"Yea, that's it. I can captivate both of them." He would save her from her own demise.

Haddox moved quickly through the people zeroing in on Mia. He shoved the guy, grabbing the piece of metal before it can lock in place. He snaked an arm around Mia's throat, coming up behind her. Pressing against her back, he felt all her soft curves. "Don't think I don't know what you are doing," he whispered in her ear, his voice rough. "If you wish to play with others, I have someone you can play with," He teased. Pulling on one edge of the collar, he slid it out from under his hand, removing it.

He was jarred from behind. His fingers slipped as the collar clicked close. "Watch who you're pushing." The man from before growled before letting the sea of people swallow him whole.

Haddox tugged at the choker, it was locked in place. "Now you are on a leash…" His worry turned mischievous as he thought about what could happen. "You can play to your heart's desire."

He moved his hand to her hip as her fingers raised up to her throat. The metal choker sat there snug around her slender neck.

"What is this?" she whispered, her voice husky with a mix of fear and arousal. "Get this off."

"Now you will have to do what I say." Haddox's eyes gleamed with wicked light as he caught Leah and pulled her close, his breath hot against them. "Let's play," he purred, his voice low and seductive.

Leah's eyes flashed with a spark of resistance, but her voice was laced with a hint of excitement. "Haddox, I don't really feel like playing with you right now," Leah whined, her tone teasing.

Haddox's gaze locked onto Mia, his eyes burning with an intense passion. "Good, because she was going to play with you," he said, his voice dripping with sensual promise.

Leah's eyes widened; she quirked an eyebrow at Mia. Shutting her mouth, Leah gave a wicked grin.

Mia's hands tugged at the choker, her face set in a petulant pout. "Take this off of me right now," Mia demanded. The music blared over head cutting her off. Lowering his head, he brought his ear closer to her lips. "We don't need it," she teased.

Haddox's chuckle was low and husky. "No, I think not. This collar will make you more... receptive to our needs. It will help you surrender to the pleasures we have in store for you. It will also help you with the tests to come. Now be a good girl and do what I say. Trust me, you want this." His words sent a shiver down Mia's spine, her eyes locking onto his with a longing that bordered on desperation.

Mia's hands dropped from the metal. He tugged both women back over to a secluded couch. The air seemed to thicken with anticipation. The couch, nestled in a quiet corner near the restrooms, seemed to whisper promises of forbidden pleasures. Haddox's hands guided them, his touch igniting a spark of passion that threatened to consume them all. As they sank into the plush cushions, the metal choker seemed to gleam in the dim light.

Haddox sat down on the couch while Leah danced in front of him, swaying to the beat of the music. She had her wings strapped down under her soft pink dress. "Sit here, Mia," he said, patting the seat next to him. His eyes barely rested on Mia before they swarmed back to the seductress that was enticing him. He beamed from ear to ear, finally getting what he wanted. No, deserved. This was how his nights should go each and every day.

Mia took a seat on the couch, her body stiff. Her hands skimmed over both Leah and his thigh, eager to touch and be a part of things.

Pulling Leah down closer to him so she sat on him more firmly, he turned her cheek to him. He kissed Leah as she laid back on him. His hands skated over her bare skin, the heat between them scorching hot as his hands roved over her.

Haddox hooked his finger around the loop in Mia's collar. He pulled her down, so she was kneeling by his leg. "Watch and yearn for us."

Twisting to the side so she could better see them, Mia pressed her lips together and gave a small nod. She licked her lips and watched them.

He saw her eyes go round as they deepened with desire. She panted and bit her lip as she saw where he touched Leah. He could only imagine she wanted his hands to do the same to her.

He loved seeing her like this; her face turned, meeting his with eager lips. Kissing Leah again, her lips tasted sweet as she leaned back, surrendering to the moment. Her legs fell open as she pressed into him, letting go of all restraint. Haddox skated his fingers up her thigh, scooting the pink dress up, showing nothing but bare skin below. He dipped a hand down, letting a finger glide down her lower lips, toying with her. She was already wet for him. The kiss intensified, a sensual exploration of tongues, as her body melted into his.

"More," Leah sighed, leaning her head back as she grinded on him.

His bulge was painfully hard and confined still. Slouching down even more, he pulled Leah up his stomach. His hand rubbed at her center.

Using his other hand, he pulled down the tiny strings that were holding up Leah's dress and released her breasts. He leaned back into the side of the enclosed couch, giving them both more room to stretch out. Her breasts were much fuller compared to Mia's small perky breasts. His hands overfilled with Leah's as he massaged them.

"Mia," he purred. Her eyes had never left them, and he could tell she was getting horny watching them. "Come here and suck me off while I play with Leah some more." He had left enough room to pull his pants down and get to work.

Mia moved forward eagerly, kneeling between his knees. Her eyes were lust filled, but there was a glimmer of something there. Her hand reached out to Haddox, caressing him, pausing as she tugged at the pant strings, undoing them.

"Haddox..." Leah whined.

He had stopped mid-motion as Mia's eager fingers began their lazy descent, making sure to brush against him, making him want more of both of them.

"Wait..." Haddox chest tightened. "Mia, come up here and kiss Leah."

Swaying her hips as she rose up, Mia leaned over them, her hand going to the back of Leah's neck, pulling her forward before their lips came together. Leah's body rubbed on his hand as she relaxed back into him. Letting him take her fully in his arms.

Haddox's gaze was fixed on the sensual display before him, salivating as his eyes burned with desire, watching their tongues wrestling together. The sound of their moans was like a siren's call, drawing him in with its raw sensuality. His arousal spiked as he strained against the confines of his pants, his body crying out for release. Mia's thigh pressed against him, sending shivers of pleasure through his body, and he cursed her for not freeing him first.

He didn't particularly care for humans in that way, but this seemed to work with Leah. That was fine with him; he was more than happy to exploit it for his own pleasure. He'd make sure he would only be with Leah in the manner that counted. Leah didn't care either way. She has had humans and Old Ones alike. She was freer and the reason they enjoyed having fun together so much.

Leah's arms wrapped around Mia, bringing her closer as their kiss deepened. Mia's hand pinched her free breast, smashing his hand between their bodies. Haddox was fascinated with them. Kissing the side of Leah's neck as he watched, Leah's voice hitched as she breathed in. He saw how much Leah was enjoying this and knew he had her.

"Mia, work your way down to my cock. I'm feeling lonely," Haddox said as he turned Leah's head to his lips.

Mia knelled in front of him. She slide down his legs and pulled at his pants. Yanking them down, her hot breath on his cock as she takes him into her mouth. Teeth grazed the underside of his cock, making his eyes bulge open. Mia's eyes met his, staring at him as she bobbed her head up and down.

Fuck! She had a pull that would not stop. This woman was making him rock solid. Her mouth was pure magic. Was he seriously thinking about breaking his rule and bedding this human? Could he do that? Throwing his head back. He almost lost it.

His hand smacked down hard on Leah's pussy, making her squeal and giggle in pleasure as his fingers toyed with her. Mia pushed his cock forward, slapping it against Leah's wetness. Mia licked his balls, massaging the shaft into Leah. Pushing him closer to Leah's pussy, the wetness did most of the work. His hips thrust him closer to his goal as he felt her line them up. Mia's hands were there, pushing him into Leah's hot sheath. Ever so slowly, each of them let out a small moan. Leah sunk down on him, her legs widening as she ground on his cock. Mia's delicate tongue continued to lick his balls and shaft as they moved in unison. Haddox used his hands and fingers to widen Leah's lips more.

"Lick her at her core, Mia. Make her come for me." His movements were already jerky. This would not last. He was on the edge and his control was slipping. But he had to make it good for Leah or she wouldn't have him again to teach him a lesson. She had done this before. It wasn't his first rodeo.

Mia crawled up between both of their legs, licking him and then her, taking her time going back and forth between them. Leah was transfixed by what Mia was doing to her, and he was equally captivated. They both watched Mia stick her tongue in where Haddox's cock slid in, teasing them both. They were both screwing her in a way, and that made him want to unleash everything he had.

Leah threw back her head, closing her eyes. As Mia's hands took over, holding her lips open and licking Leah's clit. Haddox gripped Leah's thighs, pounding into her. She swayed her hips, letting out a long moan.

She was on the brink, her body tensing around him, coiling up in anticipation of the release that was to come. Her muscles gripped and clung to his cock, holding him in a tight, pulsing vise. He thrust into her, not slowing down. Mia's hand slid up the underside of his cock as he slid into Leah. It felt amazing and almost had him coming undone himself.

They had always had fun together, but had never tried this before. Haddox was good at getting his way and getting people addicted to the type of pleasure only he provided. But he always felt like he had to one up himself and those around him. Nothing was ever perfect to keep them around for long.

"Haddox," she yelled out as she came over the edge, pushing down on him as Mia continued to lick and tease them.

Leah gripped Mia's short hair, pulling her up. She stopped her grinding against him.

His pleasure flitted away at the change of pace. Haddox's fingers gripped Leah's hips, wanting to throw her off and dive back in, finishing what he had started.

Leah's orange cat eyes blinked at him as she cocked her head. "Let the girl go party. Haddox let her have her own pleasure. While I finish with you," she purred. "I think you will have your hands full anyway." Leah leaned forward, repositioning him at her ass before lowering slowly on to him.

Haddox hissed. She was so tight, and he was so wet from her that she slid down easily.

"Yes, you like that?" Leah panted.

"You've never allowed this before." Haddox punched his hips forward each time Leah came down. She kept the pace slow, where he wanted to hammer her home.

Wrapping a hand around Leah's throat, he yanked her bottom against him. "Fine begone." He thrust in, punishing her. This would be fun.

"Maybe my friend can join us after, if you're up for it," Leah gasped out.

Mia watched them the whole time her hands touched her own legs, gliding up her stomach. Her delicate fingers roved over her shoulders, sliding the skinny straps down her arms, baring her breasts. His vision gobbled up the sight.

"Don't you want me?" Mia pouted. "I'm here for the taking." The lights overhead glared over him, piercing his eyes.

How could he say no to that? A feast for his eyes. His mouth watered with wanting. He had wanted to taste her this morning, but Leah had distracted him. He hadn't gotten back in enough time before everything went wrong. She should have never seen what his place was without his power. With power running through his veins, this would not be like last time. Flexing his arms, he slapped Leah's ass, leaving a nice pink mark there on her pale skin. "Get up. I feel like being in the middle of my favorite dessert."

Leah got up, moving to the side. A lazy smile tipped her lips as she stroked a finger over his shoulder, snuggled up on his left.

"Come here, my pet." He willed all the power into his own illusion of what he thought she wanted.

"What do you want, Haddox?" Mia glided over the last few steps reaching for him.

The lights burned into his eyes, making him blink rapidly. He rubbed his eyes. "You know what I want. Do it again! Make out with her." Clearing his vision, his hand was smacked away. Mia stood there in front of him dressed, and her eyes were filled with horror.

"Excuse me?" Mia asked.

"Do it again!" Haddox demanded he reached for her; his eyes dropped to her throat. The choker was missing. Where had it gone? Had another taken it off?

Mia looked disgusted. "Do what?" Her snide tone grated in his ears.

No, this wasn't happening again. He pulled at his magic, but it didn't stir.

"What you just did." He lowered his voice. "You kissed her."

Mia's eyes wandered over to his left, shocked. "Who?"

"What do you mean, who? Leah..." His head whipped to his left, searching the couch next to him. Leah wasn't there.

"You think I kissed Leah?" She laughed. But stopped shortly after he didn't join in. Her face fell to worry and confusion.

The music vibrated around him with a heavy bass, but he couldn't stop seeing eyes turn towards him. His pants were down and his cock was in his hand, shriveling as they spoke. Tucking himself away, he searched around the couch, wondering where she had gone.

"Listen, I came back here to check on you and Leah, but clearly you're going through something," Mia said, backing away her eyes followed his hands. "This was a mistake." She shook her head, dodging away.

Laughter erupted in his head

"You! This is all your fault!" Haddox argued, he raised up out of his seat searching for a mirror. Then he would see the thing hidden behind his eyes.

Me? I only showed you what you wanted. What you yourself were unable to achieve, being only a halfling, that is.

"Abbadon!" Haddox ground out, spittle flying from his reddening face. "Was any of that real?"

I'll never tell. Abbadon sang.

Chapter 14
Mia

Mia slipped away, fading into the crowd and away from Haddox's sight. Her fists tugged on the short strands of hair. Her hair was a dark blend, making it hard to tell the exact color. She had wanted some color added, like Battie had in her hair, but they hadn't had time for it. It was something she was open to trying later, at least.

Something really weird was going on with Haddox and she didn't want to be around him. It was like he had been talking to someone that wasn't there.

"Where are you going, cutie?" A man rumbled into her ear. The man swirled around her as he kept dancing.

Mia smiled but shook her head, trying to escape. She had enough dancing for now. Right now, she wanted to find somewhere she could sit and relax. It was another reason she had looked for Haddox. Thought she would be able to at least sit with people she had known. Now she would have to figure it out for herself.

This man looked normal enough. She had danced with some pretty interesting creatures so far. One had a lion's mane, another had wings, one even had a long tongue like a lizard. A shiver went down her spine at the thoughts that plagued her. Most of them were here to dance and hang out like her. Nothing sinister about it.

Not to say there weren't those types prowling around in the shadows. Biding their time. She steered clear of them. Turning from the man, she found herself being pulled and spun back into his waiting arms. Looking down, she saw a tail hook around her waist.

"Such a pretty little present." He smiled. Each of his teeth were sharp and pointy. "Follow me, my darling." His hands were firm. She could feel the strength as he kept her close.

Her luck had run out. She had run into one she had been trying to avoid. The music was so loud, screaming would do her no good.

They twisted and turned around, the other people losing themselves to the beat. He spun her into another's arms. Looking up, her eyes became captivated by the bright colors. This man was more bird than human and the colors of his feathers were so amazing and preened out. Many of the people in the crowd wore dark colors, so seeing someone with so many bright reds and oranges was refreshing to the eyes. Losing track of the man with the tail and sharp teeth, she relaxed into the bird's interesting dance. His bird-like legs bent at an angle and were also much longer than hers. She had to skip to keep up. People circled around her, everyone dancing with one another, grinding against her ass as she raised her hands in the air. She liked the feeling, hands sliding and touching, tantalizing her only as much as she allowed. The man behind her bound her arms in metal shackles. A tether was looped at the top of the shackles, pulling taut. As it did, her body lifted and her feet left the hard ground. The flat black slip-on shoes she borrowed dangled off her toes. The clink of metal cuffs vibrated through her arms. With ease, the crowd lifted and effortlessly maneuvered her. Out of the crowd, the man with teeth tugged on the leash she was attached to and pulled her back to him.

"Better to play with, don't you think?" he whispered into her ear.

Her dress lifted higher, with her arms above her head. The skirt was dangerously close to being indecent. She liked to tease others but not with so many stronger than her and her locked into place. Unease began to stir in her belly.

He let her feet touch the ground, just barely. She swayed there as his tail snaked around her waist. He had one hand on the rope and another on a drink.

"Here, you look like you could use a drink." He took a small sip before putting the cup to her lips.

She let the drink run over her tongue. He had drunk some, so it couldn't be all bad. The same golden liquid that she had the night before flowed down her throat. She coughed trying to spit it out.

"Drink up," he said.

He didn't give her a choice, so she had to guzzle down more of the sweet water drink. Soon the effects took hold, giving everything a dream-like quality as the edges of her sight went hazy. A smile lit up her face after every last drop flowed down her throat.

The cool drink felt nice on her parched throat. The burn from within heated her back up, mixing with the touch of people's hands and bodies. With his hands roaming over her legs and hips, a scorching pressure built from below, sending shivers up her spine. She shimmied against him, needing more contact than he was giving. The chord pulled her arms tight as she jumped into the air. Others raised their arms and hands, wanting to touch her as she passed over them.

She tugged on the straps that held her in place, wanting to move more. As he hoisted her up, she kicked out, her legs dangling in the air. The sway of her body and her limbs helped her go the way she wanted to. Raising her higher, he let her fly over the dancing crowd as a laugh bubbled up her throat. The wind cooled her heated cheeks.

The music and beat turned into a slower dance. Circling, she slowed as the same man that held the rope let it go. A sharp scream cascaded out of her as she landed. Arms cradled her body, when she landed. Gasping, her heart hammered in her chest. Feet barely able to keep up with his moves anymore, she was a swaying mess. He turned her into him and danced with her close. Growling, he sent her off, soaring again over the head of the crowd. A blue woman dressed in a black pantsuit caught her. Her black hair was cut in a short bob and her demonic looking eyes glanced at Mia in surprise.

"What are you doing here?" she muttered before unlatching the rope from the pulley system. But she kept Mia's arms shackled together.

"Who are you?" Mia asked. She had not run into her before or seen her. Did this woman know who she was? It sounded like she did.

The woman's keen eyes followed Mia's loose steps and awkward movements. "Follow me. Grey will want to see you," she huffed. Wiggling her pixie nose in distaste.

Mia tried to wiggle her nose in that cute manner, bumping into the front of her. Booping her nose with her finger. "Grey is so mean. Tell me who you are and you can let me go back to dancing." The warmth of the liquid had spread out over her whole body now.

"I am Grey's assistant when he remembers he has one." She nodded; her lips pursed in anger. "Shayla."

Mia lowered her arms as the rope slackened. She offered her hands to Shayla for her to shake. She fought with the restraint to only allow one hand but failed. "Nice to meet you." Muttering to herself, she cursed her hands.

Shayla looked at the offered hand with a raised eyebrow. "What do you want me to do with that?"

Giggling, her eyes settled on her outstretched hands. Why had she offered both her hands again? Oh right, she was meeting someone new, and it was polite to shake a person's hand, or so her mother liked to tell her. "Shake it?" Confusion poured over her. Why would that pop up in her mind at a time like this?

What was in that drink? Whatever it was sure messed with her mind.

Grasping Mia's fingers, Shayla shook the offered hand. The suction cups on the underside of Shayla's hand latched on. Sliding her hand back, the suckers slid off with ease. "Better?" She walked around the stage and kept the rope short between the two.

Her escort forced Mia to follow as she weaved through the crowd. They had rounded a bar that was in the middle of the dance arena, heading towards the darker lounging area. A cozy area where people relaxed and indulged other things. Her eyes roved over the bodies that moved together as one. This place was huge. She doubted she'd be able to find the entrance that Leah had brought her through. The building stood isolated in the middle of the forest, far from the waterfall and other houses.

Mia's eyes landed on Grey, who sat in one of those lush chairs that swiveled. His face already looked annoyed whenever someone came near. He snarled at others of his kind, keeping all at bay. Tripping over her feet, her limbs tangled with one another, trying to keep away herself.

Shayla kept moving forward, bringing her towards the giant of a man.

Chapter 15
Grey

"Grey, don't look so serious," Shayla said as she dragged Mia over, forcing her onto his lap. His horns were too large to loop her arms over his head. She put her hands in her lap.

Grey leaned back in a large chair and the soft cloth enveloping him in comfort. He had tipped his head back to relax his eyes when he sensed another moving into his space. To find none other than Shayla, he had told her to take the rest of the night off. But here she was, dragging some problem behind her for him to deal with. His eyes widened in surprise, realizing it was Mia. His gaze seemed to freeze as if time had stopped. For a moment, he forgot how to breathe. He placed his booted foot down. His mind raced through what this could mean. The chair was snug around him with no place for him to scoot over for.

The short, choppy click of her heels let Grey know Shayla was still pissed at him. "Guess what I find as I'm leaving for the night?"

Grey's eyes slid to Mia, but he didn't answer Shayla, knowing it would just piss her off more.

"Right, see, this is why I am your assistant. I am here to assist. Just because you have slowed down in teaching does not mean you still don't need help when dealing with things," she complained.

It was not the first time she had brought this up. She took her job seriously; one he had threatened to fire her from on more than one occasion. It's not like you could fire family, not really. She was a cousin on his mother's side, or so she had told him. Battie vouched for her and would throw a tantrum if she even heard that he actually fired her. He didn't care much about what people thought of him, but Battie, his sister, was different.

Mia scrambled to keep her legs and dress down as she fell into his lap. She wiggled to sit up, but only managed to lean against his chest, sprawled out across his legs.

He wrapped an arm behind her waist, helping to ease her into a better sitting position with her still firmly on his legs.

"Now that you have a handle on things. I will leave. Enjoy!" She smiled pointedly at Grey. He caught the hidden meaning. She had been in a position to help him with Mia, but now she was all his problem.

"Where are you going?" Mia called out, watching Shayla leave. Her head lolled to the side, resting against his shoulder as she looked up into the white eyes of Grey. Her eyelids drooped, as if the effort to keep them open was too much, but her lips curled up in a bashful grin.

"You are a strange bird," Grey said. His hand tightened on her hip, holding her up. She slouched a bit forward. He used his chest to keep her steady against him.

"Your kind of scary looking," Mia sighed with content as she leaned her head back. Her back hit the warmth of the chair, but she kept falling in the small crack between the chair and Grey.

"Weird that you seem comfortable with someone so scary." He scooched closer, shrinking the gap and allowing her to lean back against his shoulder.

"You don't feel scary. You just look it." She inched closer.

He watched her as she brought both hands up to his face. The cuffs made it hard for her to move. She had to bring the top of her body closer to his, resting against his chest. The tips of her fingers brushed against his eyebrows and forehead, then slipped down to his mouth and cheeks. "Right, there are the scary parts." The silky black dress rode up her thigh as she moved.

He caught the little slice of black fabric that was hidden under her dress. "What are you doing?" He raised an eyebrow. His large hands came down on the fabric, pulling it down her thighs.

"I dunno." She tried to climb over to the other side but stopped part of the way over and fell back on to him, unsure of what to do. "The drink I had…" She stretched her hands out in front of her, her hands batting around something only she could see. "It reminded me of the drink Haddox gave me before. I don't like what it does to me."

Pulling her back, Grey cupped Mia's delicate neck with his large, dark hand. His fingers gentled as they caressed the velvet black choker. "What did Haddox give you, little bird?" His eyes scrunched in confusion. His other hand circled her waist, rubbing up and down her side, his fingers tracing the curves of her body. The dress she wore was a gentle caress against his skin, the soft fabric a pleasing contrast to the warmth of her flesh. He pivoted his sight from her, looking for the golden blonde hair of Haddox. He would bite his head off once again if he found out she was in his care. Haddox always thought he was meddling in his business.

The only time he was ever in Haddox's business was when he oversaw teaching him and his brother. He had given that up after the first trial took place. Which wasn't too long ago, hence why Shayla was having a hard time with the lack of work to keep her busy. Her success largely depended on his, and why she pushed him so much lately. He didn't have the same drive they did. Not after... He wasn't wired that way.

"Haddox," he hissed.

"Whoa." Mia brought her hands up and cradled her head. "So dizzy."

"I will discover what he gave you. Once I find him," he vowed. Scanning the dancers with a calculated intensity. He knew his quarry wouldn't be among them, lost in the thrall of the music and crowd. That wasn't Haddox's style. No, he craved the spotlight, and the dance floor, as captivating as it was, wouldn't provide him with the singular attention he desired. He kept his gaze on the periphery, scanning the shadows.

"I can't deal with him right now. Can we just sit here?" She leaned back onto his chest, yanking at the dress, pulling it down. Giving him an eyeful of her chest. The slip of a dress melded to her body, fitting against her tightly, leaving nothing to the imagination.

He found himself worried about her. He didn't want her going anywhere he couldn't keep watch.

"Those dancers are making me dizzy and hot just watching them." She fanned herself. Her long lashes fluttered against her rosy cheeks.

Giving a sigh. "Of course. Well Mia, you don't have to worry with me. You are free to do as you will." He snapped his fingers, getting another's attention. A young man with a bony white skull came over with a smile plastered on his face. He knew Shayla would not leave him high and dry. One of her minions always was around when she was not. "Will you go hunt Shayla down? She should be able to obtain the key to these shackles, or if you could." Grey brought Mia's hands down so the skeleton man could properly see what he needed.

"Of course, Grey. Rex will be right back with that." The mini skeleton bounded off; he took off the top hat he was wearing before rushing off to catch up with the woman.

Oh, right, his name was Rex. This was the one that liked to talk about himself in the third person. Maybe Mia wasn't so strange next to that.

"Rex will be back shortly. Till then, try to relax." He leaned back, hiking her and the dress into the cocoon of his body. The crowd of dancers were right there in front of them, practically tripping over his long legs. Many dancers touched one another, eying them, he saw their lust filled thoughts turn to action as they danced away to a dark corner or to one of the other chairs.

Mia licked her lips, her head pulled to the side.

Grey slowly spun the chair, giving her a reprieve from the hectic dancing. The lounge was more subdued, than the dance floor. It was more daring and tantalizing than most humans were ready to see out in the open.

His hand followed the dip of her hip to the edge of the dress, making sure it was low enough and toying with the edge, right at the top of her thigh.

Her mouth opened slightly, panting, and her eyes were slitted at half-mast.

"Do you like to watch?" he whispered, his lips grazing her ear. He craved her answer. Wanted to know more about this woman that called to him. That stirred him in ways that defied his control.

Nodding her head, she sighed. Her legs straddled Grey's, falling open slightly.

Grey's hand followed her inner thigh, moving the dress to puddle in the center of her lap. "Use your words. I need to know this is you and not the drink."

"Yes," she uttered, her mouth going dry. "How would you know?" For the first time, she twisted her head to look at him, really look at him.

He watched as she scanned each of his horns. Waiting for them to land back on his white eyes. "I can tell that your mind is working with the question you just asked and if you had slurred your speech, then I would back off."

"I'm not buying it," she snorted.

"That's fair, but you are the one still on my lap." He looked down at her, she fit nicely against him snuggled into his side. He had not moved his hand from her thigh and she had not pushed away from him.

He turned their chair more; it swiveled away from the eyes of the hungry crowd. The other chairs around them were facing the same way as his and in each of them a couple were in various degrees of undress and having sex.

He saw her eyes lit up with fire beating back that dull, haze-like edge that had begun to creep in. The drinks, potent as they were for humans, he hoped that it had only been the one and her mind could fight the numbing effects. A darker concern began to gnaw at him as he wondered how many had Haddox given her and what he had done with her. If it was up to him, he would stop and find him right this moment and demand answers. But then she would be alone. He couldn't do that to her. Grey chose to use this time to get to know her, and to explore the depths of her passion and spirit.

As she rattled the shackles in front of his eyes. "I need these off. Then I can leave." Mia's eyes bore into his very soul, and Grey responded his desire for her rose.

His gaze dipped to her breasts and saw her nipples tighten and harden beneath the dress. His mouth watered with anticipation and the need to taste the salt from her skin.

She watched men and monsters alike fuck until they were spent. Grey's hand moved closer and closer with every gasp in the small circle, teasing her. If he was a gentleman, he might have offered to procure her another seat, one that wasn't directly on his lap. Could she even like the beast that lay within him? He didn't have Haddox's good looks. He might resemble a man, but the horns and white eyes said he clearly wasn't.

His fingers moved up to the apex of her thighs, but he didn't dare dip them down below yet. Would she be skittish? She had not invited him and he was afraid she would turn from him if he did much more than what he already dared. Touching the black slip of a thong he saw earlier, he could tell it was coated with sweat and her. "Have you ever enjoyed another's company?"

"Yes," her breathless answer sounded gruff. She shuffled her hands to the side, not knowing where her cuffed hands should go.

He saw the discomfort in her posture, her struggle to raise her hands up without bumping the horns on his head. He shifted back so she could lean on him easier, and has more room. She leaned back, bringing her hands up over her head, resting them gently on his chest as she settled against him. Grey lifted one foot, placing it on the cushion, blocking others view of her. They had their own cocoon here where she was mostly covered. He had moved his hand from her thighs, leaving things up to her. Her mouth hung open as she panted her eyes half slanted as she caught sight of others in the throes of passion.

"Have you ever enjoyed one such as us?"

Yes. "No," she moaned out as she stretched. "I mean... I don't know." Mia was closer to his horns and stared at the one next to her. "Can I touch it?" Her hand was already reaching for him, but she stopped short.

Grey looked at her fingers and where she intended to touch. He nodded. "Go ahead."

Her fingers didn't rush to the horn itself, but gave a tentative touch to his temple, smoothing through his dark hair. Her nails scratched his scalp, sending a shiver of pleasure through him along with a moan. He immediately curved into her touch, wanting more of her on him.

She stopped her touch at that.

He froze, wondering if he pushed too much. "Why don't you know?"

Her fingers pushed forward, skimming around the horn on the side of his head. After passing it by once, she came back to the rigid horn. It was solid and firm against his head. Her fingers tickled his scalp as they explored. Making it hard to keep listening to the words that fell from her lips.

"I was with Haddox the night before. At least I think I was. That night was so confusing it comes back in flashes, only parts of it seem real. The other parts are fuzzy and almost distant. Like a dream. He gave me many of those sweet drinks that day. Whatever was in those drinks is worse than alcohol."

Grey curled his front arm around her. Wanting to protect her from his own kind. He hated these trials, yes, it was true, but he didn't hate her. He had done a horrible job of protecting her so far. Was even part of the problem. "It is like your alcohol lowers inhibitions and lets out the real person you are inside. It's also usually used as an aphrodisiac."

"I wish I could remember." She shook her head, leaning it back against the pillowed head rest.

Unlocking the magic, he kept hidden deep inside. He pulled a bit of it forward into his fingers. Grey rubbed his thumb over two of his fingers, hesitating as he reached for her temple. "I have the power to break illusions. It might help you to remember what really happened."

Her vibrant blue eyes snapped open. The dark pupil in the center was like the dark depths of the ocean calling him closer.

"You would do that?"

"I would," he whispered.

"Yes, please." She watched as his fingers descended to the center of her forehead.

She was hot to the touch, but he let his magic cast over her. Using this time to touch her, he moved his hand like she had and skimmed his long fingers through her hair. The short strands whisked through them easily. His nails lightly grazed her scalp a second time, the strands of her hair was buttery soft. Her head fit in the palm of his hand, flexing his hand as he gave a light squeeze at the base of her neck.

She moaned out, her eyes rolled into the back of her skull.

He gave a tight-lipped smile, glad that she was affected by the small gesture as he was. Grey was mesmerized by this tiny creature. He wanted to give her something more to hold on to. "It might not come right away. But in time, you will learn the truth."

Tears flowed out of her closed eyes as she blinked them open. "Thank you," she whispered.

"Fuck!" a woman moaned out as she was being driven into. Her voice was loud compared to the whispered sighs and heavy moans that transpired in front of them.

That word alone brought both Grey and Mia's eyes back to the scene. His kind were sexual, not all humans were the same. His arm still curled around her, he let the other hand drop from the back of her head. He wanted to twist her head to his as he lowered his lips to her, devouring her there, but after hearing what Haddox had done, he pumped the brakes.

Mia leaned against his side, tucking herself into the curve of his body as she watched the others writhe together in pleasure.

"Would you want a cock driving into you like that?" Grey moved his head to the left, bringing her eyes to land on a strong male standing over a woman pile, driving into her at the edge of her seat as she took him. Pleasure written all over both of their faces as she let him lose himself inside. "Or something slower and more sensual." He swiveled to the right; the woman was riding the man while facing him. She controlled their speed as she moved up and down his shaft. A dancer slid between the chairs, gliding over to theirs. The woman laughed and kissed him before he stood behind her, sliding slowly into her ass from behind.

Mia's mouth hung open as she watched.

He found himself watching her more than he did the sexual scene. Her cheeks flushed with heat. He knew she had realized she was still sprawled out in his arms. Or was she embarrassed by the question he asked her?

"I-I know I am fine with this," she stumbled over her words. She brought her small hands down resting on them on his arm that circled her stomach. Her tanned skin was bright compared to his dark skin. "What about that couple?" Mia extended her hand to point at a pair next to them.

He turned their chair so she could see them better. The woman wore a dress much like Mia's except hers was already scrunched up to the middle, showing how bare she was beneath it. The guy's lap the woman was sitting on was at least as tall as Grey. He also had antlers, making his horns feel small compared to his.

Mia was in a similar position to the woman. Unlike Mia, her hands were not chained so she could grab onto the man's neck. They watched his hand slide between her lower lips, massaging her there with a gentle but possessive touch, dipping his fingers into her wetness. He began to toy and rub in small yet deliberate circles. She must have said something that he liked because he laughed and their eyes met theirs.

The air was heavy with the scent of sex in the air, and the tension rose as everyone watched the woman arch and wind her hands around the back of his neck, holding onto him as he pleasured her. Her body rocked in time with his movements, her hips swayed to the rhythm of his touch. He rubbed the palm of his hand as his fingers delve into her deeper. Due to the intense heat and sexual tension between them, it didn't take long before she released a loud moan, finishing over his hand.

Mia shifted restlessly in Grey's embrace; her body responding to the erotic display before them. Grey kept his hand there around her waist.

The other man kept his hand on the woman's mound, laying claim to her and all eyes that saw what he had done to her. His hand tipped her chin, silently asking for the woman to look at only him. "Do you like having others watch me claim what is mine?" His low voice rumbled out loud enough for Haddox and Mia to hear. The kiss the woman gave was all-consuming and laced with heat as their bodies moved as one. She was eager to show him how much she liked it.

"Grey." Mia's eyes drifted up to Grey's, her voice barely above a whisper.

He read the emotions there on her face, but he wanted her to ask that of him. He wanted her to admit what she clearly wanted. She bit her lip in indecision. Grey sat there patiently, waiting for her to work through the words she needed.

"Ahem." Rex coughed awkwardly. "I have the key, sir."

Grey ground his back teeth together. A twitch flicked over his cheek at the anger that flew through him. He didn't like being interrupted, didn't like that Rex had ruined this intimate moment. He kept his arm where it was even as she tugged against it, sitting up.

"Much appreciated, Rex." Grey took the key; she moved her arms down. Her thigh moved closer to the center of him, and he knew she was aware of his arousal. His solid and thick presence evident through his tight pants. Removing his hand from around her waist, he used both hands to help with the lock.

Though her leg didn't move, her eyes followed his movements. The air was thick with words left unsaid. The latch was loud as it unlocked. She rubbed at her wrists. Grabbing the rope and shackles, he shoved them over to Rex. "Get rid of those."

Rex grinned and scampered off, probably to acquire his own victim to play with that he'd tie up.

"Let's go see what Haddox was up to." His head and chair swiveled back to the dance floor in search of Haddox. Sweeping her up from his lap, he cradled her against his side, tucking her under his arm, wrapping it around as he glided through the people. They moved around him, not daring to bump into them.

He spotted Haddox lounging next to Leah in a booth. They were kissing and hugging one another, enjoying each other's company.

"I can't believe you, Haddox. Acting like this. Do you want another trial to fail all because of you? This is the last chance. If she doesn't complete this, they will wake up, and that's it we are done for. Our chances are ruined. This entire world will be destroyed."

"We're having fun," Haddox said, coming up for air and laughed.

Haddox's eyes narrowed as they landed on Mia. He shuddered. What the hell happened? Glancing back at Mia, her eyes avoided Haddox.

"Yea fun," Leah giggled. "It's all a bunch of fun. Why are you ruining it?"

"Leah, stay out of this!" Grey demanded. His eyes blazed with fierce intensity as he loomed over Haddox, his voice low and menacing. "What did you do to her?" he growled, the words dripping with a quiet, controlled fury.

Haddox visibly relaxed and breathed out a pent-up breath. "Nothing, this time." He shrugged, going back to kissing Leah.

"This time?" he grounded out. "What about yesterday? What about the drinks?"

Mia snuggled up closer to Grey, hiding behind him. Her curves melded to him even with him being so much taller than she was.

"If it was up to me, she would have a servitude necklace on," Haddox muttered.

Leah hiccupped and giggled on the other side of Haddox. "Looks like someone gave her some nectar of bliss."

Had Grey heard Haddox correctly? Them being so much closer to the bass of the music; it was hard to hear when he lowered his voice. He heard Leah loud and clear, though.

"The wine of the gods? What were you trying to do with her?" he asked. From what he could tell, he also deduced that much. Luckily, most of it had worked out of her system by now. Sleep would do the rest.

"Don't worry, she has had some before. She's fine. And you said you would stay out of my way; I'm doing this my way. I had to make sure she was on our side and not going to tank the entire thing because she hates others," Haddox growled. "It made her more pliant."

Glaring down at Haddox. "When did you give her nectar before, and what did you do to her?" His fists flexed at his side. If the memories didn't come back to her, maybe he could get the answers she needed now.

"Trust me, she wanted it and if you play your cards right, you too can enjoy the wonders of her pretty little mouth. Or more if you're into that kind of thing." Haddox grimaced.

"Did you?" The words eluded Grey; he was so disgusted.

Laughing boisterously. "Only in her dreams." He got yanked back into Leah's arms, kissing her.

Grey's angry gaze zeroed in on Mia, who still stood somewhat behind him. Her eyes shimmered, her gaze met his, then slid away.

"It was all an illusion. What you went through yesterday, you can be sure of that." Grey knew how much Haddox hated humans, but he hadn't known he had a deep revulsion of them as well.

"Yes!" Mia blurted out. Her knees gave out as she leaned on him for support. "He's been acting really weird. Let's just go."

Grey helped hold her up as he guided her out of the party. "Haddox, I think you should stay away for a time."

"Sure, she will probably be dead in the next test, anyway. She almost messed up the first test. Cheating," he scoffed. "So unbecoming," he said with disgust.

"Don't talk of things you know nothing of," Grey threw back at him.

"Says the one that helped her cheat. After reprimanding me for wanting to do the same thing. Guess the responsible one is not so responsible, is he?" Haddox yelled out.

Grey turned away with Mia in tow. They walked in silence. The party thinned and disappeared altogether. As they walked through the woods, stragglers dotted here and there through the trees, the noise gradually died down. They kept the party away from where the tests were given and where she had stayed the last couple of days.

"Something is off with him," Grey said.

"He was talking to himself earlier." She had peeled away from him once they were alone. She wrung her hands together.

"Talking to himself how?"

The woods were infused with a warm, ethereal glow, courtesy of the light stones that dotted the landscape. Areas of high foot traffic were particularly well-illuminated, with a generous sprinkling of these luminous stones. The grounds and trees were also adorned with vibrant paintings and twinkling lights, creating a whimsical atmosphere. As they made their way back, they were accompanied by a canopy of string lights, which cast a magical glow over their path.

One painting drew her forward. "I had come back from dancing with some guy and wanted to sit down and rest. There Haddox was sitting down playing with himself along with talking to people that weren't there."

"Like talking through something? Or imagining?" Grey asked. That didn't sound like Haddox.

"He was quick to anger and what he suggested was pretty lewd. It was like he was in one of his own illusions." Mia crouched down, getting closer to the painted artwork that wrapped around the tree. The groves of the wood, creating the painted scene of the wind giving it both color and texture.

"Do you have any other powers that you can wield other than breaking illusions, Mr. tall, dark, and handsome?" She slapped her hand across her mouth. Scrambling around the tree, she stayed hidden there.

Grey let her escape his gaze. Not missing a step, he continued walking, kicking the dried pine needles that laid in the dirt. Mia came away from the tree once he moved far enough away. He peered down at her, just a glance. Her cheeks were pink with embarrassment; she grumbled to herself. A smile ticked up the side of his cheek. She hadn't meant to say all that he bet. His eyes moved away from her.

"My powers aren't much of anything. Most hate that I can break illusions so easily." Glamors were a thing the less than human looking ones used. Around here it wasn't a problem. But out in the real world where a human could catch them, that was a different matter entirely. It was why he never ventured far from this place. He only went out once, and it was dangerous enough to bring his sister back in one piece. He had to keep a tight lid on his power, more so because of what his powers revealed.

"I know your sister is a healer. I guess Haddox's makes illusions and possibly heat." She fanned her cheeks as she came around the tree; they were still red. She looked away from him, not willing to meet his eyes.

"His powers are illusions. He can manipulate how the feeling or thought is perceived or seen only if it is present. So, making someone feel a certain way can be easy if he knows which buttons to push."

"Can it make something ugly into something beautiful? Or a plain dress into a pretty dress?" Mia kept her eyes and feet busy checking out other artworks some carved others made and placed along the path.

"Physical manifestations like that require a lot more power, so they can, yes, but only for a time. Each power has its limits. Haddox more so since he is only half descendant. His father was human."

"And let me guess touch makes it easier for him to pull the whammy on someone, right?"

He gave a tight nod.

"What did you mean by physical manifestations? Are there other kinds?" Mia looked curiously over her shoulder at him.

"He can infiltrate dreams. He doesn't need much power for that and turns it into whatever he so desires as long as the other person is willing."

"You said most people hate your power. Haddox and you don't seem to get along. Does he hate your power also?"

"Mine is the opposite of his. It dispels illusions or spells. It is why when I touch you sometimes you can probably think clearer. That may be the reason why we don't get along, but I think that came way before our powers came into the picture. Ever since I picked him and his brother up for extra training."

"Is that all you can do, then?"

"I told you it wasn't much of a power." Grey grimaced. While it was true that most of his kind had one power if you were born to two descendant parents, those children usually had another kind of power. One as their main and another that was weaker.

"At least no one can pull anything over on you," Mia sounded pleased.

"There is that. I have one other power." Grey hesitated.

"What is it?" Mia asked. She turned to him like she was intrigued. She had wandered closer to him as they continued down the path. They were almost back at the waterfall.

"It would be easier to show you?"

"Oh, yeah?" She looked at him with doubt, crossing her arms in front of her heaving chest. They had been walking for some time, taking their time through the woods.

"Forget it. It's nothing." Hastening his step, he turned from her. He didn't want to scare her more. He shouldn't have said anything. "We should get back. Battie will have my head if anything happens to you before the second test."

She reached out a tentative hand to his arm, stopping him. "Not only Battie, but Ashling as well, from what she said. Please show me."

"So, you were listening and not fully out when I was talking with Ashling?" Grey's worried eyes took in her small stature. She was so delicate looking, but something told him there was more to her than what met his eyes.

Giving a shrug, "I was in and out."

Taking her by the hand, he led her over to a large tree. It had vines and flowers growing along its dark, rich bark. The greenery climbing up the trunk became one with the tree.

"You don't have to keep an eye on me, you know."

"I don't?" He wore a look of astonishment. He didn't see this conversation coming. Hadn't even known she had heard them speak about her. Why was she not more furious about it?

"Do you always do what Ashling tells you to?" Her small hand folded into his larger one.

"When they are an Old One, you should take notice and listen. They have been around for eons and will most likely outlive us all."

"I thought all the Old Ones were the enemy." Stopping in front of the tree, she pulled her hand back. Her face scrunched in confusion.

"Not all, but most. She went to sleep voluntarily and helped us trap them all. She assists us by keeping them in a deep slumber," Grey said. "But to keep it up, the spell requires a sacrifice or tests to be passed."

"What does she get out of it?"

"She is not in a cage like the rest. She slumbers because she wants to and, in that room, she may create it into what she wants, whatever that may be. It is her domain."

"So, she could leave at any time. Leaving you all to fend for yourself."

"She is strongest while she slumbers. If she wakes to leave, she is the weakest of her kind, making her easy to take down and easy to capture."

"So easy to defeat."

"I wouldn't say easy, but easier, yes." Grey was happy to give her more of an understanding of why she was here. Anything to take away the pain of what he was about to show her. Cringing, he pointed to a tiny green vine growing out the side of the tree. "Look there."

She glanced at the vine and noticed the concentration that settled on Grey's face. He stared at it in complete focus. His dark hair feathered out from his head and four horns like a lion's mane. The muscles flexed as he concentrated on the task at hand. A sea of black surrounded his eerie white eyes.

The little sprout of a vine curved over to her, spreading out. She brought her finger up to touch the tip. A tiny flower bloomed from it, kissing her finger. Her face broke into a smile.

"You can make plants grow?" she said, surprised.

"Small things, yea." He watched her, and she was amazed by the tiny plant he created. Warming his bitter heart.

Her fingers caressed the flower, the vine twirled around her fingers. Even with the cooling season as it has been, these dark woods still had dark green leaves everywhere with flowers. "Nature thrives here compared to in the village."

He moved his face close to hers, peering at the little thing. Why was she so transfixed by something so small? It was a plant, like all the others. It didn't look any different to him.

"Tell me about your village." Grey wanted to know more about where she came from. What kind of person she was? She had to be strong, that much he knew. She didn't scare easily compared to the last one.

"There's not much to tell. The people there are like all the others. They fear things they don't understand or know. So, we are segregated from the open world because of it. They think so small."

"But you don't?"

She shook her head, but her eyes caught on him. She turned to him; the plant forgotten. "I had always wanted to leave. A few times I got out, but fear always won over me and I came back. I don't want to be stuck." The last sentence was whispered out as if it were a secret.

"Stuck?" He quirked his head to the side. He could understand that. A lot of the times he felt stuck here. She didn't answer. "Mia," he whispered.

"Hmm?" Her eyes were zeroed in on his mouth, her hand reached out touching his chest as she leaned in.

"Don't..." he uttered.

Mia froze, her eyes widening as she realized what she was about to do.

Why did he say that? Why didn't he just let it happen? Ultimately, he knew why. He didn't want to admit it. Mia was growing on him and he didn't want to jeopardize it with her having had that drink.

"Why?" Mia glowered. Reaching out, she steadied herself against the tree.

"I want you to be sure and not under the influence of the Nectar of Bliss. What if this is what the Old Ones want?" He didn't move away from her, afraid to break the tension. Oh, how he wanted her, but was this the best time?

"Aren't you curious?" Her mouth moved an inch closer. "What if it's what I want?" she whispered, her breath mingling with his.

"I am... curious," he admitted.

She pressed her palm to his chest to steady herself. Lifting on her toes, she closed the distance, giving him a shy peck before letting go and backing away.

His hand shot out, bracing himself against the tree curling around her. He lowered his head and angled her head up to his, capturing her lips. His kiss was sure and unhurried. He poured everything he had denied himself into the kiss.

Mia's hands curled in his shirt as she opened to him. He deepened the kiss, his tongue wrapping around hers, tugging her forward. Her back nestled against the soft moss crawling up the tree. There was heat between them, but it was a warming tingle, not a scorching flame that would burn both of them.

He pulled back, greenery caught his eye, he looked around her noticing all that he had done. His eyes widened as he stumbled back, not moving very far.

"What?" she worried. Her hand unclenched from his shirt and moved to tug at the short hair at the knap of her neck. "Is there something wrong with my hair?" she babbled.

"I..." He stood back, shocked.

She noticed his arm that was still braced against the tree had vines crawling up his arm. "Did you do that?" Mia asked.

Grey glanced at the twisted vines and flowers that spiraled around. Soft moss cushioned his hand and surrounded her, as if making sure she was protected against the bark of the tree.

"I can't..."

"Well, I can't." She gave him a deadpan stare.

Carefully, he broke away from the tree, untangling from the ropes of plants. His fingers played with a ratty bracelet he wore around his wrist.

"Maybe your powers are expanding? Do they do that?"

"Yes, when we come into our powers, but that is when we are young. I have had both powers for a very long time. This power has never, no matter how much I practice, gotten stronger than what I showed you a moment ago."

She pulled on a vine, one thicker and made of bark, yanking it out from the rest of the greenery as she brought it forward to his hands. "Here, try to make this bigger, thicker growing into a branch of the tree."

"That is outside my scope of skill." It was his turn to look uncertain. Nothing good came from his powers growing. He had spent many years testing his powers and training them. Why would they choose to act up now? Was it her? Was it these tests? He had to do more research.

"Try. For me." She frowned, her eyes turning up to him.

He concentrated on it and it barely stuttered before going limp in her hand.

"See." A surge of relief hit his chest.

Rolling her eyes. "You didn't even try," Mia said.

Glaring at her, he put both hands on the wilting vine, pushing his all into it. "This is dumb. Forget it. It's a dumb vine, anyway."

He walked away, leaving her behind.

Chapter 16
Mia

Looking down at the sad wilted vine and the fallen petals behind her, Mia gave a knowing smile. A pine cone sat next to her foot. She bent to retrieve it. It reminded her of a pinecone from another time. Smelling the brown petals, a rich earthy scent filled her nose; the spines prodded at her fingers as she turned it in hand. Had she known back then what lay in wait for her, she would have studied more with Sylvia. That way she would have been on equal footing, power wise. At least she hoped so. Giving a sigh, she let Grey walk away from her. She knew the way back and after the things they had found out together; she needed some alone time. The constant push and pull of feelings made her dizzy with confusion.

Turning back to the large tree, it surpassed all the other ones around it. The trunk was thick, her and Grey together standing side by side, barely made up the width of it. Twisting what was left of the vine around the pinecone, she attached it to the tree. The large branches looked as if they had weathered every storm. Nothing was ever going to knock it down. She wanted to stand tall like this tree, not backing down.

Brushing her fingers against her lips, she thought of their kiss. Hers was childish and abrupt, his was sensual and dangerous. How could two vastly different people be pulled together? She didn't understand it, but was glad he was nothing like Haddox. She felt calm; the drink had since run its course. But the attraction to Grey didn't leave her as it had with Haddox. Grey was rough around the edges and had a bite to him. An Alluring quality bright and heavy in her mind.

"Is there something wrong with me?" she questioned.

At least she knew the truth about what happened that first night. Turning from the large tree, she made her way back to the room at the healing center.

Bloo barked as she came out of the woods. She saw his furry little blue body against the dark shadows of the archway. Racing forward, she scooped him up in her arms. She snuggled against the soft fur. Fresh tears streamed down her face as she pushed her face against the fur.

"Okay?" he yipped.

"I missed you," was all she managed.

Bloo laid his head against the curve of her neck, wrapping himself around her. "Bloo here."

Mia laughed, "Yes you are, and I am so happy that you are. Let's go get some sleep." She carried him back to the room and set him down on the bed, relieved to get ready for bed.

She closed the door and locked it, making sure to place the chair that was near her bed in front of the door. She made sure everything was in place before letting her head hit the pillow. Once it had, she was out of it, falling into maddening dreams.

She was restless throughout the night, kicking and turning. Bloo hopped down after the second time she woke both of them with her twisting and flailing limbs.

The next morning, she got up early. Dreams had plagued her, showing what actually occurred between her and Haddox. Mia had planned to get to the door before Haddox or Grey could even come looking for her. She wanted to get things over and done with. She definitely didn't want to deal with Haddox and she didn't know if she could look Grey in the eyes and not give away what she so clearly wanted. Bloo looked up sleepily from the warm bed, the covers piled around him.

"Go back to sleep," she whispered, closing the door softly.

She made quick steps to the trial room. It was heavy as she tried to pull on it. Looking around, she saw no other early risers. The birds weren't even chirping yet. She braced a bare foot against the other door before pulling with all her strength to open it up a mere few inches. Digging deep, she pulled harder. It opened enough for her to slide through. Hurrying, she slipped through the closing door. When she scoped the room this morning, she found clothes of her size in the dresser drawers. Both warm and cool clothes for her to choose from.

As the door closed, darkness engulfed the room. Should she not have come here without anyone? No nature this time or cabin, just cold dark nothingness all around.

"The morning has barely woken, young one." Ashling's voice dripped from above. "The trial is usually not for a couple more hours."

"Are we able to start it early? I didn't want to wait for the others." She bundled up warmly since last time it was so cold with the snow and ice. The only thing that was normal for her was the lack of shoes.

"We could... Or we could talk and get to know one another." A light cast down on Mia and at the edge, she saw Ashling come forward. This time she morphed from her grandma to a young woman with long blond hair and an hourglass shape. Her dress was long and flowy, with splotches of color splattered across it. The pinks, blues, and yellows morphed with the bend of the fabric. Looking almost like flowers being blown in the wind.

"Whoa, why do you look different now? You look amazing!" Mia added on to emphasize different wasn't a bad thing.

"I wished to show you my true form. I felt you could handle it." She slowly blinked as she breathed in. "I forget what it feels like to be awake after slumbering for so long."

"Wait!" Mia stepped back and rammed into the door behind her. "You're awake? This is you?" Mia squeaked, the breath getting knocked from her. "Aren't you supposed to be slumbering with the Old Ones?" She remembered what Grey had said about Ashling, but didn't think that meant she could wake up and walk around with nothing stopping her. There weren't even guards at the door.

Giving a harsh laugh, Ashling wrinkled her nose. "On occasion, I wake up just to know that I can. I follow the rules though and stay in this room, my controlled prison," she bit out harshly. "I know my bounds." Her gaze rested on her enclosed fist, releasing it as she looked saddened.

"But what if you left and escaped?" Mia questioned, having to know for sure. Although even if she made it to the door and yelled for help, would anyone hear her before Ashling pounced on her? She didn't think so.

"True, I would be free for a time, but they would all make good on their promise and trap me for good with no way to wake from my living nightmare." A tear rolled down her cheek.

"But aren't you trapped, anyway?" At best, Mia was dealing with someone unhinged. Who could blame her? She was stuck in here for who knew how long.

"Yes, but one of my own choosing and on my own terms." Ashling looked down her nose. "Don't we all live in a prison of some sort, either of our own choosing or one we make ourselves fit into?"

Mia's lip trembled, not wanting to think like that. Her legs shook with fear. Had she left one prison to be in another? Was that what she was getting at? Or was she only talking about herself? She ended up shrugging her shoulders like she didn't understand.

Stomping forward, Ashling marched right up to Mia and got in her face. "You little mongrel, you would have wasted away in your village by either being trapped in a cage because of your wildness or married off to someone who would turn you into something you couldn't even look at in the mirror. All the while you sit there smiling, wishing to die, so it stops. All the scarring occurs on the inside, where it remains unseen, and all the pain will overwhelm you until you cannot breathe." Dark tendrils climbed up Ashling's pure white dress. She tapped a long-nailed finger into Mia's chest and kept pointing at her in different spots.

Mia's chest ached with each point. How did she know what went on in her village?

"I could have tried other things," she argued. Anger and fear warred within her, upset that it could have happened just like that and worried for the village. They were not safe if Ashling could so easily see what was going on with her and must know everything about the town.

"And they would have sadly failed you like this world has. It's sad you don't realize what you could have, what's out there to experience."

"Tell me," Mia said eagerly, pushing past the pain and moving Ashling's finger. Her fingers grab onto Ashling's shoulders, bringing her forward. Desperate.

Ashling frowned and forced Mia's hands away. "Hey, watch it!" Dusting off the dress, the tendrils scattered back into the shadows under the dress. She moved away, looking back at Mia.

Hanging her head, she stuffed down the excitement. She craved to hear, to learn something about the Old Ones other than from what her grandmother or a book told her. This would be a firsthand experience. Oh, the things she must know.

"Ashling, please tell me something about you, or the other Old Ones and this world?" She slid down the door, sitting in front of it, waiting. Mia fell back as the solid door faded away. She worried about how solid the ground was when Ashling could change anything in here with a mere thought.

"The Old Ones, as you call us, are not from these lands. We came from somewhere very far away and got stuck here while visiting. We adapted to what we were given and befriended the people who lived here. Some of us even had relations with those people and now we have descendants that help police us here."

Ashling created a background behind her as a swatch of black coated it and a dash of speckled lights blinked on. "The night sky?" Mia questioned.

"Yes." Ashling moved her hand across the color. She stepped closer to Mia, the gray stone beneath their feet.

The scene moved around them as Mia sat there. Deep blue waves crashed into the stone, the ground meeting the ocean. She looked out at the horizon, the sky and ocean melding together in the hazy distance. Something dark raised up out of the ocean, spearing into the sky breaking the path.

"What is that?" Mia cocked her head to the side, fighting her urge to crawl forward.

Ashling moved her hands, zooming in. The small rock soared over the ocean, closer to what laid beyond their reach. "Your village is but a speck on this land." The picture moved in and trees and greenery became more detailed as she pulled them all the way to her village. "There are others around the entire planet. The land we picked here is mysterious and dangerous all on its own, so other villages like yours tend to stay on the outskirts of this place. We made a home for ourselves there." She pushed away from the sea and headed deeper into the greenery.

"What happened?" Mia faltered, not sure if she meant that exactly. She needed to know more. Her mind raced with a thousand questions.

"Our group banded together to trek through this world and learn what kind of trouble we could get ourselves into. It came to our attention that your world has not yet made significant progress, as you have only a rudimentary grasp of the concepts we endeavored to teach, and they mistakenly labeled our magic as evil and flawed. We learned through trial and error not to show too much of ourselves to the masses, otherwise they turned on us quickly. Among your kind, some of us considered ourselves gods, and either received worship or fear. Neither choice was good, war always ensued in the end. Each of us had our own take on what we should do. Most wanted to abolish everyone we encountered and wipe them from the world, starting it over in our own image. This would be difficult with how few there were of us, and procreating took decades of trying."

Mia's mind reeled at the information. "Why tell me all this?"

Ignoring Mia's question, Ashling continued. "Another thing about my kind is though we populate slowly, we are long lived. Some of us are good at waiting and being patient. You do not last as long, only about seventy years, if that. With each passing year, a bit of us is forgotten meaning if you're not careful, your own kind will be the downfall of this world. The old stories must stay alive and persevere through the times."

Mia didn't understand why she was being told all this. Did Ashling know that she was not going to make it through these trials and didn't worry what kind of knowledge she kept?

"What about your descendants? Can't they keep this world from being overrun by the Old Ones?"

"When an Old One mixes with a human, a part of them melds with them, forever changing them. Our children and our children's children are more human in looks, but they can be just as vicious."

"Do you have children here?"

Ashling shook her head, turning from Mia. A stray tear fell as her hands slid up to wipe it away. She took a few breaths before continuing. "No, never. I... can't have them. Only my dreams hold possibilities for me there."

"Oh, sorry about that." Mia felt for her. Sylvia, her teacher, also couldn't have children. A few times a year, they wouldn't meet because of it.

"Course you are," she chuckled. "Everyone always says they understand, but do they ever really mean it?"

Mia's head popped up. She pulled herself up and walked over to Ashling, giving her a hug. Ashling was rigid at first, then loosened up and hugged Mia back.

"My teacher, Sylvia, also can't have children. She gets grumpy closer to certain dates and has to take some time to grieve for the loss of family and reunite with the family she still has."

"You know nothing about the hurt I endure," Ashling said.

Hugging her tight, Mia kept her arms around her for a long while, wanting her to know she meant it.

"I may not know exactly what you are feeling, but I understand how it feels when you don't have that as an option when you should. Why would I say something I don't mean?" Mia whispered.

"Many are that way." Ashling shrugged, her body trembling in Mia's embrace.

They sat like this for many minutes before Ashling pulled away. Mia let her retreat, knowing she'd had enough.

"It is why I protect the descendants so and why I vow to stay here. They are all my children, even if I have to protect them from the very beings that made it possible for them to live in this world." Rage poured over Ashling's face. The swash of color behind Ashling turned to red as Ashling panned them back out. Flames licked at the outer barrier of the town. "Some of the Old Ones made good on their promise and started taking out the humans. Including descendants who had families and bonded with the humans. It did not stop there. Fights between Old One's consumed many of your kind, getting caught in the crosshairs."

"Couldn't anyone stop the Old One's?" Mia eyed the dome that protected her village. "Is that my village in the future?"

Her lips quivered. Fighting the need to jump into the ocean and swim to help her fellow people.

Ashling's hand wrapped around Mia's wrist, holding her still. "I am the weakest of the Old Ones when I am awake. They would not listen to me, but in dreams and nightmares, I control things. It's a little harder for them to avoid me." Ashling waved her other hand and the flames disappeared and the barrier was back at full strength. "Each Old One has weaknesses. They also unfortunately have their own wishes and ideas on how things should go. For many, it was their own downfall. For others like me, they decided to lay down willingly to let their descendants live on and rest, knowing it was for the better."

She hadn't said anything about her village and the flames were gone, so she relaxed against Ashling's hold for now. She didn't really want to go back there, but would if everyone she knew was in danger. Sylvia would need her help.

"Why am I important? Couldn't anyone do these trials?"

She spun back to Mia, her hawk-like eyes perused over her body and how she was bundled for warmth. "I will let you in on a little secret."

With the sun glaring down and the waves rolling by, she pulled at the jacket. Heat swarmed her. "What secret?" Mia said carefully as she wiped the sweat from her brow.

"Remember how I said that when an Old One touches someone, it forever changes them?"

Mia nodded. Her muscles were rigid and ready to run as she feared what she may hear next.

"The person who takes on these trials has to be someone that has been touched by an Old One." Ashling waited a moment for it to sink in.

"So that means... descendant..." Mia was puzzled. She tried to recall exactly what Ashling said. But all that echoed in her mind was Old One and human.

"It could mean that yes, you are a descendant of an Old One and a human." Ashling toyed. "But in your case, it's not..." Ashling dropped.

"How..." Mia uttered.

"When you stepped into my realm here, I saw many things about you. Threads of how you connect to the tapestry of fate. It helped me decipher what trials you would need and if you are the right person for the job."

"What job? What happens after passing these three tests? No one has told me what happens after."

Waving a hand, Ashling brushed her off. "That is a discussion for another time. No, the better question you should ask is how did you come to be here? You already know part of that story."

A flash of light played behind her. She turned away from the ocean and village. Looking up at the sky, Mia saw a much younger version of her grandma. The sky had turned to blues and purples as if the sun was setting, though she shouldn't be able to see inside a room. Bringing her focus to the water that surrounded them, she looked for where the picture was coming from. "What is that?"

"A memory!" Ashling giggled with delight. A circular bowl with some kind of food popped into existence. "Want some?" she asked as she took a handful and threw some into her mouth.

She took a piece and sniffed the white circular object. It smelled buttery. She placed it on her tongue, part of it dissolved and the rest disintegrated as she chewed. The taste was light and buttery, with a hint of salt. It was pretty good, nothing like she had tasted before.

Ashling froze the image in the sky. "You're supposed to be watching this? Don't you guys have movies in your village?"

"We have some, but not many. All of those must be transported from the old country." Her father loved movies and always tried to bring one when he visited. Mia wondered if he had access to this tasty treat back in their old country. He didn't talk about his travels often. But sometimes he would share the goodies he received.

Ashling pointed to the image in the sky. Mia turned back to the memory, waiting for it to start back up.

Grandma Sky fell to her knees as she scrambled away from a tall man that was carrying a large wooden mallet. His eyes were pure black and filled with hatred. Black ooze flowed down from his eyes and ears. "Stop running, little mouse!" The man yelled out; his voice distorted with another voice on top of his. A hazy outline of a dark cloud pulsed around him. "I am Abbadon! Know my name. I want you to scream it from the top of this hill, little mouse. Warn the people below of what is coming."

He seized her and flung her to the ground, trapping one of her arms beneath his heavy boot. He leaned his weight on her, raising the wooden mallet, and slammed it down on her hand. Abbadon would wait before heaving the mallet backup and smashing it back down over her knuckles. Her lips were bloody as she chewed them together, refusing to call out for help.

"Stop it!" Mia called out, running to the edge of the rock. She took a step into the water and ground to a halt as her leg sank into the deep ocean.

"Watch your step," Ashling said.

Falling back, Mia lifted her leg out of the frigid waters. Her pant leg soaked through. The heat of the sun clashed with the chill from the water nicely. Looking over the side of the rock, the dark depths of the ocean hid what laid below. For the first time, fear shivered through her as she stared at the endless expanse of the great ocean. She had always had sand and dirt beneath her toes or a shore in sight to guide her back. Looking around, she saw none of that other than what Ashling provided. She was at her mercy.

"I don't want to see this," Mia grudged.

"And yet it happened and must be seen." Ashling stared at her.

Mia's mouth went dry. She leaned her head against the knee of her dry leg. "And if I refuse?" she asked, keeping her tone peaceful. Her mouth that was dry filled with water and her stomach lurched. The rock rose and descended with the choppy waves where it had stood still a moment ago.

"Careful. What you demand." Ashling rose into the air behind Mia. The waves pushed the rock away from the image in the sky.

Mia kept her eyes closed, not trusting her stomach enough to look. There wasn't anything she could do other than hope Ashling didn't want to kill her. The sea was tumbling the small bit of protection back and forth, as well as up and down. Her stomach couldn't take it.

"Fine, I will not play the story for now. All you need to know is Abbadon touched your grandmother. A part of him stayed with her as she grew and gave birth to her child, and her child passed it to you. A touch of his Chaos lives in you."

The waves calmed some and her rock became more solid. Enough for her stomach not to rebel. Breathing in through her nose, she breathed out slowly through her mouth.

"But... No," she gasped out. Refusing the information.

"Yes." Ashling nodded, grinning from ear to ear. "If you would like, we can start the movie again." A breeze from the ocean air lifted the blonde hair of Ashling and it fanned out around her.

Peeking out behind her elbow, Mia looked up at Ashling. She looked like a goddess. The image still paused there in the sky behind her. "Please don't," Mia begged.

"Chaos found a way. Somehow, he always finds a way. He is the main one that wants all humans to suffer. He never cared about the inhabitants of this land, only that we persevere." With a twitch of her perfectly rounded nails, Ashling blurred the image into the clouds that had rolled in. Light filtered back in, bringing the day back from the twilight they had just been in.

"But how can I stop him? What happens after I pass the trials?" Mia's wild eyes searched the turbulent stormy sky, then back at Ashling.

"The tests are all about choices. Which one will you make this go around?" Ashling dipped down her foot, barely grazing the stone. "Last time we had two wolves that you had to choose between. What shall we do this time?" She tapped an elegant nail against her perfectly pursed lips.

"Why this? Shouldn't I be tested with strength or smarts? Also, don't you have to be asleep in order to make this room come alive..." Mia fumbled, realizing that Ashling was awake and still created all that she saw before her.

"Silly girl." She swirled her hand, and they were on a luxurious beach with the sun bright in the sky and small bright clear blue waves crashed against the fine sand. A big floppy hat appeared on Ashling's head. She smiled and put on some sunglasses that appeared in hand. She turned her face up to the bright, shining rays.

Mia spread her hand in front of her face, squinting at the bright light. Everything had changed. The wind whipped over her cheeks and she could taste the salt of the ocean spray in the air. It felt so real. "But you said you were weak when awake." Mia tried to understand this being.

"Weaker, but still capable of a lot. Even stuck in here. While awake, I must lean on my audience to help paint the picture." Ashling pointed at Mia.

"I did not think up all this!" Mia took a step back, her bare foot sinking in the soft, warm sand. It added to the heat that she was already feeling with the long shirt and pants. She tugged at the sleeves, pulling them up, needing to feel the slight breeze from the wind.

"When I sleep, I can affect things regardless of what the people in the room want. With being awake, I borrow from your mind what I may or may not need. You are thinking of warm and hot things with your clothes, so it isn't a stretch to imagine a beach or ocean or even your village."

"So, it limits this second test a bit." She smiled at that.

"Partly, but I do like to be creative." Ashling gives a cruel smile. "I kid, of course. I like challenges even for myself. Should we have a choice between your mother or your grandmother?" She eyed Mia's frightened look. "No, too easy... How about choosing between a life of marriage or being locked up for your strangeness?"

Mia backed up toward the door, regretting her decision to come in here early. She should have stayed far away from here. Should have been running away from Ashling instead of wanting to talk to her. But there was nothing she could do about that now.

"No, that wouldn't be entertaining. I have already told you the outcomes of both options. Wait, go back to that thought you just had."

Mia looked up at Ashling in surprise. "What?" She squeaked.

Ashling rushed over to Mia and pounced on her. Her long nails, like talons, were out as she launched over her. Mia fell back against the floor, having been flattened out by a petite woman that was shorter than her, and mostly hair. Staring up at Ashling, she watched as her hand and fingers pecked at her hair and head.

"Go back to that thought," Ashling fussed.

Wincing, Mia flinched away, worried the Old One had lost it. Grandmother Sky warned her they were strange in their own right. "I thought things might have been different if I didn't come in here to chat with you and continued on with the trials as normal."

"Choice is unavoidable. This conversation would have happened one way or another," Ashling said simply. She sat there; Mia still pinned down with Ashling hovering over her.

"What if I don't choose anything?"

"It is still a choice, even if it is a lack thereof."

The beach faded out and a forest sprouted out of the ground. Ashling pushed off her, getting to her feet, making the surrounding scene more real with the details.

Mia struggled to sit up a dirt path with a fork in the road lay before them. The one on the right looked bright and sunny. Deep grooves marked the well-traveled road. The other way was darker and overgrown. Not a hint of a footprint broke up the ground. Yellow eyes stared at her from the dark thicket down the dark road. Fog curled over the ground and a third way appeared in between the left and right way. The leaves covered the dirt path. If you could even call it that. There was barely even a dent in the foliage. The only real tell was the trees and branches were bent as if someone had crossed there.

"Infinite possibilities branch out from one instant and a path forward is inevitable. Even standing still is a choice." More ways opened around them, showing the unlimited choices.

Huffing, Mia pondered over the many options.

A smile creeped over Ashling's face. "Oh, so wickedly delicious, trying to outmaneuver an Old One. What if there is something you could do?"

"What do you mean by that?" Mia asked.

"You should consider the possibility of being able to change a decision you've already made." Ashling danced down the bright path, then skipped through the fall leaves on the ground, switching to another.

"Impossible," Mia uttered even as she watched that it became doable.

Ashling gasped. "Are you calling me a liar?"

"No, not a liar. I just don't understand how you would do that with a choice. A physical path. Yes, I can see how you could switch to another. But a choice? I don't see how..."

"What if you had the power to change one choice that you had made? What would it be?" she interrupted.

"Changing something I have done won't change much here unless I leave the village entirely to avoid this future," Mia argued.

Ashling smiled once more. "Not even then." The forest whisked past them; the trees blurred by. A clearing came into view along with a woven tapestry. Threads of color flew in and out of the strings, the picture unfinished so you could not tell what it was quite yet. Her fingers plucked at woven threads. The strings still bunched across the tapestry. The thread swirled to life to show Mia standing on her father's boat, surrounded by the wide-open sea. A butterfly landed on her shoulder. "If you would have left by your father's boat. The woods would have still called to you; this was always your destiny."

"I could have avoided the call like I have been doing."

The thread was snipped at the end of a bubbled knot. "The call would have been too strong and it would have ended with no way to get back safely."

If it was up to Mia, she would keep Ashling busy with this debate. She seemed to like the thrill of the argument with teaching. She came alive when talking about something she clearly understood. "If this was my destiny, then why were two others chosen before me?"

Anger started to bubble up in Mia. Was it pointless to even try in this world if everything was already figured out for her? Or was there really a choice for things?

"The first person was not chosen; instead, his ancestor, who was the first human hybrid that helped put the Old Ones to rest, volunteered. He was uniquely qualified to help with these trials. He did not want to sit on the bench while Grey, his friend and Haddox, his brother, had to see to these tests. The second was an accident of sorts."

"There had to be tests before these, right? How do you know when these trials are needed?"

"I am the meter. If I can easily wake, then the spell that was used is weakening and must be fortified. If not, then the balance between the Old Ones and humans will corrupt enough where the spell will break. The strongest of them will wake first. Abbadon also known as Chaos, will always fight his bonds, being the most powerful."

"But the forest chose me? Why would someone volunteer?"

"The guardians can choose their warrior if one wants to step forward and attempt the tests. The guardians have to allow the people that chance. If none come forward, the guardians request the forest to make its choice and dispatch it into the world to pick. The guardians then watch and follow to bring that person back."

"And what happens after all the tests? What are the next steps to keep the spell strong and the Old Ones slumbering?"

Ashling huffed and rolled her eyes; she stomped her foot. "Make a selection or one will be chosen for you."

"No!" Mia yelled out. She couldn't bite back her anger or words anymore. "Tell me what happens after all these tests. What keeps the spell strong and the Old Ones slumbering?" She rushed Ashling, wanting to force her hand.

"Wrong choice!" Ashling yelled back as she took off. Running past the meadow into the darkened trees that blended into the rest of the pitch-black room.

Mia chased her until she came to the edge of the trees. She took a tentative step; her foot was swallowed by the darkness. Nothing could be seen beyond where the black shroud covered. Keeping her eyes and hands trained forward, she stepped away from the light and trees but kept it at her back, never forgetting how to get back if needed. She walked forward slowly with her hand reaching, not wanting to bump into the wall in front of her.

Many steps later, she relaxed slightly, never crashing into the wall. Laughter rippled around her. Mia wished the door would come back into the room. But she knew it wouldn't return until after the test was given. Turning back to the woods and meadow, she hedged back to the light, tired of Ashling's games.

"Ashling, you cheat! Finish this or let me go." Mia's anger grew as she became more and more frustrated.

"Me? All you must do is select a choice that you would like to make different. It's not very hard. Why are you making a thing of it?"

"Fine!" she yelled out. What if she said something, and the test had the power to make that change and it was connected to something she liked that she hadn't thought about? Mia had to give Ashling something that was relatively recent, so it would make much of an impact. "I would choose not to drink anything Haddox gave me..."

A stark bright light bored down on Mia, and everything around her turned to white. All four walls came back, and the door was there. The woods had blinked out of existence, forgotten. The room was spacious but bare, and back in the far corner was a bed, where Ashling huddled in the middle. Compared to the rest of the room, the bed looked extravagant. Filled with soft blankets and puffy pillows.

Rage filled Ashling's eyes; her fingers tangled in the blonde tendrils yanking on them. "What did you say?"

"I think Grey called it the drink of the gods or something. My first night here when I awoke, he gave me a drink that tastes like the one I had last night by some random guy," Mia babbled. Her hands played with the long sleeves, covering her hands.

"I... wait, it's there, sort of." Ashling choked on a sob as her hands curled under the blankets on the bed. "I will not make you relive any of that or show you what the change in choice would give you. If Haddox had to pay for his crime, what would you have it be?"

"You can do that?" Mia whispered.

"How would you make him pay?" Ashling whispered dangerously low. Her eyes turned fierce.

Shaking her head, she let that feeling of vengeance go as part of her crumpled. "It doesn't matter."

"Come on. This is your test, Mia. What is your choice?" She hopped down from the bed. Summoning a lime green butterfly, it flickered to life in her palm. She whispered to it before tossing it into the air. It fell, but caught on a breeze and raced to the door. It crashed through it, dissolving into the stone, disappearing all together. "Timer starts now. Answer the question before Haddox makes an appearance. The butterfly will fetch him."

"He didn't really do anything. It was all an illusion," Mia strained, taking a step forward. Ashling's short height kept making her forget how strong she really was.

"I saw. I know. But it wasn't him that showed you it was an illusion. It was Grey. A guardian doing his job. Haddox has tarnished the guardian name. And for that, he will pay. Make a choice."

Mia's mind raced. She could do anything she wanted to him; she could make him feel and go through what she went through, but would that change anything or make anything different? No. It wouldn't.

"Quick hurry, it looks like he was close by and is on his way here." Ashling danced, her fingers in the air, rushing her. "Don't you want him to suffer? To hurt as badly as he has hurt others? This is a free pass to bring all the hurt and pain you have ever received and make someone pay for it."

"Ashling, is something wrong?" Haddox's muffled words came through as he knocked on the large stone door.

"Time's up." Ashling moved up behind Mia. "Better yet, let's see you tell him what his punishment will be to his face." Her hand fluttered, and the door screeched open slowly. He glimpsed around the door into the room and she motioned him in. "Come in, come in. We are finishing up with the test."

"Oh, really?" His cool eyes held a hint of surprise. "After the last one, I am surprised she is in one piece." Pushing the door open, he raced over to scoop up Mia, giving her an all too friendly hug.

Tremors raced over her and she stopped him easing out of his arms. "Don't," Mia clipped.

"What's wrong?" Haddox asked.

"Decide," Ashling whispered vehemently, still behind her.

"Decide?" Haddox questioned.

"Tell him," Ashling urged.

"My test is to decide your punishment."

"Punishment for what?" Haddox bellowed out. His hands turned to fists, placing them on his hips.

"For taking away my choice when first coming here, with the drink."

Hard, calculating eyes studied her. She felt Haddox's gaze as well as Ashling's drilling into her from behind. Silence filled the entire room.

Haddox's normally golden eyes dimmed and his hands loosened as all his golden glow slipped out of him. A darkness settled over him. He looked more human than the Old One. "I see," Haddox uttered.

Mia's hands trembled and her legs barely held her up as she stepped closer to Haddox. "I want to make you pay. But I can't be like you, Haddox. I don't think I could live with myself knowing that." Taking a shaky hand, she cupped his cheek.

A look of doubt glared at her from his seething stance. The glow was no longer there, but the anger thrived.

"I hope whatever darkens your soul releases you before it's too late." Mia searched his eyes. "I understand you're worried I would be like the last one and not care for your kind. You felt you had to do this to get me on your side. It was wrong, though. I am not the right person for you. I can't show you what you so desperately crave."

"He won't find it if he keeps going down the path he currently is on," Ashling added.

Mia wrapped her hands around his neck and hugged his still form before letting go and sliding towards the door. Making sure there was plenty of space. She let out a held breath the further she got from Haddox. She had made herself show him kindness when she didn't know if she had it in her.

Holding her head high, Mia walked away from him. Ashling flew forward, moving to the door, she waited, holding it open for Mia.

"That will suffice for now. You passed," Ashling nodded.

Mia left through the door, hearing Ashling shut it behind her. Haddox and Ashling were now locked in that room together. She wasn't sure if Ashling would exact her own revenge or let it be with what she decided. She did not know if she chose correctly but, in her heart, it was what she felt the situation needed, regardless.

Chapter 17
Haddox

Clenching his molars, he stood waiting. He needed to finish here and charge after Mia. She sure had the audacity to blame him for something she wanted. He would show her.

We will both show her! Abbadon laughed in his head.

After the stent last night, he hadn't heard or felt Abbadon, until now. He had thought he had given up or burned himself out of magic. Hell, he didn't know how this worked if he could even get rid of Abbadon for good. Should he tell Ashling? Did she already know?

"You should be happy she let you off easy." Ashling closed the door. She stood between Haddox and the exit, not quite done with him yet.

"Happy? I did nothing wrong." His eyes shot to the door. Worry bloomed from his chest, sending adrenaline shooting through his veins.

"Oh, but you did." Turning from the door, Ashling walked back.

She only came up to his shoulders, but for a petite thing, she was scary. Being a true Old One, they were all a little crazy. Even if she was the weakest of them, he would not fuck with her.

"Mia was having fun with Leah and me at the dance party last night. If she went to find her own fun and ran into something on her own, that's on her," Haddox defended.

She was covered in a simple blue dress that came down to her knees and poofed out a bit.

"Interesting." Ashling circled around Haddox. "And what can you say about the first day when you gave her something to drink?"

Haddox gulped. He didn't like her behind his back. "She wanted it."

"Far from it, boy," she said with a bite. Her face turned into a snarl. "Remember, I have seen her memories. I know exactly what happened. The question is, when did you learn to block things?"

Sweat beaded across his forehead and trickled down his face. He worried she might see his thoughts.

Don't worry. Your secrets are safe with me, boy. Abbadon whispered through his mind.

Haddox felt drained and tired. Was still in bed when the butterfly had come to wake him. Could he be coming down with something? At least his shame was hidden for now. Though he feared that it would find its way into the light all too soon.

"I found her. I made sure another pointless death was not made before she could get to the trials. If I had to bend the rules to make sure death would not occur, then I would do it again." He turned to Ashling, not being able to handle her at his back any longer. Haddox pinned her with a glare. "I have been guarding her and getting her on our side. I've been the only guardian here for this one."

"Wrong. Grey found Mia while you were playing with Leah."

"No... But..." Confusion wrapped around him. He thought over last night Mia had left for some reason when things were getting interesting. "She was with Leah and I for a time."

"When? When your pants were down around your ankles and you were jerking into your hand?" She raised a hand to her lips as she laughed. "Did you get stuck in an illusion yourself?"

Haddox raised a hand. Red hot fury surged through him. His palms slammed into her. The amount of power behind his rage sent her soaring through the air back onto the bed that was a few feet behind them. She flopped against it, bouncing from the force.

"It wasn't an illusion," Haddox said.

"Silly boy can't even tell reality from his own illusions." Ashling's head came up, and the lights flickered in the room. "If it were up to me, I would see you killed for your actions, and still might if I so wish it. You sicken me. But I will respect her wishes and trust she knows what she is doing. I will not affect her outcome from the path it is on," Ashling raged.

"I sicken most people." Her power stuttered as it blinked away, taking everything but the bed. The background came back as he rushed toward her, tackling her to the bed. Strength flowed through his limbs as power rose from the center of his chest and came out, hovering above them. He laughed as her eyes flickered in surprise.

"Who do you have there with you? This isn't you." Confusion warped her face as she concentrated. Listening to something that he couldn't hear.

"Just me, baby," Haddox laughed. His voice lowered more than his normal tone. Moments before, the lack of power sent him spiraling. He took a deep breath, soaking in the maddening power. He felt like he could take on anything and would if provoked.

"Is there no redemption for you, then?" She frowned and her eyes scrunched closed as she searched for something.

"Why would there be? Stop trying to look for my thoughts. You won't find them." A flicker of his old self shone through. Haddox worried what she and the others would think and questioned if he should be doing this.

No! A surge of power raced through him, crushing those doubts.

He refused to be weak anymore. This power was like a drug he couldn't get enough of. They would all see what he was capable of; they just had to wait for the right moment. If only he could take the power of an Old One, then none of them would ever question him again. That was it! He had to find a way to get Ashling's power or, better yet, take all their sleeping power. A smile slipped through his cold, dark, numb persona.

She gasped. "I know what you are." Ashling glared up at Haddox. Her eyes a mix of colors, swirled together.

Staring back at her, a shudder ran down his spine. His head tilted to the side, the sound of his neck cracking echoed through the air as he stretched, the vertebrae popping in protest. The movement was almost languid, a deliberate display of relaxation in the face of tension.

"You know nothing," he sneered. His hand trailed over her petite frame, his fingers brushing against soft skin, sending a shiver down his spine. His lower body pinning Ashling's smaller form was a deliberate reminder of his physical dominance. But then his hand closed around her slender throat, his fingers squeezing tight, the touch a stark contrast to the gentle caress of moments before.

"This is my realm you are in! When I say I know, I do not lie." Her eyes sparked with anger like hot coals as the air in the room began to shift and change. The elements responded to the rising tension, tugging at Haddox's clothes. The fabric rustled and whipped around his legs.

Haddox growled, pressing down on her with more pressure and strength. The shadow he caused climbed along the stark white walls, having a mind of their own. Black sludge splashed onto Ashling's chest. He gave it a curious look but stopped short once another blob dropped into the same puddle. His free hand swiped at his face. Sludge poured out of Haddox's eyes.

"What is this?" Haddox's voice warped with another. He felt the pressure as if someone was trying to squeeze him out of his body.

Take a seat halfling, let the grownups talk now.

Hands shook in front of his bleary eyes. Haddox backed up from Ashling, more worried about his current state than the Old One. "No," his voice cracked.

What if I get you an Old One's power?

"You can do that?" Black inky mess spread over his hand. Excitement curled around his heart. He nodded. "Fine, take over, but only for this conversation."

"Haddox what did you do?" Ashling reached for him at the same time something else took over. His already pale skin grew darker as more sludge poured out of his body. She retracted her hand and the slippery substance coated the tips of her fingers. "This feels wrong." Her breath wheezed tightly out of her chest, laboring.

"Hello, wife." Pushing down on top of her with all his weight, he kept her pinned to the bed. "It won't change anything with you knowing who Haddox holds. You won't tell them for fear of messing with the cosmic balance. One minor slip can make this all come crashing down on top of you." Abbadon was hard and ready. He ground his pelvis into Ashling's. He groaned, closing his eyes in ecstasy.

Stark fear-filled eyes stared up at him. "Haddox, you need to fight him," she fought his hold, but Abbadon didn't move.

"What a nasty web of lies you have spun here." Capturing her wrists in one hand, he pulled them up above her head. "Shall we reunite with each other like we used to?" he asked. He licked the side of her cheek from her chin up to the corner of her eye, slowly, deliberately.

Revulsion contorted her face, her lip curling back in a snarl. "I've told no lies," she spat. With a violent motion, she hacked and spit in his face, the glob of spit hitting him with a wet splat. Her chest heaved with rage, her body straining against his grip.

He pushed up off her. Abbadon let the spit slide off his face, not bothering to wipe it off, the gesture a stark reminder of his indifference to her disgust. A quick jab of his fist punched Ashling's side, the blow sharp and precise.

Wheezing in, she crumbled, curling around her hurt side. "Your love was always so toxic. Look at what you have done to Haddox and Mia."

"I couldn't get him to go through with it fully, but didn't it remind you of how we first met?" Abbadon sneered. "After that you were all mine for the ruining," he gloated.

"And ruin me, you did," Ashling seethed. She struggled to sit up, pulling her legs up to protect her.

"I should have gotten rid of you long before now. Your weakness sickens me. You are like those that inhabit this world. Haddox knew who I was. I think he craves the violence I promise and the power I hold." He chuckled. "He is the perfect one to inhabit my form until my body can be restored from the spell."

"How did you even get out after last time? How did you come to infect Haddox? I saw both Grey and Haddox here before sending out for Mia. They were fine then."

Laughter rippled out of Haddox as the dark mass grew, taking over.

"Your little prodigy stumbled across my tomb. Her blood and wounds were a delicious way to wake. She was whisked away from me before I could capture her mind. This body would work for what I needed." He slid his hands down Haddox's muscular body.

"That shouldn't be possible."

"You above all should know Chaos will always ensue. The little beastie pet of hers made it possible for me to wake. Like you, I pulled memories from her mind before she could be whisked away too far. She was none the wiser. When her blood scattered across my grave." His hand snaked out to grab Ashling's foot, dragging her back to him. "It tasted so good,"

"Why didn't you take her over?" Ashling's fingers scrambled for purchase on the soft blankets, the cloth ripped from her hands as she was pulled by Abbadon.

"I knew you would sense me, my love." Ashling's slender neck disappeared behind his large hands as he wrapped them around her. "Couldn't have you stopping me before our game even started. Like you tend to do. The last two times I have tricked you."

"Careful or you will kill your ride," she managed to squeeze out. Her fingernails bit into his skin, creating half-moons.

Haddox could sense Abbadon contemplating his next move, looking down at the body he occupied. Disgust rolled through him, but was left wondering at what. "I need this... We need this," Abbadon cursed. He had to keep with this ride until he could break the stupid spell.

Haddox gasped as he heard the thought form. He tried to take back his arms to make him reach out to Ashling, but something blocked him from his body. "Help," he mumbled, trying to get her attention. His voice bounced off the same barrier. He had lost contact with body. He was a prisoner of his mind, only allowed to watch but not react.

"Only I can hear your plea's boy," Abbadon called out, his strength renewed by the desperate cries. He squeezed down on Ashling, pushing her into the bed. She fought to say more, but he was tired of her words. The thrill of her fear and helplessness empowered him. He had not done this for so long. Didn't realize how much he had missed tormenting her. His pleasure had been the only reason she had been permitted to stay alive.

Ashling went limp in his arms, he was tempted to continue choking her to death, but then who would he play with when they were all back. He could always kill her later. No, for now, she was better off alive. It wasn't like she could stop him now. His plan was in motion and nothing would derail it.

He tossed her body from him, leaving her lying on the bed. Hair, dress, and face a mess. "Serves her right," Abbadon condoned.

He stepped away from her body, taking his first real breath of air. This body was young and full of energy. Too bad it was wasted on a halfling and the young. Their descendants will never understand what they take advantage of. But he would make them all see. Show them the error of their ways. For now, he had Haddox caged, but the wording was dodgy and not something he could escape. He would be back in the cage in Haddox's head all too soon. But before he got pulled back, he would enjoy one last thing.

He uncinched the belt at his waist, loosening it.

The lights flickered off, sending the whole room into total darkness.

A single light shone down on him, sending a golden halo around him.

Ashling walked forward into the light. The hem of her dress lengthened and brushed the ground. Vines and darkness banded around Abbadon and Haddox. The inky shadow and ooze smashed into Haddox's body.

He struggled against the hold, but they held firm. The barbed vines bit into his flesh. Abbadon didn't miss having a body for this purpose alone. He fell to the ground when they tied tight, leaving only his head covered.

She crouched down, getting face to face.

"You feel that?"

Giving a noticeable nod. Abbadon had forgotten that when she passed out or went unconscious; the realm became hers. He had meant to get out of the room right away, but couldn't help himself. She wouldn't kill him, though, even when they were at their worst.

"Good, remember it. I am no longer your victim." She stared at him. "Haddox, fight him. Otherwise, you will be lost."

All the while, Haddox watched things play out in the back of his mind. Abbadon's thoughts and ideas were clear to him for the first time. *Was this what he saw when I was in control?* Anger and tears came to his eyes as he pounded his fist against the hard barrier.

Abbadon's laugh echoed around Haddox's prison.

"You have your warrior. I have mine," Abbadon's voice was low and distorted.

"How do you plan to keep Haddox on your side after this?" she teased.

"Are you enjoying your prison here?" Abbadon wiggled within the cocoon, flopping back and forth. The vines tugged him away as he tried to scoot toward the door.

"I could keep you locked up in here till after the last test. Then you will be dragged out of Haddox back to your hole in the ground."

"You know as well as I that the last test is not up for you to create with your little dreamscape. Does your warrior know that? The third test won't start unless all the players are on the board."

A tornado of wind whipped around the small room, the vines clinging to Haddox's body, keeping him in place. They morphed around him. Covering his head and silencing his mouth. But he could see. He watched as she pulled him into the shadows.

Scratches at the stone door could barely be heard over the moans and groans of the winds. Ashling turned to the door, demanding the winds pull the door ajar.

A blue furry little dragon appeared, wagging his tail and barking. "Bloo help!" He skidded to a stop as he bound in. "Friend not here?" Bloo asked.

Ashling calmed the storms, but kept Haddox and Abbadon out of sight. The twigs and thorns tightened on him. He didn't have enough air to even groan out in pain.

"No, Mia is safe; she left a little while ago. Can you do me a favor, though?" She kept her tone light and airy.

Bloo barked twice, jumping up, putting his front paws on the tops of her knees. Ashling bent down to pet the soft fur of Bloo, giving him scratches behind his pointed ears. "That's a good boy, Bloo! Can you go get Battie? Bring Battie here," she urged.

Bloo bounded off, racing out the open door.

Abbadon seethed under the vines. Though a small part of him jumped for joy. As long as his conversation with Ashling was unfinished, he remained in charge. He began plotting, he had already pushed ideas into motion. It wouldn't be long now. He sat there watching his wife pace into the darkness.

The barbs of the vines dug into him, but he tried to distance himself from the pain, numbing it. Instead, he paid attention to her actions and what would happen next. For now, Abbadon would stay quiet, hidden. Learning what this little mouse had been up to all these years.

A woman with a white coat came rushing into the room out of breath. Her hair was colorful. Abbadon searched Haddox's mind to supply the name. Battie was the sister to Grey, the other guardian that for now wasn't a problem.

He watched as she ran, colliding with Ashling. They wrapped one another up in a tangle of arms. Holding each other. He squinted at the two, his anger rising. She betrayed him. How could she? His own thoughts echoed Haddox's from the other day.

Ashling's eyes opened and stared straight at him. Her face fell into worry as she backed up. They walked in the other direction. "I need your healing powers." She ushered Battie into the room towards the bed where Ashling's true form lies on the bed in slumber.

Though they were away, the room bounced their voices back to him. He heard every hushed sigh, every quiet murmur. It helped that Haddox had not used any power today and was fully rested. He drew on that strength. He would need to escape. That was becoming evident the longer Ashling ignored him. Perhaps she thought she could honestly stop him by not letting the third test start. Because if he wasn't on the board, then the round wouldn't begin.

A blinding light emitted from the two small females as they huddled against each other. *Turn around!* Abbadon silently urged Battie. If she would have, the light made Haddox's form easily seen. Ashling wouldn't be able to hide him forever. His power was growing even in this halfling's form.

Both ignored him.

"What the hell happened?" Battie said loudly in the quiet space. "Why weren't you in the dreamscape keeping your real body hidden?"

"Don't worry about it," Ashling paced once again. "It's nothing."

"Why don't you return to your body?" Battie asked.

"I can't wake, yet. It will take time to heal." Ashling avoided. "Thank you for coming so quickly."

"That's gonna be my line later." Battie smiled roguishly.

Ashling's laughter bounced off the walls. "When did my little vixen become so brazen?" Ashling came back to sit with Battie.

"Must have gotten some of it from you when doing the healing," she pouted, caressing Ashling's arm as they sat there in front of her sleeping form, talking in hushed tones. "Those are hand bruises on your neck. Who attacked you?" Battie asked.

"Remember, I told you there are some things I can't talk about?" Ashling gripped Battie's hand in hers. Her knuckles turned white.

"Yea," Battie responded.

"This is one of those things. I can't really explain. You must trust that all will work out."

Abbadon sneered at that. Who would trust Ashling with any sort of secret? She was pitiful. So meek and powerless.

"You know you have my heart and trust," Battie said easily.

He looked at them with disgust. Anger rolled through him and it sparked something darker in him to burst forth.

"Battie," Ashling sighed sweetly. Her hand rose to caress her shoulder. Her eyes met his.

Could she see the anger writhing there below the surface? He squinted and glared at her. His ears picked up on their happy sighs.

The vines wrapped around his face, cutting his view. The last thing he got an eyeful of was the two of them kissing. Rage boiled hotly under the greenery. He couldn't believe the vegetation wasn't on fire from his thoughts alone.

Though he couldn't see, nothing could block out the sounds that they were making in the background. Whispered and hushed moans along with touches of skin to skin. A breath, a sigh, gasps, and a throaty chuckle. All coalesced in, building his anger. It sat in the pit of his stomach as he pulsed his magic at the vines and stretched the shadows.

A strand loosened. His eyes bugged out, and he snarled. If the vine wasn't pinching his lips together, he would have hollered out.

"Battie," Ashling moaned out. "Yea."

She belonged to him. Not anyone else. She was his! His! His! Damn it!

Ashling yelled out a burst of pleasure as she came undone.

What do we do now? Haddox thought. His mind caught up in the chaos of Abbadon's own swirling emotions and thoughts. *If I had sharp, dangerous wings like Mother's we wouldn't be in this predicament.*

That's it! Abbadon went deathly still and quiet. Haddox could almost feel the vines for himself, almost held control of his body again.

Imagine the wings, Haddox. Abbadon's voice pressed down on him. *Bring up the illusion and I can make it a reality for a time.*

Golden wings appeared and as they did they sliced through the vegetation being made real. The vines hold weakened momentarily, giving him enough time to escape. He stepped away from them quickly. Making his way to the still partially open door. Pausing before sliding all the way through, he looked back at the bed. Battie was there between his wife's thighs, eating what was his. Ashling laid sprawled out, gripping the dress and hair in her fists, huffing out. Her legs were limp from what she had gone through. He kept the solidified golden wings for now.

Sliding through the door, he was out of that room, away from the source of his anger. She and all of them would get what was coming to them.

"Haddox?" Angry, his voice came out garbled.

Abbadon ignored the weak attempts at the barrier that he kept Haddox behind. It was weakening. Soon he would get pulled back in Haddox's mind and would no longer be in control. "I can give you these wings long term if you give me some time to work on something."

Haddox hesitated. "It is a big ask but doable." Abbadon waited before continuing. "Otherwise, this is only something I can produce for a time." Abbadon knew of magics that could make the wings permanent, fortunately that information was also where he needed to go for the next part of his plan.

"They will look exactly like you have it now?" Haddox asked, Abbadon turning his eyes to see the edges of the wings. They were golden and splendid. His mother would cry when she saw them. They were so beautiful.

"Yes," he answered simply.

Haddox was tired. He was already having a hard time figuring out where he started and Abbadon begun. Their thoughts were muddled together. Did he even really want any of this anymore? If he could give in for a time, he would get something he had wished for ever since he was a small boy. That he was sure of. "Yes, but I need my body back by tomorrow. Leah and I have something we are meeting up for," Haddox said smugly before leaning away and falling into a slumber.

Abbadon gave a cocked smile and strode away into the woods. He had to make every moment count while he was in control. He would leave the wings till last, ensuring he would get his time to work on what was important.

Chapter 18
Mia

D irectly after leaving the testing center, Mia went back to her room. She had left Haddox alone with Ashling, and wondered what she was going to do with him. Shaking her head, he was Ashling's problem now. Worrying about someone like Haddox, he wasn't worth it. Yet a part of her stomach turned a bitter taste sat on the back of her tongue. Battie was there in her room with a large basket.

Pausing in the doorway, she sighed with relief. "Hey."

Battie turned, almost dropping the basket. "Dang! Warn a person before you sneak up on them."

"What's that?" Mia looked over Battie's shoulder into the basket to see what she had. The container was filled with different colored strings and some needles and cloth. Everything someone would need to embroider clothing.

"Leah felt bad and since you had shown an interest, she wanted to gift you with something from her stash to get you started. That way, you could personalize your clothing while here." Battie rolled her eyes.

Pursing her lips, Mia tapped a finger against her thigh. Should she take the present or send it back? Leah was hard to read. She never knew if that woman was a friend or an enemy. But after seeing her get comfy with Haddox after everything, she didn't think she wanted to be friends with someone like that.

"Leah has made great strides to battle most of her demons. But she still has a tough time letting go of the one where she has a lot of fun if someone is pleasing her. Regardless of who it hurts." Battie placed the basket on the bed, pushing it towards the middle. She leaned against the bed, stretching out her long legs. Tipping her head back, she closed her eyes.

"Long day?"

"Long life, unfortunately," Battie said, without even opening her eyes.

Silence hung in the air. Mia could tell that Battie was at the edge of her rope. There wasn't much more of her to give. She needed rest, someone to take care of her for a change. She gave a piece of herself over when healing someone, but she never took for herself. Other than getting the person's personality for a little while, that had to be exhausting to deal with. "What would you do if you weren't here doing healing?"

Battie smiled and turned to Mia; her eyes fluttered open slowly. "Interesting enough, I have done that."

"What?"

"Lived a life outside of healing. My mind unable to cope with the process any longer, I departed from the village. I left because everyone knew me for healing and wouldn't let me rest in peace as long as I was here."

"I can understand that. It must have been hard leaving your home." Mia sunk into the bed, bringing her knees up and re-laxing back in a more comfortable position.

"At first it was. I almost turned around to come back every day. It was nothing like we read in stories or heard from others that have mixed with your kind. One must go out there and experience it if they really want to know."

Battie leaned on her side on the bed while propping her head up with a hand. She kicked her feet from the bed, bouncing it slightly. She was eager to delve into this story. Her eyes shone with child-like excitement.

"What did you do?"

"I created stories and sold them for money. I spun webs of tales. In small villages, it wasn't much, but could get me some-where warm to sleep for the night. I did well in bigger towns. Cities that had many people. There I would thrive. Everyone wanted to hear about some other place than where they were." She smiled. A hint of her sharp teeth could be seen.

Mia had never realized that she had monster-like teeth like her brother. The green and pink colors helped distract from anything else that might set people off.

"That sounds amazing," Mia sighed. Even Battie had gotten to go places and see this world for what it was. She dreamed of that.

"I was pretty good at it. Stories flew out from me and there was no end in sight. Most storytellers I had talked to said there would be a time where they slowed or even stopped. But they never did. It was like a part of my soul that was bright and happy and for the first time I had reached and tapped into the power I was truly supposed to be a part of and it wasn't even an actual power like the ones they have here."

"You were meant to tell stories. There's nothing wrong with that. Why can't you do that here along with your healing?"

Battie frowned, shrugging her shoulders. "I'm too busy when I'm here and exhausted from using my power all the time that I mostly eat, sleep, and work."

"That's no way to live!"

"Tell me about it," Battie huffed.

"You have to make time for something that brings you joy in life or else you will run into that issue again where you may have to leave here."

"That would be tough to do…" Picking at a thread on her black fishnet stockings.

"How come?"

"There's… someone… maybe."

Mia sat up so fast. "Who?" She came closer to Battie, wanting to know.

Her eyes flicked to the open door, then shook her head. Mia followed her eyes. "We can close that if you need."

"It wouldn't matter with the powers that some of the people have here," she huffed and flounced onto her back.

Frowning, Mia pulled the basket over to her and shucked through the contents. There was a bit of everything. It reminded her of a large wicker crate her mom used to carry. She would have it for when they did picnics, or she had to bring in vegetables or flowers from the garden. That was back when her mother hadn't turned sour in her older age.

When Mia wasn't sure what to do or say, her fingers craved a needle and thread. Because of what she could fix with colors of thread, she didn't know how to do for people and their problems.

"Perhaps this crush can help you better be able to balance your work and personal time."

"Since it is hidden it has been even more stressful in some ways." She sat up, stretching her arms out. "You're the first person I have told."

"Why?" Going to the drawers to fetch a plain shirt, she brought it back to the basket and started to dive into a project her mind was reeling with. She concentrated on Battie, but knew her fingers would fly over the strands and fabric, knowing where to go.

"Why did I tell you? Because you aren't a part of this world, so you don't care one way or another."

"True. Well, I hope whoever it is knows what they have and treats you right."

Bloo ran in, barking his head off and growling. His electric blue fur stood on end ruffled; it gave him the look of having back plates standing on edge.

"What is going on?" Mia asked. The needle had stabbed her in her thumb, the noise had startled her so badly. She paused in her work, setting it in her lap, waiting for Bloo to make it around the corner. "Bloo here."

"Battie!" Bloo barked

"In here," Battie supplied.

"Ashling help," he yapped.

Battie raised an eyebrow. "Ashling needs help."

"Yes, yep." His claws scratched the cobble stones for purchase as he tore back around the door, shooting back out. "Hurry."

Battie's pale face went even paler. Her lips fell open.

Oh, she had a feeling she knew who the crush was now after the look she caught on Battie's face. Mia hid her smile. "Go on. Seems like your healing specialties are needed once again."

"If you need anything, Grey can, usually be found in the library. Down the ways from here." Battie patted Mia's leg before getting up. "Never a dull moment." She threw over her shoulder already out the door.

Bloo jumped up on her door front paws first and kicked the door back open wide. "Be back." He raced away with Battie.

He was back minutes later. The sides of his fur heaved with each great breath he took in. Panting. He collapsed on the cold, hard ground, melting there. "I'm guessing she got there, okay?"

Bloo didn't say anything, just looked at her. She read his silent answer well enough from his face. He was tired from the run. All that excitement was tiring for someone so young.

The next couple of hours she spent working on a couple of plain clothes she had picked out. Embroidering whimsical swirls onto the clothing, she personalized it and made it uniquely hers.

Hours later, she was bored and in need of conversation and food. Walking the hallways, she searched for something to occupy her spiraling thoughts after grabbing something to eat. They ate clean here, mostly fruits and vegetables. Plants grew inside and out of the buildings. Some of those plants held food while others were pushed to the corners and persuaded to become a decoration against the wall or a shelf if the vine was thick enough. Eventually Mia came across the room where Battie said she would find Grey.

"Whoa!" Mia exclaimed. She walked in and stopped and stared. She saw Grey sitting in a huge comfy chair that was made for his body, plus enough room for another. The vines twined among themselves, coating the ceiling. Books surround him in stacks, many lie around him forgotten. There were shelves and rows of books, along with tables. But he chose that spot in front of the warm fire to read. A large book was splayed across his lap in his hands. He looked up from it.

"How was the test?"

"Passable. Why were you not there?" She cringed in thought, rather not wanting to relive it.

"I had things to do." His eyes scanned the book, not keeping his eyes on her.

She walked around the chair, peeking out behind it, watching his strong but relaxed body. The loveseat was built for something larger than a human. She was not some small, dainty person either. In this light, Grey didn't look intimidating or mean like he had before. Ever since he had kissed her, she wondered what else she had gotten wrong about him. Remembering that night, she licked her lips. He had helped her when he didn't have to or even want to. He hated these trials or so he claimed.

"Do you need something, Mia?" He huffed.

Peering over the armrest, she leaned against the side the leather was smoothed with age but still plush and soft. She placed her chin on her propped hands and batted her eyelashes. "Battie said you are here most days and that I could find you here. What are you doing with all these books?" She toed one of the books to the side to make more room for her legs and feet so she could stand there next to him.

Grey brushed a hand through his dark, straight hair out of his way. His hands were careful around his horns, but they glided around them easily with years of practice. His white eyes peered at her as if studying her. They still unnerved her. The white part of a normal eye was black in his and the pupil and iris were stark white. No wonder her village thought of them as demonic or monstrous.

Grey frowned at the words before him. "Trying to find a workaround. How to bypass these tests and keep the Old One's from waking. Unfortunately, most of these books were written by them and why would they put a weakness of theirs if known in a book for anyone to find?" He threw the book down on the ground away from Mia. He grabbed a smaller, more normal size looking book, flipping through the pages.

Mia watched the book flop on the ground as dust coughed out from its pages. The warmth at her back made her a bit drowsy.

"I've been reading about the spell that makes up these trials. I know that the person that takes on the tests has to be a human and and have the spark of an Old One."

Hadn't Ashling said something about the first person being uniquely qualified? "Is that why your friend thought he could take on the challenge? Was he a mix of human and Old One?"

He was startled out of his reading, placing his finger in the middle of the page he held his spot. "Trey was his name and yes, though, we call them halflings." Pausing, he flexed his cheek before looking back at the pages. "That doesn't explain how the girl that came from your village was able to take on the tests."

"How far did she get? No one really talked about her," Mia prodded.

Flipping the page roughly, his eyes danced as they read. His mouth muttered words in the silence.

She waited, knowing he had heard her.

"The girl? Maybe a little younger than you, barely even started the tests before she took her own life." He pointed at a passage in the book. "It says here that a human possessed by an

Old One can transfer enough of their essence to make future children susceptible to them."

"Does that mean any children that came from someone possessed by an Old One is also a halfling?" Hadn't Ashling also said something like that? She hadn't really encompassed all that Ashling told her. She didn't connect the two originally. But now, here with Grey, it was starting to come together and make sense.

Rubbing his head, Grey flipped between two pages. "Essentially…" he hedged. "Whatever DNA makes an Old One, their presence alone can change a human enough to affect theirs and any of their future generations."

She listened to him drone on. The movements of his arms and face told her how passionate he was against these tests. She took the time to really study him up close.

Growling, he tossed the smaller book behind him and grabbed another large tome. This one looked brittle and very delicate. Mia worried Grey would crush it in his anger.

"None of these books are explaining who came up with the spell or why the tests are needed." His fingers dug into the hardcover of the book, making indents.

"Ashling when I talked to her last, she said that she was the meter." Her hand hesitantly touched his.

Relaxing his hold, he stared at Mia, really taking her in for the first time. Her clothes were accented with brightly sewn colors.

"The meter?"

She thought back to a couple of hours ago. So much had happened, and she had waited some time before coming to find Grey. "Said something about if it was easier for her to wake up, then the spell was weak and needed to be strengthened. Which makes sense. Sylvia and I also replenish the barrier that protects the village twice a year. "

Grey nodded and opened the book. Mia glanced at the scrawling written across the page; it was mostly foreign to her other than the pictures. Coming around the front of the loveseat, she moved the other books to the side, then pulled herself up and relaxed against the comfy backing. Her eyes roved over the images as he devoured the texts.

"If Ashling created the spell, wouldn't she know all there is to know about it?" Mia asked. Her head sliding to rest on his arm.

"All the books have stated thus far is that she helped with the spell, but I don't think she created it."

"Then who did?" Mia perked up with curiosity.

"My guess is the forest spirit, but who knows? If it is the forest spirit, there are no well-known texts on her other than what we have gained from years of study. She is as old as this land; she predates our ancestors even."

Mia nodded, letting her thoughts wander as he continued his search.

"I was thinking about something."

He placed a finger in the book but closed it; he didn't move much since she was leaning up against him. "What about?"

Her light blue dress straps dangled off her shoulders. She pulled them back into place. The crackle of the fire caught her attention. She noticed the beauty of the wood that arched across the stone fireplace. There were large picture bay windows on two sides, ones where you could sit in and read. All the vines pulled towards the skylight in the center. Letting in the daylight and sun.

"So, you know how last night you made all that stuff grow out of that tree?" She played with one of the big bows she had tied around each shoulder.

"Uhuh," he said absentmindedly.

"I think you need to try again."

"Again... Again?" he said a second, clearer time. "No." He shook his head and flipped open the book, he scanned the page, ignoring her.

Her eyes scanned the skylight. Looking out at the bright blue sky, she watched wisps of clouds pass overhead. She snatched the book away from him, throwing it next to one of the pillows at his feet.

"You are a rude little bird," he growled.

Raising up, she maneuvered on to his lap, facing him. Her knees tucked into his sides. "Make me stop." She shrugged, unconcerned with what he said. Watching how he treated the books, she doubted she harmed it any worse than he would have.

"What do you expect to happen?" Surprise lit up his eyes as he leaned back and let his head fall back against the dark brown, smooth leather.

"I want you to try again. Bring me that vine." She pointed up at the ceiling to the one that was dangling right above them. It curled around the rim of the glass, missing the sun.

"And if I don't?" He cocked a grin, folding his arms over his chest, blocking her from getting closer.

"See, I think you are afraid to try again." Mia swayed her hips as she raised up.

He wheezed out, unwrapping his arms. One of his hands moved to the armrest, but the other caressed her thigh.

A smile played on her lips as she felt a surge of power and confidence. If she could not make him do what she wanted with words alone, she could always make him frustrated enough to try. With a deliberate slide, she positioned herself on top of him, and the instant response of his body was electrifying. The way he became rigid beneath her, with the slightest movement, rocked her to her core, sending a wave of desire through her and leaving her eager for more.

While dancing, she had noticed how sexually charged many were here. Part of her was thrilled to find such a place to let down her hair and enjoy. Back at the village, everyone was so stuck up and you had to hide any kind of pleasure. But she could tell Grey was lonely and his defenses kept many at bay. Almost kept her from knowing the real him, if it weren't for Battie.

Air whooshed out of him as she curled her hips and leaned into him, placing her small hand on his chest. She raised back up, leaning her front against his muscular chest. His eyes dilated, the white taking up most of his eye.

Chapter 19
Grey

He eyed her, watching her closely. He inhaled, taking her into his lungs. She smelled so good, intoxicating almost. He could tell what she wanted. The woman played with fire and dared to try to not get burned. But his mind still ran fresh with the idea of what Haddox had done to her. He wanted her to know that they weren't all brutes and monsters. What experience did he have with that?

"Oh yea?" He teased.

Her breasts were so close to his mouth all he had to do was look down, but all he wanted to do was stare at her and fall into those endless ocean eyes.

"Yea, and I will prove that you can do it." She reached for his hand that was on the armrest, both of her hands encompassing his forearm, holding it up to the ceiling.

Flexing, the muscles beneath the button-up shirt he wore rippled and tensed, visible even under the fabric. The sleeves were rolled up to his elbows, exposing his forearms and accentuating them. He wanted her to feel the strength that resided in him. But was he strong where it counted? That was still the unanswered question.

He sent his power out to the tiny vine, trying to make it grow. It wobbled and only grew another inch before stopping listlessly. "I told you that is all that ever comes from it."

Shocked, her lips dipped down to his. One of her hands left his arm to caress the side of his cheek. She held him in place as she had her way with him. He smiled into the kiss, his other hand roaming up her thigh, pulling her in closer.

He forgot about the little twig, lowering his arm to wrap around her. Before he could bring it fully down, she pushed it back up in the air. She slid back away. "Try again."

He threw his power at the vine to prove her wrong. He wished he could give her what she wanted. Then beg her to bring back those delectable lips. She brushed a shy kiss over lips; it reminded him of their kiss last night. Hers timid and sweet, his hot and ferocious. How was she ever going to handle him? He worried for her, if she continued to push him as she was.

While her attention turned to the twig, their kiss forgotten, his gaze fell to her chest, captivated by the gentle sway of her breasts. His mouth watered. He wanted to take her into his mouth, devouring her whole. His unattended hand traveled up her thigh, wrapping around her waist and drawing her in. He longed for her to settle onto him, to feel the hardness that she inspired, to comprehend that his desire wasn't a casual thing, but a fierce and primal response that he couldn't control. He had never planned to be this way with her, but his body seemed to have its own agenda, reacting to her presence with a passion that he couldn't deny.

Mia gasped. As he looked up, he saw the branch tickling Mia's fingers curling down around her wrists. What the hell? It waved in the wind at him, the audacity of that little vine. Was she causing this somehow? No, she couldn't. They both stared in awe. Both their eyes traveled over the room, noticing the other vines stretching for them.

"See?" Her eyes came back to him.

"That proves nothing," he grumbled. Disappointment filled him when she did not lower her body or lips back to his. What were some stupid vines to him? When he had something like her in front of him. His leg stretched, kicking one of the stacks of books nearby. Reminding him he should be researching.

"Doesn't it?" Her mouth turned down as sadness washed over her. She pulled away from him and out of his arms.

Before she could leave the cocoon of his body, he pulsed magic into the vines above, pulling them down. They struggled to meet his touch as she tugged at the greenery that had wrapped around her wrists.

"Hold on..." The blood running to his other head was causing his mind to slow. When he focused on the vine, it fought his control. But...

"What more can I do to show you that you can do this?" Mia asked breathlessly, as she was amazed by the little magic she witnessed.

"Kiss me," he gruffed.

Mia's lips crashed into his. This time she was feverish and hot, yearning for more. He slowed her kiss, wanting to make this last.

Like at the tree, her fire worried him. She burned so brightly she could burn to ash if she wasn't careful. This time he kept his eyes open, keeping focused on the vine. Power seeped out of him, curling around him. But nothing happened yet. He let his mind wander.

With slow languorous kisses, he intertwined his fingers with her hand that was still free, raising their it up in the air. He waited a moment, picturing exactly what he wanted. Placing both of her smaller wrists in his large palm, he held her arms there. He poured his powers into the vine, asking it to wrap around her hands and wrists, tying her up so he could play with her how he wanted.

Her tongue darted against his mouth, asking for him to open up. He allowed Mia in, cupping his tongue around hers, guiding her into his slow dance. A happy moan escaped as she fell into him.

Watching, he saw the wood and vines climb over her arms and wrap around tightly. He kept the vines soft, calling moss to cover. There would be no pain here.

Lowering his arms, hers stayed trapped; he gazed upon this masterpiece before him. He rubbed her sides and pulled her down into his lap. The vines stretched easily allowing him to lower her. Strengthening them, they answered his call, so they were firmer and more unable to break and hold her weight.

"Is that okay?" Grey's rough voice caressed her neck as he devoured her. Kissing her neck giving her time to answer.

"Yes," she took two quick breaths. She tested the restraints. Her hips swirled around his head, toying with him.

"Let me know and I can unravel them if you need." He picked at one of the tied bows on the straps of her dress. He slowly unraveled the string, unwrapping his present.

"I will."

He kissed her again. Her eyes remained closed, and she relaxed into his hold.

He had the vine hoist her up in his arms, his face now level with her breasts. His fingers untangled the strings, smoothing down the fabric between his eyes and her breast. She threw her head back, arching her back to bring her breast closer to his lips.

Excitement coursed through him, thrilled at seeing her tied up. She was a feast for his eyes. His hands skimmed down her sides, his fingertips tracing the curves of her waist, the dip of her hips, and the gentle slope of her thighs. Those thighs were still perched over him, like an invitation, a sensual offering he couldn't resist.

One of his hands ran up her inner thigh, the skin smooth and silky beneath his touch. Soft sighs breathed out of her. His fingers dance their way to the apex of her thighs. And there, he found no barrier, no clothing to impede his exploration. The realization sent a jolt of arousal through him. His excitement roared to life. He cupped her core, his lips nuzzled her nipple, the tender flesh responding to his touch by hardening into a tight, sensitive peak. His tongue flicked, swiping a taste of her skin. She tasted sweet and wholly addicting.

The sensation was almost overwhelming, his senses heightened as he savored the taste and feel of her. His tongue continued to dance across her skin, tracing the curves of her breast, the swell of her nipple, and the tender flesh that surrounded it. The touch was a gentle caress, a soothing balm that seemed to calm the savage beast of his desire, even as it stirred the embers of his passion into a raging fire.

Heat poured over his hand as he rubbed lightly. Her hips danced with his movements on their own, happy moans and pleasured sighs whispered between her lips. He lowered her down on his hand as he raised his head up to capture her lips and the sounds she was making. His hand moved in time, with his tongue probing both sets of lips at the same time.

Sounds of pleasure poured out of her, egging him on. He slid a finger into her nice and slow, letting her control the pace. She rode his hand. His palm bumped nicely against her clit, massaging her when she brought her weight down on him.

His other hand snaked around the back of her neck. He couldn't get enough of her lips and mouth. She tasted so sweet he could only imagine what she tasted like down there. His hand skated up the back of her scalp and scrunched the short hairs there, tugging up slightly.

She rode him with unbridled passion, her moans muffled by his lips as he devoured her mouth. His intensity never wavered, fueling the inferno that raged within her. A wave of passion surged over her, shuddering through her, crashing into his hand and lap. As the tension finally broke, her body surrendered, letting go of all the sexual tension and fading into bliss. Sorrow crashed into her as silent tears fell down her cheeks.

Grey caught her, holding her tight, letting the vines unravel from her wrists. His hands were there, wrapping around her, holding her together.

"Shh. Here, come here." He caressed her cheeks, wiping the tears away. Giving her sweet kisses on her cheeks and head. Rocking her into him. She sat down on his lap.

He was still rock hard, there was no way of concealing what was clearly between them. Her fingers fumble for him.

He pulled her hands away, tucking them in his and placing them on his chest. "Mia, it's not the time for that. This was about you and what you needed. I've got you."

She crumpled into his chest and sobbed as she let the tears and pain that she had kept sequestered inside out.

"Alright, listen to my breathing." His soothing voice surrounded her.

He held her there, letting her get out what she needed. She took multiple quick breaths in not being able to calm herself.

"Try to breathe in and out with me."

"I can't." She fought against his hold.

He loosened it, but kept her sitting there with him. "Mia, you are safe, I promise you that. But do not run from this. Not from me."

Her eyes glistened as they met him. There was no anger or anything dark resting there in his eyes. They were kind and lonely. She took in another deep breath, letting it out slowly.

"That's it nice, deep, slow breaths, got it?"

Mia nodded weakly.

"Good, keep focusing on my breath and matching it." Grey looked down at her, worried.

"Is that what he is like to everyone? Or is it because I'm human?" she whispered out. Flinching away, she hid her face in Grey's chest.

The flames had died down and new wood needed to be added to keep it going strong. He stared at the flames, getting lost in them as he held her. Grey wasn't sure what she wanted to hear. Wasn't sure what he should tell her. "I think a part of him has always been broken. He is so different from Trey. How can two brothers be so different?"

She leaned her head against his chest, staying silent there for a while.

"You hear that? Listen to my heartbeat and the warmth of my body against yours. Know that I've got you. You can lose control for a little while." Grey could give her that much.

"Haddox wanted me to only pick strong choices to survive this."

"I am not sure what side he plays on anymore." Grey ran his fingers over her scalp and played with her hair. "All I know is you have to listen to your heart and know it will guide you to where you need to be."

"Why do you say that?"

"Trey, who volunteered for these trials, explained both of his trials to me. He had seen a pattern to them. These tests are to know what kind of person you truly are. That is why there is never a right or wrong answer, but shades of differences."

Mia rested her head against his chest. He brushed his cheek against her hair. "Who was Trey? You mentioned him before?"

Startled, Grey leaned away, distancing himself.

"He was my best friend. I knew him since he was a little boy."

"Were you not little also?"

"Many, many years ago. I am a direct descendant, meaning I age much slower. Both Trey and Haddox are halflings from an Old One and human coupling. We may appear to be the same age, but our ages are vastly different."

"Are there many direct descendants?"

"Around here there are. Since the direct descendants have a much longer life like the Old One's they tend to stay here or come back to this place. The halflings still have a longer life, but not as long as ours. They leave or travel to other places. Able to blend in easier than most of us." Mia had seen only part of their city. Only on the outskirts and here. The true heart of the town lay hidden. He would make sure she got to see who they really are as a people.

"Mmm," she mumbled, her eyes barely able to stay open.

"Rest for now. There will be time for more questions later." His mind continued to race and his heart beat rapidly. He would not disturb her, though she has had it hard enough.

Her head connected fully with his shoulder as he slid her legs to the side so she could stretch out beside him if she needed to. He pulled a book from the stack behind her that was on the seat. His eyes skimmed the pages, but he had to read over it a couple of times before he understood the meaning it was trying to convey. His mind wouldn't settle on the research any longer. Now it kept coming back to the woman that slept next to him.

Glancing around before his eyes returned to the pages. He took notice of the greenery that was lusher and more vibrant. Branches that were once frail and brittle were now strong and thick. The library had been full of browns of every hue, but now there were greens and little white flowers dotting along the ceiling, decorating the tables and bookcases. His power had done that. She had shown him what he was capable of. But she did not yet know how much of it came from her. His eyes landed on her sleeping form. So vulnerable and innocent here in his world. Without her, he doubted if that part of his power would have ever come so easily to him.

He refocused his sights on the book, letting his thoughts go quiet, not wanting to question it any longer.

Chapter 20
Mia

Mia whined as a wet tongue licked her face. Whimpering, she swiped with her hand. "Go away." Through the skylight, she knew it was early morning.

Pausing long enough for her to nod off, another lick brushed her cheek.

"Ugh!" she groaned in disgust.

Rolling away, she turned her face and body away from what was trying to wake her up. Something warm and firm stretched under her head, moving her. Her eyes popped open as she leaned back, noticing that her head was resting against a firm stomach. His dark shirt had creases in it and was rumpled from sleeping. The shirt was more than half unbuttoned, and Mia's hand was curled around the edge. Bloo pounced on her, demanding attention. Laughing, she caught him before he could do much more damage, her hand slipping from his shirt away from temptation.

Afraid to look up, she continued petting Bloo. Heat flushed her face as she remembered last night. He hadn't even cared about himself. Did he expect more from her now?

Grey grunted as he stretched out his lower legs. "Hey," he said.

Mia sat up quickly with Bloo in her lap. Bloo gently licked her fingers, playfully biting them. "Don't we have to go to the next test?" she questioned. Her stomach heaved at the thought. This would be her last test. She would either die on this test or make it through to only who knows what. Ashling hadn't let her know what happened afterward.

Grey's hand snaked out, swiping Bloo back gently. Once Bloo was out of the way, he pulled Mia over his legs and into his corner of the chair. She was between him and the corner of the large loveseat. One of his arms draped over her hip, while the top half of his body rolled on top of her.

As she laid under him, she realized the enormity of his frame compared to her small size. His eyes remained closed, resting on his side.

"I'll take that as a no." Her fingers roamed through his hair. The fire had gone out sometime during the night. The room had cooled off, but with his body and heat, she didn't feel the bite of it. She found comfort with him there. Something she didn't realize how desperately she needed.

Bloo whined and growled at Grey. He kept shuffling his legs and moving his feet. She guessed he was blocking him from trying to encroach on their cuddle session.

Mia knew she was right when Bloo came around the back of the chair and sat at the edge furthest from Grey and stared at her. "Bloo, can you say hi to Grey?"

Bloo retreated so she couldn't see him clearly behind the arm rest. Grey took the time to kick off his black boots and kick his feet over the other side of the armrest. He held Mia tight, turning her into him, nuzzling her breasts.

"No," Bloo said. She could hear the nails against the hard floor as he walked around the chair, searching and pacing.

Mia held her breath as Grey got comfortable. This chair was large enough for a human to sleep comfortably but not someone of his size. She frowned and looked at him with sympathy. She waited for him to start something after he rested against her breasts, but his head rested there solidly and didn't move. His breathing deepened. He couldn't be asleep, not with how his body was contorted.

"Please, for me?" Mia asked.

Bloo gave a small woof. Walking away, he jumped up in a chair that sat across from them and settled down with his butt facing them.

"It's okay." Grey's voice was rough with sleep and muffled by her clothes.

"Grey?"

"Hmm?"

The vibration from his chest rumbled against her back, causing her nipples to tighten. "What do the books say happens after all three tests are given and passed? Do I go back to my village or do something else?" Mia needed to know. Could she even go back and live with all she knew? That place felt so small now.

She didn't think she could ever go back. No, she would rather stay here or venture out to other places.

"Not much is written about after…"

Mia jacked her head back as one of his horns came close when he moved his head. His eyes met hers, his face so close to hers. His eyes searched hers.

"This is mine and Haddox's first guardianship. We are both new to this."

That information stunned her. She thought for sure Grey would have known more information. With all the books he had gone through, how could he not know everything about these tests? "How is that possible? What happened to the guardians before you?"

"Dead," Grey's voice cracked. Before she could utter anything else, he rushed to explain. "My father was a guardian before me. He was not a kind or forgiving man. The last set of tests before these happened when I was a small toddler, so I don't remember them all that much. From what I have pieced together, they were able to get through the tests and strengthen the spell. But shortly after that, the person that went through the trials killed himself and the two guardians alongside him. All three perished together."

"Whoa."

"You die next," Bloo barked out.

"Bloo," Mia scolded.

"He will get used to me in time," Grey whispered.

"I dunno about that." Battie walked in, her eyes zeroing in on the scene. "He seems to have pretty good taste." She twiddled her fingers through his fur before Bloo could bite her fingers. She found a spot behind his ear, making him arch back into her expert hands and forget about biting her.

"Hey Battie." Mia waved, looking sheepishly.

"What are you doing in this neck of the woods?" Grey muttered.

Rolling her eyes, she finished giving Bloo plenty of pets before walking over to them. "What a happy couple." Coming around the side, she shoved his feet off the armrest, and plopped down in their place. "I'm checking on my patient. Not that it's any of your business. What are you doing here?" She emphasized the 'you'.

"I come here all the time, little sister, and you know that."

"Do I? Must have forgotten." Battie grinned. "Why not go out and stop being cooped up in this place?"

"What about the third test?" Mia asked.

"We have some time if you want to..."

"Of course she wants!" Battie said excitedly. She threw her arms up in the air, standing and spinning around. "Good, I can come with you and stop off to see a friend." She grabbed onto Mia's arm and yanked. "Let's get you ready for the day first."

Grey hadn't moved, so Mia was pinned to the couch.

"Move, you big oaf."

Grey sighed and pushed off Mia. She watched his arms flex; she saw the corded muscles ripple. Her mind blanked on being nervous with his body hovering over hers. His leg kicked forward and stood up away from her. Before going too far away, he supplied his hand.

Mia took the offered hand and let him pull her to her feet. She popped off the couch, stumbling into him. Her hand reached out to stop her fall. Her hand met his chest, his heartbeat racing. His intense gaze captured hers and she lost all sense of anything else around them.

Battie grabbed her other hand and raced away, pulling her behind. "Come on, I got stuff to tell you."

Both Mia and Battie scampered off to her room. Battie rummaged through the few clothes Mia had been given, once they were back.

"What is all this?" There are little bits and pieces scattered around.

Mia shrugged. About halfway between the door and the dresser, she finally had come to her senses. "What did you need to talk to me about?"

"Why is there a pine cone in here?" Rummaging through the drawer, she tossed it on the floor.

Mia scooped it up, placing it on the dresser. "It was in the dark woods when Grey walked me back from the party." Her eyes bounced around the room.

Battie stopped her ferocious movements, digging through her clothes and things. "What happened in the dark woods?"

Giving a huff. "Nothing really. We argued, and then we went our separate ways back at the temple,"

"Nothing? Nothing, like what happened in the library?" Battie asked.

"Did you have to tell me something? Is Ashling alright, should I ask questions about her like you are to me?" Mia fired right back.

Battie ignored her. "This morning didn't seem like nothing, so something is going on between you two, even if it didn't happen that night." Battie bumped into the basket that Leah had given her. Its contents spilled out over the bed.

"Hey, stop it!" Mia shrieked. Scooping up the contents and placing them back in.

Battie lifted her hands above her head and shook them back and forth. "Battie don't do this, Battie calm down, Battie not too much. Take a break, Battie. Well, I don't want to!" She yelled out, pulling at the sides of her pom pom pigtails. Pink and green strands loose in her hands.

Mia gave her a curious look but put the items into the basket, allowing her time to calm down. Gathering the strands of beautiful threads, she watched Battie argue with herself. Quickly cleaning up the rest, she moved over to Battie, who was berating herself as she walked across the floor.

Something had to have happened to make her this agitated. She had been normal in the library, but every time she asked her about what happened or Ashling, it sent her overboard. What happened?

"You don't have to." Mia gripped Battie's shoulders, trying to calm her down. "What is going on with you? Tell me what happened? You said you had to tell me something."

Battie rubbed at her horns that peeked through one of the buns. She could just make out the horn in the shape of a bat wing. The chains that crisscross over her torso rattled. She eyed the dresser. "Oooo, what do you have to wear?" She creeped past Mia and headed to the set of drawers.

Rummaging, she pulled out clothes, assessing and discarding as she saw fit. She pulled out a long green skirt with black flowers.

"Are we going to talk about what happened?" Mia asked. Her head hurt trying to stay on topic with her. She hadn't even had anything to eat yet today. It was making it hard for her to concentrate.

"This will be perfect," she said, bouncing around. She swirled it around, holding it to her waist. "Not my style, of course, but it will look amazing on you." She threw it over to Mia.

Mia snatched it out of the air, looking down at the dress she was still wearing. "My clothes are so normal compared to some of your eccentric outfits."

Pulling her head out of another drawer, Battie stomped over to Mia, shaking a finger in her face. "Normal? What is normal? Do not compare us together. We are not even in the same realm of possibilities. I have my thing and you have yours." Battie's eyes went blank and distant. She played with the collar at her throat and popped her lips a couple of times.

Waiving a hand, Mia shuddered, taking a step back as Battie continued to stare off into the void. "I have lost her once again." Moving off to the side, she gathered a shirt to wear with the skirt. Changing, the silky cloth hugged her body. Mia pulled up the skirt, she swayed, liking the feel of the cloth as it turned with her.

"Shirt, we need a shirt," a strangled sob wretched from her lips as she came back to her thoughts. Battie went back to the shirts, not even looking Mia's way. "Here, this one is a plain white blouse. It will look nice with the skirt."

Taking the shirt, Battie danced away, avoiding Mia's eyes. She had already pulled on a thin tank top, but she pulled the shirt over it and tucked it into the skirt. Running her hands through her short hair, she pressed down every strand into place. "Ready. Are you positive you don't want to talk, Battie? What are you going into town for?"

Battie smiled, but it didn't quite reach her eyes. She shook her head. "I am headed deeper into our town, as you call it, to heal a friend and tell her a fantastical story."

"That's good. You love to tell stories," Mia said.

She nodded.

"My grandma does the same. She is the keeper of stories and history alike in our village. She will train someone new to take over for her soon." Mia thought if she talked about something more normal and plainer that maybe Battie would open up. Something was throwing her off.

"Keeping history alive is important. Otherwise, we forget and won't remember who is bad or good anymore." Battie's eyes were wide as she walked closer.

Taking a step back, the back of Mia's knees hit the bed.

"We must dull our mind to move on. But we must remember the despicable things done so they don't happen again." Battie giggled. "Mia, do you know a despicable thing that has happened?" Battie's hand raised.

Mia gripped Battie's wrist a little too hard. "What are you saying?" To pinpoint just one thought from her chaotic babble. "Which despicable thing?"

Ripping her wrist away from Mia clutched hands, she dodged them and closed the distance between them. Battie cupped both of Mia's cheeks and pulled her closer. She stared at her eyes, then turned her head and peered past her temple. Battie placed her temple next to Mia's. The pigtail of Battie's hair helped soften the bump of their heads. Battie's fingers became vice like her hands squeezed around her biceps. "Ahh, there it is." She closed her eyes and moaned, slumping into Mia. "His beautiful discord. Oh, how his crazy strokes my own. Ashling knows our type," she cooed.

Pushing Battie away from her, her arms and hands shook. "Ashling?" Her eyes darted to the door. She backed up into the corner of the room. Battie had never hurt her, but that's not to say that she couldn't. If she yelled for someone, would that push Battie further into whatever episode she was in? This was the first time she wasn't really acting like herself, at least not in a fun, bubbly way.

Battie scrambled forward to keep them together, pushing Mia into the corner of the walls. Her arms flailed, trying to keep Mia's hands at her side.

Fear gripped Mia's lungs, her heart raced and her movements became jerky and erratic.

"Battie!" Grey bellowed from the door. His tall form, a lovely sight to see. If he wanted to come through, he would have to bend his head so his horns didn't hit the metal frame.

Battie freed Mia from her death grip and backed away, surprised. "It wasn't... I didn't..." she was at a loss for words.

Mia stood there in the corner, not moving. She was afraid to set Battie off. Her wide eyes studied the woman before her. This Battie didn't look put together. Her hair was messed up. Her clothes were wrinkled and rough.

"Brother, I..." Her eyes filled with tears as she looked up at him, her hands playing with the chains hanging from her clothes.

"Go," he whispered, standing off to the side outside the door.

She slipped past but stopped before leaving, her head hanging low. "I'm trying."

"I know. Share it with someone before you go into town. We will stop by and come get you before coming back here."

She gave a curt nod and ducked out into the hallway.

Grey turned to Mia, who was speechless. She watched his eyes travel up and down, her attire resting on her pretty skirt. Her bare toes peeked out from the vibrant green cloth.

"Does she get like that a lot?" Mia asked.

"Sometimes if she heals a severe wound. She knows not to do that unless she can share that pain with another. Where did she go before coming to get you?"

"I think she was with Ashling. Bloo had come to get her to help with something urgent." Mia bit the inside of her lips, not saying more. She wasn't sure if Battie was open about her relationship with the Old One or if that was something that was frowned upon.

Sagging against the wall, Grey banged the back of his head against the stone wall. Tapping it a few times as he muttered to himself.

Mia rubbed her arms, red marks sprung from her tanned skin. Where Battie's fingers had dug in.

"When healing Ashling... I don't know what happens, but as you can see, something does." He stood up, dusting off the seat of his pants. He had changed his clothes from last night. The clothes he had on now were more leisurely, rather than the formal pants and button-down shirt. "Shall we get going?" He offered Mia his arm.

She glowered at him.

"I will explain more on the way." Water dripped from his hair; he shifted his hands nervously through his hair, giving it a good shake to discard the rest of the water. The tan shirt billowed out as a gust of wind whipped through the hallway. The cloudy day brought with it a nice cool spring wind.

She took a tentative step forward, raising her hand to his arm. Gripping it, she stepped up next to him. "Do her and Ashling hang out a lot? She's not a guardian, is she?"

"No, she's not." As they walked, he cast a worried look behind them, towards the way Battie had left. But they turned right to the open exit beyond. This was one of the side entrances. It opened near the waterfall.

She felt the spray of the water before she walked down the steps and over to the wooden posts fencing off the path. Leaving the arm of Grey, she leaned over the post, looking at the crystal-clear water that rushed by.

"You know she can heal others, but that is not all she can do. She also has vivid dreams; some are where she is other people. That being said, it is not always easy for her to tell where she is. If she is in a dream or reality. Ashling has helped her through it and they have been spending time together."

"Sounds like they are extremely close," Mia suggested. She tried to read between the lines to decipher whether he knew they were more than close. After she had her fill of the waterfall and its grand sight, she followed Grey down the path towards the dark woods.

"Could be. I try to stay out of her personal business and let her come to me if she wants me to know. I have protected her as best as I can, but I also need to let her be herself and figure out what that means for her."

"You care a lot for your little sister." It sounded like even if he didn't know, he knew it was up to her to make that decision. He would love her either way.

The sun peeked out from behind a cloud and kissed her skin as they walked through the trees. Buildings integrated with the scattered foliage. The cloud coverage made the woods extra dark and spooky. Through the shadows she spotted houses from Haddox's tour.

"I do. She has not been back all that long. Her dormant dream power made her come back sooner than she would have liked."

Battie has a dream power? Maybe that was where she gets all her stories. What if it hasn't been as dormant as they think it has? These questions plagued Mia; she wondered if they worried Grey as well. "Battie said she told stories."

"She did. A human captured her. He knew of the Old Ones and when she told stories about them, he got curious. Kept her locked up to study her and made her tell him all she knew." Stopping, he looked back at their tracks, the building still hidden by trees. "She still won't talk about it."

Mia wrapped her hands around his arm and leaned into him, giving him comfort.

"Battie must have gone into her dreams to protect herself, and that is when her dream power kicked in. Ashling was able to reach her there and protect her while giving me time to get to her. Ashling also kept the man at bay so he did not harm her. I may not always agree with Ashling's methods, but I appreciate her and what she has done to help us over the years."

"I know she has control over dreams and nightmares or something like that, but how did she know to reach her?" Mia asked.

"You know, I never really asked how. I will have to ask them next time I see them." Grey stopped in front of some hanging vines. His fingers caressed Mia's arm as he held her back.

"Are you sure you want to see our place?" Grey asked.

"Why wouldn't I?" She tried to peer through the vines, but they were too thick. Something in the pit of her stomach told her to turn around and go the other way.

"There is a reason why we hide this place. Not just anyone can find it, you must know it is there. Our world is going to seem strange and abnormal from yours." A tick in his jaw flexed, but otherwise, he remained stoic.

"How? You are not making me any less curious by saying those things." She tightened her grip on his arm, her breasts bumping against him. Warmth spread through her. Her determination and curiosity were keeping the unease she felt from this place in check.

He chuckled. "I suppose I didn't make it any less enticing. Well, here goes." He pulled back the vines of ivy and an entire city appeared before her eyes.

Buildings grew around and through trees and many of the buildings had glass that would protrude out, letting in the beautiful views of the woods along with the natural light. The trees were the tallest here and bundled around one large tree. The canopy created by the overhanging trees was dim, almost no light shone through. Glow lights lit the path in different colors. The air was alive with an otherworldly energy, as if the very fabric of reality had been woven with an intricate pattern of mystique. It looked as if it was underneath, burrowed under the ground. A whole city lay before her, bigger than she thought the dark woods could hide. The atmosphere was heavy with an almost palpable sense of enchantment, as if the very essence of magic had been distilled into the air.

"How?!" Mia exclaimed.

Mia pulled Grey's arm away and took a step away from the curtain, the city blinked out of a sight. Moving the vines the people and buildings trickled through. She did that a few more times, not believing it.

"We borrow some of Ashling's power to help conceal what we have built here."

"It is truly hidden." She walked down the path, looking to find another way in beyond the vines, but each time the foliage was too thick to get through. And that ever present bad feeling kept nagging at her.

"There are other paths to get in. You just have to know what you are looking for." He held the vines to the side, waiting for her to come back into the bubble of the city.

The town was huge and four times the size of her small village. Mia followed behind Grey towards the main tree. Bypassing buildings and shops along with some homes. Her mouth hung open in shock. Her mind was blown. She would have never found anything this grand, even if she did travel to other lands.

Her eyes bulged, spotting bulkier creatures dressed from head to toe in weapons. "You guys could easily overtake us with all that is here." The words flew out before she could recall them. Mia slammed her hand over her mouth, surprised.

"Don't let yourself be fooled. Most of these buildings are not in use right now," Grey laughed.

Taking another look around, she noticed further up in the trees she looked, the darker it was. Only a few specks of light glowed here and there. He was right. She would have expected this place to be bustling for the time of the day it was. That was how it was in the middle of her town around this time. But here they had plenty of space to travel down the path.

"Our numbers were much larger eons ago, back when the Old Ones still walked with us. Now our numbers are so divided even those who stay here would not give up this piece of harmony, to fight and overtake the humans. Most of them are human and don't agree with the Old One's views."

She eyed a creature that looked part lion. Hadn't she danced with someone that looked like him the other night? "Are you sure about that?" Mia pointed out.

"We do get some visitors from time to time. But as long as they don't bring war to our lands, then they can stay until they no longer want to."

"Show me more." Mia bounced up and down on her toes. Hanging onto his hand, she yanked him this way and that as she found something she had never seen before.

A small smile escaped his tough exterior as he took her deeper into the city. "More than happy to."

There were blocks of stalls and shops but most centered around the outer ridges of the largest tree. One sold colored glass and rounded metal that encompassed the glass. She stopped and admired the town and forest alike. This place was enormous; she couldn't even see where they had entered the buildings blocking her vision. Each stall had colorful cloth and their stands were filled with goods.

"This is the market area. If you need something, this is where you get it."

Mia made her way slowly around the circle, taking in all the food and gadgets. Some tables had fancy baubles and blades; others were tents with signs warning of a psychic reading happening. She saddled up to a booth that had pretty beads on a tray. She stared at a jar of smooth stones. Her fingers itched to touch them; digging down into the cool stones. Watching the colors fall off the back of her hand as she pulled it free, she grasped onto many of the stones letting them fall one by one through her fingers. One bead hopped out of the bowl, rolling to the edge of the table.

Her hand darted out quickly, grabbing it before it fell to the floor.

An old woman scooted out from behind a yellow sheet. She licked her lips, smacking them together. "That one has chosen you, quick tell it your name." The woman's fingers cupped around Mia's, steadying her as she stood.

Mia's eyes darted to Grey, who smiled. He wouldn't let anything bad happen to her, would he? He hadn't yet, at least. Up close to the old woman, Mia could tell she didn't have any teeth, but the knowledge burning bright in her eyes still worried her.

"Come now, come now. Your name?" The woman looked at her expectantly, tilting her head to the side.

She closed her fist and whispered her name. "Mia."

"Ack!" The older woman pried Mia's fingers back gently. She got close to her hands and eyed the rock. Pulling her hands apart, she stomped her feet. "Oh, fiddlesticks."

"What?" Mia looked on, worried she had gotten a bad stone or done something wrong. The dark stone had blue swirls that spiraled and dipped with the round rock.

"Oh, nothing dearie. That one there has been causing problems for me since the dawn of time." She plucked it out of her palm. "That one is not meant for you." She placed the stone back in the bowl with its like counterparts.

They all watched as the rock moved on its own and hopped out of the bowl onto the table and rolled toward Mia once more. There were two holes on either side of it, making it look like one of the decorative beads that were scattered on the table.

The old crone scooped the stone, yelling and pointing at it. "Hey, I said you were not right for her and that's final!" She glared. "Don't take that tone with me. What good will you do to her? You have been nothing but trouble for me every step of my life. I should have left you on the side of the road where I found you."

"She's talking to a rock, right?"

"It looks like a rock." Grey shrugged.

The old woman grumbled and tossed the bead across the open circle and over the heads of people walking by. Up ahead, there was a magnificent water fountain. The bead plopped into the water, sinking down into the depths. "Cool off," she muttered.

"What's so wrong with that bead?" Mia asked.

"Don't trouble yourself, dearie. Go on, you must have lots of shopping to do for a pretty little thing. A few hundred years in a cold bath will calm it down."

Mia's eyes continued to different vendors as the old woman started to pack up. "Those weren't normal beads, were they?" she whispered to Grey as they walked, making sure to leave plenty of room as they passed the water fountain.

"No, they weren't. Usually, Hildie will let a bead go with a new owner if she deems them worthy. Apparently, she doesn't like the bead that chose you."

"What do they do?"

"Different ones do different things. You would have to ask her since she is the one that finds them. They don't always come in bead form either."

"But I gave it my name."

"That's okay. She only has you do that so she can argue that you can't return it if you don't want it anymore. A receipt of sorts."

Grey tugged at Mia's hand, dragging her to the left. "Over here are non-lethal, everyday beads and jewels. These shouldn't be a bother." He turned her loose at an orange tent, pulling the flap back so she could go in.

Her frown faded away as her eyes gazed upon the glittery pieces in front of her. She walked towards the back, finding a small collection of bracelets. The one that caught her eye was a metal half link bracelet. It was plain looking except for the cat's eye in the middle of it. She took it off the plush pillow, running her fingers over the jewel and metal.

Looking over her shoulder, she noticed Grey was not with her. He was back at the entrance talking to a rotund man watching her. Though they were quiet, she could still over hear their whispered words.

"Will this cover it?" he murmured to the tent owner. His eyes crinkled at the side.

"Yes, sir." The owner nodded, his beard bobbing with his chin. He slipped the coin from Grey and disappeared behind a nearby counter.

Grey's boots echoed over the stone as he came up behind Mia. "You should try it on."

"No, I couldn't." She shook her head, putting it on the pillow it rested on.

"I insist." He plucked it back up and pushed it into her hands.

She twisted her wrist and wrapped the metal around it, flicking her hand to settle the bracelet into place. "How's it look?" Her hand was steady for him to look at.

His eyes didn't move from her face. "Amazing."

She blushed. "How much time do we have? When will we have to head back and pick up your sister?" Mia asked. She couldn't believe that he had bought her this. She had some money hidden at home, but the coin looked different from what her village used.

"I want to show you the highest building and tree we have here so you can really take in the whole city. After that, we can stop by and check on Battie and see if she is ready to leave, and then we will get you back to the test." His mouth turned into a frown as he said the last part.

Chapter 21
Haddox

Haddox had nodded off again. Blinking, he concentrated on what was happening. Abbadon was still in charge of his body and walking down the middle of a hallway. He had kept up with him for a while, still jazzed about the wings he now had. He couldn't wait till he had access to his body again to really try them out. Right now, he was cut off from his body and numb to it all.

"Abbadon?" He tested. The barrier he sat behind was weak, but he had said he would give him time to complete what he needed. He didn't want him taking away the wings before he even got to try them out.

"Yes?"

The hall he was in was dark, but he could tell it was early morning. The birds were chirping incessantly. Had he slept the night? He vaguely remembered climbing through tunnels and a large cave. Where had they gone?

"Are you almost done?" He left his hand connected to the barrier. He wasn't as tired as when he was touching it. Abbadon closed the gap, meeting his hand. A pulse of power echoed through him. The connection was right.

"Almost. You know, I could use your help with things."

"With what? How?" Hope looped through Haddox catching him off guard.

"This barrier." Abbadon raked his fingers through it aggressively. "It divides our true power. Even now I can feel the weakness leaching my strength. I will have to rest soon to recover." His eyes traveled the length of the empty hall. He ducked into one of the many balconies off the side of the building.

Haddox followed his gaze and saw they were two stories above where the waterfall crested. He watched in his mind as Abbadon tore through the flimsy barrier, creating a hole.

"Much better! Now we can talk properly." Abbadon's voice mixed with Haddox's creating a garbled tone.

Though Haddox could understand him perfectly.

"Go on," Abbadon bellowed out over the edge of the balcony for all to hear. The noise from the water below covered him, mostly.

"You can't," Haddox said hesitantly. Deep down, he knew that Abbadon was more than capable of doing as he pleased. As he heard his own voice, Haddox felt a surge of emotion swell within him. It was a small miracle, really, that he could speak at all. The sensation was so exquisite, so precious, that his throat constricted with emotion.

Facing back towards the hallway Haddox saw sparkly glass filled in the decorative sides to the door frame. The black metal work holding it in place. In the glass, Abbadon stood before

Haddox. A smirk quirked his mouth and his eyes and body were both elegantly leaning and cocked.

Reaching out with his left arm, nothing happened. He tried to reach for the glass again. His left arm lay lifeless next to his body. Trying with his right, it answered his call with ease. His knuckles ran into the metal. The force bruised his skin. He sucked in a breath and held the hurting hand to his side, holding it tight.

"The left is my side for right now. Give it here," Abbadon huffed in annoyance, lifting his left-hand palm up, waiting for Haddox to give him the right one.

Haddox gave him his hand. It was weird feeling his own skin but not having control of the other half of his body.

Abbadon's soothing cool lips bent as he kissed the wound blowing on it. An icy coolness seeped into the skin, soothing the fire that burned with pain.

"This is how it could be, us working together, not against. Your pain would be my pain and we could work to alleviate it."

What he said sounded good. But he still didn't know. He already felt like he was losing himself a little at a time with his illusions. They were slowly taking over his life, and he was having a hard time distinguishing reality from illusion.

"I could stop that from happening. The only illusions that will be seen are the ones that you want others to see. No more will your own powers try to take over you," Abbadon spoke, his voice soft and warm.

"You could? Why is this happening to me?" Haddox whined.

Abbadon looked up at the gray clouds rolling over the dark sky. "It's not your fault. Halflings sometimes have a hard time taking on the full power that comes with being part Old One. There is something every Old One needs to go through that either cancels the power out or gives you the strength to take on the full extent of the power. The knowledge has been lost to time and neglect."

Anger pulsed off him. "Ashling?" The darkness around Abbadon's reflection grew more ominous.

The dark cloud molded around him but encroached as it rolled forward. "She is young for an Old One. She may not have remembered it in and out of her dreams. But that is still no excuse to lose touch with her origins."

Haddox nodded his agreement. Too many times, they were asked to follow her advice, and for what she didn't know any more than them.

"I have found one of our knowledge bases. It is close to where the other Old Ones rest."

The Old One's resting chambers were off limits. None were supposed to disturb them for fear of waking them up. It was a tricky place to get to. In order to reach the cave, you had to swim down to find a thin crevice that you could slip in and slide through a small tunnel that went for about a mile before swimming up into a small pool that led to a system of caves. Choosing the right cave system so as not to get lost was even harder. Most of them didn't have exits. The Old One's path used to have one, but it was caved in when they were originally put there. Being a guardian, he got to know that knowledge, but Ashling never told them about any knowledge base nearby.

Haddox remembered when he was young there was a girl that had water powers. She was intrigued with anything old; they had all snuck in and found the crevice. Using her power, she helped him and a few others through. The cave system, along with traps, kept them from venturing too far. They had almost lost someone to a crumbling pit. He had never heard of any others getting as close as they did.

The location of the knowledge center was something he was curious about. He had traipsed all around there looking for another way in. Let alone anything he could have used to woo the girl. She really liked anything that could tell them about the Old One's origins. That was before she had left for the open seas. The call to water was a lot louder than anything he could have offered her or any Old One's treasure.

"Where is it?" Haddox asked after reminiscing over past memories.

"The knowledge base? You must know what you are looking for, it…"

"Who are you talking to?" Battie asked, coming around the corner. Her eyes traveled over the balcony. Her eyes met Haddox. "I thought I heard you talking with someone out here." She walked forward, peering over the edge, making sure no one had fallen into the water below.

"No, no one. Leave me!" Abbadon waved her away. "From there, we would be able to unlock things without having to finish the tests..." his voice garbled.

"Haddox?" she interrupted. "Are you talking to yourself? Or..." Battie peered into Haddox's eyes.

Haddox looked back at her, not trying to show that he was split in two. That was just what he needed for anyone to see him looking the craziest he has been. They would get rid of him for sure if they thought he was talking to himself.

"Why is one of your eyes bright gold and the other dark and dull?" Battie questioned. "Is this an illusion you are doing? I see the wings."

Elated, he gave a half smile. Pride filled his chest at being seen for what he truly was at the heart of it all. To be accepted. His gaze drifted to the wing on his right side, its presence a tangible reminder of Abbadon's promise fulfilled. He flexed his back, and the wing responded, its feathers rustling softly as he extended them. The sensation was unmistakable, a thrilling confirmation that this was no mere illusion.

"No, they're quite real." As he spoke, he fluttered his wing, the gentle breeze they created whispering against his skin. A single tear escaped, tracing a path down his cheek as he savored the moment.

With a sense of quiet conviction, he added, "You should go." The words hung in the air, a gentle but firm dismissal, as he stood tall, his newfound presence and identity unfolding like a promise.

Battie rubbed her hands together while still studying him. She raised her hands slowly before laying them down on his left hand. Abbadon's hand.

Haddox felt warmth and healing magic pour into him. Abbadon shrunk, but her hand was latched on tight. He skirted and receded within Haddox's mind, behind the protective barrier that was ripped open. He took center stage back in his body and the full weight of the golden wings. They were not butterfly in shape like he usually made them, but they were still gloriously his and he wouldn't exchange them for anything.

Make her stop! Abbadon hissed.

The longer Battie hung on, the weaker Abbadon became and retreated. Already he was not as loud as he has been the last couple of days. "Whoa easy, there." He caught Battie, her legs and knees going weak. She wobbled back and forth, mumbling.

Battie curled her hands into fists, tucking them protectively against her chest. "Ashling... everything is so bright," she moaned out. Rubbing her head, she squinted. "Haddox?"

"Are you okay?" Haddox asked. Abbadon settled behind the thin film of his mind. Abbadon would rest for now, bide his time.

"Where am I? What was I doing? I wanted to tell someone... something." Battie looked around, never settling for too long on anything. She swayed as she stood up.

Haddox hesitated, keeping his arms out in case she fell again. "You said Ashling's name. Were you with her?" He helped.

"Ashling?"

She paused; he saw her work through things internally. He was patient, not wanting to trip her up or push her. Her confusion pleased him. She sounded like him when he got confused with an illusion. Could she be a halfling like him? Did all halflings have issues with their powers? Abbadon said as much, but he couldn't remember any others having problems.

"Ashling, Ashling, to hear a heart so pure in sound," she sang. Cupping her hands to her cheek, she sighed happily. "Did you know she is ticklish?" Battie giggled.

"Shouldn't you be checking on your patients?" Haddox helped corral Battie towards the hallway. He felt Abbadon's seething anger. He wanted to reach out and strangle Battie, but Haddox couldn't allow that.

"Ah yes." The bird's sung loudly in the early gray morning. "I shall go find Mia and check on her. I will tell her about Ashling." She called over her shoulder. "Something to tell her." She kept repeating to herself as she walked down the hallway.

Haddox let her go, watching her stomp down the stairs to the first floor. The tall ceilings echoed her voice back to him even when she had turned down the stairs out of sight.

"That was close," Haddox said under his breath. "Relax a little while. I'm going to go talk with Leah. We can talk more later."

Abbadon's presence receded, his thoughts faded. A stillness followed that allowed him to focus on the changes within himself. He stood there, his muscles tensed and relaxed in a slow, deliberate rhythm, as he grew accustomed to the new weight and balance of his body. The wings, once a distant dream, now a reality, stretched out from his back, their edges fluttering softly as he moved them. Haddox pushed them even faster with sharp downward thrusts. That was enough force to lift him up slightly. He kept at it his sole focus on the sky above. With repeated flaps, he ascended. He crowed out joyfully. His eyes closed in elation took. His wings slowed too quickly, and the balcony came up too fast, jarring his straight legs. The sting of it caught him off guard, and the momentum made him tumble to the ground.

Clenching his teeth together, he hissed out a bellow he wanted to let loose. He would have to work on building strength in his wings and then also learn how to better land. Leah would help him now that he was more... He knew exactly where to find her and she would still be in her room, in bed. She never got up early and he couldn't wait to surprise her.

He struggled. His legs had tingles running up and down them from when he landed. He got his legs under him and used the hand railing as support to keep him up. Using the wall and banister on his way down the stairs, he kept moving forward, his head on a swivel, making sure no others saw him.

It was exhausting the wings at his back; they drooped a bit on the floor dragging behind him. How did others that had wings deal with them all the time? Others that called the air their home made it look so easy and effortless.

At Leah's door, he slipped through, catching the edge of his wing in the door when closing it. The thin tip of the wing was small, but there were many veins branching to the tips. The door pinched his feathers. He caught it before closing it all the way. Like when stubbing a toe, the zing of pain whipped straight to his brain. The end of the wing throbbed in pain as he held his breath. He sucked in air until he couldn't any longer. He let it out slowly, trying not to shout.

Leaning his head against the door, he stood there against the it, holding the edge of the wing. That seemed to help a bit.

"Haddox? Is that you?" Leah's sleep deprived voice was muffled under a sea of blankets and pillows.

Turning from the door, he spied her face poking out from beneath the cavern of blankets she had around her. "Leah?" He laughed and relaxed where he stood. Her room was bathed in a soft glow of blue lights. "Blue?" He was surprised by the color whenever he was here it was usually a mixture of pinks and reds and sometimes orange.

"Blue is for sleeping. We don't do much sleeping when you're here." A whisper of a smile edged her tired face. "Why are you here?" She struggled to keep her head raised.

"Look!" he exclaimed. Turning to the side, he moved them back and forth.

"Another one of your illusions?" She shook her head and sunk down on her arms, not looking at him anymore.

"No, not this time." Crossing the small distance to her bed, he pulled off a couple of the blankets. Meaning for her to take him seriously.

"That's not possible." She yawned, picking her head back up.

"And yet possible." Yanking her hand out of the cocoon, he brushed her fingers over the sensitive wing. He shuddered as her fingers met his golden shimmery wing.

Pressing into the papery thin wing, she tested it. Knowing it was an illusion usually kept her safe from this kind of thing. "You know my power. If it's not something you can believe in, then it isn't substantial. This is real though, you feel that," he urged.

"I just don't understand how." Leah crawled to the edge of bed and sat there stunned, her hands stroked the wing beneath her fingertips as they moved over them and checked closer to his back.

Haddox let her manipulate him as she explored his entire back. Every slight touch sent shivers down his spine, and every heated breath seemed to ignite a fire within. Now he could understand why Leah liked her wings being played with when she was in the throes of passion. It was unbelievably pleasurable. The gentle strokes and soft caresses seemed to awaken a deep sense of bliss, one that he had never known existed.

"Can you get me an audience with her?" Haddox asked reluctantly.

"With who?"

Haddox eyed her as she studied his back. Waiting for her to look up at him. "You know who."

Leah's mouth went to a thin slash across her face. "Your mother?" Bursting out laughing, her own rainbow wings fluttered open, cascading rainbows over the walls.

Red hot rage burned through him. He turned abruptly, swiping his wings across her face. She stuttered before recovering.

"I'm serious. She will listen to you." His fingers curled over her shoulders, pulling her up to stand in front of him. Her thin bony shoulders could easily be crushed.

Her own wings stalled. They caught the light reflecting it onto his wings. She shook her head. "She will not. Not about her halfling of a son. You still don't get it." Rolling her eyes, she tried to cast off his hands, but he held her firm. "She doesn't only hate halflings or humans. She detests males and all their egos. Why do you think she doesn't live here but in her own court of her own making?"

A burning sensation pulled his attention and hands to the side, letting her go. She jumped away, out of his reach, before he could grab her. Rubbing at the thin membrane of his wing, he massaged the burned hole. She could bend and manipulate the light, burning him easily.

"You are a part of her court, a part of her inner circle. Can you do this for me? I thought we were friends of a sort," Haddox pleaded.

"I'm only here because of the tests and she needed someone here to know what is going on. You are nothing more than a toy for your mother. To any of us. Get it through your feeble mind. If you can't be fun, you are of no use to your mother or any of her court. Including me." Her voice turned low and dangerous. Pulling out a knife from the pillow that was in the middle of the bed, she sliced the pillow in half, showing how sharp it was. Feathers floated down between them. "Would you like to see how her court would deal with you if you displeased any of us?"

His eyes furrowed in anger. "I know from experience what she would do. I have been on the blade's side of her court."

"Idiot," Leah scoffed.

Twisting the knife, the colored lights flash into his eyes. Haddox turned his head to avoid the harshest beam and moved to the side. The wind of the knife passed near him.

Confusion rippled across his face. He should have known. Always expect the unexpected. They liked to keep others on their toes. He knocked her hand back as she tried to swing back around.

She tackled him and pinned him down against the bed. Her knees pressed into his sensitive wings. Arching into her, pain radiated outward across his back.

"Such a mama's boy. You were supposed to be fun." Leah grimaced as she brought the knife up to his throat.

Haddox raised his head, straining his neck. His eyes met hers, a wildness blazed there. If pain wasn't radiating through his entire back, he might have been turned on by how wild she looked. They had acted out scenarios before, but nothing like this.

Show her what you're made of. What we are made of. Abbadon whispered through his mind.

"You could never be on the same level as your mother's court. The only reason why she went through with the pregnancy is that you and your brother might have been girls. Halfling girls, but still something." Leah folded her wings down and came closer to his face.

His lips crashed into hers with a fierce intensity, demanding and possessive. He didn't ask for permission; only took what he wanted, his mouth claiming hers with a raw primal hunger. She gasped at the sudden onslaught, but her surprise quickly melted as she responded with equal fervor, pulling him closer.

He took that small distraction to reach up with his arms and grab her wings, her thin dragonfly-like wings bent in his fists. He yanked her back, pulling the knife away from his neck. "You want fun?" Haddox asked.

Crumpling the wings into one fist, he freed his other hand. Grabbing her wrist with the knife before she thought to swipe at him.

Haddox roared in pain and anger as he threw her off him and slammed her to the bed. He banged her hand against the bed, making her drop the knife before his other hand slid to her throat pressing her down into the soft covers.

"There he is." Leah chuckled, throaty and deep. She licked her lips.

"Fine, have it that way. If this is what you wanted." He pressed down on her throat, cutting off her air. Abbadon wasn't so different from him. All he wanted to do was make them pay and didn't they deserve what was coming to them? Ashling, his mother, and even Leah all deserved this. He now saw what Abbadon was trying to tell him all along. They were afraid of the power he held and what he could do with it. Besides Abbadon, he could have that power. A smile spread across his face.

Leah's smile faltered; she stretched her neck trying to get more air but he still didn't let up.

"Abbadon, I agree to your terms as long as we are equal in this. I will share with you my body if you share your power until you can make it back to your own."

Leah's color drained from her face as she looked up into his face.

Abbadon came forth, and the barrier between them dissolved. They changed easily out of the driver's seat of the body with whom needed it. Abbadon cracked his neck and let Leah get a good breath before tightening his hand once more.

"We will make them all pay and end the tests for good," Abbadon stated.

"I will tell your mother who you are working with and what you have become," Leah wheezed out.

Haddox stared down at Leah, adding pressure. His smile never leaving his face as her eyes fought to stay open.

"You should be ashamed!" she barely whispered out before her eyes fluttered close.

He watched as she passed out. Excitement cascaded down his body. Haddox was tempted to finish her and let none be the wiser. But unlike her, he had restraint. He needed her alive, to tell them all what was coming. Because his mother should prepare for what was coming, her court would be next. First, they would deal with Ashling and these tests.

"Yes, then we will do the same to your mother's court," Abbadon agreed darkly, reading his thoughts like they were his own.

Haddox stopped squeezing and let his hand lay against Leah's neck as the vein fluttered there like a caged butterfly. A red mark in the shape of his hand appeared on her pale skin. A calm settled over Haddox when leaving the room, he made his way over to the testing doors to wait for Mia and her final test.

Many hours had passed, they had made him wait. He could hear Grey and Mia talking loudly and laughing as they walked up the path from the woods. Utter contempt for them rolled through him. What? They were friends now? Grey had never wanted to be a part of these tests, not even when Haddox's brother, Trey, joined the tests. Haddox could just make them out as he spied through the green leaves, each of them staring at one another. More than friendship shone in their eyes. What did Grey have that he didn't have? Grey deserved everything he had coming to him.

Leaning against the doors, he waited for them to come closer.

Chapter 22
Mia

Mia came around the edge of the woods. A vine tugged at the mesh of her skirt. Haddox was already there, leaning against the door. Mia and Grey had spent most of the day together, he showed her their actual town. It was surprisingly bigger than she thought it would be. After the market, he took her up into the trees to look down over the city.

"Where have you two been?" Haddox seethed.

Mia beamed. "He took me to see the hidden city. I didn't know how much there was to this place. You guys have a whole world of your own." She had been captivated by Grey throughout the day, unable to tear her eyes away from his lips.

"Like you care," Haddox grumbled. "The girl before you would have rather died than help our kind."

"Hey, that's not fair. I'm not her. Don't think all humans are the same." Mia stepped back at how cruel he was being. Everything had changed since her first day here. Grey had said mean things and Haddox the sweet one. How did things get so twisted?

"Step aside Haddox." Grey frowned.

Mia clung to Grey so he wouldn't go far; she didn't want to be left alone with Haddox again. She didn't want an illusion to be used on her. But from what she saw, he already had an illusion in full force with his golden brilliant wings standing loud and proud behind him.

"For the last test, a guardian can come with and witness the last test being done." Haddox stood firm, blocking the door.

"You both are guardians. I would like Grey to attend with me." Mia cowered beside Grey, not taking another step closer to Haddox.

Grey's hand brushed her own.

"I am the one running this series of trials. Grey wanted nothing to do with these tests, let alone you to begin with. Or don't you remember?" Haddox snarled.

Mia's eyes furrowed in thought. "I know that," she mumbled. She had literally thought that. They were so different from the two men she first met. That will teach her not to assume she knows someone by how they act when first getting to know them.

"That was before," Grey said at the same time as Mia, but petered out, not continuing what he was going to say.

"You don't need to pretend, Grey, it's fine. I will chill out on the illusions, and you can get back to what you do best." Haddox smiled.

Mia shuddered at how large the smile was. It was almost creepy looking.

"You're doing an illusion now," Grey said. He moved forward; Mia stayed slightly behind him. He flicked his finger at the wing. "What!" he exclaimed when his finger met the gossamer texture the wing had.

"That's right, not an illusion anymore," he laughed. Haddox turned, causing his wings to smack Grey's hand away.

"How?" Grey asked.

"I have my way's; don't you worry about it." He pushed the door open slightly. "Now that someone with power is here. Let's go beat your next test," Haddox cajoled.

"You don't even like her," Grey stepped up next to Haddox. Anger written all over his face.

"And you do?" Haddox's eyebrows were raised in question.

"I... Of course, I like her." Grey looked behind himself at Mia then back to Haddox, fumbling with his words.

Mia was shocked. Grey couldn't even get his words out. She thought he had felt the same as she did about him. Was this again all for show? She was so tired of being strung along.

"For a human, though, right?" Haddox asked. "They don't last too long," he sneered.

A tightness squeezed around Mia's chest as they bickered.

"I will go in by myself!" She bellowed. Stomping forward, she moved past Grey, tired of their fighting. Neither one of them wanted her from the start; she was only the chosen one for these trials. They would have done the same for any other person that was chosen. There was nothing special about her. It was good of Haddox to remind her of that. She had started to let feelings in with Grey, but maybe she shouldn't. So, they had shared some intimate moments, so what?

Raising her head, she stomped forward, giving Haddox the evil eye, daring him to try something with Grey there at her back. She stood toe to toe with him, waiting for him to make his move.

Showing a look of disdain, he eyed behind her and slid to the side, opening the heavy door in one swift move. Strength rippling down his chorded arm.

Facing the darkness, she proceeded forward, waiting for the door to close behind her. She wanted to make sure neither one of them followed her in.

When the door groaned close, the darkness didn't bother her as much as it would have normally. She stepped forward. Her bare foot sunk down a little. Grains of sand cushioned her steps, the heat soaked into her skin. The sky lightened, and a desert splayed out as far as she could see, it was filled with sand and the sun coming up over the sand dunes. The heat was already blazing and stifling and would get worse as the sun rose. Ashling's giant form hung suspended in the sky, peering down at her.

"Are you ready for your third test?" Ashling boomed out, her voice echoing around Mia.

"Yes, and this time I want nothing to do with Grey or Haddox. Leave them out of this and let's get this over with." Annoyance fluttered, trapped inside her. She had thought Grey, and she were at least getting along, but it didn't sound like he thought the same. He was just as stuck in hating humans as all the rest of them.

"So be it. Then your choice will be simple. Both choices lead to your death. How do you wish to proceed?" Ashling's voice echoed around her. "Would you like to perish now or after when the Old Ones have risen?"

Mia twisted her head in confusion. A crick in her neck was starting to bloom as she cocked her head back. "What are you talking about? This isn't like the other tests, where there was an infinite number of choices. This can't be the test?" Anger stirred in her belly.

A strong hand latched on to Mia's arm and turned her to him. Taken aback, she looked up at the wildness in Grey's eyes.

"I said..."

"No, I'm sorry Mia," he hastily said. "I refuse to watch another useless death happen when I could have deterred it. You don't deserve to die; you deserve to have so much more than this." His hands motioned around him. "To have more than I can offer."

"What do you mean?" Her heart fluttered to life, but she held it back, not wanting to be hurt anymore.

"Ashling is not quiet; I want to be here for your final test. I slipped in after Haddox left." His dark hands still covered her lower arms. His thumb caressed the soft patch of skin on her underarm.

One soft touch could not undo what he said.

"Ahh, the test is among us now," Ashling said softly. "More options have opened up to you if you so choose."

She was being cryptic. Mia knew that, and it had to do something with Grey being here now. She wanted to make this choice without one of them to cloud her judgment. And he still hadn't explained why he didn't jump to her defense before.

"No Grey, get out. I don't want you to be here." She tried to push his hand away.

"What Haddox said before that was before I knew you, before last night. Before this morning." His features fell as he relaxed his hold. "What can I do to show you that?"

"I'm a human Grey." Avoiding his eyes, she looked out over the sand dunes. Only desert surrounded them.

"You are so much more than that to me," he pleaded.

"How?" Mia asked, finally looking up at him. She masked her desire for the words her heart wanted to hear.

"Did you know Grey has also passed two of his own tests?" Ashling interjected. Ashling wore a pout as she came closer, making herself larger in the sky.

Mia understood Ashling was supposed to be the star of the show, the main attraction in these tests. But all she wanted to stare at was Grey eager to hear what he had to say.

"Tests? What tests?" Grey asked, finally looking up to see Ashling.

Caught off guard, Mia finally registered what Ashling had said, following his line of sight to Ashling.

"So many tests, so little time," Ashling sang. "First you sent her pet in with her, even if you said you didn't mean to," she said a little louder, not letting him speak. "And second, you actively accepted Mia and tried to help with these trials, even when you said you didn't want to."

"Tests, those weren't tests. Those were choices I made," Grey said. His fists clenched in anger as he took a step forward. "I am not a part of this."

"All my trials have been about choices," Mia said. She rested a calming hand on his strained forearm.

"You are a part of this, even if you don't like it. It's true that you couldn't be fully considered for the tests because you don't have any human blood running through your veins, but it is important nonetheless." Ashling turned in the sky as if distracted by something only she could see.

Whispered and hushed words fell from Ashling's mouth, but Mia couldn't discern them. Since Ashling all but placed them on hold, she looked at Grey.

"It doesn't matter. You and Haddox are not welcome here. I am a pawn to both of you, a thing to be used. I'm tired of the games."

"How can you say that? I haven't played games with you." Grey captured her hands in his much larger ones and held them between his. Her face was down turned, but he used their hands to push her chin up so he could look at her.

"What I witnessed between you and Haddox tells me all I need to know. Your view on humans has not changed. I've not changed. I am who I am and this was just something to be fleeting." Her anger slipped through her fingers as she tried to clutch it and wrap it around her. His face begged her to listen to his words.

"Oh, but you have changed. It is healthy for you to change. If you are stagnant and not growing, then what is life worth living? It is I who needed to escape the cold, stagnant place I kept myself." A blustering wind that kicked up sand blew down on them. It pulled and yanked at his billowing shirt.

Her own skirt wrapped to the side of his black pants, wanting to tangle around him.

"Great, another riddle." Mia kicked the sand after the wind died down. It kicked up a few inches before falling down the little sand hill they stood on top of.

"It wasn't meant to be." He smirked. "After Trey died." He looked up at the sky.

Mia saw how hard this was for him. She moved her head and brushed her cheek against his knuckles.

"After he died, I went to a dark space I hadn't seen in quite a while. I was surprised I still had that kind of hate and anger inside me. Studying and researching consumed me. I forgot to let anyone else in to help move me forward. I distanced myself from my sister. And anyone else who wanted to help."

Her heart broke at that point, and feelings welled to the surface. She swayed closer to him, not being able to hold her ground anymore. He was really trying.

"Then it became easier to keep people away. Mia, I thought I needed to keep you at arm's length because of these tests. But I can't," he choked up. "If you don't feel the same, I get it. But I need you to know it has nothing to do with you being a human." His hands moved to the sides of her face and his thumbs brushed her cheeks.

"If I choose anything other than me right now, it will be wrong. The strong answer was not right in the first test and I could not bring myself to lower myself to Haddox's level, but I couldn't fully forgive him either. Any choice I make ends up wrong and comes to bite me in the ass."

"It is not as black and white as all of that, but shades of gray. Stop limiting yourself to your village's standards and make up your own." He pulled her close.

The warmth from his body did not diminish the heat that sweltered within. Her arms and legs were slicked with sweat. Making everything damp and uncomfortable. "I still don't see how my choices are all important. I don't even know what this all leads up to. What happens after this last test?" The sun was making her delirious and she couldn't keep track if they were talking about them or the test.

She noticed Grey wasn't having as hard of a time with the heat. His body was not sticky or sweaty like hers was. He only looked at her and begged for her to forgive him and give him a chance. Or at least she thought that was what he was trying to say. If only there was some water or a cool breeze, then her brain could concentrate on what was important.

"Abbadon keeps the others asleep. If he wakes, he will have the strength to breed chaos into the world, giving the other's enough power to break their chains and rise. He is the first pillar, the strongest of them all," Ashling argued. "Your grandmother understood how dangerous he could be for the world." She had turned back around to them. What had her attention before distracted her no longer?

"Maybe Abbadon needs to wake and wipe the slate clean," Mia said. She didn't know this Abbadon. Didn't know his story or what he stood for. All she was basing things off was what they told her. She should have spent more time with Grey; his books would have helped her here.

Ashling vibrated in the sky as she looked down with worry in her eyes. Her mind was on something else other than them, something that she kept checking behind her. "Perhaps you need some time to cool off and think through things. Let this be a two-part test." She tapped her finger against her lips in thought. "This first test will be a collective answer for you and Grey. Will you choose death now or later?"

"Who in their right mind would pick death now?" Mia scoffed. "Can we avoid death all together?" Mia couldn't fight the test, so her feet itched to run out of this room until whatever this was caught up with her. Too bad Ashling hid the door once again.

"I have given you the riddle. You can stay here until you both can come to an agreement." Ashling ignored what Mia yelled out. Turning in the sky, she faded out.

"I will not decide something like this for someone I care about," he yelled up at the now empty sky.

"Care about?" Mia paused, shocked that he said that so loudly. Though only they were there now to hear it. She dismissed it, focusing on the riddle. "It could mean that I last a whole human life before dying if I choose later."

"Or it could mean you die tomorrow," he spat out. "Ashling! How.... could..." Grey's words cut off as he mumbled something furiously under his breath.

"Me? What about you? This is a test for both of us?"

Grey opened his mouth to answer, but thought better of it and shut it. His brilliant white eyes slid to the side as he turned from her and gave her some distance.

"How long do you think she will leave us alone for?" Mia asked, not liking the silence. She didn't care for the distance, either. Her heart squeezed, shortening her breath at the idea of there being too much distance between them.

"It's hard to say," he said nonchalantly.

"I'm still angry with you," she grumbled unable to let it go. She buried her feet in the sand, hoping to hide them from the sun. "But if she doesn't come back soon, we should walk to see if we can find some shelter. The heat and sun will make this unbearable soon."

She looked up at him, his shadow cast across her, his horns and head covering the blaring sun. It eased some, but she knew even Grey would not be able to hold back the power of the sun. Even with his tall, dark hunk of a body.

"You can be angry with me all you want as long as you will work with me on it. We can walk and talk." He stepped forward, looking back. He waited for Mia to make up her mind.

She huffed out a breath and scooched a path forward, keeping her feet under the hot sand. "You're no different from Haddox. He is more open to his hatred, but you don't have the best opinion of humans either."

"How can you say that? My best friend, Trey, was half human."

She puffed out as she tried to keep up with his long legs. "The keyword there being half human. What about full humans? Do you know many of those? Trey lived here with you guys. But do you know many humans outside of here?"

"That's not fair. There aren't many full humans that live in our city with us. Trey's father is a human."

"Because we don't last long? Or you don't try to bridge that gap?" She was starting to understand the problem.

He tipped his head to the side, allowing the sun to shine in her eyes.

She threw a hand up, blocking the harsh rays. There was cool water up ahead. She could just make it out as she squinted. Picking up their pace, they headed that way. A small oasis in the middle of this dry, dusty desert. Beautiful blue waters lapped at the sandy beach. The rocky cove that surrounded it ushered out a spray of mist from the bubbling water that slid over rocks. A couple of green palm trees surrounded the cool pool, shading it nicely.

"Some humans last," Grey croaked out.

She waited to see if he answered the second part of the question, but he only stared at the pool of water.

She stared; also, afraid it was an illusion of the heat. Her hope only increased the closer they got. The sound of rushing water grew louder, and she could hear the gentle cascade of water bubbling. She quickened her pace, her thirst for relief driving her towards the cool water.

"What do you mean by that?" She threw out over her shoulder, rushing to the small waterfall. She needed that cool water on her face. Her blistered toe ached with each step as she plowed forward.

Taking off her billowy shirt, she kept on the thin tank top she had underneath. She hiked the skirt up, showing off her bare legs and feet. She was careful to avoid getting stuck on a pricker bush as she made her way over to the water. The sharp greenery stabbed into her skin with every step

Bending down, she scooped water into her hands and splashed it on her reddened cheeks. Refreshing.

"There's a way for Old One's even halflings to share their long lives with someone."

"But you can't tell me, right?" She glowered at him from beneath the hair covering her face.

She felt his eyes on her as she took a sip from the water. Rivulets of water delved down her arms and tank top, wetting the shirt as she slurped from her palms.

He stammered.

Turning away from him, she spotted an alcove that had a little waterfall protruding from stacked rocks covered in greenery. A path took her underneath the rocks, the water came out overhead. Pulling up her skirt, she dipped her toe into the cool water. Sighing, she plunged her foot in.

"Guess I'm right," she chuckled.

"What?" He cocked his head to the side, walking closer.

The waterfall thundered down, its torrential waters crashed against the rocks with a deafening roar. It covered up what Mia was trying to say. Picking her way back over the slick rocks, she came closer to Grey, his horns too tall. He would have to crouch down to have enough room to make it through. "How do you share your long lives?"

"It's a very intimate moment. They share their life essence with one another and combine so closely. That if one dies, then so does the other. It is not a decision made lightly."

He leaned against the rocks on the outside.

She hid a smile from him. "I guess we should use this time to go over the riddle."

"She said this would end in death." He bared his sharp teeth. He looked away from her, but she saw the rage that was pent up. "What kind of riddle is that?" he asked.

"Of the two that are here, who do you think it will be?" He stared at her. "Okay, dumb question. Let's not think of the riddle now, then. What do you want to talk about?" She took his hand and rubbed her thumb over his knuckles.

"Stopping this madness. I won't be a part of another mindless death." His hand squeezed around hers, but he let it go before he tightened his grip too hard.

"Okay, we're talking about it." Sweat trickled down her brow. She could see the same was happening to him, even though the rocks helped cast a shadow for his eyes. "The heat is getting to me, I think."

Her eyes drifted towards the pool with a wicked idea. Pulling on his hand, her eyes begged for him to follow her. She hiked the skirt up higher, the vibrant green of the skirt offset with the dark black flowers she had stitched on.

His hand slid through her fingers, falling away when she walked too far. Her hips swayed as she stepped into the water.

The skirt weighed her down even more when the ends got wet. When the water was up to her stomach, she pushed the cloth down over her hips. Balling up the cloth, she threw it at Grey. It landed in a wet ball at his feet. She swam backwards, getting deeper into the oasis.

Grey looked down at the fabric and picked up the silky cloth. It slipped through his fingers; he hung the cloth up on the rocks beside him so it would dry out.

Closer to the middle, she couldn't touch anymore. She went under to see how far down it went. The water was dark and cloudy, making it hard to see the bottom. She reached out trying to touch the sandy floor. A few kicks down and she was still not reaching anything. This couldn't go on forever.

The breath that she held in her lungs caused them to ache as she kept holding it. Thinking better of it, she kicked back to the surface, her hands reaching for the air.

A crash a few feet away stirred up the dirt from the bottom. Mia was discombobulated by the sound and rush of cloudy water.

She came up coughing. Pushing her hair out of her eyes, she struggled to get back to a place where she could touch. She slammed into Grey, his chest hard and bare.

He gripped her arms, holding her up. "What were you doing?" he asked.

He sounded strained. She spotted his clothes sprawled along the beach. "I was trying to see how deep the pool went."

"You need to remember this is still a test. Something could have happened to you." He didn't let her go until she found her footing.

Her leg brushed against his bare leg. She combed her fingers through her short hair, finding her composure.

Laughing, she pushed back into the deep-water swimming away from him. "Don't you know how to have fun? Not everything can be life and death all the time. Plus, she won't let anything happen to us while we are contemplating the question." The thin strings from the tank top kept falling, being pulled by the water. Swimming to the other side, she noticed he stood there watching her. It was like he only had eyes for her. Her body heated thinking about his nakedness beneath the water. Since the water covered her up to her neck, she slipped the tank top the rest of the way off, letting it float behind her.

His dark, powerful body zipped towards her under the water. Rising out of the water, she giggled and splashed him. He towered over her even in the deep water, pulling her into his embrace. His body was warm against hers.

She placed a hand on his hard chest, keeping him at arm's length. Looking down at his dark form, she could clearly see what wasn't hidden. Her cheeks turned pink as she froze. This was the first time she had seen him in all his glory and, surprisingly, he looked like other men she had seen before. Maybe a bit larger.

"Do you see something you like?" he whispered. Taking her hand from his chest and nibbling on her fingertips, drawing her even closer. The silky slip of her legs brushed against his.

This time it was her choice, and she would grab him with both hands. She placed her hands on his free hand and brought it to her taut nipple. Shuddering against his touch, she watched his eyes widen.

"Mia." He breathed out, lowering his lips. He brushed them against hers.

The warmth from his skin sank into her. The refreshing pool was amazing in the heat of the desert. A big grin sat on her face as she pushed him into the depths of the water so she could curl her body around him. She struggled to kiss him; he could touch the pond floor and she couldn't. He wrapped his long arms around her; she took her cue and wrapped her legs around his midsection.

Mia's hands roamed up and down his arms and chest as she clung to him, her touch igniting a spark between them. Her fingers wandered higher, circling around his neck, and she pulled herself up to kiss him, her breasts pressed between them.

As they kissed, small splashes of water sprayed into her face, making her flinch. He wadded to a shallower part of the water, where he could hold her more securely. Mia's body slid down his stomach, their lips parting only briefly as they moved.

His tongue probed her lips, seeking entry, and she opened to him, their tongues melding together in a sensual dance. Her tongue danced along his, deepening the kiss.

One of his hands grasped her side, while the other held a firm grip on her buttocks. Suddenly, he stopped, his breathing hard and labored. His eyes were wide and wild, filled with a mix of desire and hesitation.

"Are you sure?" he asked, his voice low and husky, as he searched her face for confirmation.

She did that to him, and a part of her liked that. He bent over her; her arms tugged his neck and she kissed him again. Her tongue surged forward, tentatively touching the tip of a sharp tooth before running it softly across each point.

Grey sighed. The water covered their lower half, but his hard, throbbing cock was trapped between their bodies. Her fingers itched to touch him like he did her the previous day.

She stretched and rubbed herself against him. He scooted her further up.

"Grey," Mia moaned in need.

He crushed her to him, walking forward out of the water so he could get a better position on her slippery form. He hiked her up his body, putting her legs over his arms so the tip of him came free. Slowly, he lowered her onto his cock. She eased down onto his slick member, opening herself to the new sensation.

Her intake of breath stuttered as she took all of him. He filled her to the brink. Her hands on his muscular shoulders kept her close to him. He slowed, waiting for her to adjust to him. Staring down at her in his arms. Her perky breasts brushed against his chest. She squeezed around him, making his breath come out in brief spurts.

"If you keep squeezing like that, I won't be able to hold back," he hissed. Still moving slowly, she was held suspended in his arms as they both savored the moment.

She hoped Ashling would stay away long enough for them to have their fun. She wanted to see this through.

Mia slid up and down easily as she covered him with her heat, the friction heating between them. His stance was sure in the shallow water as their eyes connected and held. He was so much more than she had ever had before. This was different. He was different. She felt him growing inside her, stretching and filling her to capacity. She moaned out with delight.

Thickening even more within her, his bruising hands were heaven wrapping around her, bringing her to the brink of ecstasy. She saw him look to the left and pause.

He stepped slowly, his cock rubbing against her lower lips as he spotted a shelf near the waterfall. Holding on with all her strength, she climbed up to kiss him. Her breath jarred with every step he took. "Don't stop!" she whispered.

His hand reached out; she slid down, but he caught her before she touched the hard stone. Sighing, her eyes popped open. She saw his hand call for more moss to cover the sharp rock. A soft, thick carpet spread over before he placed her safely on the soft ledge. Grey shoved his palm up on the stone behind her, covering it with the same stuff. Leaning her all the way back.

Her hands let go of his shoulders. The fuzzy greenery was soft under her and she shuffled back, liking how much of him she saw driving into her. Vines crawled to him, wrapping around Mia's fingers and arms, confining her to the rock. Like last night, she let them tie loosely around her wrists, pulling her breasts up higher. Mia wanted everything he had to give her. The spray from the waterfall created a fine mist that speckled across her skin. He lapped at the beaded water as it collected on her stomach and between her breasts.

The vines crawled up her arms and legs, holding her open to him. He slid all the way forward, their bodies coming together. Moaning out, he lowered his lips to hers. Giving her a bruising kiss, he started to move and build rhythm. His cock swelled inside her, stretching her to the brim. The stretch touched parts she hadn't had caressed before. With each thrust, it sent tingles and shivers through her.

"Grey." She puffed out as he let up after their kiss. The vines widened her legs for him as he pounded into her, giving her his all. She tried to hold back, wanting to come when he did.

Her nipples hardened under his touch as he played and pinched. She watched eagerly as he enjoyed her.

Desperate for release, she struggled against the vines, working one arm free of the leaves. She threw her arm around him, pulling him into her body, needing the closeness of his hot skin on hers as she orgasmed, screaming his name. "Grey!" She sank her fingernails into his back, scratching to get him closer.

As they came together, he let out a primal shout, his hips continuing to rock against her. He whispered something in another language that she couldn't understand; the words lost in the intensity of the moment.

She held him against her as he continued to move, her body still responding to his. Leaning her forehead against his chest, she rested there. She was spent, her body was lax and light as a sense of happiness washed over her.

She wiggled against him. "Can you ease the vines back a little?"

"Yea, shoot, yea. Hang on." Some vines retreated, freeing her hands, but they held her legs around him. He was still thick inside her.

"Grey? Already for round two?" Most men needed a breather between rounds, but maybe he was different. This time she needed the break.

His pure white eyes looked at her through slits, she lost herself in his loving gaze. She knew he was enjoying the pleasure they had together. A shudder worked through him, sending another jetted stream into her core. Warmth cascaded through her and a wave of pleasure rebounded. She gripped onto him as a moaned sigh escaped her.

The next shudder coursed through her, and he shook as he ground into her, his lips descended on hers, kissing her with passion. His body was a torrent of sensation, and she was swept up in the intensity of what he was doing to her. A warmth rolled over her, sending her to dizzying heights in a matter of seconds before crashing. Another orgasm ripped through her as she groaned into his mouth.

She was still aware of his presence inside her, though his thickness had diminished slightly. "What is happening, Grey?" she huffed, her body radiating heat. The spray of the water cooled her off nicely.

His kiss was all-consuming, his lips moving against hers with a fierce intensity. His body was a powerhouse of sensation, and she was at its mercy, unable to escape the torrent of emotions that threatened to overwhelm her.

"As we came together, the energy from you made me thicker with each go until I finally let loose. That energy keeps us locked together along with my swollen cock until the energy works back through us, creating rolling orgasms. This can take some time to work through after the initial go. If we move before the energy is spent and my cock fully deflated, let's just say it would be very painful for both of us."

"Is that why you enjoy tying me up?"

His cock twitched, causing her to let out a happy moan. He rolled his hips, letting out a low moan as the energy shuddered down him once more. Away from the grasping vines, he pulled her into his arms, breaking free. He turned and leaned on the ledge, draping her across his hard chest. "I like your soft curves wrapped around me."

She spasmed around him, wrapping her legs around his hips, rotating them as she milked him for every bit of pleasure she could ring from him. As she sensed him beginning to withdraw, she slid up and down his length a few times, teasing out her final orgasm and taking it to dizzying heights.

One arm wrapped around her waist, holding her securely as his other hand helped her movements go up and down. Holding her as she came undone in his arms.

She collapsed, having nothing left to give. He pulled out, warmth still flowing out of him. He was spent as well. They rested against one another for a moment.

His cheek rested on the top of her head as he wrapped an arm around her. "I do like tying you up, especially with the vines I can make grow. It's a huge turn on."

"Glad I helped you develop that power?" She chuckled.

"Yes, that's for sure," he laughed out. "The other reason I tied you up this second time was so you didn't move and hurt either of us. But seeing you have to put your trust in me like this." He sucks in a breath through his teeth. "It does something for me."

Keeping her in his arms he slid down the rock facing, not even caring that it scraped his back as he sat down. She rested her head on his shoulder as shivers raced over her.

"I'll have to remember that."

She snuggled into his chest, needing some much-needed sleep after that marathon of orgasms. Giving him up was something she couldn't do now that she had him. They had to figure a way out of this mess.

That's it. They would call Ashling back from wherever she went and demand that she be given a new test, one that does not end in her or his death.

She mumbled unintelligible words, wanting to tell him her amazing idea, but sleep pulled at her. Dreams invaded her thoughts, showing her telling Grey of her amazing plan and him being happy. She thought only a moment went by when she shuddered awake with her back in his arms. Had she told him? Looking up at him, she knew she could get used to this and no, this wasn't just great sex. She had that before, but it wasn't like this. His eyes were closed, but his arms were secure around her.

"You are safe. I will watch over you as you sleep," Grey said.

Her heavy eyes pulled her under to a dream where she doesn't have to die, or make a choice between dying now or later.

Chapter 23
Mia

After Mia rested, she talked over her plan, the one she had been too tired to voice earlier. Both had decided to demand more answers before deciding later. Regardless, it would give them more time, which was what they needed. She would dive into the books with Grey and find a better way.

Something loud banged on a door and echoed around the desert. Mia scrambled for her clothes first while Grey watched. She kicked his clothes to him and he languorously put them on. Pulling up her skirt, she looked up at the sky. The sun had never moved once, hitting the peak of daylight. The whole day could have been gone or just a couple of hours. She couldn't tell how long they had slumbered.

Ashling faded back in. Her hair was a bit mussed on one side. Her booming voice echoed over the sands, vibrating the water in the oasis. "Have you both come to a decision?"

"What was that loud bang?" Grey asked, not looking as he buttoned the last button on his pants.

"Haddox is demanding to be let in. His power has increased and is pressing our time to a close here."

Grey shook his head. "No, he doesn't have that kind of power."

"He does now," Ashling hissed out.

"What aren't you telling us?" Mia stepped up beside Grey, taking his hand. She wanted to show a united front. It would be them against the world if it needed to. She would bet on them.

"There are some things you two don't yet know." Ashling shushed; she moved forward, like walking out of the sky. As she got closer, her form got clearer, and she sized down.

"Then tell us so we can make an informed decision," Grey said.

"Though Haddox is troubled in his own right, this darkness and power is not only his. He has been possessed by Abbadon's Chaos. He wants to bring back all the Old Ones and start the world anew. Now, what is your choice?" she huffed.

Mia felt closed in and rushed. It was too soon. "How... wait..."

"I can always force an answer." Ashling smiled at her sweetly. But Mia knew not to test it.

"No need," Grey said. He threw out his hand to stop her.

Mia nodded. "We choose, later."

"Perfect," she said with all teeth. Turning to Grey, her eyes zeroed in on him. "Haddox killed his brother in a jealous rage. The two deaths weakened the sleeping Old Ones and, with Mia's blood unlocking Abbadon from his prison, Chaos could infiltrate those around him. Somehow, he has gotten to Haddox and possessed him."

"When? So, all the things he has done since... It's not Haddox?" Mia asked. Her fingers fiddled with her skirt, playing with the strings on the tapestry, worrying each line.

"No." Ashling winced. "He is terrible in his own way, not as terrible as Abbadon could make him. He doesn't have the full power required to take over Haddox completely, I believe. But Haddox either doesn't fight him or has sided with him."

"How do you know all this?" Grey asked.

Ashling bit her lip, unsure. This was the first time Mia ever saw the goddess look so normal in her own realm. It ruined some of the awe she held for them. These were magical people and creatures, but at the root of it, they still functioned much like normal people. Was it wrong for them to put their trust in Ashling all this time?

"Why not release Abbadon and kill him, then?" Mia asked, tiredly.

Ashling muttered something under her breath, turning away from them. The sky darkened, bringing clouds to cover the hot sun. "Another secret I have carried. Abbadon is my husband... or was... it was so long ago. I cannot rightfully watch or take part in his demise."

"Can't or won't?" Grey bit out. His fists curled in anger at his sides.

Mia saw the tick in Ashling's jaw. She had walked away from them into the desert sands. "Why did you marry Abbadon?" Mia asked, trying to diffuse the situation.

"I thought I could save him, change him for the better. I thought I did for a time," she despaired. "But his darkness and chaos took over him, bringing him back to the man he had always been." She disappeared from the dessert.

The oasis disappeared with her existence. Leaving the cooling sand, her toes wiggled, leaving indents in the sand dune. The ground moved and weaved; Mia balanced as she wobbled, her hands stuck out at the sides. All that was left when settled was the bare concrete room with the lone bed. Greenery grew all around them, sneaking in between the cracks from the outside. The room shook as a loud knock vibrated through the room.

"We do not have time for this." Grey stomped forward towards the door.

Ashling appeared in front of the door, blocking Grey's way. "Not yet."

All the steam and fight had gone out of her. Why was she acting like this? Where was the strong, fiery creature she had met days before? Could one man destroy a woman in such a way as this? Make her look so vulnerable and weak. Mia felt in the pit of her stomach that something was wrong here.

Grey's eyes burned with hatred as his arms visibly shook, keeping his anger in check. "What do you mean, Haddox killed Trey in a jealous rage?"

Mia stepped up next to Grey, easing him back. He did move with her, but he was stiff and focused on what Ashling had to say.

"Trey had everything Haddox wanted."

"They were brothers. There was nothing Trey had that Haddox didn't!" He bellowed.

His muscles rippled under Mia's fingers. He had so much trapped strength, yet he didn't use it in the way she thought he would.

"Trey had wings, and looks to blend in enough with the full-blooded descendants. A power that was strong in his eyes. But most importantly, he had a healthy relationship and best friend. Both were with direct descendants. He gained acceptance from all kinds of humans, halflings, and direct descendants. He had no issues fitting in here," Ashling admitted.

"Why would wings be so important?" Mia remembered Haddox's illusion with his golden wings.

Grey's hand came up to hers that were wrapped around his arm and patted her fingers. "His mother. She runs her own court up north in the mountains. Although she isn't the best, Haddox put her on a pedestal. She dislikes men in general, but found Trey useful for his appearance."

Mia saw where he was going with that, not needing him to continue. She could only imagine what either boy went through.

"Trey, didn't get any special treatment. Regardless of what Haddox thinks he was no better off. Their mother is horrendous and manipulative," Grey stated.

The door burst open, banging against the wall, and making dust fall over them. The door nicked Ashling, scraping the edge of her shoulder. Haddox stood there in the doorway, his eyes pure black as two dark rivers slipping out of each eye. His wings were bright behind him. They flapped and a gust of dust kicked forward, hitting them in the face.

Mia raised her hand to block the dirt and grit. The same dark oily stuff rose above Haddox, floating and sitting behind the wings, using them as a shield.

Bloo charged in behind Haddox, growling his muzzle covered in foam because of how worked up he was. His teeth showed. He charged at Haddox's knees.

Haddox pulled his leg back before kicking Bloo directly in the face, sending him soaring into the stone door.

"Bloo!" Mia cried out.

Bloo whined, his little body crumpling to the ground once he hit the door.

Grey's arms wrapped around Mia's stomach, keeping her from launching at Bloo. She cried; her legs gave out. Grey held her up, keeping her back from Haddox, who was filling up the room. The oily shadow creature grew bigger with every step forward he took.

"It's rude to talk about someone behind their back!" Haddox yelled. "If you're going to talk about my past, then I might as well be present to make sure no misinformation is being passed around." He eyed each of them without missing a beat.

Her mouth hung open. "You didn't have to do that."

"What? Your little pet there?" He pointed. "I have been wanting to squeeze the life out of that thing ever since it followed you and Grey here."

She had let so much go with Haddox, trying to be the better person. To be kind, but enough was enough. He had no right to treat something so innocent in all of this like that. She could not let him get away with treating Bloo that way. "Where's the line Haddox? Humans can be play things but nothing else? Or should we not exist all together? If I remember your illusion right, you craved me and the things I could do." Mia's body visibly shook as she wrapped her arms around her, standing on her own. Her body was visibly cold as she went numb.

"That was some good fun. A human servicing me as one should. It was so easy to get you to do my bidding. You pretty much were putty in my hands. Looks like Grey knows exactly how malleable you can be," Haddox smirked.

Grey shoved Haddox against the wall, his large hand over his throat. Cutting off his air supply. The dark bubble rose above Haddox, not getting pinned behind the wings that were crushed between Haddox and the wall.

Haddox gave a strangled laugh as more of the liquid poured out of his eyes.

"What bothers you most, Grey? What I did to Trey or what I'm going to do to Mia?" He pushed his throat against Grey's hand, making him tighten his grip.

"How could you kill your own brother?" Grey bit out his face inches away from Haddox's, the spittle from his mouth flew out, hitting Haddox in the face.

Haddox strained against him. "He had everything! He got mothers' looks. It was him who had the power! Everyone liked him. While I got told multiple times how I wasn't good enough." Near the end, his voice distorted the shadow growing larger up the wall. He laughed maniacally as dark blobs oozed out of his mouth.

Grey took a few steps back, surprised. Mia gasped; she saw the blobs pull together into the larger one above. Facial features started to form as more inky darkness was added to it.

"Could he have been possessed back then, even?" Mia asked, trying to think of something to intervene.

Ashling came forward, shaking her head. "No, he only recently got possessed. Shortly after you came here, I noticed a change in him."

The room rumbled and shook as the shadow grew larger.

"I won't let you hurt anyone else." Grey stood with his arms out in front of Ashling and Mia. The vines plowed into the room, answering Grey.

"Yet here you are. About to lose someone important once again," Haddox taunted. "Don't worry, you won't have to watch from the sidelines this time."

Bright golden wings shone brightly out of Haddox's back; they were blinding.

Mia noticed Grey's vines halted their progress. He couldn't see. His hands were blocking his vision of Haddox. He swiped forward and back with great power, springing him forward, toppling into Grey. Haddox's hands fisted into Grey's shirt as he crouched over him, bringing him close to his face.

Grey swung at Haddox punching him in the face.

"Stop!" Mia screamed out, running for Bloo.

Haddox was stunned by the punch. The large dark thing above him was at the capacity of the ceiling. A pressure squeezed around Mia. The weight was heady; she saw Grey go down to one knee. Haddox laughed as he stretched and cracked his neck to the side. His head fell back, reaching for the dark oily mixture burrowing into the ceiling above. The shadow grew even larger; the room bulging at the seams trying to hold it all in.

The laughter ceased, but the distortion in Haddox's voice stayed like another was using him as a puppet. "You have made your choice. Now live with your destruction!" His voice boomed out.

Cowering at the loud volume, Mia covered her ears. His voice shook the very foundation of the room. From what Mia could tell, Ashling wasn't affected; she peered up at him.

"Don't do this," Ashling said.

"Be stuck here, wife! You can watch as your village crumbles around you while you are stuck inside this room, not able to help or defend them. You have let them clip your wings; cage you like some showpiece. That halfling has tamed you. Don't think I can't smell her all over you."

"Leave Battie out of it, she isn't part of this." Ashling stomped. Her hair raised up around her as she floated up in the air.

Rocks and huge blocks from the walls tumbled down as the dark mass ripped open the ceiling and punched out a wall.

Haddox made quick work of his wings and zipped out of the room, dodging the debris on his way up in the sky.

"Choice is power! They are all a part of this." Haddox smiled and winked. "Look at you still being caged, even when I have gotten rid of the jail cell." He flew off the wind from his wings, knocking more stones down.

Mia watched a large chunk of ceiling wiggled loose right over Bloo who was down for the count, lying prone on the floor.

Screaming out, she jumped forward as time passed in slow motion. "Bloo watch out."

His eyes blinked slowly, shaking himself, trying to get to his paws.

Grey struggled to sit up under the rubble that had crashed down on him. He was directly under where Haddox had exited.

The rock about kissed Bloo's little head when it stopped midair and other rocks that had fallen floated back up. They came together to form the ceiling. Building back the room that Haddox had destroyed.

Ashling's palm was outstretched and controlling the boulders as she fit them where she needed. "This is my realm, and I will not let another defile the home I have made for myself."

Bloo whined a little, calling out. "Friend."

Racing over to him, Mia pulled his soft body into her lap, his upper half draped over her lap. She cradled and cuddled him to her.

Ashling pushed the last rocks back into place, fixing the hole in the ceiling.

"Are you okay?" Mia asked. Her hands raced over his beautiful blue and black coat, making sure there were no cuts. Her hands were firm as they felt his bones to make sure he didn't have any sticking out of him. "You were kicked really far and hard."

Wincing, a strangled cry emitted from him. "Tender."

Mia eased up, going slower and making sure her hands were gentle. "Take it easy Bloo. Don't move."

Bloo's front paws strained. He tried to stand, but gave up and settled down.

Mia petted him gently, keeping him lying on her lap.

Grey was shocked when the rocks lifted off of him. His gaze settled on Mia before moving to Ashling.

His face scrunched in anger. He quickened his step, standing over Ashling. "What did you mean Battie isn't a part of this, and what did Haddox mean by her being a halfling?"

"That was Abbadon he has taken over though it seems like Haddox and he may have an understanding..." Ashling went quiet, her eyes shut but her eyebrows scrunched together in thought.

"Battie is my sister, if something has happened to her..." Grey's fists tightened at his sides as he let his stance do the threatening.

"Battie and her are kind of seeing each other," Mia helped break the ice. Grey loved his sister; he would not judge her for this. She didn't know why Battie and Ashling chose to keep their relationship quiet, but they didn't need to hide it from him.

"Alright... but she is a full descendant like me." Grey looked Ashling up and down.

"Actually, she's not."

"I'm not," Battie said at the same time. Her eyes pinned Ashling where she stood. "That was not your secret to tell."

Ashling looked down at the ground.

Mia jolted from her spot. Bloo groaned. She hushed him and tried to hold still while begging with her eyes at Battie for help. Battie padded over to Bloo, kneeling, assessing the damage before she started on healing him.

Grey turned on his boot, Ashling all but forgotten. "What do you mean you're not?"

"In my dreams I can talk with mom."

"But she is an Old One and slumbers."

"I know that." She shrugged. "She told me things... not all at once, but enough to know my father was human."

"I..." A loud explosion rocketed the ground and a plume of smoke arched over the largest tree in the woods at the center of the village. The barrier had gone down and the large tree was visible from the open door. "I'm going to make him pay." Grey ran out the door. It stood wide open.

Mia saw Haddox hovering over the trees, throwing something into the village. Clouds rolled in, large and mysterious, as Abbadon manipulated Haddox.

Chapter 24
Haddox

Haddox was getting lightheaded as they climbed into the air. Hovering over the city. He saw the people below him were curious and looking at him in all his might. His wings were stunning, and he shone with so much light. No wonder everyone was looking at him. Whispered words floated up to him and unease rolled through him. His stomach twisted and turned with their words as they stopped and pointed up at him. It was his childhood all over again. Instead of being worshiped as he deserved they were calling him names and making fun. Had he gone too far?

Taking down the barrier around the city was a rush. The power had soaked into them and jazzed him up. His mind was reeling. Abbadon swayed hovering above him. He had already grown so large; he started to create thick arms, a face started to appear from over his shoulder in the large dark black blob that was attached at his shoulder near his wings. It tugged at his back, but didn't add too much weight. Abbadon's smooth, black head swam nearby.

"Focus Haddox, remember once we are done here, we will take out your mother's court," Abbadon said.

Haddox reached out, feeling the dark goop. It stuck to his fingers at first, but felt like cool water as it slipped off when he pulled his hand back out. Only a dark shadow colored his hand. Proof he had stuck his hand in at all.

"What would your parents think?" Grey yelled out from far below. He ran through the treetops on the swinging bridge that connected two large trees. The planks below his feet wobbled as he clung to the ropes.

Abbadon stirred the clouds and sent an inky dark arm blasting out. He hit the tree on one side of Grey's bridge. The dark oily substance wrapped around the tree, and he felt a sucking sensation at his back as more vitality poured into him.

Giddiness poured through Haddox, and at his elation he crowed with pleasure. He flapped his great wings, helping the winds that blew in and scattered those below into shelter. He hooked a left, angling down at the apex of his reach, wanting to touch the clouds that Abbadon had just mustered. Flying down, he hovered in front of Grey, who gripped the ropes swinging back and forth on the barely together bridge.

"You don't think she knows? Leah ran off to tell her to prepare for what was coming," Haddox sneered.

"Why?" The rattling leaves and crashing items below drowned out Grey's voice. Screams persisted as the winds and storm got worse.

"Mother only tolerated me until I couldn't perform for her anymore. Then she kicked me out! Out of her court, out of her life. I was never enough for her." Haddox brushed his hands through his hair, standing it on edge. The vein in his forehead throbbed a headache settling in.

"Trey was right there with you, man! He was your brother." Grey mustered his way across the bridge. His boots found pockets where the board and ropes met. He spread his stance balancing. He was riding the air currents on the boards.

"Trey!" Haddox's eyes peeled open wide. "No, no, no, no. It was different for him." He laughed out maniacally. "His power covered for him and was her favorite for a long time. Until we were sent here to be with our father for good instead of just for the summers. Our boyish charms were getting too out of control for her to handle."

"Trey would have understood he would have been there for you. How could you kill him?"

Haddox watched Grey squirm. He had made it to the other side, his grip crushed through the wood at the ledge. It broke away in pieces. He stood far back next to the large tree.

"He was always better at everything I tried. He got the girl, the family, the wings... Everything," he yelled out frustrated. His wings were splayed wide behind him as his arms and top half were jutted forward, trying to make his point. "And yet he thought he could save all of us by passing the trials."

"What happened in that last trial?"

Haddox saw Grey was trying to hold himself back. But that wasn't what he wanted. The power he was gaining from the tree was amazing, and he wanted to use it to destroy anyone that got in his way. A large crack echoed around them as the tree became so brittle from Abbadon feeding off it that its heavier limbs started to break off at the top and come crashing down. It wouldn't be too long before the whole thing would fall to the ground. He smiled at that thought. People would be trapped under the rubble and chaos would ensue.

"He made his choice!" Haddox bit, gnashing his teeth together. He heard a crack in the back of his mouth when he clenched too hard. He flew closer, anger radiated all over him. Who was he to question what happened? Yea, he was there for his brother's death, but he didn't choose it. He only witnessed it and stood there shell-shocked by it all. They would never believe him. How could they? They already thought he was worthless. Why would they think he could do anything other than kill his brother?

Racing across the wooden planks, his boots thudded against the boards before Grey launched at him in the sky. He came crashing into him; barely having time to brace for impact. The momentum from Grey's body pulled him back and down. This angle prevented Haddox from flapping his wings.

Haddox threw out the first punch connecting with Grey's cheek and wrestling with him, trying to dislodge his body so he could use his wings. They were still heavy, but with the power he had gained from Abbadon, they were easier to use. The slight tug at his shoulder gave him the pull he needed to crawl over Grey. He gripped his hands around his throat. There was no other good place to grab. The behemoth came to this fight without a shirt. He spread his wings out and glided down on the air currents. Grey's huge body lunged at him and tugged him down faster than he would like. Haddox scratched his neck, his fingers not finding purchase as Grey slipped down his body and through his hands.

Haddox slowed his descent, hovering above the center of the market. At the last-minute Grey reached out, his hands gripping onto anything that passed by. Crashing into a pole that broke with the weight and momentum of his fall. Ripping through cloth as he fell through one of the tented shops that scattered the plaza. A high-pitched wail pierced the destruction. Grey groaned. Boards and food scattered as he came closer.

"Give up Grey. You lost this fight a long time ago. Even you preferred Trey over me, don't act like you were not a part of this all along." Silence answered him. Haddox looked up at Abbadon, who was whispering something as he sent the goop to another tree, leaching life and power from the trees surrounding the area.

Abbadon fell into the large tree above. He sent out his oozing mass to surround and eat at the tree. He laughed demonically as he consumed the power and life that was feeding into the tree. "Can you feel it, Haddox the power of all those that laughed at you, that pushed you to the wayside. Their life is yours now to decide whether they live or die."

Something tickled the back of Haddox's throat; the dust was heavy in the air as more and more things crashed and crumbled. Abbadon had done more damage to the city, taking down buildings and trees, reducing it to rubble. Where once large buildings sat in trees that stood the test of time. Now it has been reduced to rubble and large hills of rocks and debris. Nothing was lush and magical anymore; it was as if a war had descended upon his city and took the joy and magic from it. It was almost as sad as Mia's human village. What a waste.

"What is your problem?" Grey yelled.

A vine launched at Haddox, wrapping around his ankle. Another joined it, encircling his other ankle, getting pulled down away from the dark haze of Abbadon. The speed of the yank prevented him from breaking his fall with his wings. He crashed face first into the huge tree in the center. The vegetation grew thick, and the greenery started to engulf him. Thorns poked holes into his wings. Green and brown, thick wooden vines tied him down, binding him to the larger tree, keeping him from escaping.

"You think that will stop us?" Abbadon Pushed him to the side and took over for Haddox. Abbadon pulled even more of his sludge-filled self-up away from Haddox's body, but a thin line remained tethering him to Haddox.

Inky tendrils created a spider web network around the wide column of the tree. Sucking in and eating at the wood, it crumbled and cracked as the trunk of it dwindled down to a dry hollow center. Abbadon squeezed the center, wringing out any last juicy tidbit of goodness he could find. Unlatching his dripping limb from the center, the trees middle started to crumble and the top came slamming down hard before toppling to the side.

Grey ran as he saw the larger-than-life building and tree come crashing down. He urged the people around him to run. He even stopped for a small child and yanked her onto his back as he rushed others away from their broken-down homes and businesses.

Pulling himself up, Haddox slipped through the loosened vines and greens; their hold on him was not as strong when Grey wasn't around. He hung from Abbadon as the monstrous sludge moved over his home, searching for more delectable power to leech. Even while Abbadon consumed, he still felt tired and lethargic.

He looked out at his city; the place he had once called home and didn't recognize it anymore. Abbadon had demolished it all. No longer was there a market for business to grow and prosper. The homes that were integrated so closely with nature now were non-existent. What had he started? Maybe if this was his mother's place, he wouldn't feel like this, but this had been a safe haven compared to what he was used to.

He still remembered the first time he had come to the night market; they had been celebrating, and it was the first time he had seen people join together, laughing and dancing. Magic was shot off like fireworks, creating dazzling pictures in the night sky.

"Run, run little ones. For as long as you can, because I will get you." The larger Abbadon grew, the more his sludge filled tendrils could reach out from his center, latching on to the next tree. His oozing mass slithered into homes, seeking magical items to siphon. Tables upturned rocks and beads littered the ground, no table left unturned as the living mass pulsed with energy.

Chapter 25
Mia

Mia watched Battie take and cradle Bloo to her bosom. She helped her up and made sure he wasn't jostled too much as she moved.

"I'm going to take him to the healing center where he can rest and recuperate after the healing I did. He will be fine. Just needs some rest," Battie whispered. Ashling and she exchanged a worried glance, but said nothing more.

"I will come visit you soon, Bloo. Get better. We will take care of what is happening out here." Mia's throat twinged. Her heart was heavy with grief and worry. Haddox was out there and from what they could hear and see, he was demolishing the city. Trees kept falling and loud cracks reverberated across the distance. Grey had gone after him, but he didn't look like he was slowing him down at all. The clouds were knitting closer together, and the wind was blowing in stronger.

"You alone possess the power to fix things," Ashling stated as she continued fixing her home and setting upright things that the fight had overturned. The fight had left things in disarray. "Now that Abbadon is loose and in the open, he will cause more destruction and chaos than any of us expected."

Battie passed through the door, and paused, keeping Bloo close to her body.

Mia blinked, her eyes lost in thought, trying to recollect her thoughts after Bloo. "I can't stop any of them," Mia looked down at her hands. How could she even take on Abbadon when she felt so useless? She had shown Haddox leniency after the last test. Was that not what she should have done? Should she have been harsher? Would that have changed this outcome? And Grey? He had a right to his anger. He had horrible stuff to process. Grief didn't strike without anger. She couldn't blame him. And she was meant to stop them? Fix things.

"This is the second part of the test. One choice will lead to the Old Ones being able to get free. The other way keeps them trapped, but things could be tricky for you and the ones that care for you," Ashling commented. The room and ceiling were back to normal. She stood by the door, looking out at what was happening.

Her mouth hung open, not believing what she was hearing. "What's part of the test?" She hugged both her arms around herself, not wanting to let go or face the next choice.

"Haddox or Grey. It was always going to come down to one or the other." Ashling gave a sad smile that tipped to the side.

"That's an impossible choice!" Mia's eyes followed the smoke in the sky, staring at the trees she kept seeing fall. "If I choose Grey, Haddox will go into a spiral and let Abbadon have his way with his body, leaving him in charge to cause the chaos he so badly wants."

"That is a probability, yes." Ashling nodded. "If he has not lost control yet."

"If I choose Haddox, Grey will go into a furious rage and hate humans and me even more. He is a pure descendant. He could do more harm than good, weakening the hold that keeps the Old Ones in slumber. Getting us right back to the crux of the problem."

"You don't think you are enough to make him pause in his rage? You think so little of your time together?" A lone tear fell down Ashling's cheek.

"We just admitted to our feelings for each other, let alone ourselves. This brand-new thing, whatever it may be, no, I don't think it can stand this harsh of a test so early on."

"Then what are your other options?"

"I can't fix Haddox like you thought you could with Abbadon. He will have to make that choice to change for the better. To do better."

"You will have to figure out a way in order to keep the Old Ones at bay," Ashling said.

"You must stop him before he does something he can't take back!" Battie muttered.

"Battie!" She looked back, astonished that she was still there with Bloo. From her position, Battie stood aside, out of the doorway's line of sight. "Battie, what are you still doing here?" Stepping right outside the door, Mia scratched Bloo's little head.

Bloo barked and licked her hand. "This is important!" he growled.

"You have to stop him." Battie had tears in her eyes. "Grey is out there."

"He left in such a hurry. He was gone before I could even say anything." Mia was startled when the largest tree in the center toppled, sending a dust plume exploding up from the forest. Birds flew from their perches, screeching their displeasure.

"He's out there fighting Haddox." Battie stood there, stone cold. Her eyes were the only things showing emotion.

"Are you in shock?" Mia whispered. Glancing at her pupils, she noticed they didn't move much other than stay trained on the sky.

Mia stuck her head back in the empty room, looking worrisome. The room was plain and bare. Ashling deserved more than this. Mia knew she could make this room whatever she wanted to, but there had to be more that she wanted. Someone she craved to be out here with.

Ashling made her way to the door but didn't cross the line. "This is not the time to go into shock. You have a job to do." She raised her hand; it shook as it hung there in the air. The tips of her fingers pressed up against some invisible barrier that kept her locked in the room.

"Tell me it will all be okay," Battie said. Her voice raised. "Tell me! It was all worth it in the end."

"Battie." Ashling begged softly. Her shoulders were down and her body curled in as her arms hugged around her midsection. "He had to know."

Glaring back, Battie cocked her head to the side. "Like that, there were better ways?"

"I'm sorry."

"We will talk about this later... You know if we survive." Battie took off, with Bloo close to her chest as she jogged to the healing center.

"She'll come around," Mia broke the silence, stepping back across the threshold into Ashling's room.

"That is for another time." Ashling grabbed Mia's hand, forcing her hand to rest above her chest bone. "Now is the time to awaken your own power. And make you realize you have had it all along. Do you feel that?"

The thump of Ashling's heartbeat was strong beneath her fingers. "Your heartbeat?" Mia blinked slowly as she concentrated.

"Not that, no," Ashling said exasperated

Mia stared at her hand at the center of Ashling's chest between her breasts. She relaxed her hand, her palm touching her skin fully, and concentrated. Resting her torrent thoughts. Her breath was loud in the silence. She tried to hold it to see if she could sense something then.

"Are you ready to see the full vision of your grandmother?" Ashling said quietly.

"The one where she fights Abbadon?"

"Yes, and how she tied him to the circle. Perhaps there will be clarity in what you must do in the vision. You will be able to see and feel as she does through the vision, but also at a distance. I will only take you out at the end."

"Is there time to even do this?"

"I think you will have so much more knowledge and know what to do after, yes, we have the time." Ashling nodded her head as she cradled Mia's face.

She blew a gentle breath on Mia's face; her eyes growing heavy and her head slouched forward. Ashling's powerful arms caught her before she fell forward. Her body became listless as it floated to the floor gently.

Mia had the sensation of falling. Her hands whipped around; her long fingers and pale skin, a new version of flesh and bone.

A large man wearing a tan working shirt and well worked leather pants stood over her. He carried a large wooden mallet. Pure black, hate-filled eyes stared at her; black goop oozed from his eyes and ears. She remembered seeing the same with Haddox. Abbadon! But who was this man standing over her? Well, not her, as she took in more of her surroundings and her own clothes she started to see just the beginnings of her town. This was her grandma Sky when she was younger and had no wrinkles.

"Stop running, little mouse!" He yelled out, his voice distorted with another on top of it. A dark shadowy cloud spilled out of the man's back. "I am Abbadon! Know my name. I want you to scream it from the top of this hill, little mouse. Warn the people below of what is to come. Dark chaos has come for them."

He grabbed her and threw her on the ground, pinning one of her arms under his heavy boot. Her fingernails scratched at the tough leather of his boots, her hands all but useless in trying to pry his foot off her arm. She gritted her teeth. Her eyes flashed with fear and anger all at once.

She felt her grandmother Sky as she struggled, but could also see her face and the surrounding space, not just what she saw. It was all too surreal and a little discombobulating. One moment she was watching from her Grandmothers perspective and the next she was looking down on both of them in the field, the town in the distance. This is what Ashling must have tried to warn her about.

Mia was yanked back into Sky's body as pain radiated through her hand as Abbadon raised and slammed down the wooden mallet. Busting her hand up, tears fell, but she refused to cry. Blood stained her lips as she clenched them, refusing to yell for help.

"Tom," Sky's voice shook. "Please stop, this isn't you." She curled in and then flipped away with each sickening crunch and thud of the hammer. Her body yanked and fought to get free.

"Tom isn't here anymore, little mouse. Hasn't been for some time." He gave a cruel smile as he tossed the mallet away, pulling her up by her good hand and squeezing the bones, crushing them. "Remember how you gave yourself completely to Tom?"

Her wet eyes met his, Abbadon's face wavered through unshed tears.

Mia was in a whirlwind of emotions and feelings. She was having a hard time taking it all in and digesting what it meant. She expected a gentler introduction, but the story began at its climax. Sky's thoughts blended with her own as things unfolded.

"Tom was gone then, too. You gave yourself to me," Abbadon laughed.

The look of horror washed all the color from her face as she crumpled, his arms wrapped around her, pulling her close to him.

He danced around with her limp in his arms while having a gleeful time. "Yes, it was perfect. Your sweet body was mine for the taking. Want to know how I came to rest with your lover here?" He leaned her into a dramatic pose, as if they were performing a sensual dance. Looming over her, his body dominated her small frame, before pulling her tight.

Her body shook and swayed into him; her hands pulverized to a bloody pulp. Every time he gripped one of her hands in his, the squelching painful sound rolled her stomach. The pain was consistent and numbing as she lost concentration. He tightened his grip on her, crushing more bones, sending a sharp waking pain that pulled Sky's attention back to him.

"I will tell you the story. Your little guard here caught an Other, an Old One descendant. Him and some of his buddies have been dissecting him and learning about him for a few weeks now. When he passed from his wounds, it helped awaken me and let me break from the cage that held me for so many years. Your lover was the closest to the body at the time of death, so I slipped in with him, none the wiser. Took my time taking him over, gaining my power and bearings, causing havoc of my own within your little town. Enjoying life for a fleeting moment since it had been so many years since I had been free. My takeover was delayed because this body resisted me, forcing me to take my time gaining power."

"Tom," she cried out.

His hands constricted around her waist and hauled her up his body. "Why don't you show me one more time before I ruin everything? How much does Tom really mean to you? I'll even let him have this goodbye." Tom's eyes cleared of the dark shadows in his eyes and he looked around with surprise. The haze behind Tom dwindled as Abbadon sank back into the body.

Sky raised her hands, throwing them around his neck, and let his lips descend on hers. Her grief and pain burned as she poured all of herself into the kiss, wanting Tom to understand what she was doing.

"I take you in, Abbadon! Tom, push him out!" She yelled into his mouth, kissing him and sealing the deal. Nausea rolled through her as the possession ripped from Tom and poured into Sky. Tom's arms pushed against her, but she held onto his neck, refusing to release her grip.

Her strength was giving out. But before it did, the sickening darkness flowed into her, sitting in the pit of her stomach like a lead weight pulling her down. The pain increased enough that she blacked out, when she came to both Tom and her were sprawled out on the ground. Her head was so heavy but she focused and stared at Tom waiting for him to take a breath. She saw the rise of his chest and even the small snore that escaped his open mouth as he exhaled. Sighing she slumped back down. She felt Abbadon inside her, stretching and reorganizing her insides. Her hands were all but useless at her sides, so she struggled to sit up. She must get him out of her before it was too late.

Sky's mind rebelled against the onslaught of terrible thoughts. Her eyes landed on the spilled flowers and wrecked basket. She clung to her memories and what she had been doing. She had come out on the northern field to pick flowers. Noticing Tom with the wooden mallet patrolling the inner wall, she went over to check on him. He had disheveled clothes and mussed, dirty hair.

A whining noise emitted from her mouth before she could stop it. Scrunching her eyes closed, she doubled over and dry heaved. Wrapping her arms around her stomach, she marched forward, her eyes landing on a dilapidated house in the distance.

Grave markers littered the front yard as she picked her way carefully among the stones.

"Sylvia will help me," Sky muttered out. Sylvia knew magic and things of old. Like her, they both had researched this land and the beings that inhabited it. She barely made it to the house without screaming. Leaning against the door, she kicked at it with her shoes. When there was no answer, she mustered all her strength to kick it again with more feeling. A guttered cry garbled from her.

"What do you want?" A young woman opened the door quickly. She had a nasty growl and a mean look on her face. Her vibrant red, orange hair was down and framing her face with wavy curls. Freckles doted across her nose and cheeks.

Sky fell forward. "Help," Sky's voice broke as she slumped over.

Sylvia caught her and looked Sky over, noticing the blood that pooled and dripped from her hands. Her face changed from anger to concern from one blink to another. "We must get your hands set before it's too late. Otherwise, they won't be usable. Who did this to you?" She cradled Sky's wrists, trying not to bump them as she guided her into her home.

Swallowing past the flood of saliva that filled her mouth, she let out a groan. "There is no time. You practice black magic, yes?"

Sylvia's eyes scanned past the open door, looking for people and their weapons. "I had known it would come to this," she said under her breath.

Sky fumbled as Sylvia almost dropped her wrist. She saw the hesitation in Sylvia's actions. Her body had gone stock still. "Yes or no, on the black magic? I need help. An Old One has gotten loose." Sky could tell this wasn't just a descendant no, she had researched the Other's kind when they first arrived here in these new lands. Neighboring villages up and down the coast had all agreed the others were better off left alone unless they wanted to provoke the Old Ones.

Worry rained down Sylvia's face as her eyes came back to Sky's. "Yes," she said with reluctance. "I also have some knowledge of the Old Ones, not so much of the others."

Sky nodded her head. "Good." Though she didn't know how that would help all that much. She breathed deeply, knowing what she had to do. "Then give me something for this pain so we can take care of the Old One that will possess me soon."

Leaving Sky to lean on the doorjamb, Sylvia ran to the kitchen, grabbing a few herbs and a book before coming back. "Put this under your tongue. It will help ease the pain."

Sky opened her mouth and Sylvia helped place it under her tongue. The relief from the agonizing ache was almost instant, but the throbbing remained strong and persistent. They were running on borrowed time.

"That will do for now. The Old One that I took into me. He had possessed Tom before. I couldn't let him ruin this town and beyond. We have to put him back where he came from."

"Put him back?" Sylvia looked aghast. "I'm not even sure where he came from. I don't even know how you got him into you," she said frazzled. "Do you know magic?"

Silly laughter bubbled out of her lips. "I know of it and that it exists across many cultures. But no, I am just an artist that likes to collect stories."

Sylvia kept her distance, flipping through the pages of her book. "How did you come by this possession?"

"Abbadon, I remember that name from a story I once heard. He said he would bring chaos to our town and said Tom fought him at every turn. Abbadon, at the end, let us have a moment together and I took advantage of that time. I told Tom to push him out while I accepted him into me, begging him to use my body instead of Tom's rebelling body. We don't have much time. I feel him burrowing up, stealing my weakening body. We have to give our town a chance to survive. We have to do something." Sweat beaded across her forehead. Fear locked her legs in place; she feared it was him, not just her body shutting down.

"Magic takes time and precision to complete. This will not be easy. But I think I have a way, at least I hope." The pages rattled as she flipped back and forth between two pages. Sylvia's feet fumbled over the rug as she crossed the foyer. She grabbed a pencil and approached the enormous book that was sitting on the kitchen table. She grabbed a bag, throwing jars and candles into it that were sitting out on shelves. Next, she took time to scratch something down in her own smaller book that she carried with.

Sky leaned her head back, listening to the scratch against the paper. Her eyelids drooped down. With the pain scaled back, exhaustion was setting in. Her body craved sleep and wanted to repair the damage that had been done.

Sylvia jarred her awake, the sun much lower in the sky than it had been previously when she shut her eyes.

"You were mumbling," Sylvia said.

"We need to go," Sky urged, not sure how much longer she could hold on.

Sylvia nodded and slung the bag around her torso. "We will have to go into the dark woods." She hunched low to ease Sky's arm around her neck, helping her walk forward.

Each step was agonizing. "But how, the guards? And I don't think I can travel very far." Sky looked back from where she came to the highest hill in their village. She wondered if Tom had woken up yet or still lay up there hurt and scared. Scared, like she was.

Sylvia took Sky's arm, guiding her away from the grassy hill past her house. The guards often ignored the house bordering the woods during their searches. "Don't worry, I have another way. I have been to the woods and forest before, but you mustn't tell anyone. Promise me."

Sylvia waited for Sky to nod before going any further.

Sky looked up at her, truly taking her in. Her dark brown dress came to her knees, but she had pants and boots on. Good protection for a hike in the woods. Items needed for a spell filled the satchel. Sky trusted she knew what she was doing. "I know what the town says of you that you are the most vile and evilest person. A witch born of the dark arts. I promise if you help me save our town, you will have one person forever in your corner. You will be good in my book."

Sylvia grinned. Happiness flowed through her as she rushed forward, humming a happy tune. "Then that is all I need."

Dodging forward, she left Sky, skipping forward to a tall tree, looking back every couple of seconds to make sure Sky was keeping up.

The pain kept radiating up her arms and back, shooting straight to the back of her head, creating a headache. Sylvia's head was on a swivel as she tapped on the trunk of a tree.

"What are you looking for? The guards don't come out this far."

"Humans are not the only creatures that inhabit these woods." Sylvia pushed on the trunk of the tree hard. Cracking open a small opening, wiggling her fingers into the edge, she pulled it out, making the opening bigger.

Sky slid through, trying not to bump her worthless, stumped hands. Her knees weakened, stopping her immediately as she toppled over, slipping down in mud on the other side of the tree. "What happened?" she complained, rolling over and locking her legs together. She tried her best not to put weight on her hands.

Sylvia slid through with no issues and expertly traversed the terrain as she skated through. Hopping over the small mud puddle that formed at the base of the tree, she continued weaving in between trees, looking for something.

"I had a portal set up to get me from my side of the woods over to your side. Makes it easy to dodge around things when needed." A mischievous grin lit up her face.

"Sylvia," Sky sobbed.

Turning, Sylvia looked back at Sky lying there in the mud covered in muck. "Is he taking over? Are we out of time?" Sylvia nervously chatted, making her way back to help Sky up. Her steps were rushed and jarring.

The mud made it easy for her shoes to slide through, but that quickly dried up the farther they got from the muddy mess. "I can't move my legs," she hissed out. Worried they wouldn't make it in time.

"Hold on." Sylvia stepped away and drew a machete knife from the bag. It looked sharp and ready to chop if needed.

Sky gulped loudly. Wondering if it would be better to cut her hands off to bloody stumps. Sylvia edged closer with a wild look in her eye. Sky wished her legs worked because she would like to step back or run. She was so afraid. Was Sylvia going to end her life to stop Abbadon from taking over?

Passing by Sky, Sylvia evaded and slammed the small knife at the base of a tall leaf. "Usually, I would not make a path like this, but the circumstances being what they are, I think we will risk it." She laid the thick leaf down, then helped Sky into it to pull behind her. She hacked at the small limbs and vines that tangled. Making it easier to get through the dense woods as she yanked the large leaf with Sky on it.

"This helps. I can focus on fighting him, thank you," Sky said. She looked around, getting lost almost immediately. "Where are we going?"

"I have a place of power nearby where I have stored things to help us."

Sky seized in the leaf; Sylvia was thrown off balance. She dropped the front to rush to Sky's side. Her gentle hands braced the sides of her head, keeping it steady.

Sky coughed and rolled. "Let me free," she screeched. Something had taken over her voice. She threw her head back and her eyes clouded over. Dark tears started to fall from them.

Sylvia gasped, backing away with the machete pulled tight in front of her. She watched as Sky's eyes flicked from blue to black for many seconds.

"Hurry," Sky whispered as she came back to herself, breath puffed out of her lips hard. Sweat poured over her, and a fever made her warm to the touch, but everything was cold inside, a chill she had never felt before. The chill of death.

Sylvia's eyes furrowed. She grabbed the branch at the bottom of the leaf, tugging as quickly as she could, dragging it over the long grass out into a rocky clearing.

A circle of stones were set in front of a willow tree. The leaves of the tree tickled her as she slid through them. Sky rested on the inside of the circle while Sylvia spilled out the contents of her bag, scrabbling for the candles and items that she would need for the spell. Darting back and forth around the circle.

"What was its name?" She set up the items, placing her book to the side.

"Abbadon," Sky heaved in a breath. Her weary legs shook as she sprawled out, trying to move over to a stone and lean against it.

"I think I have something here." She ripped something out of a hollow space under the willow tree. There, Sylvia had stored many items, including some books wrapped in leather and further protected in a waterproof bag. "I found these in some ruins from the Old Ones. I remember reading about him or something about chaos." Flipping the pages quickly, she wasn't careful. "Abbadon, the bringer of Chaos. He is the strongest of them all." A snap of a twig brought her eyes up, scanning the forest. She stopped for a moment, debating, then continued to read. "The descendants will not like that he is trying to wake up."

The forest was eerily quiet as the dry leaves rustled in the wind across the dirt and grassy patches. A lone butterfly gets whipped down into their circle. Its wings are orange and black in color. It caught itself on Sky's dress. Resting there flapping its wings lazily. Sky's eyes drooped as her head listed to the side. Sylvia finished the ring of candles. She set down the other book and went back to hers, muttering to herself.

"Not the time for a history lesson." Sylvia tugged hard on her dark brown wavy hair.

Leaves blasted into the circle, clinging to Sky as she shook the chill that had settled deep in her bones. The flames from the candles puffed out as the wind gusted, creating a torrential wind around her. The butterfly flew off into the tornado of air as the leaves spun around.

When the leaves fell and she could see again, Sky had to blink her eyes multiple times to clear the dust and dirt from them to make sure she was seeing things right.

"Sylvia?" Sky wavered.

"Yes, I see her as well." Sylvia didn't move; she stood a few feet away.

A beautiful woman appeared before them. Leaves covered her in reds, oranges, and bright yellows. Her hair was as fiery in color as a flame. "What are you doing?" she raged. "The forest has called me and I see why!"

"Sky here has Abbadon possessing her, and we need to get him out before he takes over."

Sky doubled over in pain. Rolling over, she gets to her knees inside the circle, falling forward. Her hands gave out as it touched the earth. Pain seared through her. She crumpled to her side, dirt plumbed up sticking to her lips.

The woman fluttered her fingers, causing the pages of the book that was forgotten on the rock to flip harshly in the wind.

Sylvia moved to the side, sinking down into a crouch to read from the side. She set her book down and held the sides of the book open; she watched as the pages fluttered in the wind.

Waiting until it settled on one page, she read the title out loud. "Containment spell."

"That's what you will need to lock him in. This rock circle will keep him contained." The ethereal woman glanced down at Sky. Blood flowed out on the dirt already from her broken hands. "She is already bleeding, so the blood will be the key that binds the lock. I will do the last part and push him out of your friend into the cage you have set."

"Who are you?" Sylvia nodded.

Sky's teeth chattered, not being able to speak. But she was glad Sylvia asked Mia was dying to know herself. She looked at her broken hands lying in the turned-up soil and saw the bloody mess that she was leaving.

"I am the Forest. There is no time. We can discuss that later." A howl came from the depths of the dark woods.

A shiver crawled down Sky's back as her eyes roamed around the circle. She cast her sight into the darkened nooks of the bushes and trees, searching for something dangerous that would put this all to a stop. They were not alone out here. Any of the creatures that called this place home could force them to stop.

"Fine." Sylvia faltered, moving next to the woman in the fall leaf dress. "Let's do this." She looked over the spell and practiced the movements, muttering over the words.

Kneeling, Sylvia pressed a comforting hand to Sky's shoulder. The crisp leaves bunched and crunched against Sky's back. "This will be painful, but it will release him into the ground."

Sky bared down as a spiral of pain hit her, sucking in air through her teeth as she breathed through it. "Hurry," she squeaked, feeling Abbadon rolling through her, working up his final attack to take over.

Sylvia's words slurred together as Sky laid there. The Forest woman placed a cool pale hand on Sky's head, causing every synapse in her body to burn. She let out the pent-up scream and yelled out in agony. Her throat turned hoarse. It couldn't keep up with the searing embers that were bubbling beneath her skin. Black sludge flowed out of her eyes and ears. Coughing and retching more sludge onto the ground, it mixed with her blood. It oozed out of her in clumps and little streams from her face. Every part of her regurgitated what she had taken into her body.

What she had allowed into her. She listened to Sylvia's chanting voice over and over again. The spell felt like it lasted for hours when she finally slumped forward. There was nothing else she could give.

The forest woman turned Sky on her side away from the mess and pulled her up and away from the rock circle.

Sky was being cradled in the winds as she rocked back and forth. Her eyes barely stayed open. She wouldn't be traveling back tonight. Unless they had a way to carry her home without her help. Sylvia had already struggled with her on a leaf; she didn't think she would have the strength for the distance back to her home.

The forest woman waited for Sylvia to close and deconstruct the circle before crossing the barrier with Sky in tow. She set her down beneath the willow tree on the outside of the rock circle.

"Make sure she doesn't come back here or any of her descendants. If they push through the circle and bleed, it will unleash his chaos into those nearby, and he will finish what he has been meaning to all this time." Flames flickered in the forest woman's eyes as she looked down.

The glow cast across Sky's sick pallor. Sky was glad Sylvia was here. She feared she would forget all this and make it all part of a fevered dream.

Sky watched as the woman from the forest turned to Sylvia; they were at a standoff. "Now hear me, witch, I will share my power with you for a time if you will keep this transgression hidden from your kind. We don't need a war brewing up between the two, do we?"

Sky opened her mouth to say something but found after all the screaming her voice endured, it didn't spring forward like normal. Why couldn't they tell the Village? They needed to protect the city from things like this. People had a right to know of the dangers. The history needed to be kept.

Sylvia's eyes lit up with mischief. She gave a small smile. "I will keep your secret for now, but I want something more than your word that I will share your power. It also needs to last."

What was Sylvia thinking? Her eyes veered to her opened wide, begging for her to see the fear and question written across her heart and face.

Silence met them as they scrutinized one another. The sun sank inch by inch, the darkness crawling forward. "Fine, then, like a phoenix, you too will rise from the ashes with the knowledge of your previous lives." She touched Sylvia's cheek, a red splotch spreading its way over her face, down her neck, and disappeared beneath the shirt to her back. "You will bear my mark through your lives and know where it came from. As long as the mark lasts, you will share in my power."

"What of her hands?"

Sylvia looked warmed and flush, the cool temperatures not touching her. Sky shivered at the cool wind still blowing in.

"Her hands will be forever lost to her. I can ease the pain from her bones, but what you can do is what she will live with. Let it be the mark of what happened here today. My power may be great, but it can't undo what was done."

Sky was saddened by all the lost art she would miss out on doing.

"What about the village, protection?" Sky's voice scratched out.

Sylvia kneeled next to her. "We will tell them a story. One that is close enough to the truth but not enough to cause an uproar. I can work with them on a barrier."

"But..." She hesitated; it took all her strength to get that little word out.

"They would never let you or Tom survive if they knew the full story. They already want to get rid of me on a good day just because of my magic. But it will be the only thing that will be able to protect them from those who dwell here. Please Sky." Hope filled her eyes.

Sky gazed up at Sylvia, trying to read the other woman. She knew life for her had been unfair and always wished for a better life for her. But was this the way they should go? She nodded, too tired to think of much else. The edge of sleep pulled on her consciousness.

Mia was pulled away from the scene. The distorted woods muffled and cut short their words. She came out of the vision, her heart ached at what her grandmother had to go through. Her eyes stared at Ashling, who was standing in front of her.

"Now go, there isn't much time left," Ashling whispered.

Chapter 26
Mia

Mia was shoved out of the room and the door slammed behind her. Stopping, she scanned the horizon. It didn't take long to spot the path Grey had shown her to take to the city. Following it, there was a path of destruction. Something had ripped off and tore the tops of some trees.

Jumping down the stone steps, she cleared them landing in the soft grass. Cutting across to the dirt path. She didn't know what to think of the vision she'd witnessed. Her grandmother had survived something horrific. So many stories were told to her, but she didn't remember any like this. The wall wasn't even around yet. Whatever story Sky and Sylvia came up with scared the town enough to build the protective barrier. She wished she could go back to her grandmother and ask her more questions. Ask the tough questions and get to the heart of the truth. Mia hoped she had more time to do that, if she ever saw any of her family ever again.

She kicked into high gear and bursted toward the hidden grove. She didn't know how long she had been in the vision. Smoke still gathered over the trees, a large opening where the large tree used to stand, now let in sunlight in the darkened town. Knowing both of them, they would still be alive but bloody from a fight. Adding Abbadon into the equation, she wasn't sure where the city stood, let alone Grey and Haddox.

The wind whipped through her hair as the branches grabbed at her skirt, trying to hold her back. She tore it away, ripping some of the cloth from the branches, and kept going. Birds screeched through the forest. Other little critters scattered and ran past her their homes had been invaded. They were clearing out, trying to find safety.

Slashes cut through the wall of ivy and vines. Pieces of foliage covered the forest floor. The trees were slashed in half and left lying on their sides as well. She saw the whole town from where she stood, where before she couldn't until going through the veil. Something broke inside of her, the twinkling lights that dotted the pathways were crushed to a fine gravel. Sadness creeped up from the center of her chest. She doubled over in pain and anguish. Her fingers skimmed the broken edges of the splintered wood.

Images of Haddox played out in her mind of what he had done. Him flying in from above, a shadowed mass taking over. The rubble was great and she could see some didn't escape in time forever pinned under the foliage and rubble. Each strike hammered into her heart. With everything he broke and destroyed, the monster growing out of him would have gotten larger and larger. She couldn't believe the destruction. Her mind came up blank as she stared at the massacre.

What was she going to do? Ashling said the vision would help her decide what she needed to do. But she had no ideas. None whatsoever. Jagged rocks slammed into the dirt nearby as they came flying in from the center of the city.

Her eyes landed on a dark huge mass of a monster. His focus was tearing into a building that was wrapped around a tree. Smashing it to pieces, huge amounts of stone were torn from it and chucked over his shoulder. She watched the piece get flung in the air and career into a home, demolishing it in an instant. The monster let out a terrible roar as it swiped at a nearby building, bringing it crashing to the side. From here, she could not see Haddox or Grey, only Abbadon and his chaotic destruction.

"Mia! Good, I caught up to you. What is going on?" Battie called out to her.

Mia shook her head, having no words as Battie raced up from behind her. Her steps slowed as she saw the horror of the entrance to the city and then beyond.

"Here, put these on." She tossed some boots to Mia.

"Ashling showed me something that was supposed to help with this. But I have no clue what I'm supposed to do," Mia gasped.

"Ashling wouldn't have shown you something that you didn't need. There has to be something you overlooked. You must save Grey." Battie pulled at the broken vines to the tree, throwing them to the ground in frustration.

"The choice is between Grey or Haddox. But what about Abbadon? What happens to him then?"

Battie froze after walking by. "Choice? Choice?" she repeated. She slowly turned her head back to Mia, glaring. "What choice? Grey is the only option."

She sputtered. Obviously, Mia wanted to say the same, but Battie hadn't had to go through the past two tests, either. Her choice will determine what happens. If the world gets demolished or lives to see another day. How could anyone person decide that? Words eluded her, so she decided to keep walking and hope Battie would follow in silence.

"Mia!" Battie yelled after her, following. "Wait." She tugged on Mia's shoulder, spinning her to look her in the eyes.

Mia faced her head. "What Battie? What do you want me to say? Grey raced after Haddox and I'm still in this test. Stuck between a rock and a hard place."

"He's my brother." Battie looked at her with hope in her eyes.

"I know. I care for him as well." Mia looked at the city, worried about what was going to happen. The path forward was laid in rubble. She moved through it, slowly climbing over large rocks and broken houses and trees. "The problem is," she paused, making sure Battie followed behind. She had a feeling she would need Battie's help by the end of this. "Each choice I have made so far has not gone according to plan."

"What do you mean?"

"My first test was of two wolves. I chose the strong wolf, thinking it would be the best option, but it bullied the other wolf into fighting and it won. I barely escaped with my life," she huffed out. Her hands were roughened from the loose gravel that chipped away from the stones as she climbed over them.

Battie batted at leaves as she jumped from limb to limb on the fallen tree bouncing over the large downed tree. "And the second test?"

Leaving Mia behind to follow. "Was weird all together. It started off one way and then ended with deciding what I would do with Haddox because he took a choice away from me the first night, even if it was an illusion." Mia made it to the top.

The tree limbs hid most of what surrounded them, but Battie had already hacked a small clearing. She saw most of the main path had carts overturned. Food and trinkets littered the streets. Bodies had been trampled. Limbs poked out of a downed house. None came to aid. All had either fled or were hiding, hoping nothing fell or demolished their hiding spot. She was afraid to stop and check if the person had passed already or was on their way there. She couldn't help them, not right now.

"Battie." She pointed to the hand she saw poking out of a pile of rocks and lumber.

Battie moved to the hand, her eyes fierce and focused. She pressed two fingers to the underside of the wrist. She shook her head and moved away. Her head darted this way and that, checking to make sure there weren't others.

Mia's mouth had gone dry at the lost life. She slid down the tree, landing on a lower limb, hopping down to the ground.

"I couldn't do to him what he had done to me... I just couldn't. Even if this is all my fault." Her knees nearly gave out, but she struggled through. She needed to accept her decision, and all that came with it.

"This is why people hate making decisions," Battie gritted between her teeth.

"Tell me about it. I put off making some hard decisions and choices for months, even years, because I didn't feel like I would like either outcome."

"Yet life still found a way to make you decide something." Battie rolled her eyes. Kicking a rock down the road, it landed at the base of a home left untouched.

Staying clear, they didn't wish to disturb it or draw Abbadon's attention.

They were getting closer to the center of the city. More and more things were unrecognizable to what they started out as or belonged to. Small fires had started with all that had gone down.

"And this third test is now your choice on who lives Haddox or Grey?" Battie asked.

Mia pushed what they had been talking about to the back burner as she took in the bleak outlook of what had been done to the city. Was Grey even still alive? If he couldn't stop Haddox, how did they expect her to?

Her eyes were glued to the swash of darkness in the sky, hoping he wouldn't turn and spot her.

"That is what is weird. She gave us a test saying Grey and I had to make a choice together. Said he has had his own decisions and tests to do. The third test was to choose death now or later. We chose later."

"Then the tests should be done. Right?" Battie stopped; anger rippled down her face. "Why is he even here, then?"

Mia shrugged. "After we made that choice, Grey took off after Haddox. You know she gave me this last test between Haddox and Grey. One will lead to the Old Ones release and the other will keep them trapped."

"She can't change the rules like that. That's not how this is supposed to work!"

"She didn't talk to you about it?" Mia questioned.

Battie's eyes widened; half crazed as her fingers squeezed around the metal chains that crisscrossed over her shirt. The baggy black pants hugged her slight form as she tossed her head back and yelled up at the sky.

Abbadon turned to the sky. He crawled over the tops of buildings and trees that remained. Searching for what had made the sound.

Mia ran and grabbed Battie, pulling her back into a hidden alcove between two trees. The branches scratched her and Battie as they scrambled back.

"Don't," Mia whispered. She placed a hand over her mouth as they both watched Abbadon. One of his fists came down on a house, crushing it into pieces. Screams could be heard from inside. The dark haze shuttered and pulsed as it gained more mass. Another of its tentacled arms shot out to a tree and latched on, draining it. Reducing it to dried splinters and dead leaves. His mass got larger and larger as it fed.

Battie pulled down Mia's hand. "Look. That thing is coming out of Haddox and with each death, each drained tree, he is becoming stronger and more real in this world."

"That thing is Abbadon," Mia shook her. She was distracted for a moment, looking for Haddox and Grey. She couldn't see them from where they were now.

"And Haddox allowed him to be here. We must stop him." Battie turned to Mia, her hushed voice whispered incessantly.

"How? How do we stop that from destroying?" She bounced on her toes, the leaves rustled as she shook out her arms.

"I'll worry about slowing him down. You worry about saving my brother!"

Mia wrapped a hand around her upper arm and felt the adrenaline that coursed through Battie. The vibrations were small but still jittered in her hand. She worried her lip as she looked at the broken city. Dark clouds huddled near Abbadon's distorted laugh erupting out of him and Haddox.

Battie dashed out of the shrub, rushing forward. "You can't go in there!" Mia screamed out. The wind stole Mia's scratchy voice. Her fingers clung onto the netting of Battie's shirt; her heels dug into the loose soil holding her back.

"Let me go," Battie said, deadly quiet. Her eyes slid to Mia as she gave a vicious look. "Before I make you."

"You don't mean that?"

"He is my brother and has lost enough! I will not leave him to deal with this on his own. These are my friends, people I have grown up with. Don't think Abbadon will stop here; he will consume the entire world before he is done."

"I know all that." Mia was getting annoyed. She knew how important this was to Battie, to everyone that lived here. Her putting more pressure on her was not helping.

"Find a way to put him back in the ground he came from. They did it once before you can do it again. I will distract him and keep them busy." She slung her shoulder away, the cloth ripped in Mia's hand.

Shreds of the cloth came loose in her fingers as she closed them, keeping the tendrils of strings. She had tried. Grey would be furious if Mia let anything happen to his sister. They were both cut from the same tapestry.

Battie steered around broken stones darting through the wreckage. She yelled out, dragging Abbadon's attention away from where Mia was still hidden.

"I can do this. Think Mia, what can I do?" She stomped forward down the stone covered street. Leading to the center of the city. Her eyes scanned the sky and ground, bouncing back and forth.

Thinking back to when her grandma took him into her and put him in the ground. She agonized over the details of what she had seen. "She didn't do it, though not alone. The forest spirit had helped to push him into the ground and Sylvia cast the spell." There was so much pain, it was hard to remember clearly. Being so fresh, Ashling had given her no time to process. "I have no spells that I know offhand and the forest chose me, but isn't here like she was for my grandma."

Time had passed by quickly as she searched for a way to contain the situation. She had finally reached the center of the town. The way had been slow going, having to dodge Abbadon in the sky and the rubble he had left in his wake. The once colorful market was now covered in rubble and desolate. Haddox and Grey fought on the other side of the market. A whole severed tree trunk laid cracked in half. The downed tree leaned against others trapping homes under its weight. The homes closest to the trunk were demolished, others down the way were only partially destroyed. Leaving hope that some had survived. Abbadon had moved closer to Haddox and Grey.

"Mia," a high-pitched whine called out from the rubble close by.

Her eyes scanned the wreckage, searching for who had called out to her. Vibrant pink hair waived in the wind and a dusty green shirt peeked out of some boards and rocks. Battie? She was the only one Mia knew who wore those colors together.

"Battie!" She raced to her, throwing the debris out of the way to get to her. "What happened?" Mia looked up, searching for Abbadon. Instead, her eyes landed on Grey. He spotted her as well, with surprise written across his face. He must have heard her call out Battie's name. Worry dotted his brow as he wrestled with Haddox. They were locked in a struggle.

Haddox laughed. Mia caught the moment Grey's blood boiled and a dark calm stole over him.

Mia shook her head. Looking down at Battie, a large stone had her pinned. She mouthed the words. "Don't," she begged him not to do this.

His dark gaze turned to Haddox as Grey struck out. The shadow above grew with each punch Grey landed. Going full out Grey kept hitting him and not holding back. He wasn't paying attention to Abbadon like she was. He couldn't see that his anger wasn't helping the situation. Couldn't see past the bloodlust that had taken over him. He thought the worst had happened to his sister, most likely. They were too far away to hear her properly. It didn't help that Abbadon kept continuing to morph and demolish the city, making communicating impossible.

Battie's hand reached out to Mia's and held on for dear life. "You must stop them at all costs. This can't continue. I can't... He is the only family I have left." Tears filled her eyes as she coughed.

"Did Haddox do this to you? Grey is making him pay." Mia searched for a pole or something she could use to leverage the large stone off her. "Abbadon looks like he is feeding off of their fight."

"No, Abbadon wouldn't even let me get close." Battie's eyes turned fearful. "Grey has to stop. He can't finish this, only you can. He must let go of that pain and hurt Haddox caused."

"What are you talking about?" Mia had thought she was going to have to yell at her to save her brother again. "Right now, he is thinking the worst thing has happened to you. I don't think he is going to be thinking clearly. I won't be able to reach him like that." She struggled to get Battie into a better position.

She hissed out in pain, and Mia lowered her down to the ground. A rebar pole pushed through her stomach. She had landed on it and the rock had trapped her there. Blood oozed out slowly.

Battie's hand flickered with a warm glow and faded as she tried to heal herself. "Never could heal myself as I could others." She laughed, her hand shaking.

"Battie don't talk like that. You have to get up. I need to find something to roll this boulder off you, and then we can get you back to the healing center so you can heal."

"There's no time. It doesn't matter."

"Of course there is. There is always time," Mia sobbed. She had to make it through, or Grey would never forgive her. Battie was the only one that had been nice to her from the start. That had helped her just because she had the power to. More people needed to be like Battie, even if she was a little kooky.

Battie's forceful hands came down on hers. "No, you don't understand? If you don't stop Haddox and Abbadon, then the world as you know it ceases to exist. Everything will come to an end. Including me. He won't even allow the direct descendants to live. Not even Grey. That is how much his perfect utopian means to him. He wants to be the sole person, the one that everything starts from. He wants the respect and the worship to be all his. Ashling thinks he won't even wake all the Old One's, only the ones that were most loyal."

"Did Ashling tell you all of this?"

Her eyes faded as she looked off into the distance; she could just make out a part of Abbadon's fizzled out lower half. Her face looked as if she was witnessing a great horror. "I have dream walked with some of the Old Ones. Abbadon, he's something so unreal, so nasty." She shuttered. "Ashling blocked a lot of that part of her past out."

"That still doesn't explain," Mia interrupted.

"Ashling," Battie called out. "Ooooo so pretty," she squealed. Delirium slipped from her lips. "Ashling once mentioned a woman from the dark forest."

"What does that mean?" Her hands moved over Battie's stomach, keeping pressure on the wound. Could she be talking about the same woman from her vision? Phoenix? Her eyes were drawn to the battle between Haddox and Grey.

"They did it out of love." Coughing, Battie fought to keep talking. "Love is the answer! I love Ashling!" she bellowed out.

The pressure jarred Mia's hand.

"Without love, we are doomed." Blood poured out of her lips as her eyes rolled back into her skull.

"Battie!" Mia screamed. She held her hand, squeezing it tightly. Battie's hand was listless and lax. Leaning over her friend's chest, she listened for a thud before finally sighing in relief. She was alive for now.

She would not last much longer. Her skirt was splattered with blood, Battie's blood, and ripped to shreds. She straightened her back and rolled her shoulders. As she quickly walked across the city center, her boot landed on something round, emitting a loud crunch. A green butterfly swooped in, fluttering in front of Mia's face. She backed up, looking down at where she had stepped. The dark bead was staring at her, surrounded by other colorful beads. This must have been where the old lady's cart had been. No old lady could be seen though.

Everything looked different than it had. She was shocked by the gentle reminder of the beads from her earlier excursion. The butterfly swirled around the bead; a small plant curled up from the middle. Did the small bead hide something all this time? She studied the small leaf coming out of the bead and she couldn't tell what kind of plant it was. How could a plant help? The butterfly landed on the bead in her palm.

"What are you?" She had remembered seeing a butterfly before the woman appeared in the vision. Who was she? Was she every butterfly? This one was green and yellow, not orange and black. Was it only certain ones?

"Help it grow," a woman's voice was carried in a gust of wind.

The butterfly flew off, leaving the plant and bead in her palm. She closed her hand in a loose fist, spotting Grey.

She ran as Haddox launched at Grey. Their bodies collided and tumbled away.

As she grew closer, Haddox and Grey fought, not paying her any attention. Abbadon didn't notice her yet. The rage and destruction he fed off made him bloated and top heavy. He pulled his heavy form from tree to tree and house to house, searching for more life and power.

Chapter 27
Grey

G rey winced under Haddox. Abbadon's distorted laughter bubbled up, Haddox threw his head back and laughed, joining him as he landed punches on Grey. His wounds throbbed in time with his heartbeat.

"I will make you pay for what you have done," Grey coughed out.

Haddox was pulled away as Abbadon climbed up on top of a building. He flapped his wings, stretching the distance between the two monsters.

Grey couldn't believe how Haddox could let him in like that. Take over. Now Abbadon was destroying their home. Before being tackled, he glimpsed Mia. He wasn't sure if he had heard her right or not. He could have sworn he heard her call out Battie's name. But she shouldn't be here; she should be back at the healing center, healing those who had escaped. Thinking up a plan on how to survive. This wasn't something he could think about clearly right now.

He smeared coughed up blood over his cheek and mouth as he struggled back up. His body was sore and a cut on his leg gushed blood. Grey wasn't the only one battered and bruised though, Haddox also had taken quite the beating. His golden shine was missing, he more resembled his own gray pallor than his own tanned golden skin.

"Abbadon!" Mia yelled out.

What the hell what she doing? There was no way she could fight him. Grey's eyes searched for her fervently. She sounded close, but the dust obscured his sight. Parting through the clouded dust, Abbadon toppled over another building. He had lost count of how many had been destroyed. He had always thought their city was large, but year after year, it felt smaller. The crash covered her voice blocking the words she uttered up at him. Looking defiant in her own right.

Mia dashed away from a large boulder that was lobbed in her direction. It was close, but not on top of her. She made her way over to him, racing over the dirt as it kicked up behind her. When she got closer, Grey looked over at her. She didn't have powers like they did. What could she possibly do that they didn't have the power to? His heart squeezed at the thought of Haddox hurting her, anger kicking up in his gut once again.

"Mia!" he called out when she got close enough. Ducking under a piece of cloth that created a hidden alcove between two stones. Haddox was a little preoccupied for the moment, trying to gain enough distance from Abbadon. "What is going on? We did the last test and answered her question. Why didn't Abbadon go back to sleep?"

She clung to the shadows, trying to stay hidden. Abbadon roared and growled, searching for her. Buildings kept toppling over as she skirted into the hole with him.

"Battie's pinned and stuck, but she is still alive," Mia blurted out.

Relief flooded through him. Grabbing her to him, he bent and brushed a kiss across her dust covered lips. "Thank you."

"Ashling added a second part to the test after you left. Has anything like this happened before?"

Grey shook his head. "A second part?" His hands smoothed over her arms, down to her hands. One was curved into a fist. He hadn't noticed any scars or cuts, but still, he wanted to put his mind at ease. Curling a finger behind her closed fist he nudged at the fingers there.

Pulling her hand away, she brought it up so they could both see in the cramped space. "I found the bead from earlier at that woman's stall. Inside was a seedling."

"A seedling? How is that going to help?" He pushed her hand aside. The little plant would die soon if they didn't stop Haddox and Abbadon.

"I..." she stuttered, peering down at the plant in the palm of her hand.

"What was the second part of the test? If we can complete the tests, we can send Abbadon back to slumber." Grey shook her, trying to get her attention.

"Help it grow..." she whispered. Her eyes left the seed poking her head out of the cloth covered hiding hole.

Grey stuck close to her. He would lay waste to this entire world if she got hurt when he could have done something to prevent it. Holding her back, he stopped her from rushing forward.

"What are you talking about?"

"If I place the plant somewhere, do you think you can get it to grow?" Mia asked. Her eyes never left outside.

She was tracking Abbadon's movements, and so was he. "What does that matter? He will reach out and suck the tree dry. I have been watching him do that repeatedly. There is no stopping him."

"Haddox is his weakness. He is still tethered to him. Look at him." Watching Haddox they watched as he flew away from Abbadon. He would reach a limit away from him and slowly be pulled back. His frantic, wild eyes searched the depths of the rubble. "Abbadon is draining him even now. I have a plan, but we must go now. Divide and conquer. Distract Abbadon for me."

She darted forward before he could stop her to ask her what the plan was. He had no idea what this woman was up to. He watched as her tiny silhouette headed to Haddox. Ducking under the cloth so his horns could clear.

Abbadon turned and saw her dart across. Pulling himself back over to the center, Grey interjected and cut his sight off from Mia. He asked the trees to lend their strength, at least the ones that were left. He didn't know how corporeal Abbadon had grown; Grey had enough power to destroy, but could the vines even grab onto him? Throwing out his arm towards the foggy mass, he coaxed more from the forest. The vine encircled Abbadon, but his upper body was too massive to do much use. Abbadon's massive hand slammed into him, his shadow claws gripped around him, squeezing the air from his lungs.

He felt the breeze as he was thrown back into a wall. His head thumbed loudly as it connected with the side of a broken concrete building. Pinpricks of starlight skated across his eyes as his vision blurred.

The pain from his ribs pressed into his lungs as Abbadon increased the tightness of his hold. Not able to get enough air to call out, he tried to pry at the fingers that were around him. Fingers slid in the sludge, Abbadon's form became more solid.

A growl emitted under some rocks nearby before a small body launched with a loud warrior cry as he bit into Abbadon's dark shroud of an arm. Bloo shook his small body, tangible dirt and leaves flung from his blue fur. Claws dug deep into Abbadon's sludge. His hackles were raised, making his fur stand on end.

Abbadon reeled back and his grip lessened. Grey fell to the ground in a slump. Abbadon raised his arm back, whipping Bloo back and forth, shaking him loose. His other arm raised up in a fist.

"No," Mia coughed out weekly.

Grey sought out Mia, looking to see how she fared. It hurt for him to inhale a stitch in his side, struggling to learn how to breathe once more. Haddox had restrained her, keeping her back from rescuing Bloo.

Bloo was rattled, clinging to Abbadon's arm as his fist came down on Bloo. Mia cried and sank to the ground. Grey watched Bloo launch through the air. He moved quickly, dashing forward, catching him in his arms. Fire and cinders burned around the marketplace. Abbadon inhaled the fumes. The smoke hid him and his movements.

Grey darted out of the center and into a side street. Mia screamed in terror. Abbadon continued his rampage, the building that was behind him still intact; it busted apart as Abbadon's arm punched through the wall. Racing away, Grey looked down at Bloo wrapped in his arms shivering. The once bustling market was desolate and a wreck. There was no safe place that he could place Bloo. Worry gnawed at him. He had heard Mia scream out and wasn't sure if she needed him. He kept running through the streets, jumping over stones that blocked the way, trying to keep ahead of Abbadon. He kept circling back, trying to find a way around Abbadon.

Between one moment and the next in his running he was grabbed by his horns from up above and flung. Bloo was jostled from Grey's arms, landing in the dirt ladened alleyway. His body slammed through a crumbling tree. Even though the tree was mostly dead and drained by Abbadon, it still hurt. A tug at his horn pulled him through the dirt. He hung before the monster.

"Even a direct descendant like you has no chance. Pathetic," Abbadon sneered before whipping Grey forward.

He soared overhead and bellowed as a piece of his horn broke off, launching him farther across the market. Crashing into the ground, he slid, then rolled until he slammed into an overturned cart.

He opened his eyes, barely making out Mia; she was still crouched at Haddox's feet. Her mouth hung open as her eyes met his. He could tell it was bad from the look on her face. Pain radiated everywhere; he didn't want to move. Launching at Haddox, Grey watched her legs and arms circle around him. She held on tight as he swirled around his wings, fanning out the feathers.

As they twirled, Grey saw Mia was holding something in her hand. They shared a look. "Make it grow," Mia mouthed to him. She brought that hand up to her mouth and grabbed it with her teeth, careful of the plant growing out the side.

A knife glinted in Haddox's left hand. It was poised and ready to strike into Mia. Abbadon roared above them, making the already teetering buildings shake and trees rustled because of the vibration.

"I accept you for who you are and take you into me," Mia mumbled into Haddox's mouth.

Grey moved forward, grabbing the knife away, tossing it to the ground and yanking his wings down, keeping Haddox pinned between himself and Mia. His heart broke at seeing Mia smash her mouth into his enemies. But he could tell that she moved the bead from hers into Haddox. He fought his hold as he tried to backpedal. She gripped the back of Haddox's head, keeping their mouths locked together.

He was locked in his own personal hell, watching them together. It took every part of his strength to not whisk her away. The adrenaline rushing through him was making his mind unsteady. He had almost forgotten what she wanted him to do and why she was kissing him in the first place.

Make it grow.

Grey reached around Haddox and found Mia's clenched hand. He caressed her fingers, asking silently for her help. She relented and opened her palm to him. He held on to her as his other arm came around Haddox's throat, pulling him back. He found the plant there at the back of Haddox's throat and begged it to grow straight down. The seedling responded to the magic; it spread down Haddox's throat cutting off part of his air supply. Sinking into him and latching on with sharp thorns.

Haddox staggered back, trying to cough and regurgitate the plant. His face contorted in pain. Still, Grey didn't let up, pouring more of his power into the plant, asking it to reach for the sky. Wanting it to wrap around Haddox and Abbadon both locking them away to never see the light of day.

Mia pulled back. Her eyes wide, lashes spread apart, glued to the plant poking out of Haddox.

Relief poured through Grey; he leaned his head against Haddox keeping his head tilted to the side. "Keep going, grow big and strong to lock this one and the monster attached to him," he whispered to the plant.

With all the pain that radiated over his body from battle, the pull of the magic was nothing compared to the throbbing of his missing horn. A gut-wrenching sharp needle dove into his mind accompanied by a shrill whine drilling in with the pain. It was a good thing he had a physical arm looped around Haddox because he didn't think he would be able to concentrate enough to find him by sight.

He fought his tired eyes, forcing them to crack open. He noticed dark tar like sludge flow over Haddox and Mia; she tightened her grip on Grey's hand, grabbing his attention. Haddox shook his head and chomped at the vine growing out of his throat, trying to bite off the vegetation. Grey continued to pour as much as he could into the vine, growing. Using his weight, he pulled his arm tight against his trachea, trying to keep his mouth from opening wide enough to bite through the vine. Mia's hand slipped from his as she also tried to force his mouth to stay partially open.

Without sticking his fingers in Haddox's mouth, he didn't know of a way to keep his mouth open. Haddox bit clean through the vine and kept his mouth shut, smiling. His body still fought to cough; he became wild like a bull, bucking them both, trying to break their hold.

The sludge that slid down over Haddox covered his hands, making him slippery. He held his breath; it reeked of old dead carcasses and sulfur.

The sludge had a mind of its own, though, crawling over his skin. Moving toward Mia, climbing her arms and prying at her closed mouth. He watched in horror as the sludge tightened on him, trapping his arms as Abbadon struck out. All that he was came raining down on Mia, she was totally covered in the dark muck, Abbadon zeroed in on her taking hold of the situation.

"You are the one I wanted all along. With you, I won't need this halfling anymore!" Abbadon garbled.

"No," Haddox mumbled, his arms bulging against his restraints.

It was the only thing Haddox truly cared about. Himself. Haddox's wings were getting too heavy for him to lift the more Abbadon poured over on Mia. Grey didn't know what to do other than keeping the vine alive. It fought and struggled against the closed teeth. The plant curled back around searching. It found another passage, this one ripe for the picking. He smirked; nature would always find a way. The plant dipped out of Haddox's nose and grew around him, locking him in place.

One problem down, the next one felt impossible to even attempt. He fought the greasy sludge, but it pounced on him every time he got free.

"Help me," she belted out. Able to claw enough of the ooze away from her mouth. But she wasn't looking at him. Her eyes remained fixed on Haddox.

Hopelessness racked Grey's body, Abbadon keeping him pinned. "What are you doing?" Raw pain tinged his words.

Haddox's eyes locked onto his, a calculating glint burning in their depths. "I will take this one last thing from you," he said, his voice low and menacing.

Grey knew he was thinking through his options. His eyes lit up with the old golden mischief that Grey had seen on him over the years. What was he up to? What plan was he concocting in the scheming mind? With Mia allowing Abbadon, there was no way that Haddox would survive, none of them would.

"The only way to stop him is for me to block Abbadon's entry to Mia and let the tree grow around us all," Haddox whispered out.

Grey watched as Haddox's arms snaked around Mia, pulling her closer. Her hands smudged the slimy ooze away from her mouth, keeping it at bay. Haddox rushed forward, their lips colliding together.

Grey froze, and the vine stuttered, stopping its growth.

Mia's fists curled tight, pushing up, clearing her eyes. Her wide eyes met his. He saw fear and pain there all at once. But mostly terror. Right before the dark sludge poured over her eyes, he saw the crinkle of her eye at the corner. There was love there before it covered her from his sight.

Grey hollered out in pain, sending it all out into the world. He had never felt a loss like this before. Giving his own dark thoughts only a moment to contemplate letting the world suffer this dark plague before he righted his mind. He didn't want her sacrifice to be for nothing. Mia wouldn't have wanted it that way. His sister would have also tanned his hide if she knew he had thought such a thing. They were both too good for the thoughts he harbored.

Pouring all that he was into the magic vine, strengthening it and coaxing it into a magnificent tree. One that would put the previous large tree to shame. It gained speed and strength with his last-ditch effort, plowing up and around Mia and Abbadon. Perhaps this last thing he did would wipe him out as well.

The sludge shrank around Mia's face as the bark solidified around her. Grey plastered his chest to Haddox's back, getting closer to her. He gently pushed his palm out to caress her uncovered cheek, and she sunk into his hand. He had enjoyed their time together and was sad he hadn't given her more of his time. The vines curved around Abbadon, drawing him closer to Haddox's disappearing form. He moved the vines to cover his face and to give him time with Mia before losing her to the tree.

"Grey, what are you doing?" she blurted. Thick, hardening bark covered her body, restricting her movement as she stretched her neck.

"I want more time with you." He gazed at her face, painting it to his memory. He would never look upon her face again after this. She would only be a memory. "I wanted more time with you."

"You understand why I had to, right? We have to show them a different way..."

Grey inhaled sharply.

"You must show them a better way. If you don't, our fates are all sealed." She nuzzled her cheek against his hand, pinning it to her shoulder.

Grey shook his head in confusion and anger, wanting there to be another way. His hands loosened around Haddox as the tree rooted in place. Now that roots were planted the tree started taking over. Growing branches and thickening its center to encompass the behemoth of a monster above. Time was ticking. The tree needed to grow larger and move the woman before him, covering her up as well. But he couldn't.

"I don't know how," he whispered out. Letting a tear fall, he closed his eyes, afraid of the last moments he had with her. Afraid of what he might do. He'd just found her. Why did he have to always lose someone he was close to? First it was Trey, now Mia. When would his heartache end? He only hoped Battie survived through this all. If not, then all would be lost.

Abbadon let out a massive roar that shuddered the entire ground. He clawed upwards, but the vegetation surrounded him and swallowed him whole.

Stepping back, Grey's foot caught on a knot the tree was forming; he fell into the hardening bark.

"Mia?" The bark had almost covered her entire face. He wasn't ready to lose her.

"You know what you must do?" she whispered out.

"No," he mourned.

"Our love is a seed, and it has to grow."

"There has to be another way," Grey growled.

"That is what I learned here. There are many choices that we can make. But all outcomes are not the same. I have made my choices. Now it is up to you to make yours. This doesn't work without you."

Grass near the roots poked through the upturned dirt and between the broken boards and stone, it grew lush and tickled his ankles, swishing in the wind.

"I don't want to make this choice," he uttered. He stomped, blades of grass bent around his foot. Twigs sprang forth and wrapped around his legs as if holding him while he unraveled.

"You can't come with me." Mia frowned.

"I thought you said it was up to me?"

"Your sister will need you," her voice broke. "Look at them." Her eyes saw past him.

He looked behind him. A couple scurried out of a half-broken home trying to help a neighbor that was struggling with debris.

"They will need you," Mia said.

"Battie is still alive." Grey said it more to remind himself than anything. His heart thumped heavy in his chest and his adrenaline dipped with the fight ending.

"Yes, but she will need healing along with everyone else," her voice got softer the more she spoke. "Abbadon must never be able to destroy this world. There are too many wonderful things in it."

"You are wonderful."

She couldn't turn her head away from him, but her cheeks blushed with color. The branches bloomed and stretched out and the wood moved, rising.

He allowed the tree to take her from him. His fingers trailed down the bark, dotting the wood with flowers and vines. She deserved the forest at her feet. Drained but determined, he gave his all to help her do what must be done.

Green shoots of leaves and colorful flowers sprouted from the wood, decorating it as the tree grew enormously.

"I love you," Mia whispered as the wood closed around her.

"Don't do this!" Grey yelled out. His legs gave out as he sunk against the roots of the tree. Large and encompassing, they arched over him. The trunk taking up most of the square, the marketplace laid in tatters around them. The destruction evident, the world just got a whole lot heavier without her. Nothing would ever be the same.

Huddled in the alcove of the roots, Grey cried out, curling his fists into the soil. Magic trickled out of him, keeping the tree and vegetation thickening. He did not cut it off for fear of Abbadon escaping. Part of him wanted to spend all that energy weakening himself, hoping for an eternal rest much like the Old Ones.

He felt lost, empty with not telling her how he felt when he had the chance. His thoughts spun, and the emotion leached out of him, making him numb.

Chapter 28
Mia

"Am I dead?" Mia asked as she came to. Everything around her was misty and out of focus. Bright colors blurred around her.

"You are transitioning. You have passed your trials. Now we wait." Ashling's head poked from the side as she smiled down at her.

"I thought I had passed them before?" She righted herself, looking around. Pink and white fluffy clouds surrounded them as they floated in space.

"You did, but there is another that must complete his."

"What? Who?" Mia asked.

"Mia, you silly child. You were given impossible trials; ones you could not win alone. While you had the ability to make a choice, the outcome ultimately relied on others, not you. Grey also had tests."

"Oh?"

"It was never truly about the choices you made. Rather, what you could accomplish despite that choice. Like with the first test."

"I could have picked both wolves, feeding and strengthening both. They would have been stronger together."

Ashling shook her head. "The wolves represented Grey and Haddox. Those wolves don't clash well. But Grey had his own test. One that brought him back to the thing he detested. Could he do it even after it took a close friend?"

"Is it normal for the guardians to also be tested?" Mia asked. Had she been lied to this entire time? Was she not the chosen one? Was that why everything went wrong in the end?

"Now you're getting it!" Ashling smiled.

"Then why didn't it work when Trey was tested if this was Grey's test all along?"

Frowning, Ashling swam through the clouds. Concentrating and picking her words carefully as she spoke. "That test was for Haddox. Even with Trey, Grey chose to keep his distance and research instead."

"Okay, maybe he helped me around the first test, but the second one he wasn't even there for. How was he tested?"

"The second test with Haddox was more about the strength you had. Grey might not have partaken in your test, but he still had his own. He chose you over his research and stopping the tests. You helped him see there was something deeper to the world more than finding an answer and stopping something that was inevitable. If he wasn't brought into the mix, Abbadon wouldn't have been able to be sealed away. Without his added strength, things might have taken a turn for the worst."

"I could have done something more with Haddox so he wouldn't have let Abbadon in."

"Even the small amount you showed him changed him. It was just enough. You planted the seed, and Grey helped it grow. He chose in the end what was right."

"But..."

"We must protect our own energies and boundaries or risk losing ourselves. You picked wisely," Ashling interrupted.

"Ashling!" Battie complained as she soared in from a puffy cloud, her dark demeanor coming through even in the bright and colorful clouds.

"Battie!" Mia perked up. "You're not hurt!"

Battie gave a deadpan stare to Ashling. "You didn't tell her."

"I was getting to it," Ashling complained. She rolled her eyes as she rolled to her side, fluffing up one of the clouds to lounge on.

"Mia, this is a dreamscape one Ashling helped me create. So, I can appear however I want too, really." Battie stomped through the clouds dispersing them and towered over Ashling's lounging form. With a wave of her hand, the cloud moved and tipped upright, making Ashling stand and sending her flying in Mia's direction. "Now tell her."

Ashling harrumphed, stopping midair dangling close to Mia. "Your choice was right, because Haddox was able to doubt Abbadon enough to allow you guys to stop him. He could have given up all the power to him. But he didn't."

"He is still a selfish prick, though," Battie grumbled.

"Him being selfish, kept some of that power from making Abbadon unstoppable," Ashling intoned.

"Why was the third test so crazy with different parts to it?" Mia wanted all the answers she seemed to be giving and with Battie here, she could make sure she didn't speak in riddles. It was her time to get to the bottom of things.

"Picking death later helped scoot the battle where it needed to be. Your choice only influenced the battlefield. The people you brought together are what helped both of you tip the scales in your favor. If another choice was made, would you have found the seedling?"

"So, you can predict the future. Then why not explain what needs to be done?" Anger rolled through her. She was starting to see why Grey had been so against these in the first place.

"Sadly no, but I have been at this long enough to know." Ashling looked as if she was about to say something more, but thought better of it. "If I explained what you should do, would you have done it or fought it as much as you fought your mother? This was the only way for you to learn to accept what happened and learn from your choices."

Mia wrinkled her nose. She moved away, climbing a hill of clouds, not liking Ashling hovering over her. Lording this knowledge over her. "If I'm not dead. Then what happened with Haddox and Abbadon?"

"Abbadon is back to his resting state," Battie reassured.

"But Haddox, like you, is in a sleeping dream much like this one," Ashling said.

"Not exactly like this one," Battie argued. "Ashling watches over him and makes sure he is learning and growing so he can get the peace he needs one day."

"What happens next, then?" Mia asked. Ashling would be the best one watching over Haddox giving him choices. She hoped he changed for the better.

"Sadly, next is again a decision out of your control."

Yawning, Mia stretched. The clouds lengthened and softened, cushioning her steps and slowing her down.

"Let the girl rest for a while," a voice chimed in softly. A soft green glow from a fluttering butterfly appeared, growing clearer as the light grew near.

It transformed from a butterfly to a beautiful woman, the same one from her grandma's past. Her dress was different from the reds and oranges of the fall time leaves. Now it was vibrant greens of fresh leaves.

"You are the woman from my grandma's memory. You helped Sylvia tie Abbadon to a circle of stones."

She curtsied and smiled.

Ashling came forward, hugging the woman. They embraced for quite a while before Battie coughed. Ashling let go. Backing away, she made her way back to Battie's side. Picking up her hand, she intertwined their fingers.

"This is the mother of your forests; she has been here before all others have come to live on her planet."

"The mother of the forest," she said in awe.

"There are many legends of the forest that were forgotten, but it doesn't make them any less real." Ashling nudged Battie.

"Do you have a name?" Mia struggled to remember what Sylvia had called the forest.

"You can call me Janani. I have been monitoring you for many years, child." Her voice was surreal. It had a melody to it as she talked.

"Why?" Mia hesitated.

Ashling tsked at Mia, her brows furrowed in her direction. "Don't bother her with such questions."

Mia looked between Ashling and Janani. She bent her head lower. "Not to mean any offense. But why would you watch over me?" she whispered as her eyes flicked between Ashling and Janani.

"Thank you for your assistance and helping her get ready for what was needed," Janani said to Ashling. "Can I speak to her alone for a moment?"

Ashling frowned, but nodded and bowed as she and Battie retreated, slowly fading into the clouds floating away.

Janani's body was slim and agile as she coasted over to Mia. The soft puffy clouds pulled Mia down, so she slumped against them, losing all energy. She was zapped. The light pinks and purples made this place seem surreal and dreamlike.

"You want to know why you were chosen? Even when the tests were about you and Grey." Janani asked.

She nodded; her fingers twirled in the clouds at her feet. She pulled at it, the feel and texture much like cotton wool.

"You were curious when your village sided with fear." Janani dress rustled as she sat beside her. "An adventurous spirit that knows no bounds. Your heart is light and forgiving. Anger crashes against you like a storm in the night. It reminded me of when I was young and still new to this world."

The wind rustled through the leaves, pulling some of them loose. The leaves swirled and flipped and, as they tumbled up higher away from the clouds, they changed into moths and butterflies. More and more flew from her dress as they swirled around, finding a place to land and keeping their wings down. They scooted close to one another and formed a picture of Mia when she was a child.

"You would tell me the most wonderful stories when you thought you were alone." Janani waited for the butterflies to form another picture. "You would strain to hear my voice whispering in the wind." She giggled.

Mia's eyes traveled back to Janani. Janani's dress exposed her lower half, revealing space where legs should be. Mia tried to look away, but her eyes kept getting pulled back to the disappearing dress.

"And when you grew frustrated, you would bend what rules you could." A defiant little Mia stood on the beach, looking at the wall that divided their beach from the great unknown.

"I fought the waves many times to find a way around." She focused on what Janani said rather than her lower dressed form with no legs.

"Yes, you did. And eventually you succeeded." Janani smiled.

"I was so tired after all that swimming that I could not go back the way I had come. I followed the wall back, hoping to find a guard or reach the entrance and be let back in. But before that happened, I found a small break in the wall."

"There hidden amongst the thick grass. A small crack if pressed. I asked the wind to part it for you so you could visit whenever you wanted." Light shone in her eyes as her smile reached them. Some butterflies flew back from the picture and became smaller. But they reattached to her, creating legs instead of the dress again.

"You asked the wind?" Mia blushed and ducked her head, embarrassed as she got caught staring.

"Yes, I didn't want to be rude. Wind can be very sweet when asked."

She talked about the elements like they were real friends. Mia had to remember that even though she looked human, she was far from it. Ashling was even cautious around her. She wondered what times in her past she was guided to do something.

"Ashling said you were the mother of the forest, so you were here before the Old Ones came?"

She tinkled with laughter. "Did you know that it is hard for those of us with endless lives to stay connected to the world? To not harden our heart towards others. We forget how carefree and childlike we were. How simple things can bring us so much joy." Getting up, she walked to the butterfly picture. Her hands brushed the tips of the wings, and they crumbled to dust, raining down and silencing the bright color. "You reminded me of a time long ago."

It was hard to follow Janani's thoughts. Her words were more like riddles than Ashling's tests. But she sat there hoping she would come around to some form of answer she could understand. Or even wanted.

"Perhaps it wasn't that long ago. Time isn't as important as it is for someone like you."

"Can you tell me about the tests?" Mia tried to corral her back to the topic she wanted an answer about. If not for her, then to tell Battie so Grey could give up his relentless research.

"The tests were more glorified back then; it was more about the renewing of the magic and spell rather than being dangerous. But after your grandfather decimated one of the Old One's sleeping chambers, Abbadon was no longer under that spell."

"What?" Mia asked, astonished and confused. Abbadon had said as much about Tom, her grandfather. But the tests before this one were more like the spell they did to renew the wall.

"Oh, people would get hurt sometimes during the tests beforehand, but not too badly. It was mostly about seeing if you were worthy. Nothing to the extent that happened in your test and the two before yours." Janani backtracked.

"But why me?"

"After the last death, right before yours, Abbadon sent out a warning that I felt being the heart of the forest. It made me shudder in fear at how close he was last time to getting his wish.

He sent out his warning to me that he would succeed next time. I knew you were meant for this; you were your grandma's child."

"How did he not possess me when he clearly possessed the other woman before me and my grandpa?"

"In your grandfather's time, Abbadon was weak and new to being outside his body. Tom was in close proximity. But since he had little to no strength, and the human resisted, it took him some time to take over completely. He bided his time."

"But why didn't I get possessed then? He would have been stronger than that initial time." Mia was frustrated. She shoved up from the moving clouds to burn off some of the energy.

Janani floated up and hovered in the air, keeping pace with her. "You have practiced magic with Sylvia. She put protections on you that avoided that very thing from happening."

"Didn't matter. In the end, he found a more willing host with Haddox."

"Your family has been touched by an Old One and because of that it passed down to you from your mother. Making magic something you can handle. That is why you were pulled to things and places outside the wall."

Every time she learned about something in the past, it only made things confusing in the present. "So, what now?" Mia demanded.

"Now we wait."

Chapter 29
Grey

"**A**re you feeling better?" Ashling murmured.

Grey's eyes popped open. He groaned out as he untwisted from the chair he had fallen asleep in. The warmth of the library had made him too comfortable. How could he have fallen asleep? Passing a hand over his face, he covered a yawn and stretched his sore bones.

"Yes. I hate that my healing power can't work on myself," Battie said.

"Powers can be so fickle sometimes." Ashling scrunched her nose. Gazing longingly at Battie. "So much has changed in a very little time. How is the building of the new temple?"

A migraine beat at the sides of his head. "Can you guys go somewhere else to chat about things?" Now that Ashling was allowed out of her room, she stuck mostly by Battie. Their voices and the light shining through the skylight grated on him.

"Well…" her head whipped around. "That reminds me, Grey. You should really see the progress we have made."

"What progress?" Things had changed drastically after the battle. It had only been a month and already people were moving on like nothing happened. He couldn't do the same.

Wouldn't! Everyone was happy about what Mia had done, capturing Abbadon and Haddox within the huge tree that now took up most of the room they had for the market space. But she had also been trapped with them. What kind of monster was he to trap her with those two?

"Tell him what you created and the story that goes with it," Ashling pushed, bumping her hip into Battie's.

His dark hair hung over one of his eyes. He studied Battie intensely as they talked. She hadn't said as much but he knew she was reclusive for a reason. With Ashling's freedom, he noticed their time together had increased. He was glad that she had someone, because he couldn't be there for her like he should. He had failed Mia, and he was now failing his sister.

Tugging on one lime green pigtail that hung down, Battie picked up books from the floor and put them on the tables away from Grey. "It's a place to celebrate her victory and to remember who Mia was."

"I feel horrible for arguing with her when I should have been telling her what she meant to me. Now she will never know," Grey interrupted.

"You should come see it. You can tell her what you didn't have the chance to." Battie paused.

Grey saw the shared look between Ashling and her. There was definitely something going on. He loved his sister and would do anything for her. Ashling was never the problem, just the tests. Getting to his feet, his bones were sore from how he had twisted them while he slept.

"She's dead Battie. She won't hear what I have to say," Grey said solemnly. He moved past her to the hallway, leaving them to continue chatting. Nausea bubbled up as he moved. He couldn't remember the last time he had eaten. He would get something before going back to his room. At least there he would get some peace for a little while.

"The humans must hear of her story... they all should," Ashling blurted, her voice raised.

Grey froze at the open archway.

"That's my plan, to travel and make sure all know what Mia has done for the world and each of our kind," Battie whispered.

Tipping his head back, he swiped his hand through his hair, shuffling it back. His hand bumped the broken horn. It still ached if he wasn't careful. He turned to the room but held his tongue.

Ashling frowned, she plopped down in the large chair, tucking her legs up next to her. She stared up at the ceiling. "When do you plan to leave?"

He saw frustration etched in Ashling's body, her muscles held tight and rigid. He wondered if it was at him or Battie. It wouldn't surprise him if it was aimed at both of them.

"Soon, I wanted to wrap up some things here..." Battie slouched back in the same chair next to Ashling. "I am making sure you can come with me. That way, we both can see the world."

Her leaving wasn't news to him. This was something Battie had talked with him about. She had asked for his help on how to get Ashling the freedom she deserved. She had proved that she was on the descendant's side on more than one occasion, but this really had solidified things. That part wasn't the struggle. Others that lived in the village were having a hard time with her not being close by, in case anything went awry. There were going to be checks and balances, set in place.

Ashling's eyes got large and round as her small heart-shaped mouth hung open.

"I'm not leaving here without my nurse, who has taken care of me."

Battie's one arm was wrapped from shoulder to fingertips. It had to stay in a cast as she healed. The human way. Grey smirked.

Ashling blushed. "I thought we weren't serious," her voice got quiet as she did a double take.

"What do I know? I'm batty," she winked. Battie's hand reached out to Ashling's that laid between them.

"Do you think I will really be able to go with you?" Ashling's voice quivered.

"Yes, it will be good for you. You need to be around people and learn our ways. Perhaps even learn more about your own kind. We can no longer fear the knowledge Old One's once held."

"What about the tests?" Ashling questioned.

"No more tests," Grey growled. "That will be my only focus while you are away. It was a spell to be renewed before Abbadon was unleashed so we will continue to search for another way.

You and Battie will work on strengthening the bond between humans and our kind in order to stave off needing the tests in the meantime."

Ashling shared a look with Battie. One he had caught; Battie shook her head.

"What?" He was getting tired of them all walking on eggshells around him.

"It's just, Haddox shared a memory with me before I sent him to dreamland."

The surrounding tension thickened. It was bad enough he would never see Mia again, but then he had found out Haddox was still alive and held in a coma. His humanity was the key to binding Abbadon in place. Or at least that was what Ashling had told him. It seemed like the rules kept changing. It was why he wanted to oversee the research, because then he could know for sure.

Battie threw her hand out, bumping against Ashling.

"He showed a database near where the others slept, one that Abbadon had messed with. I've left a map of where to find it in my room. You can start there and work on recovering the lost knowledge directly from the Old One's themselves instead of through the second-hand knowledge written here."

"Great!" Grey's muscles tensed, ready to sprint back to her room and find the map.

"It's not going to be as easy as that." Ashling rubbed her soft cheek against Battie's shoulder.

He waited.

"Janani said she would help you with the language in my stead."

Doubt radiated through him. Janani was new to him. She was neither human nor a descendant. And she was the one that helped Mia figure out how to trap Abbadon and Haddox. But she was conveniently missing.

Battie nuzzled her nose against Ashling's.

He felt awkward staying for their intimate moment. He backtracked out of the room; they had forgotten he was even there. His back connected with the wall right outside in the hallway as he stayed to overhear. His heart ached at what he no longer had with Mia and how he missed her.

"What made you decide to invade more than my dreams?" Battie asked.

"What made you decide to throw caution to the wind and face me?" A soft hush of fabric whispered in the silence.

"Mia made me stop and think about what I really want for my future."

"Did she? Your brother wasn't worried like you thought he would be."

Silence filled between Grey's ears. Sounds of kissing and rustling of clothes filtered through. He held his breath, not wanting to make a sound.

"With you like this, I almost forget you are one of them." Battie's voice was low and throaty.

"I chose the right side, that's all."

Battie must have done something because he heard Ashling yelp in surprise.

"Battie!" she hissed.

"There is more to it than that."

"Fine. Like Janani, I try to stay connected to the world in different ways, so I do not harden myself to it as so many of the others have," Ashling sighed. "There were others like me who wanted to help but didn't have the power or cunningness to. They are locked away with the others for something they didn't choose or want."

"Perhaps there will be a way to free them in time. Or maybe they will be given a test of their own that will decide their fate."

"I doubt Grey would help after everything," Ashling whispered.

Unable to take any more, he slid away from the conversation down the hallway. He ached to have Mia with him. He had only just gotten used to her being around when she was taken.

His mind was numb to the thoughts circling in his mind. He blindly walked down the hallway. It was still early and wasn't busy. Most were helping in the village with the destruction that was still being cleaned up. He hadn't been back there since the day everything happened. He hadn't been able to.

Something round and furry launched in his path, bringing him to a stop.

Bloo whined and limped. "No," he howled.

Leah came racing after him. "You have to stay off your paws. Battie will have my head if you don't let yourself heal."

"Leave him alone."

Leah shrank back. "Then can you get him to rest?"

Grey scooped up Bloo, who settled in his arms immediately. Grey held him close to his chest as he made his way into the room he had scattered out of. Papers were strewn about on the bed around a basket in the middle of the floor. Looking around, he spotted the half link bracelet he had gotten Mia sat on the dresser. "This was her room?" He must have gotten turned around, not realizing where he was.

"Well yea. Bloo wouldn't leave her bed for a long time and wasn't eating. We got him to eat again and now he won't rest. He keeps getting re-injured." Leah huffed.

He grabbed the bracelet, keeping a hold of it. "Get out."

Bloo snuffed out a breath through his nose with finality, staring at Leah.

Not staying a second longer, Leah whisked herself out of the room on rainbow wings.

Grey didn't care if he was being harsh. This was her room. Her place and they didn't need to mess it up. They didn't understand that Bloo and him were hurting; they were all just happy to be alive and that it wasn't them in his situation.

Setting Bloo down on the bed, his fingers brushed at the clothing set out on the bed. She had sewn designs into her clothes that she hadn't put away yet. Bloo laid on the clothing, rubbing his face against it.

"I miss her too," he choked out.

Looking at the papers, they were patient documents, probably for the next tenant that would need this room. To accommodate his thicker wrist, he widened the bracelet's clasp. He would wear the bracelet since she could not. He grabbed the pillow, hugging it to his face, inhaling deeply, hoping to catch her scent still lingering there. She had not slept here long enough for it to be infused with her. He hollered out as he threw the pillow through the doorway.

"Why are you still so angry?" Battie asked, poking her head in the room.

He tossed the papers off the bed. His lungs tightened, squeezing his chest. He was so empty, and no one understood it. He couldn't unleash all that he felt. Pushing things down and concentrating on the next step only made him feel numb to the pain. Which wasn't what he wanted, either. "Because, Battie."

"Why?" She came up behind him, resting a hand on his shoulder.

"I didn't tell her I loved her," a sob burst out of him.

"She had to know you felt the same," Battie explained.

"What if she didn't?" His blurry gaze landed on his sister.

"Then go to the tree and tell her exactly what you want her to know. Tell her how you are feeling and what losing her felt like. Pour your heart out and let her know. You can see for yourself what we have been working on. Everyone has pitched in."

"I can't..."

Battie pursed her lips. "Follow me." She took his hand and made him follow her. She glanced back before leaving fully. "Bloo, you rest. If you do that, I will bring a treat back for you."

Bloo set his head down on his paws and closed his eyes.

How Grey wished he could accept defeat like Bloo did. To lay down and sleep until someone came and bothered him.

They walked in silence down the dirt path. The barrier had not been repaired yet, the vines still cut and branches had been moved back, making the way larger. Boulders lined the edges, marking out sections. So many people were loitering around talking. Making plans. Their hushed voices quieted once they saw Battie and him. Most bowed their heads in respect.

"They decided that the market will go closer to the entrance rather than around the tree. The market will be a natural defense as well."

Moving past the large group and sectioned area. They took a cleared side street into town. Other roads had not been cleared yet. Houses and trees still laid in rubble. Dirt covered faces stared at him from partly broken homes. Still, he could see where progress had been made.

Sunlight blinded him once they got to the center and where the largest tree now sat. The sun shone off bright white stone. A large book lay open. Getting closer to the white stone, he noticed it wasn't plain marble. There was a picture that had been painted across it. On the left page was Mia's village, then in the next section, there were the two wolves from Mia's first test. The next panel showed Haddox. On the right page, it showed

Grey and Mia together. The next panel was Abbadon, in his monstrous form hovering over a bunch of little people. Then the last panel showed the tree, as it was seen today. Looking at the tree, it still looked unfinished, and there was a small part of the page that was left untouched. He wondered when Battie would have time to finish it before leaving.

"You have done so much in such little time, Battie!" He hugged his sister close, wanting her to know how much he loved her. He wasn't going to let her go without her knowing, either.

"Thanks. It took the whole village. This will be reserved for reflection and teachings."

"There is still so much to do." Anger riled through him at the destruction that still littered the ground. They had cleared some parts up here and closer to the tree, but they had to wade through a lot of it to even get to this part.

"There's one more thing I want to show you." She pulled at his hand she still had grasped in hers as she guided him down the dirt path.

They walked around, away from the front of the tree. It took a while to get to the back of the tree; it was humongous and spanning the whole circle that the market had filled. Passing people on their walk, he saw some groups that left trinkets near the tree and others who prayed before it. "They show their love for what Mia and you helped create to keep our village safe."

At the back, pods of flowers lined up on one of the large roots. Greenery and shrubs, from the forest, latched onto the roots, wrapping the wood and shooting up the sides.

"Make it bloom," Battie nudged Grey forward.

Looking up at the gigantic tree, he wondered if she was in there looking down on him, seeing what a failure he was. Or did she dream like Haddox did? They never really explained. He wouldn't let them. It would have felt too final, letting the last of his hope go.

He curled his hands up into fists. "I am so angry!" he growled out. He looked around, noticing none had followed them back this far. A tear trickled down his cheek. Kneeling in front of the tree, he reached out a hand, touching the vine to the closest largest flower pod. "Not angry at you... Never at you." He hung his head in defeat as he sobbed against the tree. "Look, I'm talking to a tree. You at least deserve some flowers." Letting the magic trickle down his arm, he added to the beauty of the dark tree.

Surrounding the bud of the huge flower, he peppered more flowers up and down the side of the tree. He opened himself and his magic up to the tree, begging for it to answer his call and show him the beauty of the flower in the pod. He barely felt his power anymore, but here, being this close to where she last was. It was quick to answer.

"I promise to renew the flowers every spring and think of only you and how you united us over something we didn't even deserve." His fist struck the hard bark, barely causing a dent.

"You should see the way Battie has stepped up to make sure your story is told. Says we must combine forces to make sure both the Old Ones and humans survive. I will try to do better."

His fingers spread out, unclenching his fist. The rough ridges and deep grooves of the tree were easy to grip in his giant hands.

Looking up at the giant flower pod, it wiggled and started to open at the top. It was getting ready to bloom. Surprised. Grey made his decision to let go of the anger and opened his magic and heart to love, the love of missing her. The flower burst open and something laid there in the middle of it.

"Mia!" Grey sprinted over to her, scooping her up in his arms, holding her close.

"They made me wait for you to make your choice." Her eyes fluttered open and a hint of a smile lifted her lips.

"I love you, Mia," he whispered to her. Kissing her cheeks and hugging her close. His body shook with happiness. "I will prove to you in every way I can how much you really mean to me."

Coming Soon...

Don't miss the next novel in Raquel Gabrielle's A Soul Saga. Keep reading for a blurb of what book four will bring:

Shade's story is about to unfold...

In the shadows of a world he barely understands, Shade walks a treacherous path. Recently transformed into a human, he bears the weight of a grim duty: betray the one he was sworn to protect, steal her magic, and save her from her own destructive power. All while learning what his true purpose is. By his side, a tiny, fiery spirit named Taz burns brightly. She is a firecracker and the only thing holding him together, since he has no soul. He keeps coming up against dead ends and the feeling of being lost.

Enter Natasha, the Ice Queen herself...

Or so she would like people to think. Cold and calculating on the surface, she hides a fiery determination to protect her own. Together, they forge an uneasy alliance to dismantle the forces threatening their world. But as they delve deeper into the shadows, they uncover a web of deceit that goes far beyond their initial suspicions. Natasha's own father is entangled in the plot, and the true scale of the danger is far greater than they imagined.

The one thing Shade and Natasha have in common other than their enemies is their agitation with Alexia. Each for different reasons. Both of them must navigate a labyrinth of betrayal and intrigue. As they close in on their quarry, they find that the line between friend and foe blurs.

Acknowledgments

As I stand on the precipice of this book's release, I am struck by the journey that led me here. The past few years have been a whirlwind of growth, learning, and discovery, and I am eternally grateful to the many people who have shaped me into the author I am today. To my readers, your unwavering support and enthusiasm never cease to amaze me. You are the fuel that keeps me writing, and I am honored to have you on this journey with me.

To my writer group and critique partners, you have been an invaluable source of guidance, encouragement, and tough love. Mar and Maegan, your insights and unwavering support have been instrumental in helping me navigate the challenges of this book. Zivah, my ride-or-die critique partner, you have seen this story through its darkest hours and its triumphant moments. Your keen eye for detail and unwavering belief in these characters have made this book so much stronger. I am forever grateful for your friendship and your dedication to this story.

Allen, my rock, my partner in crime, and my assistant in all things, your support knows no bounds. You are always there to listen, to brainstorm, to roll up your sleeves and dive in when needed. Your enthusiasm for my stories is infectious, and I can't wait to share my next adventure with you by my side.

To the readers who have taken a chance on my words, thank you from the bottom of my heart. Your support means the world to me, and I am humbled to have you on this journey. Here's to many more adventures together.

About Author

When Raquel Gabrielle is not conjuring up magical realms or crafting characters, you can find her in Oklahoma with her husband, dogs and cat. With a passion for adventure that rivals her love of writing, Raquel is always on the lookout for the next great story - whether that's in the pages of a book or the secrets hidden in the shadows of the unknown.

She mostly writes Urban Fantasy and Paranormal Romance, a fusion of myth, magic, and mayhem, with a healthy dose of romance and intrigue thrown in for good measure. But don't be surprised if she veers off the beaten path from time to time - after all, the best stories often begin where the map ends. Raquel invites you to join her on her journey where the boundaries of reality are pushed, and the possibilities are endless. For more information about her books and writing, you can join her newsletter at www.RaquelGabrielle.comor on her Facebook

author page Raquel Gabrielle

Scan for Website   Scan for Facebook Page

I hope you have enjoyed the book. I would love to hear your thoughts. Please take a moment to leave a review. They are so important to indie authors like me.

- Link Tree – RaquelGabrielle

- Ream Stories (Like Patreon) – https://reamstories.com/raquelgabrielle

facebook.com/RaquelGabrielleAuthor/

instagram.com/raquelgabrielle/

tiktok.com/@raquelgabrielleauthor

goodreads.com/user/show/153277018-raquel-gabrielle

bookbub.com/authors/raquel-gabrielle